WARRIOR'S SURRENDER

BY

Elizabeth Ellen Carter

Acknowledgements

Thank you to editor Kyle Lewis.
Also to my husband who enthusiastically worked through
plot points with me and came up with terrific ideas.

And to wonderful authors Noelle Clark, Susanne Bellamy, and
Eva Scott for your never-ending encouragement and support.

DEDICATION

To my darling husband, my hero.

TABLE OF CONTENTS

Prologue　　9
Chapter One　　14
Chapter Two　　21
Chapter Three　　31
Chapter Four　　40
Chapter Five　　46
Chapter Six　　53
Chapter Seven　　61
Chapter Eight　　69
Chapter Nine　　78
Chapter Ten　　85
Chapter Eleven　　93
Chapter Twelve　　100
Chapter Thirteen　　108
Chapter Fourteen　　115
Chapter Fifteen　　122
Chapter Sixteen　　128
Chapter Seventeen　　137
Chapter Eighteen　　144
Chapter Nineteen　　150
Chapter Twenty　　158
Chapter Twenty-One　　164
Chapter Twenty-Two　　170
Chapter Twenty-Three　　180
Chapter Twenty-Four　　186
Chapter Twenty-Five　　194

Chapter Twenty-Six 199
Chapter Twenty-Seven 207
Chapter Twenty-Eight 212
Chapter Twenty-Nine 219
Chapter Thirty 224
Chapter Thirty-One 231
Chapter Thirty-Two 239
Chapter Thirty-Three 245
Chapter Thirty-Four 252
Chapter Thirty-Five 259
Chapter Thirty-Six 267
Chapter Thirty-Seven 274
Chapter Thirty-Eight 283
Chapter Thirty-Nine 293
Chapter Forty 301
Chapter Forty-One 311
Chapter Forty-Two 321
Chapter Forty-Three 329
Chapter Forty-Four 338
Chapter Forty-Five 348
Epilogue 360

* * *

About The Author 364

PROLOGUE

Durham, England—1070

The flare of a pitch-soaked torch lit the corner of the timber long-house. Lying on the floor, the torch's yellow-orange flame licked greedily at the timber, igniting it. Roiling black smoke billowed up, filling the room and obscuring the entrance to the hall. The acrid smell mingled with the bitter, metallic tang of freshly spilled blood.

Sebastian coughed and doggedly followed his Norman lord through the rapidly thickening miasma within the burning building.

The young man's heart pounded wildly.

The excitement of the battle fought through the afternoon still thrummed in his veins. And although he knew the foe was well and truly routed, there were still dangers as the rebellious Saxon earls of Northumbria fiercely defended a retreat that brought them all closer and closer to the Scottish border.

As a squire, Sebastian took his role of guarding his lord seriously. Even in this still unfamiliar country, he protected the flank of the warrior both on foot and horseback, using his training, agility, and skills to ensure the forces of King William of Normandy vanquished their enemies.

William was the newly crowned king of England and Sebastian had lived and fought for him in this land for two years, but never before traveled this far north. Here the wild moors were strewn with rocks and sharply cut escarpments covered with gorse and purple heather. It was without question one of the most wild and beautiful features of this uncivilized region.

Sebastian adjusted his sweat-slicked grip on the pommel of his sword to keep it from slipping from his grasp.

"Seb!" his lord called through a smoke-rasped throat. "Outside!"

Sebastian rushed to where he had last seen the door.

One or two well-aimed kicks saw the hinges give way. A roar of air rushed in, fueling the flames, which grew in size and heat, propelling the two men outside.

Screams of terror and pain filled the night air as the Norman knights laid waste. Not even this village's only stone building—a church—was immune from the ransacking and arson.

Sebastian knew a number of his compatriots had broken ranks, that some of the screams he could hear came from women being raped in the flickering firelight of destroyed houses and outbuildings.

Disgust filled him at the thought. Fighting men in the field of battle was honorable. Raping, looting, and pillaging like the worst of the Vikings was vile.

Despite the heat from the fires, the burden of the mail across his chest and legs, and the fatigue of many hours of fighting, Sebastian kept his eyes on his lord, watchful for threats. They reached another corner of the burh, marked by a boundary palisade of sharpened logs.

"The hay barn," said the knight. "There may be more men hiding. Secure it. We'll need fodder for the horses tonight."

Sebastian nodded and ran in the direction indicated by the older man, toward a large two-story wooden structure with an opening large enough for a laden hay wagon to pass beneath.

Here, the smoke was less choking and the sound of the battle in the heart of the village faint. It took him a moment to adjust his senses to the absence of noise.

The barn door stood ajar and Sebastian entered. He allowed the tip of his sword to point to the ground as he paused to catch his breath and listen.

A shuffling sound toward the back of the barn caught his attention and he brought his sword back up. An animal? Too large to be a rat. A pig or a sheep, perhaps?

He moved forward cautiously to investigate. Even an agitated goat could still inflict injury if it was too distressed. Moonlight streamed in from an aperture propped open in the long wall, revealing the stacks of baled hay on the hard-packed earthen floor. The shuffling noise behind one tall stack drew him farther into the barn.

"Come out, little goat," he called softly. "I won't hurt you...."

This time the sound of metal scraping against metal accompanied the sound of the movement.

Fatigue fled. Sebastian was on alert. He readied his sword and cautiously edged around the corner of one of the baled stacks.

Just two sacks propped in the shadowed corner.

He breathed a sigh of relief and chuckled until one of the sacks wriggled and a tow-headed boy aged not more than four peered out at him. What Sebastian thought was a sack in the low light was actually a voluminous cloak.

The child whimpered and turned his face away.

"Do not cry, I will not hurt you," he assured the child in halting Saxon, a tongue still foreign to him.

He crouched forward to offer a reassuring hand when a scream erupted close to his ear. Sebastian turned in time to see a blade wielded by a feminine hand plunge toward him. He rolled and the blade skittered harmlessly across the links of armor that covered his arm.

On his hands and knees, Sebastian became aware of a third person. He regained his feet and brandished his sword to deal with a new threat—a Saxon knight.

The man's surcoat was intricately decorated. A blue ground, the color of the summer sky, overstitched with bright yellow interlinked squares. This was a man of status, perhaps an earl.

He was dressed in quality armor, but blood streaked down one thigh. The stub of a spear shaft was clearly visible through a tear in the mail.

The knight, bearded and grizzled, ignored Sebastian and shuffled painfully toward the boy and the second figure, a flaxen-haired girl.

No, a young woman maybe about fourteen years of age, Sebastian realized as she stood to her full height.

"Faeder!" the boy child cried.

"Hush, bairn!" the old man gritted out against the pain of his wound.

Angry at allowing himself to be ambushed, Sebastian positioned himself ready to fight. He was confident he could best this injured knight no matter how experienced the man was, but there could be others here, and against two or more he would be dead.

He backed away from the boy, his eyes never leaving those of the knight who looked at him with open contempt and limped the last few steps to stand between Sebastian and his two children.

"Stay away from my family. I will fight you to my last breath, Norman dog," he sneered. Sebastian understood the rapidly delivered insult. He'd heard the curse enough times in the two years since leaving his childhood home in Normandy.

"Seb! Where are you?" called a voice from outside the barn. It was his lord.

"Here!" he responded.

The girl turned the boy to her stomach, forbidding the child to see the scene foreshadowed by his call. She glanced at her father with concern, then turned her eyes to Sebastian, an expression of nervous expectation crossing her face before setting in determined resolution.

Sebastian looked back at her. He had sisters and brothers. And he would fight to his last breath to protect them too. He could not fault a father for protecting his family.

The Saxon Earl's sword dipped. Because of his injury, exertion had weakened him. A feverish sweat broke out over the man's face and lingered on his graying beard.

He needed a physician, Sebastian realized. There were monks in an abbey a league away who would help.

The young Norman addressed his instructions to the girl. Her cornflower-blue eyes refused to show fear of him; her father and brother would need her bravery and strength if they were to survive this night.

"Go! Get out of here!" he hissed. "I will buy you as much time as I can. Do you understand me?"

The girl's eyes widened in surprise and she nodded.

Sebastian turned and strode away from the Saxon family toward the door by which he had entered.

"What's keeping you?" his lord demanded from the doorway, peering into the darkness within. "Is the barn empty or not?"

Resisting the urge to look back, Sebastian answered, "Yes! It's empty. Just bales of hay."

CHAPTER ONE

Northumberland, England—Late summer 1077

The late afternoon sun met the tops of the trees in the west, casting golden slivers of light across the meadow. From his vantage point on an adjacent grassy rise, Sebastian de la Croix, baron of Tyrswick, scanned the tree line ahead and waited for the appointed time.

With grudging reluctance, he considered how well his enemy did to choose this place and time to parley. As the lowering sun shone in his eyes, Sebastian could be caught unawares by a well-aimed arrow.

However, years of battle experience had drilled into him the rules of leaving nothing to chance and turning disadvantage to advantage. Thus, he had come early to the rendezvous and even now his men flanked the field, hidden from view by the very shadows his enemy perhaps hoped to use against him.

Satisfied his orders were being carried out, Sebastian nudged his large black horse forward to the campaign tent that would host this meeting.

In battle he would have worn a hauberk, but as a sign of the good faith the request for parley demanded, Sebastian wore only light protection.

His head was bare and a breeze ruffled his coal-black hair. Over a shirt, he wore a sleeveless leather aketon, a padded garment ordinarily worn under his mail. It was no match against an arrow or a crossbow bolt to be sure, but it was protection enough for a close-quarters encounter.

He dismounted and handed the reins of his horse to one of his men-at-arms and wondered about the man he was about to meet—

the dispossessed Thegn of Tyrswick, Alfred, whose land and holdings Sebastian now owned by fiat of William the Conqueror himself. The meeting came somewhat as a surprise. It was popularly believed Alfred and his family were either dead or in exile in Scotland because, until six months ago, none had seen or heard of him since the mighty battle in York that ended with defeat for supporters of usurper Edgar the Atheling.

During his many battles these last few years, Sebastian had distinguished himself as a squire in his lord's service, earning his spurs as a knight and coming to the notice of the king himself for bravery and a reputation as a cunning military strategist.

In the aftermath of the Harrying, a deadly six-month rampage from York to Durham that saw the systematic slaughter of one hundred thousand people, King William sought to secure his kingdom along the Scottish borders. He needed men he could trust rather than leave in place Saxon earls who pledged fealty with one hand and plotted treason with the other. Thus it was five years ago, just after his twenty-third birthday, Sebastian had accepted elevation to baron from William the Conqueror, and land along the Scottish border to protect with his life and, more importantly, his honor.

Now the new baron of Tyrswick waited for the noted warrior who wanted to reclaim what Sebastian now owned by right and by deed.

* * *

From the cover of the trees, a man only a few years older than the young baron watched his quarry and cursed him.

Then he cursed William the Bastard of Normandy and, for good measure, cursed Lord Drefan for making this parley necessary.

Wheeling at the sound of a snapping twig, Orlege held his sword at the ready until he recognized the approaching Larcwide, his fellow man-at-arms.

"Make the most of holding that steel," Larcwide commented dryly. "The next metalwork we will see is iron around our wrists and our legs. That's if we're lucky."

Orlege gave a short, bitter laugh, but fatigue and hunger made the effort halfhearted at best. It had been nearly a full day since any of them had consumed more than weak herb tea.

"Any sign of Lord Drefan and his reinforcements?" Orlege asked the older man hopefully, as he had every day for six months.

Larcwide shook his head regretfully.

Orlege sighed and turned back to point to the man some distance away who was entering the deep-blue-and-red striped tent erected for the meeting. It looked obscenely festive under the circumstances.

"Look at him, strutting about wearing nothing but an aketon!" he spat. "If I had a long bow I could end his worthless life and bring honor back to Alfred's family."

"If you had a long bow…" Larcwide mocked. "If you had a long bow you would be signing all our death warrants for certain, including Lord Brice's and Lady Alfreya's. This way there's a chance Lord Brice might see a healer and we might at least have one decent meal before we're hanged."

At the mention of Alfred's son, the man-at-arms's temper subsided.

"I sat with the lad last night," Orlege said. "Infection has set in on the wounds. He will be lucky to survive a sennight."

"Aye," agreed the other man. "Come." Larcwide slapped Orlege on the back. "Let us see how Lady Alfreya fares before she has to parley with that Norman dog."

As they walked back to camp, Orlege considered how far their fortunes had fallen.

Their advance party had been one hundred men strong just half a year ago. They had been modestly equipped but sustained by the promise of rapid reinforcements and reprovisioning from Scotland by Lord Drefan, cousin of Edgar the Atheling. Their lord, Alfred, had been certain of taking back his home by the end of spring.

Then they lost forty to skirmishes against the new lord of Tyrswick, a man who clearly knew the skill of warcraft well. Among the fatalities had been Lord Alfred himself, killed by an arrow within the first month of direct engagement.

Spring turned into summer and Lord Drefan's promised support failed to appear. Another forty-five men and their women melted back over the border to try their fortune on a venture more assured of success.

The rebellion might have ended right there if not for the faith Lady Alfreya placed in Drefan's promises of support and her determination that her younger brother would take his rightful place as earl of Tyrswick.

It was to her, not the boy Lord Brice, whom the men looked for leadership over the past three months.

Now at twenty-one summers old, Lady Alfreya commanded this guerrilla band of thirteen men, planning strategies that over the past four weeks had centered merely on staying alive.

As the small clearing came into view, Orlege regretted Alfreya hadn't been born a man and Brice a girl. She had the temperament and fortitude of a warrior, while her ten-year-old brother was a sweet lad with no fight in him.

Now, they lived like outlaws on land they once owned and worked, avoiding the determined pursuit of de la Croix and his men, and forced to forage and steal food that would be increasingly scarce until autumn, with its promise of the harvest and better hunting.

A ragtag group of three weather-worn canvas tents provided their shelter.

Orlege and Larcwide approached the largest of these.

* * *

Inside the tent, Frey removed a hard-stone ring set in silver and an elaborate enamel brooch from her small timber and brass-work casket before closing the domed lid and returning the box to its sack.

She stood and fastened the brooch to the cloak that had once been her father's. The blue enameled jewel, with intricate interlinked squares picked out in gold, was designed to instill no doubt the wearer was of power and substance.

Frey surveyed her appearance the best she could. Her light blonde hair, the color of primrose, was braided and tied with a leather thong so it fell just above her waist. Over a long shirt, again formerly her father's, she wore a hauberk that came to her knees. The hauberk was unfamiliar and heavy. It had belonged to a young squire killed several months ago.

Her success with the crossbow over these months relied on her ability to move quickly—something she could never do wearing armor—but now it was necessary to do so.

Over the dead squire's tunic of chain mail, Frey wore her father's surcoat bearing the armorial of the House of Tyrswick.

Hose covered her legs and her feet were clad in sturdy boots of soft brown leather, the only thing of value she owned now. Everything else had been abandoned or sold in order to survive.

Frey looked to where her younger brother lay on a narrow cot that occupied nearly the width of the tent itself. The boy watched her through half-lidded eyes.

Frey worried her lower lip with her teeth.

He is so weak, she lamented, and she had nothing to nourish him, let alone ease his fever. "*Oh God,*" she prayed, "*Brice is but ten summers old. Don't take him away from me too.*"

The boy shuddered despite the heat, and the violence of his movement steeled her resolve.

"Frey?" Brice's voice was thin and reedy. "Does Lord Drefan come? Is that why you are so anxious to go in my stead to greet him?"

Frey swallowed back tears and coughed to find her voice. She crouched down to draw a hand tenderly across his forehead. It was slick with sweat, darkening his fair hair.

"I am going to meet with someone who will help us," she told him.

How could she tell her brother they were defeated and the only way any one of them would survive was to throw themselves on the mercy of their enemy? Brice would now never be earl of Tyrswick.

Would it be a blessing if he died never knowing his inheritance had gone forever?

Frey rebuked the thought. No! Brice must live, with as good a future as she could negotiate for him.

"I'll be back before nightfall," she promised, nodding to further affirm her words.

"Frey, do not treat me like a lytling," he said, annoyance evident in his voice. "I am lord of Tyrswick and I should be the one to greet Lord Drefan." He sighed, the effort of speaking nearly too much. He curled his hand around his sister's fingers and gave them a weak squeeze.

"He should ask me for your hand first," he added quietly. "It is only proper."

Frey didn't answer but squeezed his hand in return.

Eight months ago, she would have gladly put aside misgivings to accept the marriage contract for the sake of her father and brother, but now, since Drefan and his promised armies had failed to appear, she put no faith in any man's pledge.

"I have to go, brother," she whispered. Frey squeezed his hand one more time and left the tent. She spotted Orlege and Larcwide approaching a few yards off. She squared her shoulders and walked toward them confidently.

"Is the baron waiting for us?" Frey called some distance out.

"Aye, my lady, he waits at the edge of the meadow as you requested," answered Orlege.

The rest of Alfred's band gathered near to listen.

"Then let's go through this as we agreed.

"Grimbold and Sar, you attend to Lord Brice. Orlege and Larcwide will accompany me. The rest of you wait at the edge of the woods.

"Do not act except in my death or incapacitation, and then do everything necessary to protect Lord Brice."

The men nodded readily though Larcwide was slower to respond. His reticence was not missed by Frey, who arched an eyebrow.

"Is aught amiss, Larcwide?" she asked.

In the absence of her brother's taking his rightful role, she was leader. She would not let her men-at-arms forget. They would just have to overlook her sex.

"It's not right, my lady. One of us should be going instead." He crossed his arms as he spoke, and Frey recognized the sign of resistance from living in such close quarters with him for half a year.

Larcwide was as dear to her as an uncle; she had known him since infancy and knew he had only her family's welfare at heart. And she knew his objections. He had voiced them three days earlier in front of the men.

Her response had been to brandish her knife and threaten to slit his throat from ear-to-ear for his rebellion.

Frey had hated to do it, but if she did not stand firm on her resolve, she would lose the respect of those who remained. How would it serve Brice if she gave in?

She looked at him sternly.

"It is not your position to question the decision of the clan leader, Larcwide."

The man's lips drew to a tight, colorless line.

CHAPTER TWO

The sound of a long clear whistle cut across the meadow and Sebastian looked up at the signal from one of the parties at the left flank.

A moment later, a young squire by the name of Robert rushed to the tent. "My Lord, three men approach!" he said.

Sebastian nodded, allowing the young man to recover his breath.

"Describe them, lad," demanded Gaines, Sebastian's captain.

"The two on either side are warriors, most likely men-at-arms, but their armor is incomplete and neither is wearing a helmet. Their clothes are faded and dirty."

"Then our battles with these rebels *have* had an effect," observed Gaines. "They could be offering for surrender."

"If that were so, they could have had it months ago, and with favorable terms," Sebastian pointed out. "But Alfred's message specifically said he wanted to parley, not surrender." The young baron shook his head thoughtfully. "No, they are playing some game, but I mean to end it. I will not have rebellion foment on my land. Enough blood's been shed."

He moved to the front of the tent to watch the party make their way down the hillock and across the open field toward them and scanned the tree line looking for others. By his count, nine men waited at the crest.

The three approaching were now at the edge of the lea.

Robert was right. The two men on the flanks had the bearing of experienced warriors, but were clearly undergoing hardship.

Sebastian turned his attention to the figure in the center.

The man was dressed in bright armor and a clean surcoat, although the design was hidden by a scarlet cloak. Sebastian frowned. Something wasn't right.

"Gaines!" he yelled. The man rushed to his side. "Look at them. What do you see?"

"That's not Earl Alfred," the knight observed after a moment.

"Agreed. So who the hell is it? Alfred's eldest son and heir was said to have been killed twelve years ago. There is supposed to be a much younger son, but if that's him, he's tall for a lad who can be no older than ten."

Sebastian concentrated on the figure.

The gait was confident, but the armor ill-fitting. The hem of the surcoat fell to the ankle when it should have been at the knee. The scabbard did not sit as it should.

And the shoulders were not as broad as a man's, so the figure under the cloak must be a youth—yet there was something about the way he walked that seemed so much like…

"A woman," announced Sebastian.

Gaines looked at him as if he had taken leave of his senses.

"Our guest is a woman." Sebastian nodded back at the trio.

"What kind of trickery is this?" Gaines demanded as he identified the feminine form for himself.

At that moment a breeze swirled, lifting the hood back from the woman's head, revealing her face for the first time. Sunlight painted her pale hair with gold. Another gust pushed the volume of the cloak away like a sail, fully revealing the surcoat on her slender body.

The garment was sky blue with an embroidered gold cipher of interlocked squares.

Sebastian straightened in surprise and frowned. Unease coiled in his gut.

"Earl Alfred had a daughter, did he not?" he asked.

"Aye, but she was killed months ago," answered Gaines. "Identified by her ring. She was interred in the crypt at Tyrswick." Gaines paused and looked at his lord quizzically. "You ordered that yourself."

"And so I did," agreed Sebastian grimly. "So the question remains… who is this woman?"

* * *

Frey saw two men from the blue-and-red-striped tent step forward to watch them approach.

One was a knight in armor, his head covered by mail and his features so stony, he might as well have been wearing his full helmet.

The second man—the baron himself, Sebastian de la Croix—was bare-headed, wearing only the aketon for protection.

He looked young for a baron, Frey decided, but then that was no less than what Drefan had told her. William the Bastard installed young, inexperienced men to take charge of England's border regions in contempt for the true rulers of Northumbria.

Frey's father had been in his cups that night as he heartily concurred with Drefan's declaration, boasting that one middling Saxon warrior could easily defeat six of the best from France.

Now Frey knew from bitter experience her father exaggerated. He fell with an arrow through his neck, and his body lay not in consecrated grounds at his ancestral home, but in a glen a mere league from where she now walked.

She had prepared his body herself, allowing no one to see the thegn until he was cleaned and dressed, and everything Alfred had been— father, husband, earl, leader, lord—was memorialized with a hastily erected pile of stones.

Frey swallowed the bitterness of the memory, knowing it could not help her now, not when Brice's life was in the balance. She would bury her loathing for the invader as deep as she had buried her father.

Twenty yards from the tent, Frey halted. Orlege and Larcwide stopped with her.

"Wait here," she told them before walking alone toward the tent, unsure whether or not she heard Larcwide mutter another complaint under his breath.

Each step forward was a trial, every beat of her heart warning her to turn back. And yet for Brice she would do this thing.

The knight to her right looked implacable; his hard, chiseled face and dark mustache might have been hewn from rock, and his eyes lay in shadow, so Frey turned her attention to the man on her left, whose eyes and face she could see and read.

Strangely enough, seeing his eyes gave her courage. It meant he was a man, not a monster. At least that's what she told herself as she called to the men.

"I am Alfreya, daughter of Alfred of Tyrswick, the sister of Brice who is now, by virtue of the death of our father, earl of Tyrswick," she announced loudly in French to the party of Normans. "I am the one who called for parley."

She heard a murmur go through the gathering of the baron's men at the sound of her voice. No doubt they were surprised. The call for parley was unusual enough under the circumstances, but that it should be called by a woman as a leader was unheard of.

"Have you proof of your claims?" yelled the knight.

Surely the ability to speak their hated Frankish tongue fluently ought be proof enough of noble birth, Frey fumed, but she nonetheless stopped a few feet away and unsheathed the sword she wore.

The knight stood to attention with a hand on the handle of his own sword, alert to potential threat. The baron merely stood with his arms crossed, his expression fixed.

His lack of reaction ignited her spirit. *"He means to humiliate me,"* she decided angrily. *"He won't get that satisfaction."*

With energy, she tossed the sword in the baron's direction, smugly satisfied with the look of surprise on his face. He stepped back, deftly catching the sword by the grip and turning it so he could see the hilt consisting of interlinked squares engraved on quality steel.

Frey was satisfied with the grudging respect that fell across his features as he examined the blade. She knew as well as he did that it was an expensive weapon made for a man of means. Without question it had belonged to Alfred.

"The sword is insufficient proof," he told her, stepping forward and presenting the weapon back by the pommel.

Frey had anticipated a challenge to her identity but was taken off guard by the return of the sword. She wasn't sure whether it was out of respect or whether, in this man's opinion, she posed so little threat to his person.

"I have further proof," she said, pulling the large, masculine ring from her thumb and holding it up for the baron to observe. "I hold the seal of Tyrswick."

He held out the palm of his hand. Frey refused to pass the ring.

Sebastian caught her wrist in a rapid movement and pulled her closer. Frey's shoulder collided with his broad chest and she gasped in surprise. Her heart beat loudly in her ears.

The grip was sure, but not cruel. Frey licked her lips nervously. This man exuded raw power; it would be a mistake to underestimate him.

After her initial expression of astonishment, a neutral mask shuttered her appearance.

Sebastian raised her hand slowly until sunlight glinted across the surface of the ring. Deep-cut depressions in the carnelian revealed its function as a seal. Interlocked squares and the word "Tyrs" were reversed in the relief.

He pulled her closer and she heard him take a deep breath as he saw for himself the truth she held in her hand. The baron straightened and his fingers brushed against her rapidly beating pulse in a light caress as he released her wrist.

Frey smiled at him triumphantly.

"Are you ready to begin negotiations, my lord?" she asked sweetly.

He gave her an assessing look.

"There's just one problem," he said before pausing significantly. "Lady Alfreya of Tyrswick has been dead for the past two months."

Frey paled and rocked back on her feet.

No, this cannot be! What manner of trap was this?

"She wore a ring as proof of identity when her corpse was found," he continued bluntly.

"Diera? Oh dear God in heaven, what have I done?" she breathed, lapsing into Saxon.

"Is that your real name, girl?" Gaines interjected.

"No!" Frey yelled at him. "I am Alfreya of Tyrswick!"

The men who accompanied her shifted forward and Sebastian's men responded in kind.

Without looking behind, Frey raised an arm upward and her two men stopped their advance.

"At ease," Gaines ordered, and Sebastian's own men stood down.

Frey wavered in her resolve for a moment. Tears welled but did not fall.

"What was she doing near Tyrswick?" Frey asked herself out loud before addressing her interrogators.

"Diera was my maid. I gave her a ring as both a token of remembrance and to use for trade should the need arise. She left with the others three months ago. They were supposed to have crossed the border back into Scotland."

"Do you still hold that you are Alfred's daughter?" the baron asked.

His question was delivered softly, as though motivated by compassion, but Frey knew that could not be so. Normans had no compassion.

"I am," she avowed without hesitation.

As Frey looked defiantly at the men, the daylight changed from gold to pink as the sun retreated farther down the sky. The shadows deepened, heralding the beginning of twilight.

"Then let's parley," Sebastian announced suddenly, stepping aside from the entrance to reveal a small wooden campaign table and two stools within.

Frey walked into the tent and sat on the seat he indicated. A page dashed forward, placed two small horn cups on the table, and filled them with wine before rushing away.

Frey's mouth watered at the rich and fruity bouquet. Nearly five months had gone since she last tasted grapes. There had been no wine since their party left Scotland.

The page returned with a tray of cheeses and dried fruit, and just the sight of it made Frey's stomach spasm with nausea. It had been more than a week since she and her band had eaten anything more filling than pottage made from a single rabbit they managed to snare and plucked wild herbs.

Meals since then had consisted of a weak broth made from whatever they could forage. They always went hungry at night.

Now, she ignored the food and took a small sip of wine, just enough to wet her lips.

The Norman baron before her watched every movement with great interest. She felt as though he were a hunter watching his prey—silent, certain, deadly.

She would rather have dealt with the knight; at least he wore his contempt for her openly. The baron, on the other hand, kept his own counsel and that made him dangerous.

Frey decided she needed to be especially careful of this man.

"I have come to negotiate a truce," she announced.

Sebastian offered a wry smile. "Have you indeed?"

"I have," Frey replied firmly.

"Why ask for a truce? Surrender now and we can all go home in time for supper," Sebastian reasoned sarcastically.

Frey bristled and a run of insults came to mind, all with the voice of her father. "Norman dog, thieving bastard, plunderer, despoiler, bitch-wolf's son."

"Brice, the rightful earl of Tyrswick, was injured five nights ago by a snare," she told him heatedly. "His ankle is broken and the puncture wounds from the trap jaw have become infected."

Sebastian shifted on the stool and Frey took it as a tiny tell that indicated he appreciated the gravity of the situation she described. A seemingly minor wound might easily grow hot and puffy with poisoned blood, malodorous pus, and fluid leaking from the hole, invisible demons heating the body until it was feverish and weak. Infections were a serious business indeed, killing men faster and in greater numbers than were slain outright on the field of battle.

"My brother needs a physician," Frey continued. "There is an abbey three days' ride from here. I want a truce without harassment and without arrest so my men and I can move him to St Cuthbert's and entreat the monks to tend him."

Frey watched the baron take in her words. As she finished, he sat up straight and folded his arms, his expression turning from benign disinterest to hostility.

"What advantage do I receive for the truce?" he asked icily. "Since spring, you and your company have stolen livestock and game from my villagers and been responsible for the deaths of ten of my men as well as committing treason against the Crown."

He looked at her with contempt. "For that you ought to be facing the executioner's blade, not making travel plans, *Lady* Alfreya."

Frey slammed a flat palm on the table. The platter and cups leaped but remained upright.

"And for *that* reason I cannot agree to surrender!" she yelled. "With a truce, you would be bound by the rules of combat chivalry, but with prisoners you would be within your rights to treat us as you wished, even hang a dying ten-year-old boy."

Frey glanced sharply around, now aware every man in the tent looked at her with astonishment. All of the promises to herself that she would negotiate as the equal of a man evaporated like this morning's dew because of her loss of temper.

Grudgingly, she pulled her focus back to the baron whose expression remained unchanged.

"Please, I beg of you sir," Frey whispered, as close to humiliation as she had ever been in her life. "I just want my brother to live."

***

Sebastian regarded her. Lady Alfreya thought like a man. No, like a *warrior*. Reluctantly, he found himself impressed and suddenly considering her manner and appearance.

Despite her fiery temper, which she seemed to work hard to control, Earl Alfred's daughter had grown comely, although a little on the thin side. Her figure might best be described as willowy, but her outstanding features were her hair, the color of newly harvested hay, and her bright blue eyes, which examined him with caution.

"Then what *do* you bring to this truce?" Sebastian finally asked.

"Our band now numbers but thirteen, all of whom are good men and loyal to my father. They accompanied us to Scotland when William the Bas—" Frey corrected herself, "…when the *king* harried the north.

"They are local men and without my father to lead them, all they wish now is to go home to the families they haven't seen in four years. They will cause no further trouble; you have my word on that."

The baron shook his head.

"Your little rebellion has gone on for months even after the death of Earl Alfred," responded Sebastian, "and you yourself speak of their abiding loyalty to your late father. So forgive me, my lady, if I require more than just your word."

Frey nodded. It seemed his objection was not unexpected.

"Then I offer myself as surety," she said simply.

"A hostage," Sebastian stated blandly.

Not an unusual offer, he thought. King Malcolm of Scotland's eldest son, Duncan, had technically been a hostage of King William for the past two years, yet by all accounts the lad was well treated and, indeed, educated alongside William's own sons.

So, Lady Alfreya was taking a gamble on what kind of man he was. Interesting.

"If you deem it such," she shrugged in an attempt at nonchalance. "And yes, these remaining men are loyal to my family, but they will do nothing to give you cause for retribution on me or my brother.

"You have my word of honor."

The quality of the dying light streaming through the entrance of the tent shifted again from pink to a dull, lifeless gray. In the glen, the noisy evening chorus of birds seemed preternaturally loud as they returned to their trees to roost.

Sebastian didn't need to look back at Henry Gaines to know the man's thoughts.

He'd fought alongside this knight for five years. Knowing what the other was thinking wasn't a supernatural gift; it was one developed by necessity over time to assure survival in battle.

He heard a sigh of resignation from Gaines as he made his decision and spoke.

"Show me the boy," Sebastian ordered.

CHAPTER THREE

Frey sat straight-backed on the stool. The baron had agreed to the truce? He hadn't said so directly, but if he hadn't, why did he ask to see Brice? If he wanted to force surrender, he could have his men round up their band in short order. Even a Norman would know she wouldn't dare risk leaving her brother too far away.

Sebastian de la Croix stood and Frey did likewise.

"Give me your sword and the seal," he told her. "You won't need them again."

Frey did not comply.

"Not until you agree we have a truce," she answered.

Sebastian gifted her with a half smile.

"Congratulations, Lady Alfreya, you negotiated well. You have your truce—and never let it be said that I hang ten-year-old boys for the sins of their fathers."

Frey unbuckled the scabbard from around her waist. She handed it and the sword to him ceremoniously.

"Neither let it be said the Tyrswick family is without honor," she replied, handing over the ring with equal formality.

Frey followed Sebastian to the opening of the tent, where he gave orders briskly and efficiently.

"Gaines, organize a litter and get Lady Alfreya's two men to bring the boy here. Make sure they're accompanied by two of our men," he said. "Send Robert back to the village with some coin to see what food and drink can be purchased. Tell him to fetch the friar too. We camp here tonight. I want to see the condition of the party before I decide what to do next."

Gaines paused stony-faced for a beat before nodding stiffly and moving away, barking orders of his own.

Frey watched the byplay with great interest.

Gaines had just made it clear that he believed his lord to have been too indulgent to agree to this meeting in the first place and was further out of his mind to contract a truce. The knight would not have shown mercy to the rebels.

Without looking back, merely expecting her to follow, Sebastian walked around the tent to where his horse grazed quietly at the back. In a quick, graceful motion, he mounted the steed, then looked down at Frey and extended his hand.

"I will walk with my men," she told him, shaking her head.

"Get on the horse *now*," he growled in a flash of anger, "or I will tie you up and throw you on."

His irritation simmered with each long second she stood immovable.

"You do not want to test me, madam," he said, his voice low and menacing.

Frey looked at his hand as though it were a poisonous snake before she reluctantly held out her own.

Even wearing a hauberk of mail, she was pulled swiftly onto the horse as though she weighed little more than a sack of vegetables. He settled her across his lap, arms trapping her effectively to his chest.

Her struggles seemed to amuse him as she sat straight in an attempt to put some distance between them, but that gesture came to naught as soon as the horse stepped forward. To secure her seat, Frey was forced to reach an arm around his back in a parody of an embrace.

The hard muscles of his back played under her hand with the movement of the horse beneath them. His firm thighs pressed hers intimately.

This was wrong. Dangerous.

Frey swallowed her panic as he leaned forward to speak directly into her ear, his words causing gooseflesh to rise on her arms.

"We may have a truce, my lady, but there are many more questions I have before I'm completely satisfied."

"Then satisfy yourself quickly my lord; we are not far from our encampment," she told him softly.

The man laughed and leaned in closer.

"Know this of me, princess. I am never satisfied quickly."

Frey felt a flush of color rise in her face, betraying that the double meaning of his words was not lost on her. He straightened in his saddle. It might have been to her advantage to maintain an illusion of innocence. His knight may believe him to be a sentimentalist, but he was clearly no fool, and her every word, every reaction, might weaken her position if she did not guard herself.

As they rode, he questioned her thoroughly, first about the location of the camp and the number of men, which she had already told him was thirteen. She realized he was probing again to see if the detail changed. He asked of their physical condition and the number and state of their weapons, then about the battle that killed her father.

Frey did her best to give equally thorough and detailed answers. As much as she regretted the necessity, she knew it was essential to allay the baron's suspicions if she were to ensure Brice received the treatment he needed.

Fortunately, the conversation came to an end before he asked *how* she knew so much about her father's fateful last battle.

The fact was her band's six months of war without reinforcements and fending for themselves had forced Frey to learn a new set of skills a world away from the domestic arts learned in the solar with the other women of a noble household.

It would not do for Sebastian to learn she had been on the field of battle that day and that she was one of her father's most accomplished archers, deadly accurate with a bow and a knife. Moreover, she enjoyed putting these skills to use. Many a day, her aim was the only thing that furnished what little meat they had consumed in three moons.

As they arrived among her men, Frey saw the meager band through the eyes of the stranger she rode with.

They were men bearded and roughly dressed, poorly nourished and dispirited. The Normans could have driven a sword through the lot of them and found little resistance.

One by one, their heads dropped at seeing her in the arms of their enemy. Their rebellion was truly over now.

All of a sudden, sitting high up on a horse sat ill with Frey. She pushed the baron's arm aside and slid down from the steed. The man athletically dismounted behind her.

Frey attempted to ignore his presence at her shoulder as she approached Sar, a big young lad who guarded the entrance to her brother's tent.

"How is he?" she asked him, forcing his attention to her rather than the man behind her.

Sar hesitated, glancing again at the large Norman warrior for a moment.

"His fever's not broke, my lady," he answered at last. "He's more often than not asleep and then he is in delirium and it don't abate even when he wakes."

Frey slipped past Sar to enter the tent. She knelt beside her unconscious brother's cot, taking his hand in hers, her attention divided between listening to the boy's labored breathing and the baron addressing Sar outside.

"What has the boy been treated with?" he asked in Norman, then, following a moment's uncomprehending silence from Sar, he asked the question again in Saxon.

"I don't know," said the lad. "The Lady Alfreya tends to him herself."

Good, thought Frey, say as little as possible. Better to give nothing away. Then she groaned as the youngster added, "…or sometimes Larcwide does. I don't know what potions he's had, but it won't have been much because we don't got much."

She heard the baron grunt in response and enter the tent behind her. As he did so, Brice's eyes opened and he weakly raised his head and smiled at him.

"See, Frey," Brice whispered, "you were wrong to worry. Your Drefan did come after all."

Frey tried to shush him. Sebastian stepped forward to get a better look at the heir of Tyrswick.

The lad's skin was sallow and the dark circles under his eyes made them appear to sink farther in his head. Sebastian removed the leather gauntlet from his right hand and reached down to feel the boy's slick and clammy forehead.

Frey glanced up surreptitiously at Sebastian. The easy smile he had given her brother when touching his forehead was gone as he looked to her, instead replaced with a grim line.

They both knew Brice's only hope was to be delivered into the care of the monks before his condition worsened. His body was close to defeat. Untreated, he would be dead within days.

The youngster took the baron's ministration without complaint, looking up at him in the tent's dark shadows as if he were a saint or an angel.

"You took an awful long time to get here," he murmured, "but I prayed and you came."

Sebastian ruffled the boy's hair in response and Frey felt the man look at her, but was determined to ignore him until she could master the roiling emotions that threatened to spill over. She kept her attention fixed on her brother's face.

"We're going to get you well, Brice," said Sebastian, "but I need a moment of your sister's time."

He placed his hand on Frey's shoulder and gave a gentle half rub, half squeeze to draw her attention. She gritted her teeth. If he showed kindness, she would break, so she frowned at him as she stood.

"Ha, ha! I know what for," Brice offered in a singsong voice. "I'm earl now, Drefan. You really ought to ask my permission before you kiss my sister again."

"Brice!" Frey admonished, color rising again to her cheeks.

***

If the boy's condition wasn't so grave, Sebastian might have laughed. He couldn't help himself. His interest was piqued for more than one reason. To begin, who was this expected Drefan who had been a long time in coming? And what was the Lady Alfreya's interest in a man familiar enough to kiss?

Looking at the young woman who glared at him intently, Sebastian intended to find out.

He meant what he told her. He never satisfied himself quickly, and now he had even more questions. However, there were her men to deal with first.

"My lady, you ought to speak to your men on behalf of your brother," he advised softly. "Let them know what is to follow."

Frey's rigidly correct posture softened somewhat and she nodded in agreement. Glancing again at her brother, whose eyes were now closed, she closed her own in a quick prayer before imperiously walking out of the tent, every inch the noblewoman.

Sebastian followed, sticking close behind her.

While in the tent, a pair of Lady Alfreya's men, under the guard of two of the baron's own, arrived with a litter.

Sebastian watched as Lady Alfreya gave terse orders for young Lord Brice's transportation, and when he added instructions of his own, the men hesitated, looking uncertainly to Alfreya for confirmation before they commenced their task.

He learned their names—Orlege and aforementioned Larcwide— and determined he would watch those two. As trusted men of the earl's family, they might still be dangerous.

Alfreya watched with concern on her face as the two Saxons entered the tent and emerged a few moments later, carrying the young earl of Tyrswick on the litter, heading under escort down to the camp.

Sebastian scanned the remaining men, all tired and defeated. They looked as though they craved nothing more than a belly full of warm food and a decent night's sleep. Well, that he could grant.

He accompanied Lady Alfreya as she went from man to man, thanking each for his sacrifice and loyalty. Finally, she addressed them all, assuring them there was nothing more to be done but rebuild their lives as she hoped she and Brice might.

At the end of her speech, she looked up at Sebastian.

"I know not what else to say," she whispered, looking tired and surprisingly vulnerable.

Compassion stirred in his breast.

Sebastian gave a brief nod of acknowledgment and stepped forward, looking the weary and haggard men in the eye.

"This will be the last night you will sleep outside under the stars not of your own choice," he said.

"On your pledge of fealty to me and to William the Conqueror of England, you will receive food tonight and my guarantee that as long as each of you are lawful and productive members of your villages, you will have amnesty and no cause to fear harassment from me.

"However, if you are lawless, your lives will be forfeit.

"If you have love for your late lord and any regard for his children, you would do well to consider it or it will not bode well for them either.

"What say you?"

With varying degrees of reluctance, the men voiced their assent, then one by one they were brought before Sebastian to swear their oath before him, witnessed by Gaines and the local friar who had returned from the village with Robert.

Finally, Sebastian told the men that, in the morning, the friar would subject them to a census and arrange their return home. He dismissed them with an order to "go and eat your fill."

The men turned their attention to the meadow from where the almost forgotten aroma of roasting mutton wafted.

"Baron, a word in private if I may," the friar called.

Friar Dominic was a small, nuggetty man who appeared to Sebastian, judging by his lined mouth and eyes, to have seen more of life than most.

Gaines had once joked that a single dead-eye stare from Dominic would have the devil himself flee. Sebastian was hard-pressed to disagree with the assessment. However, the friar's sharp mind and forthright manner also made him one of the few Englishmen Sebastian trusted enough to confide in.

"Gaines, escort Lady Alfreya and ensure she and her brother have sufficient to eat," he instructed his man at arms. He watched her follow Gaines in the direction of the camp before turning to the clergyman. "Yes, Dominic?"

"What are you planning to do with Lord Brice and Lady Alfreya?" asked the friar.

Sebastian gave a short laugh and turned away, starting down to the lea where flames from half a dozen braziers flickered an orange blaze, casting distorted shadows of men setting up the last of the encampment. A quarter moon added a weak glow to the new night. Sebastian could just make out the shapes of Gaines and Alfreya about twenty yards ahead.

Despite the difference in their heights, Friar Dominic kept pace with the taller man easily.

"What do you think I should do with them?" said Sebastian crossly at last. "Put their heads on a pike? Flay them? Send them to London to be locked in White Tower?"

"Strictly speaking," considered the friar, "you'd be well within your rights to do any of those things, according to the powers given to you by King William."

"What are you trying to tell me, Dominic?"

"Is it my place to tell you anything?" the friar asked.

"It hasn't stopped you in the past," retorted Sebastian in good humor.

"So, you're convinced this woman is the daughter of Earl Alfred, despite the fact you just buried a woman of that name not two months ago?"

"You performed the rites; you identified the signet ring."

"I did."

Sebastian stopped and gave a long, drawn-out sigh.

"Speak plainly, will you, Dom? It's been a long day."

Friar Dominic came to the point.

"Since we buried the girl whom you believed to be Lady Alfreya of Tyrswick, you've taken a personal interest in trying to find the man who brutally murdered her," he said. "I just want *you* to be certain, for *your* sake."

Sebastian gave a curt nod in acknowledgment.

"She carries Alfred's sword, seal, and surcoat. That alone would be enough to commend her," he said. "Even without them…she speaks French fluently, and her skills in command and negotiation would have convinced me soon enough."

The two men continued their walk down the hill.

"She is a beautiful young woman, is she not?" ventured Dominic after a moment.

Sebastian did not answer, but the friar had his attention and continued. "You've secured the loyalty of the remainder of Alfred's men—or at least their oath of loyalty. But what of his children?"

"From what I've seen of young Brice," Sebastian replied, "it will take one of God's miracles for him to see the next full moon. And as for that woman…"

"His sister," Friar Dominic corrected.

"Sister, then," Sebastian acknowledged. "She has offered herself as my hostage in exchange for her brother's care."

"Putting herself in your hands? She's braver than I gave her credit for," said Dominic, openly irreverent of the baron's authority. "But that does bring me back to my original question. What are you going to do?"

Sebastian shrugged, but the action was lost in the darkness.

"That all depends whether our murderer was an opportunist who happened across the girl at random or whether Alfreya was the intended victim all along."

CHAPTER FOUR

Sebastian's man-at-arms stalked down the hill, seemingly heedless of whether Frey followed him or not. Losing sight of the baron behind them in the darkness, Frey concentrated on keeping up with the knight whose long strides took them rapidly toward the camp.

A dozen more tents had sprung up in the couple of hours since Frey made her truce with the new master of Tyrswick. What started in the afternoon as a gathering of not more than thirty people now swelled to double that number as the curious from the nearby village arrived with food and drink. The meadow had taken on a carnival atmosphere.

Frey could see some of her father's men sitting around a fire, some laughing and with smiles that had been absent for many, many months. A yell of recognition, laughter, and the sound of hearty backslapping drew her attention to another part of the field. Two more men were in animated conversation with a group of villagers with whom they were well acquainted.

The smell of meat cooking was almost unbearable. Frey's mouth watered at the sight and aroma of two fowl roasting on a spit, and she stopped in her tracks. Gaines was paying attention after all. He stopped too, a few feet away.

The old woman turning the spit handle looked up and grinned. "Ye'll be waitin' a while for these dearie, but there's plenty o' stew t'be 'ad," she told Frey, indicating a pot suspended over a nearby fire.

"Thank you," said Frey, and the old woman shuffled off to fill a bowl for her.

Frey called to Gaines and the knight turned to her reluctantly, as though she was beneath his contempt.

"Have all the men eaten?" she asked.

The man looked around and shrugged. "I suppose so," he told her, then turned away with a disinterested air and walked off, his work of escorting her to the camp over.

Frey sighed. The care of the men, at least with respect to food and drink, was another responsibility taken from her shoulders. For months the routine had been the same. Stay one step ahead of Sebastian de la Croix and his soldiers, hunt for food, and find shelter from the changeable northern weather.

Now it was over and Frey wasn't sure how she felt about that.

The old woman returned with a steaming bowl of stew and a lump of bread.

Frey thanked her and glanced about until she saw Sar. The youngster stood glumly by the entrance to one of the tents, his presence indicating it was the one in which Brice rested.

Sar stood to attention as she approached, then his eyes wandered down to the bowl in her hands. He stared covetously.

"Have you eaten yet?" Frey asked.

The lad shook his head, and Frey handed her meal to him.

"Finish that and you may be lucky to get some roast meat," she told him. "I'll stay with Lord Brice."

Sar didn't need to be told twice. He managed the ungainly feat of dipping the bread into the stew, eating, and running toward the spit all at the same time.

On lifting the flap of the tent—the baron's own, she realized—her nostrils were assaulted by the thick scent of an incense of myrrh, rose, and frankincense. A censer more typically used in a church sat by the entrance flap in the gloom. Clearly the friar had been here first.

Had he given up on her brother too, merely offering the last rites and abandoning him to his fate?

A lamp glowed dully, offering just enough light for Frey to identify the location of her brother's cot.

She approached and observed an earthenware jar by the edge of the bedding. She removed the lid and sniffed the contents. Despite the heavy odor of incense in the air, one by one the ingredients identified themselves to her—honey, rosemary, and a citric tang she guessed were crushed feverfew leaves.

She relidded the jar and lifted the edge of the blanket. Brice's ankle had been rebandaged and the dark, sticky fluid that oozed from the edges had the same odor as the unguent in the jar.

Nearby, a bowl contained the dregs of a clear broth. If Brice had eaten more than a few mouthfuls, she would be grateful.

Perhaps she wasn't the only one who believed her brother could be made well, after all.

Frey brushed his cheek affectionately and kissed his forehead. He seemed to be sleeping peacefully, with no sign of the fever that had plagued him earlier.

There was nothing more for her to do in here, so she stepped out into the night air.

Nothing more to do. The thought echoed in her head.

Instead of the relief she expected to feel, a hollowness settled instead. Once she safely delivered her brother into the hands of the healing monks at St Cuthbert's, her goal would be accomplished. But what then?

For the first time in her life, Frey found herself devoid of purpose and with no idea of what the future might hold. From the entrance of the tent, she watched the activity by the fires and felt estranged from it.

She needed solitude.

Frey turned her back on the camp and walked into the darkness, away from the comforting warmth of the firelight, the smell of food, and the sound of conversation.

The inky evening cloaked her in its embrace.

She sat on a fallen log and allowed a tear, the first she had permitted since her father's death, to fall.

"Damn you to hell, Drefan!" she cursed in a hoarse whisper. "You said but for my father's determination to win back Tyrswick, we would be wed.

"Now my father is dead, perhaps my brother also soon enough, and my life and future are in the hands of a Norman enemy.

"My father paid you handsomely in gold but you and your promises of troops and arms are nowhere to be seen.

"Traitor, thief, liar… Is this what it means when you vow love?"

* * *

Frey's tears were long dried before anyone intruded on her privacy.

Larcwide approached, holding a joint of meat in one hand and a bowl of stew in the other.

"Eat, my lady," he said, handing her the bowl.

"What makes you think I haven't already eaten?" she grumbled, but nonetheless accepted the meal.

The man-at-arms shrugged and sat down beside her.

"I know you too well, mistress," he responded, giving her a nudge with his shoulder while he helped himself to a large mouthful of roasted sheep. "Go on, humor me. At least pretend to eat."

Frey huffed. She dipped a piece of bread into the bowl and popped it in her mouth.

It was heavenly. She chewed slowly, savoring the flavors of onion, herbs, and beef.

Larcwide watched as Frey scooped two more mouthfuls with the bread before he returned to chewing his joint.

They sat in companionable silence until Larcwide's meal was nothing more than scraped bone, but he observed Frey's still unfinished meal as he interrupted her reverie."Your father would have been proud of you today," he said.

Frey shook her head and snorted derisively.

"Yes, he would," Larcwide argued. "It's a true test of a warrior's mettle to know when the battle has been lost and negotiate the best outcome. You did that today. A few of the men are reunited with their families; the rest have been promised employment gathering the harvest, and so far none of us have been hanged, boiled in oil, burned at the stake or clapped in irons and that's more than anyone expected, so…well done."

Frey accepted his thanks with an awkward shrug of her shoulders and a nod. After a moment she turned her head and considered his profile.

"What of yourself and Orlege?"

"You can't see us being farmers or shepherds?" he asked lightly.

Frey shook her head.

"What about a swineherd?"

Frey laughed as Larcwide punctuated the question with an oink and a squeal.

He smiled too, at hearing his mistress laugh, she surmised.

It had been too long.

"You still haven't answered my question," said Frey, unaware of his distraction. "You and Orlege are warriors. You're no more a farmer than I am a scullion."

"Perhaps our new lord could stand a few replacement knights for the ones we took in battle and you could get used to washing dishes?"

Frey's look told him what she thought of the idea.

Larcwide grinned and forced a half smile from his mistress.

"Now, don't you be worrying about us, my lady. Battle-hardened warriors always find employment."

The conversation came to an end and each remained in silent contemplation for a while before Frey broached the subject that troubled her. She looked back at the camp and started to feel the pull of its warmth, camaraderie, and certainty. She blinked and looked away before she spoke.

"Do you think the outcome would have been different if Lord Drefan delivered the troops and arms as promised?"

"Only God knows," he answered truthfully, and paused before going on. "Mayhap yes it would, which would mean more war. King

William has already shown how far he will go to assert his authority. But then perhaps no, which would mean all of us dead in battle or by the noose, and you destined for something much worse than death.

"This way, your men begin a new life, Lord Brice will receive care, and you can be married to someone more worthy of you than Drefan."

Larcwide punctuated the end of his speech with a forceful spit.

Frey started. She had never before heard anyone of her men, let alone Larcwide, venture a negative opinion of Edgar the Atheling's cousin.

"So you put more faith in a barbarian Norman like the Baron Sebastian than a fellow Saxon?" she questioned.

Larcwide issued a long-suffering sigh.

"I'm a simple man, my lady," he told her. "I judge men by what they say and by what they do. Lord Drefan promised troops and aid. He didn't deliver. Lord Sebastian promised full bellies and an amnesty. He's made good on the first promise, and that's one more than Drefan."

CHAPTER FIVE

"Then came Peter to him, and said, 'Lord, how oft shall my brother sin against me, and I forgive him? 'till seven times?' Jesus saith unto him, 'I say not unto thee, until seven times: but, until seventy times seven.'"

Friar Dominic closed the ancient text—one painstakingly hand copied and bound in leather—upon a tree stump and drew breath to deliver his sermon. Earlier that morning he had announced a service of reconciliation and thanksgiving after the break-fast, as well as the hearing of private confessions.

Gathered in close were both Alfred's and Sebastian's men and a few of the villagers who weren't occupied with morning chores.

"Our Lord places an extraordinary amount of emphasis on forgiveness, not only from our Heavenly Father for our own sins, but also in that we should emulate him and forgive our brother. Not just once, not just twice, but many, many times over," said the friar.

"Many here have been both trespasser and trespassed upon. Forgiveness is not an act of emotion, but an act of your will. Now is the time for forgiveness, now is the time to leave behind enmities of the past to build a new day and a new life, exhorting ourselves to follow Christ's example."

Dominic nodded to Sebastian's young squire, Robert, who was serving as altar boy. The young man solemnly opened up the traveling sacristy and the friar retrieved a small silver salver and chalice and held them both to the heavens. The morning sun seemed to give him a beatific glow.

One by one the camp, both Saxon and Norman alike, filed past to accept the sacrament.

Frey remained where she stood at the back of the crowd. A dozen people filed past and accepted the Eucharist. Then came Sebastian's turn.

Frey watched the baron bow his head and kneel. She saw a man of superior height and strength to the friar, nevertheless humbling himself to acknowledge something greater than himself. As Sebastian knelt before God, she knew the only other he would do so for would be King William himself.

For reasons she struggled to understand, this observation made her angry.

This man killed my father and ruthlessly hunted us for months, and now he seeks reconciliation? she thought. *God may forgive him, but I don't know if I can. I don't know if I want to.*

As she argued with herself, Larcwide's words from last night popped into her head. *"He's made good on the first promise and that is one more than Drefan."*

Yet when has a Norman done anything other than pillage and destroy? she asked herself bitterly.

Then, unbidden, a fragment of a memory—surreal, as though a dream—resolved itself in her mind's eye, of a young Norman, who had stood before her and then lied to his lord to afford her the chance to save her wounded father and young brother.

Frey shook her head to clear the image. Two acts of kindness from Normans. What should she make of it?

She waited until the last of the men joined the communion line before adjusting the hood of her gray cloak, the closest thing she possessed to a veil, and taking her place.

Maybe, if she prayed harder, she could learn to forgive.

* * *

Midmorning passed before the makeshift camp had been completely dismantled. Many of those who had stayed overnight were long departed, including Lord Alfred's men. They were to accompany the friar back to the closest village, where they would stay until all the neighboring priests could check their parish records to confirm their identities.

Before Dominic left, Sebastian directed him to write a missive to the abbot of St. Cuthbert's, telling him to expect the arrival of a gravely ill child and asking the abbot to identify and vouch for the accompanying cipher. Using the ring surrendered to him by the Lady Alfreya, Sebastian added a wax imprint, accompanied by his own seal.

Now, Robert was on his way, with instructions to make all haste.

The only remainders of the six-month-long, ill-considered rebellion were the injured boy; the young woman; and her two men-at-arms, Larcwide and the younger one, Orlege, who had accompanied her to yesterday's parley.

The two men claimed no family and no skills apart from martial ones and were steadfast in their duty to protect their mistress.

Although it rankled him, Sebastian couldn't fault their loyalty. They were doing exactly as he would expect them to. Lady Alfreya, on the other hand, was the most unpredictable, difficult, frustrating female he ever had the misfortune to meet.

His plans were clear at this morning's breakfast. She would go back to the village with Dominic, who would then arrange a suitable escort to take her back to his keep. There, she would be a companion to his sister and behave like a proper noblewoman until he could figure out what to do with her.

But the damn woman stubbornly refused to go, demanding—and quite loudly, too—that she should accompany her brother.

He ground his teeth as he recalled the conversation. She had waited until he had turned and begun to walk away before answering.

"No."

He halted and slowly turned back to confront the one who dared disobey him.

"It wasn't a suggestion."

His voice was cold and angry, an ill temper made worse by the peripheral awareness that Gaines, along with Alfreya's two men, had stopped to watch the confrontation. He knew such a look and tone of voice was warning enough for his own men, all of whom knew better than to gainsay him, but this young woman refused to show any fear.

She folded her arms in defiance and looked him directly in the eye. "We had an agreement," she told him.

"And so we do," he replied. "Your rebellious rabble have returned to their homes without retribution, and your brother is about to receive the care he needs."

"Our agreement was for *my* men and I to transport my brother to St. Cuthbert's."

Sebastian frowned. Was the woman addle-witted?

"Where the hell do you think we're going?"

"I said my men and *I*, Baron. Although I thank you for the cart and the escort. You need not trouble yourself further on our account. I'm sure you're a very busy man."

She turned as if to dismiss him. Sebastian didn't let her get far.

He grabbed her by the elbow and, as he spun her back around, damn if she didn't smell like wildflowers.

"That's not the only promise you made, princess," he intoned softly. Sebastian had to confess to a deal of satisfaction in seeing a shiver run through the girl. "As my hostage, everything you do concerns me."

Her rich blue eyes flickered nervously, and the tip of her ripe pink tongue emerged to wet her lips.

He was mesmerized, and the arousal that smoldered in him burst into flame when her reply came, low and husky.

"Then I suppose you'll be accompanying us, my lord, because no force in heaven or earth will make me leave my brother."

So now, enduring the first defeat of his military career, Sebastian watched her issuing instructions to his own men about how best to secure Brice's litter in the cart.

Only when the job was completed to her satisfaction did she climb nimbly on board, despite being hampered by the skirts of the green kirtle she wore. At least it was a more appropriate garment for her sex than the hose and surcoat of the day before.

Once seated, the imperious chit looked him directly in the eye and announced they were ready to go. Like two faithful puppies, Orlege and Larcwide scrambled up beside her.

Sebastian clenched his teeth and bit down on the string of curses that threatened to bubble to the surface. He mounted his horse angrily and nodded to the cart driver.

Two of his men rode ahead and set the pace. Sebastian waited until they and the cart were out of sight before he urged his own horse to walk. Perhaps if he didn't have to look at Alfred's daughter, the murderous feelings welling up inside him might ebb.

"You're making a mistake with her," said a voice beside him.

Sebastian glowered at Gaines who had ridden up alongside him.

"I don't recall asking for advice," he answered.

Gaines continued, ignoring the warning tone in his lord's voice.

"You've been too easy on the girl," he said, looking straight ahead as he spoke. "You should have showed her who is master now over these lands. How can you demand the respect of Alfred's men when you let her get her own way?

"Word of your softness will have spread across the barony by the time we return from this fool's errand, my lord. It would have been better to let the boy die and hang the lot of—"

The knight stopped speaking abruptly as the sword pointed at the side of his neck touched his skin. The rolling rhythm of the walking horses caused the tip of the weapon to leave light scratches on his flesh.

An involuntary shudder ran through the man. He glanced cautiously along the blade to the hilt and then along the arm that held it; up to the face of its owner, whose green eyes glinted dangerously.

"Care to repeat those words?" Sebastian asked with deceptive calmness.

Gaines mutely shook his head as much as he dared with a blade to his neck.

"Then don't question my judgment."

With that, Sebastian sheathed his sword and urged his horse into a gallop.

* * *

Frey smiled back at Brice, who bravely allowed his leg to be cleaned and freshly slathered with the honey-and-rosemary ointment. He even accepted the redressing of his wound without complaint.

Now, as they got underway again, the jostling of the cart along the rutted path elicited only the occasional wince of pain from the boy.

Aided by Orlege, Brice sat up partway and managed to drink a few mouthfuls of weak beer.

"How far have we come?" he asked. It was the first complete and coherent sentence from him in two days.

"About fifteen miles by my reckoning, my lord," answered Orlege, holding a hand across the boy's brow to protect his eyes against the glare of the afternoon sun. "My guess is we'll travel a few more before nightfall and arrive at the monastery on the day after tomorrow."

The knowledge seemed to both satisfy and exhaust Brice, who merely nodded and closed his eyes.

"The wound is looking a lot better, my lady," Larcwide observed softly.

"The unguent Friar Dominic left does appear to be having an effect," she agreed, glancing back at her brother. Indeed, the swelling was much less than it had been two days earlier, but the bruises around his ankle were like gathering storm clouds of dark blues and purples.

Frey spoke softly to ensure Brice didn't overhear. "I don't know what other damage has been done. I'm afraid he might now be lame."

Larcwide gave a curt nod. Lameness was no less than might be expected considering the injury and the subsequent time the lad had been immobile.

"What I don't understand, my lady, is where the trap might have come from," he said quietly and earnestly. "You know Orlege and I don't let Lord Brice out of our sight, and I vow to you there was no snare there the previous day when we went out scouting."

Frey sighed. "I know we agreed at the time that Brice's injury was simple misfortune, but I have to admit we experienced a lot of 'simple misfortunes' in the fortnight before Brice's injury."

Larcwide frowned, considering Frey's weighted observation.

"It was always small things," she continued. "The guy rope that went missing, the knife that disappeared. Our underestimating the amount of food we had in store. It could all be explained by carelessness or a foraging animal or simple bad luck. And yet…"

"You don't think it was Lord Sebastian and his men, do you?" he asked, surprised.

Frey gave the matter serious consideration and looked around. Two of the baron's men were ahead of the cart, too far away to overhear.

And, despite racing past like the devil himself was chasing him at the start of their journey, Sebastian de la Croix had since dropped to the back of the caravan, bringing up the rear with his man Gaines. The two had since fallen back farther and had yet to round the bend.

Apart from inquiring of Larcwide about Brice's condition at their midday meal, Frey had not laid eyes on the baron for hours.

"No, I suppose not," she admitted at length.

Larcwide endorsed her decision with a nod. "He is a trained warrior with far superior numbers and resources. What need has he to play petty tricks?"

"None, I suppose," Frey admitted. "But if not him, then who?"

CHAPTER SIX

The lengthening shadows and the sounds of birds heading for their roosts marked the end of the day's journey. Sebastian glanced up at the graying sky for the moment, then continued with the work of unsaddling his horse. Was it only this time yesterday Lord Alfred's rebellion finally came to an end?

He meant what he told Lady Alfreya. There were more questions he wanted answers to, but they could wait until the lad was delivered safely into the hands of a healer.

Sebastian studied the two men who showed unflinching loyalty to Alfred's children. He caught the eye of Orlege, who was helping Larcwide erect a small lean-to. The man looked back at him with suspicion and ill-disguised hostility.

"You!" Sebastian ordered. "Accompany me."

He watched Orlege glance at Larcwide, who give a brusque nod of assent. Orlege walked toward him indolently.

The man was perhaps three or four years older than Sebastian and built like what he was—a soldier, broad across the shoulders with well-muscled arms accustomed to holding a sword or a battle axe.

He would ordinarily be dangerous to face in battle, but a month of privation had dulled his edge. Sebastian believed Orlege recognized his diminished state also and resented it.

Sebastian rummaged through one of the saddle packs and brought out a pair of hatchets, one of which he lobbed to Orlege.

The man deftly caught the tool and adjusted his grip, making a couple of practice swings while a cold smile spread across his lightly whiskered face.

"Ah, for months I've longed for the day I stand before you armed," said Orlege, again weighing the heft of the tool.

At the exchange, Larcwide looked up, cursed the young man under this breath, and stood, ready to intervene if necessary.

He glanced over to the cart where Lady Alfreya was tending to Lord Brice. She remained unaware of the tension, so too were Sebastian's men, who were occupied with the horses and building shelter for the night.

Sebastian was unmoved by Orlege's threat, watching him with arms crossed in front of his broad chest.

"And if I didn't have confidence in your love for Alfred's children and your oath of fealty to me and William, you'd be already dead where you stand," he warned Orlege.

Sebastian turned his back and walked from the clearing into the wood as he did so, calling back, "Come. We need firewood."

Orlege trembled with fury, hatchet still in hand. He lined up his aim.

"Let it go," murmured Larcwide, who now stood at Orlege's side. "Let it go, for Lord Brice and Lady Alfreya's sake. It's over now. It's done."

Orlege let his hand drop and a shudder, almost like a convulsion, shook him from head to foot. He blinked his eyes rapidly to clear them of the emotion that threatened to leak out.

Larcwide clasped Orlege's shoulder and then shoved him in the direction Sebastian had taken.

"Go," he said. "We need firewood."

Sebastian knew he had taken a risk with Orlege, but it was calculated, and he knew he was right to trust his instincts with both of Alfred's men. He could see that Larcwide, being so much older and at the end of his soldiering life, was a much more practical and pragmatic man. He would be an asset on the training field.

He stopped walking and rubbed the blade of his hatchet before glancing across to where Orlege now stood a few yards away, surveying a large deadfall bough. Soon, the rhythmic sound of metal striking wood began.

Sebastian suspected Orlege was a good man too. So long as he could learn to master his temper. In this new England, Saxon and Norman together would find their place in time; Orlege if not in his service, then certainly in the employ of another baron.

The thought of Alfreya crossed Sebastian's mind. Wasn't she as much a warrior as her two men-at-arms?

And yet she pledged homage to no one.

A voice in his head, which sounded suspiciously like Gaines, mocked him. *"Women make vows of submission and devotion to husbands, not to barons and kings."*

Sebastian struck a knot with his hatchet and the jarring resonated up his arm to the shoulder, proving a welcome distraction from his thoughts.

But it was a short-lived distraction. Sebastian's curiosity about this woman burned bright. Even his dreams last night were about her.

Dreams about the sound of booted feet echoing around a stone crypt. The body of a young woman lay on a slab of stone atop the tomb in which she was to be laid to rest. The midnight blue of the freshly laundered dress she now wore made the pallor of her skin even more pronounced. The kirtle had been one of his sister's cast-offs. At least in death the girl would be afforded the dignity she was denied in her last moments of life.

Here, in the quiet of this holy place, she looked at peace, as though asleep.

Sebastian, in his dream, found himself drawing closer.

Golden hair that once would have been this young woman's crowning glory had been butchered. Her closed lids were sunken, made shapeless by the lack of eyes beneath them. They had been gouged out by the same creature who defiled her before slicing off the four fingers of her right hand, the mutilation mercifully covered by her left as she lay prepared for her eternal repose.

Sebastian's hand reached out and touched her cheek tenderly, as a lover might, ignoring the small cuts and bruises that marred what would have been a pretty face.

He leaned in. "I have never forgotten you," he whispered into her ear, then drew back to look at her one last time.

Her eyes were open! And they were the color of cornflowers.

Hair that had been chopped away, now lay across her breast in a long fair braid, a much lighter shade than it had been before.

And in his dream Sebastian cried out silently.

Against recollection of the nightmare, Sebastian gritted his teeth and hacked at a log all the more furiously.

"There are easier ways to get kindling," Orlege called.

Sebastian halted and blinked up at him as though he just emerged from a trance. Orlege's expression on him remained bemused. Sebastian straightened and looked around to see who else might have witnessed his display, then gathered wood in his arms.

"Don't be long," he told Orlege, and began walking back to camp.

Although spoken softly, Sebastian heard Orlege's muttered words clearly enough.

"An odd one to be sure. A man who is so controlled one moment and crazy the next."

No doubt Orlege would gossip with Larcwide about what kind of lunatic they had delivered their mistress unto.

* * *

Frey busied herself about the campsite. The activity was a welcome relief from the jolting of the cart and the restlessness of her thoughts. The routine had become second nature to her over the past few months and she took comfort in it.

She smiled, recalling the surprise on the faces of Sebastian's men as she shouldered her share of the responsibilities for setting up camp.

The last of the meat from the previous night's feast, along with some vegetables and the fresh herbs she had foraged, sat in a small iron cauldron, licked by the compact, brightly burning fire beneath it.

Tomorrow, they would need to hunt, not so cautiously as she and her men had while avoiding capture, so they were more likely to meet with success. A brace of rabbits would be adequate until they reached St. Cuthbert's.

She checked on Brice who now slept, having done so since this afternoon.

The afternoon sun disappeared completely, leaving only the weak light of a waxing moon waiting to take its preeminence in the night sky. Frey could hear Orlege and Larcwide taking in low voices. She approached and the men ceased their conversation, their expression hidden in shadows.

"At your service, m'lady," Larcwide greeted formally.

"Come now," she chided. "After all this time you've suddenly remembered your manners?"

Neither man spoke, and Frey was instantly suspicious.

"What is it that has you two gossiping like washer women?"

Again silence.

Frey stood at ease and folded her arms. She looked at Larcwide, who met her stare with the practiced ease of someone who had been under its scrutiny often.

Frey turned to Orlege, who gazed at the ground.

Aha!

Sensing a wavering resolve in the object of her inspection, Frey shifted position and concentrated on the weak link.

"Is there something you'd like to tell me, Orlege?" she asked pleasantly.

Reluctantly he looked up at her, opening his mouth and closing it without speaking, as though unsure of the words.

Frey frowned.

Eventually he spoke, muttering, "No, m'lady, 'twas nothing" before turning on his heel.

She swiftly faced Larcwide.

"What's going on?" she demanded.

Larcwide glanced at the younger man before answering her.

"He's fine. He's seeing threats where there are none," he said.

"I don't understand. A threat to whom? To Brice?"

Larcwide shook his head.

"There is no threat," he explained. "He's jumping at shadows. When one has been in a state of war, it can be difficult to adjust to not being in that way. He hasn't learned that there is a time for war and a time for peace. Now is the time for peace."

Frey wanted to take Larcwide at his word, but later that night she found herself sitting with her back against a log, watching Sebastian with his men on the other side of the fire. She noticed he was watching her with equal contemplation.

There was little in the way of conversation among the group; their meal was consumed in near silence and an air of unease drifted into camp, thick and heavy.

It was unbearable.

Frey left the campfire and sought out the gloom. After checking on Brice, who remained soundly asleep, she found herself drawn to the horses tethered under a spreading oak. One of the animals eyed her, lifting its head with a tussock of grass in its mouth, which it then chewed meditatively, watching her approach.

Speaking softly, Frey reached out and stroked the muzzle of the big beast.

"It's easy for you," she grumbled. "You know what you have to do— eat, sleep, walk, trot—carry your rider from place to place."

The horse twitched its ears, then bobbed its head in agreement.

"Ebon is a very sympathetic listener."

Frey wasn't startled. She heard the approaching footsteps and turned to the owner of the voice.

The baron stood a yard or so away with his arms by his side. He now approached her as cautiously as she had approached the black stallion she now patted. The thought of Sebastian considering her a skittish mare struck her as amusing.

She offered him a shy smile, which he returned on his approach toward her. He had a nice smile, she noted. It suited him.

"I talk to him too," he said softly, stroking the horse down its flank with long, firm movements. The muscle beneath the stallion's glossy black coat twitched with the contact. Ebon clearly approved of the gesture and nudged Frey's hand for more petting at the muzzle.

"He never argues, never judges, and never gossips."

"Does he offer sage advice?" asked Frey.

"Hmm…" Sebastian pretended to consider his answer. That earned him another easy smile from Frey.

"He remains silent; most of the time it is good advice for people, too."

"Only most of the time?"

"Sometimes it is good to speak out."

It was Frey's turn to nod.

She wanted to speak now, but a large lump had somehow taken up residence in her throat, making it difficult to breathe. She concentrated on stroking Ebon's nose instead.

There was silence.

If Frey closed her eyes, she could imagine she was here all alone, but, oddly, the thought brought her no comfort, just a deep ache that cut across her abdomen.

Then she did close her eyes to guard against the pricks of newly formed tears reaching her lids.

Without sight, she could concentrate on the sounds of the crickets, the rumination of the grazing horses, and the occasional sound of summer-nesting nightjars searching for their evening meal.

During the course of the evening, a breeze had sprung up and the hem of Frey's skirt eddied around her ankles. She ought to have felt cold, but Sebastian, a couple of feet away, blocked the wind.

She found it comforting and, despite the fact that he was her enemy and the usurper of her brother's title, something within her yearned to reach out and touch him.

But she did not.

After long minutes, Frey opened her eyes and met Sebastian's own, steady and empathetic.

"It's hard sometimes," she whispered.

Sebastian nodded.

"I know."

CHAPTER SEVEN

The party of nine was on its way before the sun emerged over the treetops. Sebastian told the band that, if they made good time today, there was every chance they could press through to St. Cuthbert's before nightfall.

The news brought a smile to Brice's face and, with it, a look of undisguised gratitude from Frey. She wasn't sure what it was about last night, but it seemed this morning the tensions in the camp had eased. Even Larcwide and Orlege fell into step with the rest of the baron's men. The camp had been broken down and horses saddled as quickly and as efficiently as though the men had been working together for years.

The contrast between them, however, remained; for today, instead of faded and patched clothing, de la Croix's men wore blue-gray surcoats upon which a bloodred lion rampant was stitched.

Sebastian's surcoat was lavish. A rich shade of sapphire with the lion proudly displayed in red satin across his chest. The whole tableau struck Frey as surreal. Only a few days ago she hated this man, simply because of who he was. A Norman.

Developed in the months consumed by avoiding his relentless hunt and staying alive, her hatred of him was such she could have taken his life without a second thought or a moment's regret.

Now his kindness and honor were forcing her to reassess everything she was taught to believe about the invaders.

Could Larcwide have been right? Was now a time for peace? A time to lay down arms?

Something Frey once heard returned to her memory.

To everything there is a season, and a time to every purpose under the heaven:

A time to be born, and a time to die; a time to plant, and a time to harvest;

A time to weep, and a time to laugh; a time to mourn, and a time to dance;

A time to keep silence, and a time to speak;

A time to love, and a time to hate; a time of war, and a time of peace.

Frey allowed herself a bitter-sweet smile in recollection. She had had her time to hate and her time of war, and she was weary of them both.

A time of peace she could embrace, not only for her sake, but also for her darling brother as well.

But love?

No, she had tried that once and her heart and soul had been laid to waste like the brutal punishment King William meted out during the harrying. Every building, every living thing killed and burned, the ground salted so nothing could ever grow there again.

"Drefan, you destroyed my hope and you destroyed my love," she told him in her mind.

Never again.

Learned responses of antipathy toward the new Norman rulers had been deeply ingrained by her father and fostered at the court of the Scottish king Malcolm, who entertained the Saxon malcontents and fed them hope for their rebellion…as much for his own amusement as it was to harass the English.

Would she be disloyal to the memory of her father and to the heritage of her brother if she learned to forgive as Friar Dominic entreated? What might it be like to start over again without this burden of hatred?

Frey sighed and glanced at her brother, who lay sleeping. A fine sheen of sweat glistened across his little blond brow. First things first. Until she could see him well, she could see no other future.

So lost in her thoughts, it took Frey several moments to realize Ebon trotted alongside the wagon. She looked up at its rider.

"Lady Alfreya," Sebastian greeted.

Missing the mischievous winkle in his eye, the formality of his tone disappointed her for a reason she couldn't account even to herself.

"My Lord Sebastian," she responded coolly.

His lips pressed into a narrow line of displeasure. Good.

A puff of frustration passed his lips.

"Do you ride?" he asked, his tone mild.

The question took her off guard.

"I do," she answered with curiosity etched plain on her face.

He was up to something, she knew. Strange, but her frank regard seemed to please him.

"Good," he approved. "Be prepared after the noon meal."

And then Sebastian galloped to the head of the procession, where he stayed until the sun shone overhead and they broke the journey for a midday repast.

Afterward, Sebastian selected a mount for Frey and, suitably clad in hose under her skirts and a surcoat over her chemise, she found herself seated on a chestnut gelding belonging to Talbot, one of Sebastian's young knights. Talbot, now seated alongside the carter, was barely taller than Frey herself, and she suspected Sebastian had picked this mount for that reason.

As Larcwide on one side and Sebastian on the other adjusted the height of the stirrups, Frey smiled down at her brother, who opened his eyes briefly.

For a moment the young boy looked about wide-eyed, unsure of his location and indeed unsure of who was in front of him, before he recognized his sister. He struggled to sit up, aided by Orlege.

"Where are you going, Frey?" asked Brice, his voice reedy and thin.

"Just for a little ride, my brother." She smiled.

"Does Drefan accompany you?" he asked, his voice filling with worry.

"No, my sweeting," answered Frey, unable to keep a dark edge from her voice before hastening to soften it. "With Lord Sebastian. Remember our host, the baron?"

Brice nodded wearily, his eyes closing.

"He's nice. I like him," he said with a sigh before sleep claimed him again.

"The lad shows good sense," agreed Sebastian, cinching the saddle's girth strap and causing the horse to shift its weight.

Frey gave him her most haughty expression. It only seemed to amuse him even further. Adroitly mounting his own horse, Sebastian gave her a winning grin.

"Ready to ride, princess?"

Frey knew only one answer to that. She looked him directly in the eye with a slow, broad smile.

* * *

Frey's expression caused Larcwide to groan audibly. That look spelled trouble for the baron. It was within him to feel sorry for the Norman.

He shook his head sorrowfully as he watched Frey urge the horse to a canter, putting yards between her and Sebastian, who took off in pursuit.

Talbot turned to him, concern clear in his young eyes.

"Do you think it is safe for your mistress? I mean, my b-bow and arrows…," he stuttered.

"What are you saying, lad?"

"I left them on the saddle."

Larcwide clasped the lad on his shoulder as he laughed uproariously.

"Lady Alfreya is quite capable, my boy, and as long as her temper is not roused, your lord will be safe too."

Not wholly convinced, Talbot offered a meek "oh" in response, and Larcwide laughed even more.

Orlege caught Larcwide's eye and two men eased themselves to the back of the cart so as not be overheard.

"What do you mean by allowing her alone with that man?" Orlege hissed.

"It is far past the time the girl to be wed."

"You're the wrong sex to be playing matchmaker."

Larcwide merely shrugged, but Orlege wasn't satisfied.

"We were at war with de la Croix not two days ago. Did it never occur to you that he might take vengeance against Alfreya now he has her alone?"

Larcwide turned and gave Orlege a long and steady stare.

"No, it did not," he punctuated emphatically. "Besides, *he* is the law of these lands. He could ravage her before our eyes with none of us able to lift a finger in aid. As it is, he has seen to the fair treatment of our men and taken upon himself to personally give safe conduct to Lord Brice. He seems to be a just man, and Lady Alfreya could do worse than to be wed to him."

Orlege's eyes were as wide as platters, his flaring pupils ringed with gray.

"But he's…*Norman*!" He hissed the last, wary of being overheard.

"And Drefan is Edgar the Atheling's cousin. Would you see her wed to him?"

Orlege slumped in response to Larcwide's well-made argument. Drefan was not the man Lord Alfred had been convinced of.

In the face of all that was said of Lord Drefan, he had never heard a murmur of complaint about Sebastian de la Croix from his men.

Though there was his behavior last night as he and Orlege gathered wood…

Larcwide sighed.

He was generally a good judge of character, but he was also an old man who was tired.

Was he accepting a convenient solution to an inconvenient problem?

* * *

Frey laughed joyously, reveling in the sensation of a fine horse moving beneath her and the sound of steady, thrumming hoofbeats of Sebastian and Ebon closing the distance.

On this late summer's day, billowing white clouds drifted aimlessly across the blue sky. Frey slowed her mount to a walk and then to a halt to take in the landscape, gazing at the rolling hills of the northern English moors she loved.

Immediately before her, yellowed blades of tall grass undulated gently with the breeze. Farther down the hill, the grass was shorter and greener, marking a nearby stream hidden in the dense thicket of trees at the bottom of the vale.

She knew this place well. Their journey would take them down into this gently sloping valley, through a grove and around the Tor, which would put them within ten miles of St. Cuthbert's Abbey.

She turned to Sebastian.

"Thank you," she said. "I haven't enjoyed myself so much in such a long time."

"Not as much as I have enjoyed watching you."

Frey frowned, not understanding.

"You have a good seat."

She saw his grin widen as understanding of the double-edged compliment dawned on her.

"With charm like yours, I'm sure all the ladies of court just swoon in your presence," she retorted.

To Frey's surprise, Sebastian laughed without rancor or malice.

"And a razor wit like yours must have suitors running," he offered.

"Aye, usually in the opposite direction," she agreed with a self-deprecating grin as she rediscovered the sense of humor she had almost forgotten was hers.

"Not all though," she continued. "Those I have been aware of considered my father's favor and my dowry adequate compensation for enduring a wife with a shrewish disposition."

"Is that how you see yourself?"

Frey considered the unexpected question for a moment.

"It is how others see me," she reflected. "I have come to the conclusion one can never be a good judge of one's own character."

"Perhaps you are right. I've learned people are very good at presenting more than one face."

"You speak a truth there," she agreed.

Sebastian's eyes drifted over her form. She ought to be offended by his appraisal, but she was not.

Frey imagined what he saw there.

A woman in plain, almost peasant robes but with an aristocratic bearing. It was proper that she should cover her head, but in the pleasant afternoon sunshine, with her thick blonde hair already braided, she had not bothered with the hood, suggesting—nay, confirming—her defiance of convention.

She was aware, though without self-possession, that when dressed in the finery befitting her rank, she was considered a beauty. High cheekbones, a slender nose, and a firm jaw gave structure to her soft skin, left lightly golden by the sun. Her straight posture allowed the makeshift riding clothes to drape attractively over her silhouette.

She could not hide a flush of color in her cheeks, however, as his gaze took in her well-formed breasts and small waist, moving down to the flare of her hips and shapely legs encased in a fine leather boots.

"Would you like to know how I see you?" he asked at long last.

Yes, she would, but she'd be damned if she told him so.

An unladylike snort was her reply. "You weren't even aware of my existence until two days ago."

"Oh, I think you'd be surprised how well I know you."

Skepticism was written plainly across her features, but Sebastian was not put off.

"A wager then?" he offered.

Curiosity replaced skepticism.

"What kind of wager?"

"The fastest over a mile."

"What do I get when I win?"

Sebastian grinned at Frey's boast and she returned it.

"Anything you want," he replied.

"Really?" she asked, drawing out the word to emphasize her disbelief.

"Name it and it will be yours," he affirmed.

Her eyes narrowed.

"It's a trick."

"No trick, just you and me on horseback, the fastest over a mile, from that milestone," he said, pointing to the ancient Roman marker they had just passed, "to the next."

"What do you claim in the unlikely event of your victory?"

"Anything *I* want."

CHAPTER EIGHT

Before Frey could ask him to explain himself, Sebastian was off at a gallop, and, needing no encouragement, her gelding followed Ebon's lead.

The thought of what "anything" might mean should she lose spurred Frey to concentrate on the race.

The landscape disappeared in a blur of multihued greens and yellows as she raced along the path, its grass kept short by frequent four- and two-legged wanderers.

For hundreds of yards she gained on Sebastian, looking ahead to find the fastest way down the hill. The path ahead zigged and zagged between a thicket of trees edged by low-growing ferns before disappearing to the right around a tall rocky outcrop, just a couple of hundred yards later.

And there, just before the turning, stood the foot-high milestone that marked the end of the race.

She whispered encouragement to her mount, keeping pace with its tattoo of hoofbeats with a rhythmic strike of the reins across the animal's shoulders.

"Come on, come on, come on!" she urged as she felt the heat of exertion radiating from Sebastian's horse, now alongside hers.

Then, offering Sebastian a winsome but fleeting smile, Frey redirected her horse to draw a straight line across the meandering path and make a straight dash for the marker.

He saw her strategy only a split second later, but, by then, it was too late. The gelding was in front by a head and then one yard and then five.

Victory belonged to Lady Alfreya of Tyrswick, who acknowledged Sebastian's exaggerated applause with a bow from the saddle as his mount started to slow from a full gallop.

By the time Ebon had transitioned to a canter, both horse and rider disappeared from Frey's view around the collection of massive boulders.

She wielded her horse around to stand by the marker stone, then leaned forward to rub its neck in appreciation of his efforts and to wait for Sebastian's return.

Lingering in the dappled shade, Frey breathed in deep, refreshing lungfuls of air, her heart beating rapidly from the exertion and the excitement of the race. She listened for the sound of returning hoofbeats and the accompanying jangle of a bridle.

There was silence but for the wittering of birds high up in the canopy of leaves and the steady sound of the chestnut horse grazing beneath her.

"Where on earth could your master be?" she asked her mount softly.

The beast ignored her and carried on eating.

Frey dismounted but held on to the gelding's bridle for support as feeling returned to her lower limbs.

Taking a few tentative steps away from the horse, she peered as far as she could around the tumble of russet and ocher rocks flecked with gray flaky lichen and tall, thin tufts of grass.

"Does the baron of Tyrswick sulk like a child when he's bested by a woman?" she called out.

She waited for a response.

When it came, Frey's blood turned cold.

A sustained howl broke the silence and was joined by a chorus of similar cries that seemed to be all around her. Frey turned in a circle but could see only the trees.

Her horse had stopped its grazing and took a step back, ears flicking in one direction, then the other.

With hands cupped to magnify the sound of her voice, she called out.

"Sebastian!"

There was no reply save the call of the wolf pack.

Gooseflesh needled along her arms.

With greater calmness than she felt, Frey walked back to the horse and soothed it with soft words and a few strokes down its neck. It settled enough for Frey to unbuckle a leather quiver of arrows from the saddle, which she then secured across her back before releasing the bow, which she placed over her shoulder.

She cautiously mounted the horse, managing not to frighten it any more than it already was.

With a quick snap of the reins, Frey prompted the chestnut gelding to a slow, cautious walk.

She knew as well as anyone that a wolf pack was a force to be reckoned with. She had seen an entire flock of sheep slaughtered along with their lone shepherd, all defenseless against the relentless attack of a ravening group.

No wonder the Crown offered convicted murderers the option to avoid execution by becoming wolf hunters, she reflected. Such deadly and methodical killers were these beasts that the human killers rarely survived their first hunt. Now, from almost completely all around the large rock outcrop, Frey could hear the howling increasing in volume.

She extracted an arrow from her quiver and set up her bow, clenching her jaw in the struggle to maintain balance in the saddle of an unfamiliar mount without the control of the reins.

"We're allies, you and I," Frey told the horse. "We have to work together."

Using pressure from her left knee on the horse's shoulders to simulate the tug of the reins, she caused the animal to move to the right, taking the last corner wide in the hope she could see what danger lay ahead.

Some one hundred yards away, blocking a path made narrow by two massive boulders, she saw a pack of gray wolves, perhaps a dozen of them, with teeth bared and ears lying flat back. They surrounded Ebon.

Beyond the narrow path, blocking the way forward, Frey observed, was a landslip. Fresh, too, from the color of it.

Sebastian, his face grim, remained in the saddle with his sword drawn, masterfully controlling an increasingly frightened mount as the wolves snapped and snarled, circling in one direction as the black horse circled in the other to protect his flank.

As the horse moved round, Sebastian swung his blade, slashing at the pack. The tip of his sword dripped with blood, but the wolves, accustomed to affray, held mostly just far enough from his reach and reacted not to the pain of his occasional strike.

Then Ebon reared, his front legs catching an unwary wolf, knocking it to the ground, whereupon the horse stamped his powerful hooves. The wolf offered up a series of distressed, high-pitched yelps before scrambling away from the fight, injured and surely dead by nightfall.

The horse kicked out behind in response to another attack.

Frey lined up her target, a gray wolf lining up to leap on Ebon's hindquarters, as she heard Sebastian yell, "Leave here!"

She ignored him and let her arrow fly. It hit the wolf high in the side of its torso and the animal fell to the dirt, dead.

At that, some of the younger and more timid beasts fled into the surrounding forest, where numerous and densely packed trees offered an ideal hiding and regrouping place for the canines but offered little comfort to a rider on horseback.

The sound of the baying was horrible, loud and increasingly higher in pitch as calling wolves competed with the yowling of the injured members of the pack.

Frey quickly drew another arrow and readied her aim for a second shot, but her horse reared as it, too, became the focus of an aggressive beast running in from the flank.

Frey scrambled for the reins. Her arrow fell to the ground, splintered by her panicked mount's hooves as it spun around.

Feeling herself losing her seat, Frey kicked her feet free of the stirrups and allowed herself to fall from the horse.

Soft earth broke her fall and Frey, though slightly winded, hurriedly regained her feet.

She turned rapidly, seeking the location of the wolf. It lay dead—trampled by the gelding that now galloped rapidly away, back along the path.

A quick mental inventory confirmed her further good fortune; nothing was broken, it seemed, although she knew she would be bruised. And also unbroken was her bow.

She bent and grasped one of several arrows spilled from the quiver, quickly nocked it, aimed, and released. Another of the wolves surrounding Sebastian fell, mortally wounded.

Another glance about to ensure she was not being outflanked herself, then Frey quickly dispatched another.

Only a few wolves were now left, but those remaining were emboldened and roused by the smell of the blood of their kin. In a split second, one of them leaped up at Sebastian, snapping at him with slavering jaws before falling back. Pulling away from the wolf's attack so abruptly, the baron was forced into a barely controlled dismount lest he actually fall from the horse.

Riderless, Ebon split the center of the pack and galloped past Frey in the direction the chestnut gelding had fled. Blood ran freely from its wounded flanks, spraying her with bright red droplets as it passed.

In a cloud of dust kicked up by the horses and in the lengthening rays of the afternoon sun, Frey found it difficult to see.

She tried calling Sebastian's name, but her voice came out as a hacking cough instead.

Nonetheless, Sebastian's occasional grunts of exertion followed by canine yelps of pain reassured her he was still standing, still fighting.

Then a low, ominous growl to her left brought her focus back to her own immediate surroundings.

Just six feet away, two large amber eyes considered her. A wolf closed in, its chest close to the ground as it half crawled toward her.

Frey swallowed her fear and, with shaking fingers, slipped the nock of another arrow onto the bowstring.

As the wolf bared its teeth, she steadied her left hand and tensioned the sinewed bowstring slowly, taking it back as far as her strength would let her.

When the wolf launched itself, Frey released the arrow.

It hit the animal's throat.

The beast slumped to the ground, the arrow head protruding grotesquely from the back of its neck as blood spurted from a severed artery for several tremulous beats before ceasing.

Breathing again, Frey turned to where Sebastian did battle for his life.

Standing with legs apart and sword in hand, his face half hidden in the afternoon shade, he looked as fierce and frightening as the Norman soldiers she and her family fled in Durham.

The bodies of several wolves lay around him.

He wore a snarl Frey thought he must have stolen from the wolves. Then a deep growl forced its way through his set jaw.

"I ordered you to leave!"

With a cry and his sword raised, he sprinted toward her.

Frey was rooted to the spot, unable to move, mute and fascinated by the display of masculine aggression.

Sebastian reached her in scant seconds, shoving her aside. Frey tumbled, losing both bow and quiver, but as she fell she caught a glimpse of silver-gray fur, heard a yelp of distress, then nothing save the sound of her own ragged breathing and the birds high in the trees, unmoved by the slaughter on the ground.

Scrambling to her feet, Frey took in the scene in front of her with growing trepidation.

Where she stood moments before there now lay a wolf splayed over the body of Sebastian. The blade of his broadsword jutted through the fur of its back.

A deep red stain spread and pooled on and around him.

Before coherent thought could form, Frey watched with horror as the wolf trembled and raised its head to look at her, then huffed once, twice, in huge body-shaking tremors.

A scream lodged in her throat.

Frey's fingers grasped at air as she reached across her back for her quiver before realizing that her weapons lay useless on the ground. She took a couple of staggering steps away.

A grunt more human than animal broke the silence.

The gasp was Sebastian's as he pushed the dying wolf from on top of him. The four-legged brute tumbled to the side and stilled.

With heaving chest, his lungs filling with air, he rose to his feet with his back to Frey.

The baron extracted his sword from the corpse, wiped the blood from the steel across the dead animal's own pelt, and sheathed the weapon. He turned at the sound of a soft whimper Frey belatedly recognized as coming from her. His eyes that glittered hard emerald with fury just minutes before were now moss green, softened with compassion and tenderness.

A few steps closed the gaps between them and Sebastian enfolded Frey in his arms. Hers quickly snaked out from between them to cling to him tightly.

He felt solid and real. For the first time in a very long time, Frey felt safe.

They held each other for many minutes. And where Frey rested her head on his chest, she could feel his heart beating, quickly at first before settling into a slow, steady rhythm.

"Are you hurt?" he asked gently.

Unable to form the words, Frey shook her head vigorously in answer.

He stroked her hair and whispered soothing sounds into her ear and, as he did, second by second, tension ebbed from Frey's shoulders, down her spine, through her legs, until it seemed to her that she stood only because he held her.

"Cry if you need to," he whispered. "There's no shame in it."

Although she did not need his permission, her body accepted the release anyway. She wept silently, with body-shaking shudders that lessened with every passing moment.

Not all her tears were the result of today's battle. Months, indeed years, of emotion bubbled to the surface and evaporated in the warmth of Sebastian's arms around her.

When she had stilled, Sebastian pulled back slightly and tipped Frey's face up to his.

Despite the weeping that had streaked lines through the dust on her face, he looked at her as though she was the most beautiful woman he had ever seen.

She wondered what it would be like if he were to kiss her, and a stirring of arousal accompanied the thought playing itself out in her mind.

Frey licked her lips, leaving them slightly parted. Sebastian's eyes flared with desire.

The first touch of his lips to hers was gentle and soft.

Her lips parted farther, willing him to continue.

He did, capturing her bottom lip, tasting its fullness, touching it with his tongue. Hers mimicked his and his mouth opened to give her questing tongue access. She sighed and pulled herself closer to him.

Frey gloried in the sensation of Sebastian sliding his arm down her back to her waist, raising goose bumps as he did. His other hand stroked lengths of fair silky hair that had come loose from their braid.

This was right and necessary, she told herself. Could there be a more fitting way to affirm life than to glory in the sweet sensation of passion?

She pressed her breasts against his chest, wanting to feel more of him. He indulged her, dropping a hand to her buttocks, pulling her close to feel his hardness before his hand drifted up the planes of her back to her shoulder blades.

Frey offered a disappointed mewl as his mouth left hers, but it was to trail kisses along her cheek until they reached the shell of her ear. His breath brought rolling shivers down the length of her body.

She could feel his lips part again. "Don't ever disobey me again," he whispered.

Frey started as though doused by a bucket of cold water, washing away arousal to drip anger instead. Sebastian dropped his arms to his side and, holding her away from him, looked at her implacably.

Frey answered his expression with a glare. He continued to look at her steadily and unmoving.

Her ire simmered and boiled; a river of a great many fine Anglo-Saxon curse words, which no well-bred lady would admit to knowing, threatened to break its banks.

Frey opened her mouth to open the breach when another voice filled the air.

"Sweet Jesu! What the devil happened here?"

CHAPTER NINE

Frey started and looked wide-eyed at Gaines, who held the reins of the two runaway horses in his hand. The man looked like a giant astride his gray mount and with a mien that was just as fierce. Taking in the scene, he dismounted, unsheathed his sword, and looked about with the alert and probing air of a soldier well used to enemies lurking in the shadows.

Frey ignored both men and went to the riderless horses, examining them for injuries.

The chestnut had emerged from the encounter with the wolves completely unscathed, while Ebon bore several scratches on his limbs and flank. Nothing too serious, but they would nonetheless require treatment.

She was only half listening to the conversation between the baron and his man-at-arms. "I was taking Ebon for a gallop when I encountered this landslip," said Sebastian, walking to the fall of thick, loamy rubble and rocks.

He picked up a clod and sniffed its earthy dampness for a moment before dropping it and looking up at its origin.

"Then I was surrounded by a dozen wolves," he continued distractedly, looking for a way up to the top of the cutting. "And we had to fight our way free."

Sebastian used tussocks of grass for hand- and footholds to make his way up the eight-foot-high escarpment.

Gaines frowned but remained on the ground.

"We? Who else was with you?"

"Our guest is an excellent archer," Sebastian called down. "Lady Alfreya dispatched at least three of the wolves, possibly four, on her own."

Gaines muttered some response to the revelation, but Frey couldn't quite make out the words. Even if she had, she doubted they would be complimentary.

Having finished her examination of the horses, Frey looked up and her expression immediately matched that of Gaines, an askance look as if to say, *What on earth is that man doing?*

As Frey peered up at Sebastian, Gaines lost interest and turned his attention to the carnage around him.

"It's a sorry shame we don't have time to skin these brutes; they'd fetch a pretty penny at market," he commented ruefully. He began dragging the carcasses off the path one by one.

Sebastian grunted in assent, distracted by his investigation.

"This slip was recent, the churned-up soil is still moist," Sebastian commented while descending in a half slide back to the path. "But we've had no rains recently that would account for it."

"Your timing was a good bit of luck really, the wolves aside," offered Gaines. "If the slip is that recent, you could have been right under it when it fell."

Tension edged its way up Frey's spine. There was no such thing as coincidence. She thought once again of the little unexplained mishaps that had dogged her and her party for months.

"Good fortune, indeed," responded Sebastian.

Frey caught an edge in his voice that hinted at suspicion of something more than the timely intervention of Providence.

She slowly turned on the spot, looking in all directions for something that would provide answers.

The forest yielded none.

"Send Talbot and Baldwin to clear the path," Sebastian ordered crisply. "I am not happy about being in such an exposed position another night. We press through to St. Cuthbert's Abbey, even if it means arriving after nightfall."

Frey could see in Sebastian the master tactician at work and, without further question, Gaines remounted and set the gray into a gallop.

Sebastian looked at Frey for the first time since their kiss.

"My lady, I would have you tell Larcwide and Orlege to redouble their vigilance over Lord Brice," he said.

Disappointment at his tone bit deep, but by now Sebastian had made his way over to Ebon and was checking his mount's injuries for himself. He did not see the flush of anger and embarrassment that colored her cheeks.

Without another word, she gathered together Talbot's bow and remaining arrows.

The ride back to their party, which had been steadily making is way down the valley toward them, was made in merciful silence.

Frey warred with herself.

Isn't this what she wanted? That this Norman treat her as an equal warrior for the benefit of her men and her brother?

"What about how he made you feel as a woman?" a treacherous part of her mind whispered. A throb ran through her as her body remembered their kiss.

"It was never like that with Drefan, was it?" it reminded her.

"No, a thousand times, no," she told herself firmly, trying to shove the bitter memory back to the part of her mind in which she had kept it under lock and key for nearly a twelvemonth.

Sebastian turned to glance at her, and Frey realized she had spoken out loud. She raised her head and looked back at him, daring him to say something.

He didn't and, after a moment, turned away.

Brice should be your only focus, not trysting with the enemy, she told herself, more quietly this time.

But it was becoming increasingly difficult to consider Sebastian an enemy, though to think any more kindly of him than a man simply doing his duty was dangerous indeed. She stared at his back as their horses walked along.

He was so different from Drefan. Drefan was witty and charming. Sebastian was serious and sober.

Frey let her mind wander back two years to when her family first met Lord Drefan. He was already a favorite in King Malcolm's Edinburgh court while the rest of the displaced Saxon aristocracy was merely tolerated.

Tall, fair, and devastatingly handsome, he told all that he was the indispensable right hand of his cousin Edgar, who was still being persuaded by King William's disaffected son, Robert Curthose, to contest the English throne from his new home in Flanders. It had been rumored, on the basis of his looks and reputation, that Drefan had bedded almost every noble woman at Malcolm's court, but Alfred advised his young daughter to ignore spiteful chatter and welcome their new friend.

And what a friend he was.

Drefan would engage in mock battles with Brice and run through the halls neighing and whinnying loudly with the boy on his back, playing at being his trusty steed. He would drink late into the night with her father, enthusiastically listening to his stories of bygone battles and flattering him on a military career cut tragically short due to a pikestaff through the thigh.

That wound, attained during William the Bastard's harrying, cost Alfred dearly. His health never recovered from the blood loss and wound. Wine, ale, and mead at every meal—two or three goblets' worth—made the pain more manageable, but his limp was pronounced. Scotland's cold, damp weather left him such agony on some days that he could not leave his chamber.

On these occasions, the only medicine that would dull his pain was what the Scots called *uisge beatha*—"water of life"—made by local monks from a fermented grain according to a recipe the Crusaders brought back with them from the Holy Land.

As always, Frey recalled, Drefan was there, very attentively listening to her drunk father wax lyrical about the wealth Tyrswick held. Why, the gold he carried with him was merely a trifle compared to the fortune his land could raise. Crops that could feed a multitude, sheep the size of cattle, cattle the height of horses, trout as big as a hunting dog.

If he could only mount an army to deal with those thieving, gorbellied bastards, Alfred had told anyone in shouting distance, then *he* would be able to single-handedly raise the coin for the rightful king to take England back from those Norman dogs.

Thinking on it now, Frey was ashamed of herself. She had been embarrassed by her father when he was in his cups, but there too was Drefan, offering her a wry smile and a wink to tell her he understood.

Was it any surprise she had thought herself in love with him?

Like the time when Larcwide sheepishly approached her to say that the men had not been paid for well nigh two months, it was Drefan who offered coin from his own purse. Grateful beyond measure to this family friend, Frey asked how she could possibly repay him. She assured him her father did indeed have some gold but would be completely insensible to answering to its location until he emerged from his drunken sleep.

Drefan looked her from the top of her head, covered as it was with a pale blue veil held in place with a plain silver circlet, down to the hem of her skirt, a smile spreading across his handsome features.

"I'm certain we can find a way to repay your debt," he assured her.

A deep shudder of revulsion brought Frey back to herself.

She straightened in the saddle and brought her horse up to a trot to match Ebon's gait.

"I know you suspect foul play," Frey said when she reached Sebastian.

He glanced at her before looking ahead again.

"On the road today…the wolves," she pressed.

"What makes you say so?" Sebastian eventually responded.

"The landfall was no accident."

Sebastian slowed Ebon to a walk and shifted in his saddle to give Frey his undivided attention. When he spoke, he made no effort hide his irritation.

"So you say. I want to know why."

Larcwide had counseled her to put their series of campaign misfortunes down to mere bad luck, but she was not convinced.

Surely the run of calamities should have ended.

But after today…

"Things happened before we met," she started, and was met with skeptical expression.

Frey took a deep breath and started again.

"It's hard to explain," she breathed.

"Try. Because that 'accident' nearly cost us our lives."

Frey bristled.

"It would have been convenient, would it not?" he said, voice low, steady, and unmistakably angry. "The baron of Tyrswick killed while out riding, the heir of the original estate ready to take over? Perhaps you lied when you said the rest of your party fled. You may have men ready to ambush me."

Frey was horrified.

"You cannot think we had anything to do with that? Do you think me so desperate and base I would use a gravely ill boy as a lure? Maybe you think I strangled Diera with my own hands?"

"Men have done worse to obtain what they want," he replied, grinding out his words through clenched teeth.

Frey was livid. How dare he question the integrity of her men, moreover to insinuate they would be so evil as to arrange the murder of her only friend in the world?

"All of my men gave their oath of honor and allegiance to you and William," she responded vehemently. "Those who had no one to vouch for them agreed to be bound over to keep the peace. What more can you demand of them?"

Sebastian paused, drawing air into his lungs so his chest rose. Frey imagined him silently counting. When he spoke, it was clear he was in control of his temper once more. "I don't know what to think, Alfreya."

She started at Sebastian's use of her first name.

"But I do know you're still keeping secrets," he continued, "and I mean to have them."

His eyes that normally sparkled green were now as black as Whitby jet and they seemed to speak to her heart. There was more here than anger or lingering alarm from today's encounter with the wolf pack. A warrior of Sebastian's stature would have seen more than his share of danger.

Unbidden, she found herself drawn into those eyes, dark pools that appeared so calm on the surface, but beneath which she saw an intriguing glimpse of the complexity of the man.

Gazing at him, she took in his lips, firm and full, and her own tingled with the memory of them meeting hers. The urge to lay open her heart to him beat powerfully in her breast.

As much as she told herself she hated the thought, Frey knew she was indebted to his kindness and acknowledged he deserved to know it all. A recitation of facts she could give him; anything else was beyond her, despite the pleasure his eyes, his lips, and his hands promised.

"What do you want to know?" The question came out breathless.

A small measure of triumph flared in his eyes before his expression cooled.

"Everything," he told her. "I want everything."

Frey pursed her lips. That was exactly what she was afraid of.

CHAPTER TEN

"Frey. Wake up." The familiar voice stirred her from her sleep. She lifted her head and looked around. Everything seemed in order. Brice lay sleeping deeply in the cart just a few feet away. Dear sweet lad. She loved him as much as if he were her full-blood brother, not just the half they shared with their father.

Indeed, she loved Brice more than her full-blood elder brother, which she knew was a sin she really ought to repent of.

The gentle tendrils of sleep were reclaiming Frey once more when the voice called again.

"Wake up!"

This time the voice was insistent and Frey awoke with a start.

Instead of the gentle rocking of the cart where she last recalled laying her head, she awoke under the shade of an evergreen yew, her pillow a gathering of dense and springy yew branches covered with her robe.

She stood.

Brice was nowhere to be seen.

Frey's eyes fell upon a figure in a forest-green cloak standing about ten feet away. With the hood of the cloak covering the head, Frey couldn't immediately tell whether it belonged to a man or woman, but the identity of the voice that called to wake her, she suddenly knew.

"Diera?"

"Frey. Wake up."

Frey started. The voice came not from the cloaked figure but from right beside her.

Turning, she found Diera exactly as she had last seen her, dressed in a practical brown kirtle, her long hair the color of the goldenrod flower, several shades darker than Frey's own, plaited and lying across her shoulder and over her right breast.

Diera's doe-brown eyes were liquid with spilling tears, and Frey felt her heart breaking at the sight. She loved Diera as a sister. In fact, they often were mistaken as such.

"Hush, my dove, what's wrong?" Frey asked. Diera did not answer but encircled Frey firmly in her arms.

"Are you afraid?" probed Frey.

Perhaps it was the figure in green she feared. Frey twisted in her friend's hold, intending to yell at the cur who would frighten a girl.

The robed figure was no longer there.

Turning back, she returned Diera's embrace with emotion.

"You're here! I was told you were dead!"

Frey rested her head on Diera's shoulder and felt the comfort of a feminine hand soothing her back.

"Why would anyone be so cruel?"

Again, Diera did not answer, but lay down, tugging on Frey's hand, urging her to share the yew twig pillow.

"You're tired," she said at last. "Come, lie by me."

Frey complied, but, lying on her back beside Diera, she did not close her eyes at first, instead looking up into the heights of the great tree, watching the sun and shade ebb and flow with each movement of breeze.

Hypnotized by the motion, Frey's eyes closed against the dappled sunlight, and she took comfort in holding Diera's hand, feeling more peace than she had in a very long time.

Perhaps she slept. Frey couldn't be sure.

But when she opened her eyes again, she was certain of one thing, that some amount of time had passed and the bright sunny day was now cast in the strange half-light that heralds a soon-coming storm.

As if to confirm this, a gust of wind tugged at her skirts.

The hand that clutched hers was icy cold. Frey squeezed it to gently wake her friend.

"Diera?" she whispered. "It's time for us to go home."

There was no response, and an agonizing dread flowed slowly through Frey's being.

Thunder rolled in the distance as Frey scrambled to a half-seated position and stared.

Diera's beautiful long hair had been chopped off, wispy strands left behind waved in the rising breeze. Her eyes were carmine, the size of pennies, from which tears of blood dripped down her cheeks as if in everlasting regret.

Frey's view was drawn to Diera's right hand, which lay across her stomach. At first she thought her friend was clutching something, but then she realized the hand would never hold anything again. The fingers were missing. Only the thumb remained.

Frey shuddered violently as the dread turned to horror and demanded a voice.

Heaven vented its fury at the desecration with flashes of angry declamation and weeping from the skies, but even that could not drown the piercing scream that came from Frey's own lips.

"Frey! Wake up."

A familiar voice pulled Frey from her sleep.

Although now fully awake, she could still hear the terrible cry linger and covered her ears against it. Frey opened her eyes to then find Sebastian looking at her, his expression a mix of concern and confusion. She turned her head and looked at Brice.

Beads of sweat on the boy's brow glistened in the torchlight as the cart and the rest of the Tyrswick party passed through the gates and into the grounds of St. Cuthbert's Abbey.

True to Sebastian's word, they had pressed through the afternoon and now stars were appearing in the last of the twilight sky. For a moment, it seemed the terrible screeching returned, but Frey recognized it now as the gate being closed for the night on its rusty hinges.

When it ceased, all she could hear was the sound of their own travel—walking horses, jangling bridles, rolling wheels of the cart along the grit-covered drive—along with the footsteps of two monks with lanterns lighting their way to the main abbey complex.

The sound of lowing cattle and the bleating of sheep and goats protected in their enclosures for the evening was a comfortable and familiar sound. Frey now felt safe.

Brice's hand felt warm in hers and that felt right too. She brushed her brother's damp hair from his forehead.

"Almost there," she whispered in his ear. The boy didn't stir.

"Aught amiss?"

Frey shook her head, not yet willing to answer Sebastian's gentle inquiry.

Despite her bitter accusations that afternoon, he made her feel safe too, although she would rather kiss the king of England than tell him so.

He was tired, she observed.

Long shadows hid much of his face. The dark growth of beard and slightly hunched posture in the saddle added to the appearance of exhaustion. In the split of his surcoat, she could see his bandaged calf and, in the center of it, a dark spot like a bull's-eye from the worst of the wounds received from the wolves.

Perhaps they were wounds he sustained while saving her life.

That was another unpayable debt she owed despite the fact she herself saved his life with her timely arrival this afternoon.

Frey wondered how Sebastian felt about that.

The cart rolled to a stop at a familiar outbuilding—a long, narrow rectangular structure made of timber and thatch that stood several hundred yards from the main building.

Frey reflected that she knew St. Cuthbert's Abbey well, standing as it did less than two days ride from Tyrswick.

St. Cuthbert's was largely self-sufficient and represented a way point for pilgrims heading to the famous Holy Island of Lindisfarne.

Not only did the monks raise sheep and cattle behind the sturdy stone walls that survived the Viking raids, but they also grew crops to feed themselves and a growing number of orphaned lads they furnished with a home and an education.

It was hoped some of them would take holy orders. Those who decided against a life of prayer and worship were highly sought after by the newly elevated Norman aristocracy, who desired trusted men who could read and write Saxon, French, and Latin to manage their new estates.

Frey watched Sebastian dismount and hand the reins over to Talbot, who took Ebon along with his own mount and Gaines's horse to the stables.

Sebastian moved stiffly and Frey wondered whether his wound had reopened.

With the help of Orlege and Larcwide, two monks hoisted Brice's litter from the conveyance. The four men walked through the door at the end of the building and disappeared.

Frey was about to follow when she felt Sebastian's restraining hand on her arm. From the door through which Brice had been taken, the abbot himself, dressed in his voluminous black robes, emerged.

"Greetings and peace be with you, although we didn't expect you until morning," he said pointedly. "We've only just finished Compline and many of our brethren have retired for the evening.

"Forgive our untimely interruption, Father," replied Sebastian, "but we were beset by wolves this afternoon so we felt it best to press through to safety."

The man's expression changed at the news.

"Then you did the right thing, my son," he agreed. "Apart from the lad are there any others who are injured?"

"No," said Sebastian.

"Yes," said Frey.

The abbot looked confused while Sebastian appeared annoyed. Frey ignored him.

"Father Abbot, the baron here has suffered an injury that might benefit from treatment. I believe he may have been bitten."

The abbot looked alarmed. A wolf, a dog, any bite may be serious.

Sebastian turned to her angrily. "It's nothing more than a scratch."

"Nevertheless, it would be good to let Brother Halig examine the wound," determined the abbot.

Frey crossed her arms, satisfied in spite of Sebastian's mutterings. Their host turned to Frey.

"And where is your attendant, my lady?"

Frey blinked and cast her eyes downward.

"She has recently passed away, Father."

There was an awkward moment's silence.

"I see. Then it wouldn't be appropriate for you to bathe in the balneary alone," the man said briskly, getting down to business. "I'll arrange for one of the brethren to bring a tub to your room."

He turned to Sebastian. "Baron, let your men know they will wash before they eat. One of the novices will show them where they will sleep this evening."

* * *

The door closed soundly behind Frey, followed by the rasp of a bolt being thrown home.

She stared at the bare wooden door blankly for a moment. It was the first time she had been under a solid roof in nearly six months. It felt foreign.

The white-washed walls were unadorned but for a crucifix. The cell's small window was covered by wooden shutters. Her door was bolted for her own protection, so she was told. Yet sleeping in the open air with quick access to the small knife she kept strapped to her ankle as well as her trusty crossbow, made her feel much safer than being locked overnight in this sanctuary.

Still, the tin bath from which alluring curls of steam rose and beckoned her to join them was very tempting indeed; so too the narrow cot that was to be her bed. Narrow though it was, it did have a real mattress and the softest woolen blankets Frey had felt since Scotland.

On a stool by the bed was a bowl containing hearty stew, a small loaf of hot, freshly baked bread, and a goblet of wine. It smelled delicious, but Frey could not yet be tempted by it. A rectangle of goat's milk soap lightly scented with lavender flowers tipped the scale in favor of the bath.

She undressed and examined herself the best she could in the single, flickering candlelight.

Her muscles were stiff from unaccustomed horse riding, not to mention the fall, which left her hip, left arm, and—from what she could feel—her left shoulder mottled with multicolored bruises.

Slipping into the still, warm water and drawing the soap along her limbs slowly, Frey sighed contentedly. Even the sting of her several scratches felt less acute.

With her body at rest, her mind started on the tasks ahead.

Tomorrow, she would talk to Brother Halig and the abbot about Brice.

Although Frey had freely used Brice's assumed title to rally her father's men and to deceive Sebastian into doing what was necessary, there were important things both men needed to know that would affect any decision made about the boy.

It all depended on whether Sebastian's forbearance could be further counted on.

He had shown a great deal of goodwill to them thus far, much more than Frey knew she had any right to lay claim to, but she pushed him nonetheless. Not for her own sake, but for those she had a responsibility toward. Once she had seen to the security of Brice, Larcwide, and Orlege, then she would give some thought to her own future.

Frey closed her eyes then, almost without thinking, pressed a finger to her lips to recall the pressure of Sebastian's mouth on hers that afternoon. In the gentle embrace of the warm bath water, it was easy to imagine his hands on her once more.

She felt a stirring of desire but tamped it down ruthlessly.

Because of Drefan, and to no small measure her own father, her past allowed only one option for her future. But what did that matter as long as her family was safe?

* * *

Sebastian sat on the bench more or less patiently as a monk applied salve to the deep scratch on his leg and re-bound it.

If he couldn't be active, his mind could, so Sebastian took inventory of his responsibilities.

Prior to bathing and eating, he had seen to his men's accommodation. It was odd how he now included Orlege and Larcwide as *his* men, when they were quite clearly attached to their mistress.

As for his two charges, he had seen little of either.

Brice was safely in the hands of Brother Halig, renowned across four counties as one of the finest healers of the North.

Where Alfreya was concerned, the abbot seemed a little unsure how to handle an unaccompanied young woman, so, in the interests of her safety and reputation, she would dine alone, bathe alone, sleep alone, and remain alone until morning.

The abbot proved most adamant on the matter.

Little point if the horse has already bolted, Sebastian thought darkly. Who knows how many men have had her? That's what Gaines would tell him if he gave the man leave to speak his mind on the subject.

Sebastian tried to reexamine his uncharitable thought, but again came to the only conclusion the evidence would allow, even considering how protective Orlege and Larcwide were of their Lady Alfreya.

He recalled he'd twice heard the name Drefan from young Brice's lips. With the recollection, a flicker of emotion he was hard placed to identify touched him.

Sebastian needed to know all there was before he could put his plans into action.

The monk finished dressing his wound and departed. Sebastian watched him go and raised a halfhearted prayer for forgiveness.

CHAPTER ELEVEN

The spell of fine weather was over. Even the gray clouds, poured out flat and featureless across the sky, were halfhearted about their work, sending down miserable, drizzling rain in fits and starts. The sun tried its best to break through at dawn but, in the face of overwhelming resistance, settled for providing what comfort it could to those below with a weak half light that made the difference between noon and eventide impossible to differentiate.

Frey spent part of the morning sitting with Brice while a novice, only a couple of years older than her brother, sat on a low stool by the bed to read to him. Frey could see Brice was fascinated by the tale and she felt a twinge of guilt that her brother never learned to read nor be schooled in all the ways expected of a son of an earl.

They both listened as the young novice read the feast-day story of St. Alfreda and St. Ethelbert, two young lovers who lived three hundred years earlier in this same county.

Ethelbert was a devoted man of God who trained missionaries, when he met the beautiful Alfreda, daughter of King Offa of Mercia. So struck by her kindness and her increasing interest in the Christian faith, Ethelbert determined to ask for the young virgin's hand in marriage. However, Alfreda's mother, Queen Cynethritha, was jealous of her daughter's interest in the young man and arranged his murder. Horrified, Alfreda departed the court and retired to the marshes of Crowland, where she lived as a hermit until her death.

When the tale ended, Brice gave a sidelong glance at his sister. Frey knew what he was thinking. The similarity of the name struck her too.

The novice looked up from the book in response to a call for assistance by Brother Halig and left Alfred's two children alone to talk.

"Are you going to live in a swamp, Frey?" he asked worriedly.

Frey sat on the abandoned stool and ignored the question. She stroked her brother's fine pale hair, which had grown far too long, and brushed it out of his eyes.

"We should ask if they have some shears to trim your hair so you look like a boy and not a girl," she said gently.

Brice shook off the hand, a sure sign he was feeling much better.

"You do not answer my question, sister," he told her crossly.

Frey considered her answer and decided to give him a version of the truth.

"No, I will not go and live in a swamp. I might live in an abbey like this one."

She watched him think about her answer and her heart softened. She decided to ask the abbot which convents weren't too far away. Brice was her only remaining relative, and she would be heartbroken if she were never to see him again.

Frey became aware of Brice now scrutinizing her, and she glanced down at herself.

She was dressed in a kirtle with long, tightly fitted sleeves that flared at the wrist. The garment was originally violet in shade, but now, being soft and well-washed, it had faded to a lilac hue. Her pale hair was covered by a light muslin veil.

She certainly looked different than the woman she was just seven days ago, one who wore hose and a short tunic like the men, a woman who wore her hair uncovered and waged war.

"I do not see you as a nun. You're too stubborn," Brice pronounced at last. "I think you should marry."

"If I'm too stubborn for God, then a man would hardly take me for his wife. Did you think of that?" she asked, struggling to hide a smile.

His expression immediately became downcast. "Well, no…"

"Then a nunnery is the only place for me to go."

Frey patted his hand and stood. She could hear the quiet shuffling of the monks heading to the chapel for their noon-day devotions, and she wanted to talk to Brother Halig before he departed.

Brice tugged her hand urgently.

"Promise me you won't marry Drefan."

She halted. What did Brice know of the arrangement made by their father and Drefan?

Not that it mattered now. Even if Drefan turned up today with legions of men and pledged his life to her on bended knee, she would spit in his face before running the gutless coward through.

"Why not?" asked Frey, curious to know Brice's objections.

To her knowledge, Drefan's perfidy extended to naïve young women and desperate, displaced earls, not to the young boy who once considered him a big brother.

"I did not care for the way he looked at you," he answered seriously.

"And how did he look at me?"

Brice's forehead puckered and his fingers plucked at the blanket as he concentrated hard on his answer.

"As if he had secrets to keep from you."

Frey's expression of surprise at Brice's words was lost in the sound of a follow-up question that came from behind her.

"What secrets were they, my lord?"

She turned and scowled at Sebastian; he flicked his eyes in her direction for the barest moment before turning his full attention to Brice.

Frey fumed. How dare he intrude on a private conversation? Adding to her annoyance was the realization that Brice was not at all concerned at seeing this giant of a man move toward his bed.

Brice shrugged helplessly.

"I don't know…just secrets." Then, deciding on his answer, Brice tilted his head to meet Sebastian's eye. "Like he knew a humorous story but decided it would be more fun not to tell it."

Sebastian nodded his understanding and damn if the man didn't look as though he *did* understand. It was as though she had missed an entire conversation that had taken place in front of her.

From a pocket in his *bliaut*, Sebastian withdrew a small, dark-gray bundle of fur and dropped it into Brice's hands.

"A kitten!" the boy exclaimed.

"Yes. I was told he was old enough to leave his mother, but he still needs someone to care for him," said Sebastian.

The kitten mewled and kneaded the bedclothes with tiny claws. Brice stroked the little creature carefully. He looked to Frey for confirmation. May he keep the gift?

Frey kept her gaze fixed on her brother. If she looked at Sebastian he might see how much this act of thoughtfulness affected her. How dare Sebastian confuse her like this! She was furious with him just a few moments earlier.

She smiled at her brother and gave a short nod.

How could she refuse him this? He had nothing in this world he could call his own. She would never refuse him.

"Ouch! Stop it!" Brice gave the tabby a tap on the nose in answer to a particularly enthusiastic nibble.

She cleared her throat against the tumult of emotions that plagued her.

"Uh, he will need a name," Frey told Brice, who no longer looked at her but instead played with his new pet.

"I'm going to call him Grindan."

Frey laughed, and Brice did too.

"That's a perfect name," Frey agreed.

Sebastian looked confused and, tempting though it was to leave him in that state, Frey decided to put the man out of his misery.

"Grindan is a Saxon name. It means 'sharp.'"

Sebastian joined in the laughter.

* * *

Sebastian didn't laugh now.

In fact, if Frey met the man for the first time today, she would be absolutely convinced he had not laughed a moment in his poor, misbegotten life.

His expression was new to her—fixed and grim. She had not seen him wear it the past three days spent in his company. As a result, it filled her with unease.

Frey smoothed down her kirtle and touched her head rail to ensure her veil held in place.

The action gave her a few moments to take in the room and the anteroom off the great library of St. Cuthbert's. It held not only their handwritten illuminated Bibles, but also copies of the Anglo-Saxon Chronicles and generations of local lore of which her family history was a part.

A monk who was to be scribe for this interview sat at a scarred and ink-stained desk, ready to begin. The light from the window behind him may have suited writing, but it cast all of his features into ominous shadow.

The sound of a throat being cleared drew Frey's attention to Abbot Brother Ranulf, head of St. Cuthbert's Abbey.

"We are here to officially confirm the identity of a young woman who claims to be Lady Alfreya of Tyrswick, the only daughter of Earl Alfred of Tyrswick, and a young boy who claims to be Lord Brice of Tyrswick, the younger son of Earl Alfred of Tyrswick."

The abbot paused and the room fell silent apart from the scratching of pen on parchment.

"Do you swear by the holy book at your right hand that all you will tell us today is the whole truth, so help you God?"

Frey's affirmative answer rang out clear and unambiguously and she was invited to tell her story.

This is what was recorded:

Alfreya, aged twenty-one summers, is the oldest living child of Earl Alfred of Tyrswick, whose family has held these lands for generations. She is the second issue of Alfred of Tyrswick, who was slain in battle during spring in the Year of Our Lord 1077, being the 11th year of the reign of William of England.

The fact of Alfred's death is testified to by the baron of Tyrswick, Lord Sebastian de la Croix, who holds these lands by deed and by right from the rightful king of England.

Furthermore, the lady confirms that Alfred's firstborn, a son christened Edmund, was born in the winter of 1053. No other children were issue of this holy union, Alfred's wife having died in childbirth in the winter of 1065.

At the age of 8 years, Edmund, heir to Tyrswick, was fostered to the earl of Alnwick. He was believed killed at the Battle of Stamford Bridge in the year 1066, along with his lord, fighting alongside King Harold to successfully repel an invading Viking force. Edmund's body was never found.

The scribe looked up, waiting for Frey to continue her recounting. She glanced to where Sebastian sat on a long wooden bench in the shadows and waited for the question she knew would be coming.

"If your mother died in 1065, then who is the mother of Brice?" he asked.

Frey heard the abbot straighten in his chair.

"You may wish to think about your next answer very carefully, my dear," he instructed gravely. "We have no record of Alfred remarrying nor of a second male child being registered as his issue."

"Brice is Alfred's son by his hearth wife, a woman by the name of Rheda."

Sebastian let out a long hiss of surprise and leaned forward into the filtered light that poured through the library window.

"Congratulations," he said. "If your purpose was to withhold this news in order to make a fool of me, then you've succeeded admirably."

Frey shivered as though the words themselves were falling snow. His expression was now completely closed off to her, but Sebastian's bitter words lit a spark of anger.

"I beg pardon, baron, if my deception has wounded you, but do not expect me to be sorry for it," she answered with passion. "Whether we share full blood or half, Brice is still my brother. To see him whole and my father's men returned to their land by any means other than in chains is my *only* concern, and I will use *any* means necessary to guarantee it."

Abbot Ranulf looked shocked. The defiant stare Frey intended for Sebastian was unleashed on him instead as she continued.

"My father already made provision for Rheda and Brice. He had Edmund for his heir, but after his death, he decided to claim Brice in full and name him as successor. That's why we were in Durham." She glanced at Sebastian, accusingly. "Then the harrying came."

The abbot recovered his composure. He nodded to the scribe, who still paused in his work, awaiting confirmation that this uncomfortable revelation was to form part of the official record.

"And the reason you accompanied your father, my dear?" he inquired.

"I was there to be married."

"To whom?"

The question was asked by Sebastian.

"I don't know," she shrugged at him. "I wasn't told."

Sebastian uttered a curse, the first she'd ever heard pass his lips. The sound of the bench scraping loudly against the stone floor echoed through the library as he stood and stormed from the room.

There. It was out. The complete truth, so help her God.

Frey felt sick.

CHAPTER TWELVE

Sebastian's departure marked the end of the interview. The abbot was satisfied Frey's claims were true and her account would be added to the official record. The only thing that remained was to plan for the future, and that required prayer and contemplation. Abbot Ranulf told Frey he was planning to do both and advised she do the same.

Her form of contemplation involved a walk in the walled grounds of the abbey, avoiding the occasional shower of rain that punctuated the day. The monks at work at their labors, some in the field, others tending animals, still more indoors educating novices and translating books, all paid her no heed, leaving Frey to walk unescorted.

She was drawn to the stables in the eastern end of the compound.

"Ebon is a very sympathetic listener."

A dozen horses were stabled here and she recognized those that belonged to Tyrswick.

Ebon stamped the hard, packed dirt floor twice in greeting. Frey snagged a brush hung on a peg protruding from a post and started grooming the black stallion.

"What do you think I should do, Ebon? Am I really too mulish to be a nun?" she whispered into his ear.

The horse nodded his head.

"That is a not comforting answer, my friend. Do you think I should be more specific in my query?"

Ebon huffed out a breath in response and Frey continued brushing, dropping to her haunches to brush down the magnificent beast's legs, pleased to see yesterday's scratches were healing.

The action was both purposeful and relaxing—two of the things that Frey sorely needed to soothe her spirit.

Once or twice, a monk walked into the stable to access one of the adjoining storage rooms for some purpose or another, but no one disturbed her occupation, indeed probably wouldn't have seen her in the afternoon shadows.

So when another set of footsteps crossed the threshold, she paid them no mind until she heard a man speak.

"You know where he is now? In the slaughterhouse, taking out his frustrations with his fists on a side of mutton. All on account of a slip of a girl whom he ought to bed and have done with."

A second man responded. She knew his voice. It was Gaines.

Frey paused her work and listened.

"She has him bewitched. I tried to warn him about her, mind, and he nearly severed my head."

"He's usually an even-tempered man but he's not been right since they found the body of that girl."

Gaines grunted in agreement.

The anonymous voice continued, "Witchcraft, that's what it be, and I'll go on saying it. What kind of woman dresses like a man and leads a battle? A witch, that's who. And I reckon it was she who summoned up the wolves as her familiars. That's why she was able to kill four of them with Talbot's bow and arrows."

A melodic clanging of metal stirrups and the squeak of well-polished leather punctuated the conversation as the two men removed saddles from the tack room in the far corner of the stable building.

"She ought to have burst into flames the minute we passed through the gates of this holy place."

Gaines responded with a half-amused grunt.

"She may not be the devil's daughter, but she is a Saxon one," he answered. "I for one will be glad to see the back of her. She's been nothing but trouble.

"Aye, she's comely enough to look at, but with no lands and no dowry, she'll have no choice but to take the veil. Either that or marry some wealthy old widower who won't care that she's not a virgin."

"Still, if the baron doesn't want her, I'll be happy to ride her," the other knight sniggered. "I'm sure she's been well broken in by those men of hers."

Four stalls over, the sound of timber beams scraping through iron loops indicated the men had opened two enclosures.

Sure enough, the slow and even clopping of hooves could be heard as the horses were led from the stable, their steps enough to drown out the rest of the conversation.

Once sure they had left the yard, Frey rose to her feet. A few quick blinks cleared her eyes of the rage that suffused her being.

She had been scolded once as a child for listening in on adult conversations. Her father's steward squeezed her arm and pulled her away from the door of the long-house. Even now, Frey stroked her arm unconsciously in memory of the bruises the steward left.

Ebon nudged her shoulder and Frey responded with a stroke along his nose.

"Nothing more than a Saxon witch-whore…is that how they all see me, Ebon?" she whispered. "Even Sebastian?"

Ebon was silent on the subject.

* * *

Blood dripped from the cloths that covered and padded Sebastian's knuckles. Beads of red fluid fell to the sawdust as he pounded the flesh of his opponent.

Anger and frustration—his near constant companions for days— were now being transferred, blow by blow, to the side of mutton that swung on a meat hook in the abbey's slaughterhouse. With each punch, he was grateful for the physical action that allowed his mind to consider things less tangible.

Yes, Frey's deception about her brother rankled, but he could see its logic. It was a very clever ploy on her part to gain the cooperation of someone she did not know. He set that subject aside to reflect on the revelation that Frey was in Durham to be married.

Well yes, he argued with himself, why should that not be so? She was of marriageable age. Most girls of her years were already married or promised. That topic would not so easily dissipate though.

It continued to gnaw at him despite the reasoning he applied to it.

And what of this man Drefan? Surely he could not be Frey's intended. She claimed not to know the identity of the man she was to marry and he was inclined to believe this. So was Drefan her lover?

Sebastian delivered the carcass so powerful a punch that it jarred along his hand and arm all the way up to his shoulder.

Frey had a lover.

He returned to that point again and again, touching it like a bruise. It hurt.

He jabbed again with increasing speed—left, right, left, right—until the length of chain on which the meat was suspended rattled and danced, bouncing adjacent slabs of mutton waiting to be dressed.

Soon, Sebastian's lungs demanded air and his arms and shoulders screamed for relief. He steadied his breathing and, with each exhalation, slowed his punches.

He sensed rather than heard or saw that another person had entered the butchery.

"When I heard you were taking your frustrations out on a side of mutton, I thought you were feasting, not fighting."

Sebastian acknowledged Frey's presence in the doorway with a half glance before turning back to his makeshift punching bag.

The smell of wildflowers and lavender broke through the charnel house stench of blood as she approached.

She stood a foot away and stared at his hands before gently reaching across to touch them. Sebastian pulled them away, letting her believe the action was caused by physical discomfort.

"How much of this blood is yours?" she asked, placing her hands behind her back. Out the way of temptation.

Sebastian unwound the strips of rag that protected his knuckles.

"Very little."

He raised his hands to examine them front and back. His fingers were indeed unbloodied and he flexed them with a little effort. They were undoubtedly bruised though.

"Just as well," she said with a touch of humor coloring her tone. "The abbot ought to be thanking you for tenderizing the meat."

"Is there a reason you're here?" he snapped, and felt a twinge of guilt as a momentary look of hurt flickered across her face.

"Ebon was worried about you."

He turned away before a smile at her jest could reach his lips.

"Thank you. I'll tell him he worries needlessly."

With his back to Frey, Sebastian walked over to an oak water butt, dipped his hands, and sluiced his face.

"Actually, there is a reason why I sought you out," she continued.

Sebastian scrubbed his face and straightened.

He waited, but no explanation was forthcoming. He turned.

Frey looked at her feet as though collecting her thoughts. She looked tired, dejected, defeated. This was not the woman he met four days ago.

"Well?" he said, impatience coloring the word.

He saw it the split second it happened, had seen it before. A spark of spirit glowed to life like an ember in a breeze. Deliberately she raised her eyes and skewered him with a look.

Odd. He felt rather proud of her at that moment.

"Firstly, I've come to apologize for my deception over Brice," she started. "I see now you are a man of honorable intent and kindness despite…"

"Despite being a Norman cur? A *forhergian*, a *dysig*, a *helsceaða*?" Sebastian mocked. Yes, he was aware what some Saxons still called him—a despoiler, a fool, a devil.

* * *

Frey merely blinked and folded her arms, uncowed by his fit of temper.

"Actually, I was going to say despite being an *ealdor*—a leader—though in your case, *dysig* is also appropriate."

"Is that all?"

Frey shook her head; there was more.

"No doubt you'll be overjoyed to learn I have decided to join a convent. I will have Abbot Ranulf recommend one as soon as I know from Brother Halig how my brother will fare. You will no longer have care of me, nor need to linger on the unpleasant memory of Alfred of Tyrswick and his children."

Frey held out her hand and waited for Sebastian to clasp it as warriors did as a sign of good faith. Sebastian stared at it as though he had never seen one before, then slowly raised his eyes to hers.

"Where do you think you're going?"

The question came out as a growl. It reminded Frey of the wolves they killed the day before. She frowned, dropping her hand.

"I just told you. A convent."

The last expression Frey had expected to see from Sebastian was a smile, which started slow and spread wide. She started to smile in return until she realized something else lurked behind that expression.

"I do not think so, princess."

"Don't call me that! And besides, where else can I go?"

"You pledged yourself as my hostage."

Frey saw a flash of surprise at her laughter in response.

"That was when you had no idea my men were virtually unarmed and near to starving," she said. "Now they're back home tending their hearths, they have no stomach for making mischief. You saw them yourself. Do you honestly believe any of them could raise a rebellion?"

Sebastian took a step toward her and Frey stood her ground by keeping her eyes firmly fixed on his.

"I know nothing of the sort," he said, taking another step. "When headed by a competent leader, especially one with your attributes, I can easily imagine men ready to fall in behind at any time."

Frey was mesmerized; she could not recall ever seeing eyes that shade of green before. She blinked and he was three paces closer. Close enough to touch in fact. Her fingers tingled in anticipation.

"I gave you my word," she whispered as Sebastian closed the final distance between them.

"Sometimes actions speak louder than words," he said, trailing a fingertip from the back of her hand, along her arm, and up to her shoulder.

A shudder of anticipation ran through her, its cause unmistakable. Sebastian's hand continued up her neck to the back of her head, beneath the veil that hid her silky blonde hair from him.

Despite closing her eyes, Frey's lips anticipated Sebastian and parted of their own accord.

Unlike the frantic mating of lips from yesterday, this kiss was soft and unhurried and deepened as Frey let Sebastian take the lead.

"You and I still have much to discuss," he said in hushed tones in her ear. "And I told you I am not a man to be satisfied quickly."

The promise implicit in those words sent a flood of desire to her loins and Frey clung to him tightly, her body urging Sebastian on as his lips conquered her ear lobe and her neck.

Her imagination took flight as she imagined them coupling, his strong body covering hers, moving above, filling her with the sweet ecstasy her friend Diera assured her would come from an accomplished lover.

Not like Drefan, she recalled involuntarily. In her mind, the warmth and softness of Sebastian's touch was no match for the power of this older, well-traveled memory.

Frey trembled and halted.

Sensing her sudden lack of responsiveness, Sebastian stopped. Pulling back, he saw silent lines of silver tears. He touched one with a finger and paused in wonder at them.

"I do not understand what you want of me," she explained in a breathy plea, and her agony was made complete when Sebastian stood straight and put a few paces between them.

"It is no wish of mine to make you cry," he told her softly.

"Then what?"

Any answer Sebastian may have given was lost when his squire Robert barreled through the door of the slaughterhouse, eyes wide in panic.

"My lord, come quickly! Baldwin and the Saxon have come to blows!"

Sebastian spared a glance at Frey and followed Robert, who sprinted out of the yard before Frey could ask which Saxon was fighting.

Frey followed.

CHAPTER THIRTEEN

The melee was over by the time Frey caught up with Sebastian and Robert. Orlege struggled in the arms of a brawny, brown-robed man, snarling at the back of one of Sebastian's knights who was being escorted a safe distance away by Sebastian and Gaines.

Frey found it strange the knight should turn back to grin at Orlege even as a livid bruise formed over his eye.

"Orlege! What happened here?" she demanded.

Her man-at-arms ceased his thrashing and shrugged off the monk who detained him. His chest still heaved with violent emotion.

"Naught to concern you, m'lady. Just a disagreement among men."

"About what?"

Her man-at-arms was silent but kept his eyes fixed on where Gaines and Sebastian were questioning the man she heard named as Baldwin. Frey felt as though time had slipped backward and she was once again forced to fight for the respect of her men.

"I demand an answer!"

Orlege turned a dead-eye stare on Frey and each word of his response was coldly punctuated.

"I no longer answer to you, Lady Alfreya."

He returned his attention to Sebastian, who was still in deep discussion with Gaines and Baldwin.

Orlege thrust a chin in the baron's direction. "If I have to answer for this," he said to Frey without looking at her, "I'll answer to my new liege and not to a mere woman." At that, he stalked off toward the chapel.

She lost sight of him as he rounded the chapter house.

The small crowd that had coalesced around the fight dispersed, the monks returning to their daily chores while a group Sebastian's men appeared to drift away in embarrassment at witnessing the scene playing out in front of them.

Fury blossomed in Frey so intense and so cold her heart and lungs felt frozen in her chest. She keenly felt the absence of her bow.

By God, she would she would make Orlege pay! How dare he undermine her authority in front of Sebastian's men?

Frey determined to have answers, and if Orlege would not give them to her, then she would get them from the other man. She had only taken a couple of steps toward Sebastian, Gaines, and Baldwin before Larcwide grabbed hold of her elbow.

Frey tried to shake it off, but the older man's grip was unyielding; so too the expression he wore.

"What's the meaning of this?" she demanded.

"Leave it be, my lady. It is over."

Larcwide's words were soft but full of authority.

"It is not over," she argued. "One of my men comes to blows in an abbey, of all places, and I demand to know why."

The light misting drizzle that characterized the day so far started up again, and Frey reluctantly followed Larcwide to shelter under the stone-arched doorway of the chapter house.

After a moment, the thick oak door opened and Abbot Ranulf stood there, his mouth a taut line of disapproval.

"My lady, I'm going to ask your man to escort you to the library."

His tone brooked no argument. He looked past them and out of the door. Frey turned at the sound of three pairs of booted feet running toward the chapter house and out of the rain now falling steadily.

The abbot looked pointedly at Larcwide, who turned, walking toward the door on the far side of the hall. Frey swallowed her annoyance and followed. Larcwide closed the portal after her, but despite the thickness of its timber, she could hear every angry, clearly enunciated word from the abbot.

"Baron, this is a place of peace and of godly contemplation, not a tavern. If you cannot control your men, then you will leave!"

Sebastian's answer, whatever it may have been, was lost as Frey was forced to quicken her step and keep up with Larcwide, who was making his way across the courtyard that linked the chapel and chapter house complex with the two-story library and dormitory building.

He stopped at the foot of the wide stone staircase spiraling upward to the library as the sound of bells from the chapel tower marked Nones, the third hour of afternoon, and drew Frey aside as she caught up.

The library not only housed books and local records, but also was where young men learned to read and write by painstakingly copying texts. Now, as the last peal decayed, the sound was overtaken by that of dozens of footsteps belonging to the young scholars and the manuscript copyists spilling out and walking briskly to the chapel.

When the last left, Larcwide ascended the stairs, Frey following a step behind.

He looked tired, thought Frey as they climbed. Shafts of light from the slits in the outer wall made the crevasses that lined his face seem even more pronounced.

They entered the library itself. Two small fires burned brightly in hearths situated midway along the long walls. The walls were whitewashed and large mullioned windows comprising multiple panes of diamond-shaped glass allowed in copious amounts of natural light even on a day as gloomy as this.

Six rows of desks with four stools at each dominated the center of the room. At each place lay a sheet of cream parchment. Dark blue ink, still wet and glistening on the page, drew Frey's eye. Each sheet shared the same words, the same lines.

She paused, listening for the sound of Sebastian and the abbot ascending the stairs. There was silence.

Walking down the left-hand aisle, Frey passed shelves upon shelves of books and manuscripts, titles lit by the windows opposite.

She fingered the titles as she walked by—Bibles, stories of saints, legends of yore, and local histories. Frey had a decent command of

Latin thanks to nearly six years in Scotland. There had been precious little else to occupy her days and the scholars paid to keep the exiles' offspring out of mischief did not care if one more joined in their studies.

At the far end of the library, her attention was caught by a raised platform upon which stood a beautifully carved desk. On it, in turn, sat a large, elaborately bound leather volume.

Frey opened the cover. The beautifully illuminated frontispiece was decorated in vivid red, green, and blue inks, as well as gold leaf. It read *Historia ecclesiastica gentis Anglorum*—The Ecclesiastical History of the English People.

Larcwide sat on an abandoned writing stool, scraping the legs across the timber floor as he did so. Frey walked back toward him, deciding the time for answers was now.

"Do you know why Orlege got into a fight with one of Sebastian's men?"

"I haven't spoken to him," he answered, rolling a pen up and down the writing slope.

"Then take a guess."

Larcwide placed the pen back into its recess and remained silent.

Frey closed her eyes and sighed, recalling the conversation she overheard in the stables. Without question it was Baldwin who spoke of her so vilely. When she opened her eyes again, she found herself the subject of Larcwide's careful regard. His gray eyes watched every response. It was evident her man-at-arms had drawn the same conclusion.

"Surely Baldwin wouldn't be so careless of his own hide as to repeat the same crudities in front of one of my men?"

"What we witnessed speaks for itself, don't you think?" Larcwide shrugged. "Now the question is what the baron will do."

Sounds on the staircase meant the opportunity for private conversation was at an end.

"Will you speak to Orlege?" Frey asked. "I will speak to the baron."

Larcwide nodded his agreement before rising from the stool as the monk and Sebastian entered. Frey made eye contact with Larcwide once more and gave a slight nod. Larcwide left the library.

Seizing the opportunity to control the direction of the conversation, Frey spoke first.

"Brother Abbot, I wish to convey my deepest regret over the action of my man-at-arms. I can assure you it will not happen again, and I will speak to him immediately."

Frey halted her speech on observing the look the abbot gave to the baron.

Frey gave Sebastian her full attention and dread welled in her.

"Orlege is no longer here," he told her. "I've sent him back with Gaines and two other men."

Frey was incensed. "You have no right!"

Sebastian's answer was measured, but anger clung to each word.

"I have every right to deal with my men as I see fit."

I no longer answer to you, Lady Alfreya.

Orlege's words had wounded, but Sebastian's delivered a death blow.

He pressed the point.

"They *are* my men, are they not? You were a witness to their oath of loyalty three days ago, *were* you not?"

Frey acknowledged with a curt nod, then said, "But it is still my responsibility to see they are treated justly."

"Do you have reason to believe the baron is unjust?" interjected the abbot.

Frey forgot he was in the room.

"No," she admitted.

"The circumstances that bring you to us are unusual to say the least. Even before your arrival I have made no secret about the concern I have for your welfare," Brother Ranulf said.

"I have sent a messenger to London asking the Crown to find a husband for you. Perhaps the man to whom you were pledged still lives."

Frey looked at him with desperation.

"Have I no choice in this matter? I have heard of such places as double monasteries where men and women share the same orders. I wish for Brice and I to go to one of those."

Brother Ranulf shook his head with some sympathy.

"Those houses no longer take new initiates," he said. "The matter is truly out of my hands. Despite your father's intentions, he did not declare Brice as his heir, which means you are Alfred's only legitimate claimant.

"The Crown will want to see you safely wed to a Norman. England is still home to a number of malcontents who would use you, willing or not, to produce an heir to contest Tyrswick."

Frey never before considered her sole value lay in the sons she could produce.

"Surely as a nun, I…," she began.

The monk again shook his head.

"Kidnappings are still rife, and your beauty as well as your bloodlines would be enough temptation. Under those circumstances, we believe the most satisfactory arrangement is to have your brother train here as a scholar until he has decided whether or not to take holy orders."

Brother Ranulf paused, waiting for Lady Alfreya to process his news.

"Obviously, I cannot stay here until someone returns with news from London," she said.

"Very true. That is why the baron generously offers you his protection and his home until then. You will depart on the morrow."

"I understand," answered Frey mildly.

Oh yes, she *did* understand. The kiss in the stables, isolating her from her men-at-arms, added up to only one thing in Frey's mind.

It would be a cold day in hell before she would let Sebastian use her the way Drefan had.

If Larcwide remained in the room, he would have known her change in demeanor boded no one any good. But he was not here and the abbot did not know her. So, while he probably congratulated himself on a job well done, Frey turned to look at Sebastian, silently hurling epithet after epithet in a rage that grew stronger by the second.

As though he could hear her, Sebastian's lips quirked into a brief, mocking half smile.

Ah, the taste of those lips on hers in the stable—soft, full, and tempting. Did the man take a sadistic delight in her predicament?

Aware she was the focus of both men in the room, Frey kept her eyes fixed on Sebastian's face and dipped to a low curtsey.

"I hope to one day repay the baron's generosity," she said.

CHAPTER FOURTEEN

With the sound of morning activity behind her, Frey stealthily brushed past ferns still dripping with dew to make her way to the brook. She could hear it babbling not twenty yards from where they camped on their first night since leaving the abbey.

Frey had shared her news with Brice the previous afternoon and she left the infirmary unsure what had pleased him most—the fact he was to stay at St. Cuthbert's or that she was to marry.

During the first day's ride, Frey determined to avoid Sebastian as much as possible and stayed close to Larcwide who, to her surprise, was mounted and armed with a short sword.

It proved not difficult to avoid the baron. They had departed St. Cuthbert's Abbey without him just as the bells tolled to mark Terce, the third hour after dawn. He caught up with them when they stopped at noon and then rode ahead with his knight until the day's light evaporated.

Two tents had been erected for that evening's rest and, with quiet economy of words, Sebastian told her she would be sharing the tent with him. Frey swiftly looked at Larcwide.

To her surprise and dismay, the older man never looked up, instead continuing with his meal of mutton, with which they had been provisioned by the abbey.

There was no alternative and, although well used to sharing her sleeping space with others—her father and brother most recently—Frey found she had not rested well with Sebastian de la Croix lying just an arm span away.

For a start, the man was huge. Although the tent was his own, it somehow seemed too small with him in it. She slept with her stiletto at hand but, as she thought about it now, strapped to her thigh, it didn't offer her much comfort.

She lay awake for some time, waiting for his touch that never came. After a long while, Sebastian's slow, even breathing indicated he was asleep and lulled her into a restless slumber of her own.

Frey had to get away to find a moment's solitude, and she took her chance now, while their party was having a morning repast and breaking camp.

The sun lit the rest of Frey's path as it emerged from behind a passing cloud. Through the small clearing in the trees, she could see the light dancing playfully over the water, which chortled merrily as it slipped, splashed, and tumbled over rocks on its way downstream.

Kneeling on the grassy bank, Frey dipped her hand into the water, feeling the pull of the current through her fingers. Cupping her hands to capture a generous mouthful, Frey drank quickly, relishing the sweet coldness as it traced down her throat. Another scoop washed her face thoroughly.

With a quick glance back to the camp, listening intently to the sound of men talking and the occasional jingle of metal as tents were dismantled and horses resaddled, Frey calculated she had time to quickly wash. Perhaps now she could be rid of the feeling that Sebastian had touched her all over yesterday, even though he only actually touched her once and that was when aiding her into the saddle. With him so close, even the air in her nostrils didn't feel like her own.

Frey quickly unlaced her boots and then the bodice of her kirtle and placed both on the grass beside her. Her chemise undergarment was actually her father's own tunic, and the cream linen fell in soft folds to just above her knees.

She stepped down into the water and hissed as the cold liquid swirled about her legs. Once acclimatized, Frey sluiced water up and down her legs and thighs, where goose bumps rapidly formed. She unlaced the chemise and shimmied the fabric down her arms where she tied the sleeves around her waist at her back and tucked the hem over the secured fabric.

The sun felt wonderful on her skin, bringing warmth from the top of her head down her shoulders and arms to her back and breasts. Frey stretched her arms heavenward, drawing a draught of sweet air deep into her lungs before bending to stretch her fingertips into the water and began washing away the previous day's worth of travel. Her nipples puckered and grew hard from the chill of the water.

A cloud scudded across the sun, plunging the glen into shadow. Frey halted her ablutions and listened. The birds still twittered, the sound of the camp at work still echoed through the trees, but her instinct told her something was amiss.

"Do not stop on my account," an amused voice instructed her from behind.

Frey jumped and turned swiftly to find Sebastian standing by her abandoned boots and kirtle, his arms folded, standing at ease. Dressed in black boots, dark green hose that fit snugly over his muscular legs, and a gray tunic, he looked ready to ride.

Frey glared up at him and, with fumbling fingers, struggled to untie the sleeves of the shirt to cover her nudity. Her anger bloomed as she realized the whore's-son-bastard found her predicament amusing.

She managed to set the hem of the chemise down to her knees and stepped up onto the bank.

"Have you looked your full, yet?" she sneered.

Frey glared as Sebastian raised his eyebrows, registering mild surprise. What did he expect her to do? Scream? Faint? Hardly. Living in close quarters with her father's men over the past six months had long disabused her of any notion of privacy.

The tension from yesterday's interview at the Abbey, then sleeping so close to Sebastian needed a release, so she turned her anger on the man she deemed responsible for it.

Frey stretched out her arms, fully exposing her naked front. "Well go on, look! Don't skulk behind trees like a callow youth. Be a man."

Sebastian's eye flickered across her form before returning to her face.

"Get dressed," he said through gritted teeth before turning his back to her.

Frey allowed herself a small smile of triumph. Sebastian looked murderous.

Good.

Frey turned her back and worked at the sleeves again until she felt the knot slacken. She pushed the sleeves back up to her shoulders and tightened the laces on the neck when she was grabbed from behind and slammed violently against a man's hard, broad chest.

"Just be careful when issuing orders, princess. Some men aren't content with just looking," Sebastian hissed in her ear.

Frey shuddered, but it wasn't all in fear. Misinterpreting her movement for a struggle, Sebastian tightened his bear hug. Her arms were pinned to her side.

"Let go of me, you Norman dog," Frey demanded.

"Living too long in the company of soldiers has coarsened you," he told her. "It has also made you forget men can be very, very dangerous when their base natures are not in check."

Frey stilled herself, trying to quiet a flash of panic, and waited for Sebastian's next move. She gravely miscalculated this man. He could take her now, even slit her throat where she stood, and there would be no one to gainsay him.

Believing Frey to be quiescent, the baron loosened his grip and she used the slack to reach under the hem of the shirt for her knife. Sebastian was quicker, trapping her hand. As she struggled, he stepped forward, forcing Frey's legs to buckle.

"Yield!" he ordered. Frey continued to struggle.

"Yield to me."

By the time her knees hit the ground, he had liberated the stiletto from its sheath and tossed it aside on the grass, out of reach.

Sebastian dragged Frey up by the elbow. His sensuous mouth a thin, hard line. His eyes raked over her body slowly and brazenly. Frey felt more exposed than when she was nearly naked. Awareness of his masculinity hummed through her. Reflexively, she licked her lips.

"Don't ever let me catch you exposing your ample charms to either your men or mine," he warned her, the threat all the more potent for having been spoken softly.

Did that apply to himself too?

In a fleeting moment, images of them together flickered through Frey's mind before she squelched them firmly.

Sebastian broke the spell by ending eye contact, glancing instead at her abandoned boots, kirtle, and knife.

"If you're not fully dressed and following me by the count of twenty, I'll put you over my knee." He turned and stormed back to the camp.

Frey did as he ordered and rushed behind, appearing at the camp slightly flushed.

The baron glared at her, his mood seeming as black as his mount, which stood ready saddled for the day's ride.

Larcwide and the other knight exchanged mutually surprised glances before hastening to complete their tasks.

Frey mounted her own horse without attempting explanation.

* * *

Sebastian knew he set a brutal pace, not sparing anything except the horses, as the party of four made their way toward Tyrswick Keep.

He longed for home and the routine it afforded. In less than seven days, his world had been upended thanks to Lady Alfreya.

What a mess, he thought.

He knew Gaines believed he had taken leave of his senses and even more so ever since the discovery of *her* body.

No one, not even the king himself, knew the reason why Sebastian so readily accepted Tyrswick in the isolated wilds of Northumbria.

Sebastian could have asked for a more advantageous title closer to London or one with prestige on the Welsh border, but he wanted the north where the smell of the heather and the brine of the North Sea air would remind him of a beautiful brave girl with flaxen hair and bright blue eyes.

She had looked like an angel in the midst of that hell of burning buildings and anguished screams. Her courage saved her brother on that night too.

He kept their brief meeting as a treasured memory for years, then made his home here with no expectations of seeing her again. The girl was most likely wed, dead, or otherwise in exile, he had reasoned with himself.

Whenever he sought feminine company, her blue eyes and soft, berry lips filled his thoughts as he plunged himself into willing flesh. It had been nothing more than a harmless fantasy a country boy from Normandy could indulge himself in.

But when the brutalized body was discovered, his fantasy crashed into a mean reality. The young woman wore a small gold ring engraved with interlocking squares.

Sebastian and his men spent days riding from village to village, fruitlessly inquiring if any young women were missing. When Friar Dominic confirmed the ring was marked with the Tyrswick cipher and would only be worn by someone of status, Sebastian insisted the earl's daughter be buried in the crypt, befitting her rank.

Despite obvious misgivings, Friar Dominic agreed to perform the rites out of loyalty and friendship to the baron.

Sebastian alone mourned her and could tell none the reason why.

If it was known he had allowed a rebellious Saxon earl to escape the harrying, then his own loyalty to King William would be suspect.

He could never allow that to happen. There were too many ambitious young knights waiting for such regal displeasure with an incumbent. They would circle like jackals for a taste of their own title and lands.

And now, just six days ago, he learned the woman—the fantasy— he loved was not dead. As she stood before him that late afternoon, he didn't know whether to rejoice or throw up.

The girl he remembered from Durham had blossomed into a woman more beautiful than his memory could conjure. She was alive and whole, with a fiery and passionate spirit that resonated with him.

The living nightmare of seeing the other girl's brutalized body, believing it to be her, could begin to recede, but now the question was what to do.

It was clear that Frey did not recognize him as her savior that night in the hay barn. Instead, he was just one of the many Norman invaders who destroyed her home.

The abbot was right. Frey needed to wed, for her own security as much as for England's.

Sebastian came close to offering for her during the interview yesterday. Twice he had tasted her lips and felt her soft curves beneath his fingers. The thought of someone else enjoying her filled him with an unreasonable fury.

Then this morning, seeing the unclothed perfection of her body hardened his resolve.

As well as other parts of your anatomy, he chided himself.

Sebastian de la Croix had a reputation for being an intelligent and measured man, never one for letting his passions rule his head. To the best of his knowledge, he had only ever done one impulsive thing in his life.

Now he was about to do another.

CHAPTER FIFTEEN

Frey was certain Sebastian smirked when he looked back at her. And why shouldn't he? She must look like a gawping fool. Her only consolation was that her own quick glance at Larcwide revealed his eyes equally wide and jaw equally slack.

This was not the Tyrswick they knew.

She recognized little of what existed in her father's time, of the long-house she called home. It was gone and in its place was a stone tower, four stories tall, seemingly hewn from a single rock.

Tyrswick had grown from just an isolated selection of thatch-roofed timber outbuildings by the tributary on the River Tyrs, to a tidy little village that even boasted its own flour mill.

On recognizing the baron, villagers paused in their field labors and rushed to the road to wave. From somewhere in Sebastian's surcoat, a fist full of coins emerged. He tossed them a safe distance away from his horse and the local children whooped and hollered as they scrambled for the coppers.

Those unable to leave their chores stopped just long enough to either nod or tug their forelocks before continuing their work.

Before the party of travelers, Tyrswick Keep rose.

Frey had only seen buildings this big before in Durham and Edinburgh, never before emerging out of the green English landscape as this.

Larcwide reined his horse closer in to Frey's mount.

"Look at how Tyrswick prospers, my lady," he said, his voice low but clearly in awe.

"It does," she answered, watching the spectacle of Sebastian's homecoming. "Have their affections been bought so cheap they no longer remember my father?"

Larcwide looked at her disapprovingly.

"A man wants a roof over his head and food to fill the bellies of his wife and children," he reproved. "Why should he not cheer?"

"All of a sudden you've found Frankish blood in your veins?" Frey demanded.

"Give the man his due, Alfreya."

Frey stiffened at the use of her first name.

Larcwide held the young woman's gaze steadily. She knew this was a battle of wills she would not win.

"The war is over," he said. "You should be happy your people fare well."

"But they're not my people anymore, are they?" Frey rejoined peevishly. "They probably look at us and wonder why two ragamuffins ride horses."

Before Larcwide could answer, Frey felt a hand touch her leg.

An old woman with wisps of gray hair escaping her cap held a hastily gathered offering of flowers up to Frey.

"Not all have forgotten ye family, mistress," she said.

Frey stopped her horse to accept the bouquet and held onto the crone's hand, touched by her words.

"We 'eard about yer miraculous return from the dead, and I say Tyrswick's doubly blessed to have ye back where ye belong."

"You remember me?" Frey asked, almost overcome with emotion.

The woman smiled, exposing gaps where teeth used to be.

"Every night in my prayers, my lady, both you and yer brother. Now you're back for good."

Filled with compassion, Frey squeezed the hand with sorrowful affection.

"I can't promise that..."

"I can."

Frey had not noticed Sebastian double back to them. Astride his horse, he looked every inch the imposing lord of the manor, yet there was humanity and affection in his voice as he addressed the old woman.

"Lady Alfreya *is* home for good," he vowed.

The old woman's gap-toothed smile brightened. "You've made an old woman happy, Sebastian de la Croix."

Frey wasn't sure what shocked her most—the old woman's familiarity with the baron of Tyrswick or his declaration that she was home.

They rode on together for a short distance until Frey could no longer resist addressing the matter.

"You ought not make promises you can't keep," Frey told him as they approached the outer bailey gate.

"What makes you think my promise is hollow?"

Frey straightened in the saddle and met his eyes directly.

"The fact that the Crown decides my fate and not some minor baron in a forgotten, far-flung corner of the kingdom."

Let him mull on that insult, she told herself.

Sebastian didn't seem in the least bit perturbed; the blackguard even grinned. A twinkle in his eye hinted further at his amusement.

"You underestimate my influence at Court, princess," he said. "I've never been refused anything I wanted."

He watched her keenly and then with satisfaction, seeing the heat and arousal flushed through her, coloring her skin.

"And what *do* you want?" she said.

She had asked him that question before, in the maelstrom of conflicted emotions when he kissed her in the abbey's slaughterhouse, and she believed she knew the answer.

Yet the previous night, when they were alone in his tent, he could have taken her. He had not. To Frey's shame, she almost wished he had, even if only to prove to herself that desire was just desire, devoid of meaning, like an itch that must be scratched to find relief.

"All in good time, ma chere," he added, then urged Ebon to the front of the party, having the honor and the right to be first across the drawbridge and into the inner bailey.

The thunderous clatter of horses' hooves on wood subsided as the last of the party entered the protective embrace of the keep's formidable stone walls.

Stable boys came forward to steady the horses as their riders dismounted.

Frey glanced down at the one holding the reins of her mount. To her surprise, it was Orlege, who muttered a greeting before looking away.

She was about to speak to her man-at-arms when firm hands encircled her waist, lifting her from the horse. Even without seeing, she knew it was Sebastian.

Orlege tossed her an unreadable look over his shoulder as he led her horse away.

As Frey was lowered to the ground, she saw Larcwide walk up and thump Orlege squarely on the back. Orlege turned and the two men greeted each other warmly before they disappeared toward the stables.

Sebastian beckoned her and she followed him through the main doors of the keep.

Frey suddenly found herself filled with loss. Brice was now being cared for and with a future far beyond that which she could possibly offer him. Orlege and Larcwide seem to have accepted the patronage of a new lord. Indeed, Larcwide seemed positively delighted by the prospect.

Sebastian made his way past the guard's living quarters, the smell of sweat attenuated only a little by the smell of fresh rushes on the floor and the scent of pine resin boiling from the log that burned brightly in the fireplace.

Frey hastened to follow, momentarily losing sight of him as he ascended the circular stone staircase.

She only caught a quick glimpse of the great hall as they walked past another floor, a series of sleeping chambers accessed from a central corridor.

Frey mounted the stairs to the final floor and almost bumped into Sebastian's back. She stepped back and glanced around. It was a surprisingly light and airy room, thanks to the doors that opened out into the roof of the forebuilding.

Two or three walls were covered by sizable tapestries with armorial motifs. Benches and chairs were covered with comfortable-looking low pillows. Behind her to the left, separated by a thick wooden partition, was a spacious chamber that Frey guessed belonged to Sebastian himself. By the time she finished her inventory of the room, she felt five sets of eyes on her.

Pride wouldn't allow her to be cowed in front of this audience, so she acknowledged each one in turn with a direct stare of her own.

First, an older woman with silver-gray hair neatly, but not expensively, gowned—must be the nanny to the pretty, high-born girl beside her who was aged about fourteen years, Frey supposed. The girl's stare was a frank appraisal of Frey's own appearance. Approving or disapproving, Frey could not tell, but some kind of conclusion must have been drawn because the girl sat back and drew her lips into a tight line.

Like the older woman, the next woman was fashionably begowned, but not as elaborately as the woman next to her on the left, which told Frey they were, in turn, companion and mistress.

Even if that were not clue enough, the jet-black hair, the peculiar shade of green of the eyes, and the finely drawn features left Frey in no doubt she was in the presence of Sebastian's sister.

Suddenly, she was conscious of how she looked. Her hair, which she wore in a single braid, was coming loose from its ties, and small strands tickled her cheeks. Frey's tunic was dusty from riding and she smelled of horse. Frey was aware that Sebastian watched her but refused to look up at him.

Judging by the expressions in the room, she supposed they might think her some crofter's spawn, not the daughter of the man who once ruled this land.

She straightened her back and acknowledged their presence once more, this time as Lady Alfreya of Tyrswick.

"Lady Rosalind Villiers," he said, addressing his sister formally, "I would like to introduce you to Lady Alfreya of Tyrswick."

Frey heard a gasp of astonishment from one of the other women but elected to maintain eye contact with the one in front of her whose own momentary look of surprise was quickly replaced with a warm smile.

"Forgive us if we seem ill-prepared for your arrival, my lady, but until a few days ago, we believed you to be dead," said Rosalind.

"I shouldn't wonder at your surprise," Frey responded. "Until a few days ago, I had no idea I was supposed to be dead."

She curtsied and Rosalind rallied herself to stand. Frey realized the woman was heavily pregnant.

"Please, don't stand on my account, my lady. See to your comfort."

Rosalind smiled gratefully and eased herself back into her chair.

"I want to forestall any gossip here and now," Sebastian stated briskly. "Lady Alfreya is here under my protection and she is to be treated as a guest."

"Of course, brother," said Rosalind. "A place has already been prepared for her in Heloise's chambers."

Sebastian stepped forward and kissed his sister warmly on the cheek, murmuring "thank you" in her ear as he drew away again, his voice so low Frey thought it likely she was the only other in the room to have heard.

She watched as Rosalind patted her brother's hand affectionately and could not miss the woman's brief, appraising glance in her direction.

She wondered what Lady Rosalind Villiers thought of her.

CHAPTER SIXTEEN

Frey surveyed the room that she was to share with Lady Heloise Villiers, sister of Rhys Villiers, earl of Goscote, therefore sister by marriage to Sebastian and Lady Rosalind.

Frey undressed, ignoring the young woman's frankly curious assessment. There was something in the set of the mouth and the reservation in the girl's welcome that suggested that her presence here was not a welcome one.

She washed away the dust of two days' travel and knew what kind of image she must present—an object of pity. A noblewoman who lost everything she had, nice clothes and jewels, forced to give up every worldly comfort because her father dared to rebel against the king of England.

Oh yes, and life as an outlaw had ruined her figure.

Instead of the soft curves enjoyed by noble ladies at court, her body was lean and muscled, not like a man because her waist and hips dipped and flared as they ought, but muscles could clearly be seen along her arms, while her buttocks and thighs were hard and lean.

Frey's musings were cut short when a servant entered the room. Heloise had already completed her own ablutions. She now sat on a stool and let the maid comb and dress her hair.

Frey ignored them and examined the three garments laid out on the bed. They were all she owned.

None of those kirtles were suitable for a guest dining in the Great Hall of Tyrswick Keep. She would be indistinguishable from the servants in those faded rags.

Seeing that she hesitated in her choice, Heloise called out.

"Come now, my lady, you don't want to look like one of the serving wenches. Let me see if one of my gowns will suit."

Heloise shrugged off the maid to rummage through her coffer, missing the pained wince her artless words caused to flitter across Frey's face.

"There," the young woman said, pulling out a kirtle of dark blue.

By the way she was holding the gown, it was clearly not a favorite. Indeed, it was plain compared to the heavily embroidered rose pink dress she wore tonight, but it was clean and presentable.

"This should fit you."

"Thank you, Lady Heloise," Frey replied with as much forced grace as she possessed, "that is most generous of you."

Heloise sat back down to allow the maid to finish her hair. She looked very pleased indeed by the compliment, as though she had accomplished some great task.

Frey slipped on a cream undertunic before tentatively drawing on the borrowed gown. It fit, but only just. She loosely tied the stays on the waist. The hem was short by a good two inches above her ankle.

For a moment she reconsidered Heloise's offer, but one look back at her own clothes told her the girl was right. Frey swallowed her discomfiture and wondered if Sebastian would realize she was making an effort to fit in.

Having finished Heloise's coiffeur, the maid turned her attention to Frey. She only got as far as plaiting two braids before the sound of a ringing bell floated up from the Great Hall below. In haste, the girl pinned the plaits lopsidedly to the crown then rushed away to continue her work downstairs.

Frey straightened and repinned her hair before positioning a gauzy yellow veil with a borrowed silver head rail, and donned her red cloak to follow Heloise down to the Great Hall.

The noise assailed Frey first, followed by the smell of roasted fish and freshly baked bread.

Men and women milled around the tables, waiting for the baron to arrive before they took their places. Frey looked for Orlege and Larcwide but could not see them among the housecarls and others who customarily dined at the hall.

Frey stood with the other noblewomen to the left of the raised dais where the baron and the family would dine, a little uncertain of what might be expected of her.

The hubbub in the room died down a little as Sebastian entered the hall, accompanied by Gaines, squire Robert, and a couple of other men whom she did not recognize. Sebastian seemed to be seeking a particular face among the noblewomen who waited for escorts to the raised platform. He found it and smiled.

For several heart-stirring seconds as Sebastian crossed to the group, Frey thought the smile was for her and she returned it, but his eyes slipped past her to the person on her right, and he extended his hand to her.

Rosalind took it with a smile of her own and allowed her brother to seat her to the right of his own chair; Robert followed close behind with cushions for her lower back.

Gaines offered his arm to Frey. Her escort was clearly not happy with his duties.

To her surprise, she was placed on Sebastian's left, a position of high honor. A glance at Heloise suggested she'd expected Frey's honor to be her own. Heloise was a picture of dismay as Robert escorted her to a seat farther down the table.

Servers placed trenchers of roasted fish and filled cups with wine. With the head party served, the rest of the hall, including the servants, sat down to dine.

Frey spotted Orlege and Larcwide and a couple of more familiar faces in the crowd, including Friar Dominic's.

Gaines, still the reluctant escort, slid a wooden platter with a hacked-about piece of fish and a torn piece of bread toward her. She thanked him. He grunted in response.

Frey felt Sebastian brush her shoulder as he turned to serve his sister. Overhearing their conversation, Frey smiled wistfully to herself. She missed the easy banter with family and she wondered how Brice fared. Her heart ached for her brother.

Her reflection was broken by a demanding pounding on the table, and Sebastian rose to his feet and tugged on her arm.

"What are you doing?" she hissed.

"Time to stand up, princess. Show people you're home," he said softly.

Frey reluctantly stood.

The babble of voices died down as Sebastian spoke.

"I present to you Lady Alfreya of Tyrswick, daughter of the late earl. Alive, whole, and now our guest."

A murmur went through the crowd before a few isolated handclaps turned into an ovation.

Frey bowed her head in acknowledgment before sitting, somewhat embarrassed by the attention.

Sebastian spared her one last glance before turning his attention to assisting his sister with the second course—a pie of beef, rabbit, and pheasant. The hall thundered with the sound of a hundred fists banging their approval of the meal as it was served.

As the evening wore on, Frey shucked off her cloak and looked about for her taciturn dinner companion, who had slipped away as seating arrangements lost their formality.

She spotted Gaines a moment later. He sat with a few of his men at the lower tables.

Sweethearts separated by their duties during the day took the opportunity to sit side by side while children played in and out among the tables, followed by the dogs that eagerly foraged for scraps in the rushes on the floor.

In Gaines's place, Robert now sat to serve her from the tureen of stewed fruit and clotted cream, the final course of their meal, but his eyes were on one of the household maids who blushed becomingly every time she glanced over at him.

Frey searched for Sebastian and cursed herself the moment she became aware of the direction of her thoughts. Nonetheless, she continued to look about. He wasn't at the tables where he had stopped earlier to share a word with one of the servants or to slap one of the knights on the back with the easy camaraderie that seemed so commonplace here.

Instead, she found him seemingly in deep conversation with Friar Dominic at the entrance to the Keep's chapel at the end of the Hall. It also appeared Lady Heloise had left the hall early.

Lady Rosalind leaned along the table to Alfreya.

"Lady Alfreya, since I appear to have lost my escort for the evening, could I persuade you to assist me from my chair? I find with the babe, my balance on the stairs is somewhat lacking."

"Of course, my lady," Frey replied. "After such a long and trying week, I would like to retire early myself."

Frey helped Rosalind to her feet and together they negotiated past the tables and benches and the branches of glimmering lit candles in freestanding iron holders at each end of the dais, then down the treads to where Gwenda stood to assist her mistress to bed.

* * *

Sebastian remained unaware of his sister's retirement as he listened to Friar Dominic's news.

"There's evil stalking the land, Sebastian."

"Dealing with evil is your domain, Dom."

"But when the devil uses the hand of man, then it becomes your problem too."

Sebastian sighed; this was news he did not want to hear this evening.

"Where did it happen?"

"The village of Elmcarden, about three days' ride from here. I heard about it from the local priest."

"And the girl was killed in exactly the same way?"

"The nearest I can tell."

Dominic paused for a moment before plunging into the telling.

"The priest performed the last rites on the girl after they found her. She went missing and her parents were sure she had run off with her swain, but when the young man returned with the rest of his hunting party vouching for his whereabouts, the villagers started search parties."

Subtly, the friar drew Sebastian farther into the darkened chapel to prevent their conversation being overheard.

"When they found her, the lassie's hair had been chopped off and her eyes gouged out. The fingers on both hands were removed and clothing cut away.

"And, yes, the local wise woman examined her and she had been most grievously used."

Sebastian nodded, absorbing the facts. He didn't really need a detailed description of the girl's injuries; he knew how the Beast, as he had taken to calling the murderer, defiled his victims.

He'd seen it himself.

He'd placed a woman in Tyrswick's crypt with just those injuries. His dreams had been haunted with visions of her ever since.

Friar Dominic was right. If there was evil by the hand of man on his lands, he was responsible for stopping it. Even as a battle-hardened veteran, the thought of a woman being brutalized that way angered him. His right hand clenched as though it held a sword. It didn't and that was probably just as well, he thought. Vengeance thrummed in his veins.

"I'll send men on patrol at first light tomorrow," he said.

"That's some small comfort for the family," Dominic observed.

"Short of catching the Beast in the act, what is it you expect me to do?" Sebastian retorted angrily.

"Calm yourself, Baron," the clergyman soothed. "It was not meant as a criticism, but your men will need to do more than simply tear around the countryside. The last thing you want is for innocent men to have suspicion thrown on them."

Sebastian sighed and nodded once.

"You're right, of course. I'll ensure they are visible but their enquiries discreet. At this point, events that happened before the girl's disappearance are more important than those following."

Dominic clasped Sebastian's shoulder, looking at the younger man with a sympathetic expression. "I'm sorry to be the bearer of bad news on your first night home."

Sebastian accepted the gesture in the spirit it was given, but part of him resented it too. Dominic was assiduous in never interfering in baronial matters and yet, as someone old enough to be his father, there were times when a comment was more than just a friendly observation.

Sebastian scrubbed his face and pondered his next course of action. Tonight he would have loved nothing better than to call for a jug of mead to be brought to his chambers where, in a semidrunk sleep, he might forget the Beast and the destruction he wrought.

But he cast his own wishes aside. To be a man and a leader of men required self-sacrifice.

He would talk to Gaines about men who could be trusted.

Sebastian scanned the crowd for his man-at-arms when, at the far end of the hall, flickering in the candlelight, the vision from his nightmare stopped and looked directly at him.

The woman with hacked yellow hair.

A midnight blue dress.

One hand folded in front of the other to mask mutilated fingers.

Sebastian struggled for breath as though he had run hard. He looked about the room and no one was paying the specter any heed. The more he stared, the more pain tightened his chest.

Sebastian surged forward. As he did so, a man a little unsteady on his feet bumped into him. The man offered his profound apologies and, as Sebastian stepped around him, he saw the apparition round the stairs to the sleep chambers.

He picked up his pace, taking the stairs two at a time until he touched her.

Flesh and blood. Not spirit.

Sebastian grabbed Frey's hand and spun her so her back slammed against the wall. He snatched the veil from her head. The circlet clattered noisily down the stairs while the head covering floated its way after it.

Frey's own pale blonde locks, neatly braided and pinned, were intact, her face marked with surprise and annoyance.

He pulled her right arm between them and stared at her fingers, unsheathed like a cat's claws, ready to strike out.

Fingers and a thumb, all where they should be. One, two, three, four, five…as Sebastian counted, his pulse slowed, but his anger continued unabated.

"That dress," he bit out, "take it off."

Frey lifted her jaw, not afraid of him—defiant instead.

"So that is to be the way of it?" she hissed. "You tell your sister that I am a guest, but I am to be used as a whore?"

Sebastian in his controlled fury did not trust his voice. His fingers increased their pressure on her wrist and he dragged her up the remaining steps and propelled her into the hallway and around into her chamber.

Heloise squeaked in alarm at the noisy intrusion. The maid who combed out the young lady's hair jumped. At the terse command to leave, the servant scurried away.

"What is the meaning of dressing like that tonight?" he demanded.

It seemed Frey had lost her fear of him and some of her anger; her voice when she answered was more perplexed than aggrieved.

"Admittedly the dress is not the best fit, but Heloise was kind enough to lend me something of hers, which—"

Sebastian turned his ire on his young sister-in-law.

"Why in hell's name would you do such a thing, Heloise? Do you hate me that much?"

Frey continued to stare at him as though he had lost his mind, but at least she hadn't burst into tears as his young sister-in-law instantly did. Frey turned to the girl and placed a comforting arm around her. She turned back to Sebastian, her face contorted with fresh anger.

"Get out!"

Sebastian reacted as though he had been slapped. His eyes flickered between the two women, who stared wide-eyed at him as though he were a mad man.

He stiffly bowed and muttered an apology before backing out of the chamber. Walking back down the hall, he went only a few paces before he heard the chamber door close heavily and the lock slide home in noisy rebuke.

And at the sound, he felt relief.

CHAPTER SEVENTEEN

To claim she had slept would have overstated matters considerably. The best Frey could say was she dozed at some point after the final sounds from the Keep were extinguished along with the tapers.

Heloise cried herself to sleep and Frey could offer little comfort to her, having no answer to the girl's oft-repeated question of what she had done to upset Sebastian so. Frey was just as bewildered by Sebastian's behavior last night. It was clear Heloise was devoted to her brother-in-law and the thought of displeasing him distressed her.

She offered to go find Lady Rosalind, but Heloise clung to her tightly and, between jagged sobs, begged her not to.

Frey heard the birds noisily herald a new morning. Knowing the last vestiges of sleep were lost to her, she arose and peered through a slit in the window shutter. As the portcullis chains rattled at the lifting of the gate, Frey glanced back at Heloise, still sleeping soundly, then returned her attention to the scene outside.

Through the ingress, three liveried knights, one bearing the Tyrswick standard aloft, galloped across the drawbridge into the outer bailey, through the gate, and into the village beyond.

A fourth man, whom Frey had first assumed to be the gatekeeper, did not reenter the keep's walls as expected, but instead also crossed the drawbridge to the outer bailey, following a path toward the crypt at the eastern wall.

A shaft of morning light fell on the man's features, confirming to Frey what she already kenned from observing his stride. Sebastian walked unaccompanied and purposefully toward the vaults.

She checked again that Heloise did not stir and backed away from the window, threw a kirtle over her chemise, and hastily tied her boots. Frey nimbly descended the stairs to the sounds of Tyrswick Keep stirring into life, but it was not so busy that it observed her leaving.

It took a moment for her eyes to adjust to the gloom inside the chapel. Thin streams of light revealed no occupant, and at first Frey thought she may have mistaken Sebastian's destination.

At last, a voice spoke from the darkness.

"Has Heloise forgiven me yet?"

Frey started in surprise but moved toward the apse, her boots echoing noisily. She spotted Sebastian sitting on the front pew, staring at a spot on the ground in front of the altar. She sat alongside him, but his attention remained fixed ahead.

"She adores you. I think she would forgive you anything."

They sat in silence for long moments while the chapel began to fill with the light of the emerging morning. The sun strengthened its claim on the day, illuminating the inscription on the stone that consumed Sebastian's attention.

est anima mea quiescit

My soul is at rest.

The carving was crisp, Frey noted. Whoever lay beneath the slab had not been there long. To have been given such a signal honor meant it was someone very precious to the baron indeed.

As the light pushed back the gloom, it revealed more of the carving—four interlinked squares, the cipher of Tyrswick family.

Her family.

Frey swallowed with difficulty.

"Who is interred here?" she asked softly.

Sebastian did not answer. He might as well have been fashioned of the same wood as the pews for all the movement he showed.

Realization slid like a knife between her ribs.

"Diera?"

The question came as a sob.

Sebastian's shoulders slumped and Frey had her answer. She pressed her fingers to her lips to stop the cry in her throat. She swallowed it down.

"Tell me," she asked hoarsely.

The answer was a curt shake of his head.

"Damn you! Tell me all!" Frey punctuated her demand with a closed-fist punch to his shoulder.

Before she could land another strike, Frey was held fast in Sebastian's arms, and her frustrated remonstration manifested itself in body-shaking sobs.

"She was my friend," Frey gasped.

Sebastian loosened his grip and looked at her for the first time since she entered the chapel. His expression was anguished. The fleeting brush of his fingers against her cheek as he straightened sent shivers through her.

"Her body was found just outside the village two months ago," he said, his voice low and even, yet his focus again fixed on the stone on the floor.

"How did she die?"

Sebastian shook his head once more.

"I need to know."

He turned his face to her, eyes bright with anger.

"You do not need to know! No one needs to know what evil is capable of!"

Frey blinked away tears. How could she convince him that it was not out of morbid or prurient interest she asked, but rather something that pulled at her very soul.

"Please…I dream of her."

Sebastian pulled himself straight once more. Frey saw in his face the war being waged within. Tentatively, she reached for his hand and with her touch he exhaled.

He accepted the contact, her hand in his.

"She was slain by a monster not like anything I have seen in battle, not like other transgressions I've seen," he said.

"Raped?"

Sebastian nodded and then continued.

"But that was not the worst of it. The fiend gouged out her eyes and hacked off the fingers of her right hand, then left her by the road, posed as though she slept. He even chopped off her hair."

Frey gasped at his words. Her dream! Exactly as her dream!

She shuddered, recalling every detail of the nightmare she experienced the night they entered St Cuthbert's. And then there was last night—Sebastian's strange behavior as he stared at her right hand and then yelled at Heloise.

Frey blinked and found herself subject of Sebastian's scrutiny.

"Why?" she asked.

"That's a question for Friar Dominic. He knows the mind of God better than I do."

Frey shook her head.

"No. I mean why did you lay her to rest here?"

"What remained of her clothes showed they were finely made, not rough peasant cloth, and she wore a small ring on her right hand, engraved…"

Sebastian paused, a puzzled look on his face in response to her agitation.

"No," she said, "I mean here! Not in the village churchyard but in *your* family crypt. Why here?"

Heat and cold washed over Frey in waves. She feared she knew the answer and wished she did not.

If Sebastian answered, she did not hear. Frey's ears buzzed suddenly as though she stood in the middle of an apiary. A deeper memory tugged at her consciousness before playing before her like a vision.

They had been separated from their men that night in the hay barn. She held on to Brice so tight, wanting to shield the little boy from the violence and fearing he had already seen too much. Papa had been hurt, but he shepherded them into the building and ordered them to stay where he put them.

Then suddenly there was the young man, dressed in the armor of the invaders, who looked nearly as scared as she.

"Go! Get out of here," he had warned. "I will buy you as much time as I can."

In the years since, the memory of that night had faded and might have disappeared altogether like a will-o'-the-wisp had it not returned at Friar Dominic's sermon just a few days before.

Frey pressed her recollection further but could not recall whether she had seen the color of his eyes. She was sure she had not in the feeble light, but her mind's eye conjured up the young knight's face.

She knew that face!

Although matured by age and responsibility, there was no mistaking the fullness of the mouth and the determination of his jaw.

It was Sebastian de la Croix.

When Frey's mind returned to the present, she became conscious of being alone in the chapel.

Sebastian, it would appear, had withdrawn. Perhaps he was as uncomfortable with the implications of his revelation as she was, Frey mused.

Stunned by the realization Sebastian had been their unexpected benefactor those distant years ago, she considered how strange it was that…what? Guilt, perhaps? Might drive such a proud man to treat her vanquished family as his own.

Then his description of the outrage suffered by Diera came back to her, and she could only pray her friend's soul really was at rest, her life taken in a way so wholly unnatural. It demanded justice; it demanded revenge.

She hoped no other family would have to experience such a thing.

Frey slid off the pew and sank to her knees, where she traced with her finger the inscription and the Tyrswick cipher that marked Diera's last resting place. A small patch of the stone was soon darkened by falling tears.

* * *

It seemed to the man lodging at the Red Lion the addition of new faces would normally be the subject of intense scrutiny in the village of Elmcarden. However, the monthly markets coincided with the arrival of the band of traveling tinkers and merchants, including himself, so outsiders earned only a particular type of disinterest.

Even now, the tavern keeper and his family paid no heed to faces, only orders, and they were simple enough—ale or cider, roast or stew, room and a bath.

With only passing notice did anyone pay attention to three knights on horseback stopping at the green.

It would seem knights from Tyrswick Keep were always welcome in Elmcarden, and why not? They always had coin to spend, were mostly well-behaved, and the man on whose authority they acted was, from the traveler's casual enquiries, fair and just.

On recognizing the livery, the majority of the drinkers went back to their business with the exception of an ill-kempt young man who glowered resentfully at the party. The young man was unaware he was being observed. If he had, he might have been more circumspect in showing his animosity.

He would be useful.

The traveler had watched the young man for nearly a week; so alone and without direction, he appeared, but so filled with anger since that bastard, usurping baron had the lad cashiered from his service.

Now was the time to approach. Ensuring his cloth cap covered his pale locks, the man stood with two fresh ales in hand.

"Here, young man," he greeted, putting one of the pints in front of him.

The recipient of his largess looked at him, silent and suspicious.

"You looked like you needed one," the man shrugged.

"I know nothing's for nothin'. What's this going to cost me?"

142

He ignored the question and sat across from the tall young man whose dark hair and overtly masculine good looks, he assumed, probably never left him wanting for feminine company. He also looked like one who'd never given regard to the source of his next meal. Until now.

A nod toward the window drew the young man's attention back to the knights outside tending their mounts.

"Look at them. Coin in pocket and little hard work for it," offered the older man.

"I used to be one of them," the younger replied bitterly.

"Is that so? What happened?"

"My lord was bewitched."

"Really?"

"As I live and breathe. Bewitched."

"Then you've been unjustly treated, to be sure!" the man said. "Ah, whose men are they?" he added, as if he didn't know.

"The baron of Tyrswick's."

A shove of the mug toward the young man and this time it was accepted. He took a long draught of the amber fluid.

"Are you in need of work?"

"Aye," he eventually answered.

"Then I have work for you."

And, with that, a gold coin was slid across the bench.

The former knight looked up at his new benefactor, then back down at the coin. After a moment's thought, he picked it up and slipped it into his leather pouch.

"Who do I have the honor of addressing?"

"My name is Drefan."

"I'm Baldwin."

Drefan smiled.

"Yes, I know who you are."

CHAPTER EIGHTEEN

The passage of weeks was marked by the turning of autumn leaves from green to vivid shades of red and yellow and the sun losing its summer sting. Providence smiled on Tyrswick this year. A bountiful harvest not only guaranteed the villagers would have plenty to eat over the frigid winter months, but also ensured plenty for sale and trade.

Despite rapidly approaching her time, Rosalind reveled in her role as mistress of Tryswick Keep, employing both Heloise and Frey to be her arms and legs.

Heloise seemed proud to be so honored and took her responsibilities seriously—perhaps too seriously for the likes of some of the more experienced household servants.

Frey was also happy to have domestic activity to fill her days and gladly joined the rest of the household women in preparing pickled and jellied meats and making candied fruits and preserves to be placed in the cold stores of the Keep's basement.

The abundance of good growing was also evidenced in the generous amount of honey and beeswax gathered, and quite a few of the young female servants were delighted to be taken away from their regular chores to make up beeswax candles, which were much more pleasantly aromatic than the usual animal-fat tallows.

What resentment or disquiet anyone at the Keep may have felt at Frey's unexpected return to the land of the living disappeared when they saw her willingness to not simply give orders, but to work just as vigorously as they.

And those servants who were there when her father ruled Tyrswick were simply happy to see their mistress back home.

As Frey crossed a sunny courtyard on her way back to the Keep, she noted with approval the rows and rows of trestle tables boasting a cornucopia of fruit to be dried in the sunshine.

She stopped briefly to turn her face to the sun and breathe in the sweet scent of ripe fruit. She was content, more at peace than she had been over the past seven years. However, the knowledge that soon she would be married off to a stranger and leaving her home yet again nagged at her.

Sebastian's promise of six weeks ago that she was home for good echoed through Frey's mind. He had yet to explain himself, but in seeing such a well-run keep and a prosperous village which produced a magnificent harvest, she was beginning to appreciate that Sebastian was a man capable of getting what he wanted.

On reaching the entrance to the Keep, Frey was stopped by one of the household servants.

"My Lady Rosalind has asked if you could join her in the solar," said the girl.

"Is she well?" Frey enquired. "She doesn't suffer with birthing pangs yet?"

"Not that I am aware, my lady."

Frey was not the only one keeping a watchful eye on Rosalind, though not all the concern was welcomed by her.

Some weeks earlier, the baron had questioned the amount of physical activity she was doing and received a tongue-lashing in response. Rosalind refused to be confined and insisted on taking long daily constitutionals with Heloise and sometimes with Frey.

In fact, Rosalind put such a flea in Sebastian's ear about his nervous hovering that Frey didn't blame him for gladly taking his sister's advice to be about his own business. Since then, he had occupied himself almost solely with holding sessions of his seigniorial court or riding out to the villages under his domain.

So busy had he been, in fact, that Frey and Sebastian only managed to speak a few words to one another in passing, and they were merely everyday pleasantries.

Now, as she ascended to the upper floors, she noted the smell of sour rushes from the Great Hall, which assailed her nostrils this morning, was gone. The sodden rushes had been cleared away and, following a thorough scrubbing of the stone floor with lye, fresh rushes mixed with fragrant dried lavender and fennel lay in their place.

In the solar, the floor had been similarly scrubbed yesterday at Rosalind's direction, and not without a few grumbles from some of the serving girls about it not being spring and "how odd women get when they're on the nest."

Here, however, the rushes were not simply strewn about as they were in the Great Hall; instead, they were woven into thick mats nearly covering the floor from wall to wall. Frey observed the newly completed tapestries adorning the walls and considered wintering in this room would be no hardship indeed.

"There you are!" Rosalind exclaimed. "A messenger arrived today bearing two missives for you, my dear."

Heloise hovered by her sister-in-law's elbow, glancing at the handwriting before sitting back down and picking up a piece of needlework.

The first was obviously slow and laboriously written. Frey smiled. It was from her brother.

Brice was being encouraged by his tutor to practice writing. This was the second letter she'd received and this one had only half as many ink splotches as the first. Frey smiled at his progress.

"News from your brother?" Rosalind asked, looking up from her spinning.

"Indeed. He has taken his first steps without crutches but is frustrated that he cannot run like the other boys. He says Brother Halig tells him 'that the trying of your faith worketh patience.' He also hates learning Latin."

Frey scanned farther down the page and continued.

"He writes that his kitten, Grindan, the one Sebastian gave him, was very brave and chased a fox harassing the chickens, but, with the threat dispatched, the hens turned on him and Grindan ran up the abbot's robes and hid in his cowl."

Rosalind laughed heartily and Frey joined in.

"Oh Alfreya, you shouldn't make me laugh in my delicate condition!"

She struggled to her feet before anyone could offer assistance and waddled off to the privy.

"And what of your second letter, Mistress Alfreya?" inquired Heloise.

Frey set aside Brice's letter and picked up the second. She didn't immediately recognize the hand. She broke the seal and unfolded the parchment.

It contained just seven words in a neat, economical script.

I am coming for you, Alfreya.

Drefan

Frey stared until the strokes on the paper shimmered and blurred; only when she heard the paper rustling in her trembling hand did she remember to breathe.

Heloise looked at her with a mixture of surprise and intense curiosity.

"Is aught amiss?"

Frey swallowed and glanced up at the girl, blinking owlishly at her.

"No," Frey finally answered with a shake of her head. "Nothing amiss, but I shall lie down for a while."

She excused herself and left the solar, sidestepping Rosalind, who reentered the room.

Rosalind watched the pale and distressed Frey disappear down the stairs at a clip.

"Was there bad news in her brother's letter?" she asked.

"It was the other one," came Heloise's fading voice.

* * *

Larcwide wasn't difficult to find. Frey followed the rhythmic sound of a staff being using used to tap out a beat to which two squires practiced their timing and stroke play, brandishing wooden wasters instead of more dangerous steel swords.

Not wishing to distract them, Frey stood out of their eye-line at the edge of the quadrangle and watched Robert, along with another young squire, run through the sword drill—parry, thrust, fend, parry, thrust, fend. It came to an abrupt end when Robert's opponent sensed Frey's presence and glanced around. Robert landed a bruising blow to his arm and the young man yelped.

"Concentrate, lad!" Larcwide yelled, although a twitch at the edges of his stern mouth told Frey he didn't consider the infraction a serious one.

With the lesson disrupted, Larcwide dismissed his students and offered Frey his full attention.

"You're too soft on them," she teased.

"That's not what you said when you begged me to teach you how to use a short sword," he answered with a smile.

Although Frey had seen little of Larcwide, and even less of Orlege, she was pleased the easy relationship between them still remained.

"How can I help you, my lady?"

Frey's smile disappeared.

"I received a message from Drefan."

Larcwide's eyes widened in surprise.

"When?" he hissed. "What did he say?" He glanced about them to see if there was anyone to overhear and pulled her into a shady corner to ensure they were unseen.

Frey relayed the one-line message and the frown on Larcwide's face deepened.

"You know this is over, don't you my lady? No more rebellion, no more grand dreams of restoring the Northumbrian dynasty. We are all, Saxon and Norman alike, a part of one England and probably stronger for it."

Frey didn't object to Larcwide's speech. He spoke as a beloved family friend and she appreciated his candor.

"I know, I know," she nodded. "Even if I were of a mind to wage war—"

"If Drefan had landed a sizeable army with siege engines, there would have been news reaching us."

"What do you think he means?"

"I know not… Have you spoken to the baron? Does he know of Drefan?"

Frey hesitated and Larcwide gave her a look that brooked no dissembling on her part.

"Some. He knows we were waiting on him to supply us, and he may suspect Drefan and I had an attachment," she said.

"But nothing of your contract to marry?"

She shook her head. "I never saw such a contract. For all his drunken talk, I do not believe father ever made the arrangements."

Larcwide said nothing immediately, though Frey could see from the set of his jaw he had other thoughts he wasn't willing to share. And then, as though coming to the end of a long deliberation, the man-at-arms finally nodded.

"I'll speak to Orlege about finding the messenger. You'll be pleased to know Orlege has been persuaded being well paid and well fed is a better proposition than having his head on a pike," he said. "Now, I have to go and earn my keep, and you, my lady, should tell the baron all."

Larcwide walked away without a further glance.

Frey shuddered in the cold shadow of the thick stone walls and stepped out into the sunshine without knowing the entire exchange had been observed.

CHAPTER NINETEEN

The servants were thrown into a frenzy of activity just a few hours later with the unexpected early return of Baron Rhys Villiers and his men from London. His arrival may have been unexpected, but it was most certainly welcome. Tyrswick Keep took on a festive atmosphere for the return of the baron's brother-in-law and friend.

The cook promised a menu fit for royalty. He consulted with the butler over which wines, ales, and meads were to be fetched from the buttery and demanded the services of a couple of the stable boys to help turn the large roast spits.

The scullions and servant girls who complained earlier about Lady Rosalind's cleaning fit were now grateful their workload was light compared to the rest of the household.

"Ho! We thought you were at least another week away. Why didn't you send word?" Sebastian called over the din of booted feet, hooves, and the jangle of armor and bridles in the outer bailey. He clasped arms with Rhys in a traditional greeting.

Rhys was only a year or two older than his host, and about the same build—tall and muscular, well used to wielding a broad sword as well as a battle-axe. He shared his sister's coloring, hair a shade of chestnut brown with light blue eyes.

"I could say I was anxious to see my wife before the babe is born, but I'd only be telling a half truth," he answered. "I have word from London for you and then gossip reached me on the road that I couldn't believe so I decided to press on."

"Well, whatever news you have cannot be so burning as to keep you from your wife any longer. Go see Rosalind. Gaines can settle your men in."

With a familiarity of square Norman Keeps and this one in particular, Rhys didn't ask where his wife could be found. She would be in the solar.

Despite being tired from many days on the road, he bounded up each flight of stairs with the energy of a youth, but, when he emerged at the top floor, the first woman in his arms was not his wife but his sister, who threw herself into his embrace.

Heloise greeted him with kisses and dozens of questions about court. Who had he seen? What did they wear? What was the gossip?

Over her shoulder, Rhys shared a smile with his wife before answering the most urgent of Heloise's questions.

Her nanny, Dorcas, recalled something important and asked Heloise for her assistance. The girl didn't notice the grateful look both Baron and his lady gave the servant as she and Heloise left the room.

Rhys sat beside Rosalind on the settle and kissed her fingers and then her lips tenderly, ending the caress with a stroke of her hair and cheek.

"I've missed you, my beloved," he whispered.

"And I you. I prayed you would be back before the babe was born."

"You look well and I trust my son fares well?"

Rosalind smiled, taking his hand and placing it on her belly. "He does indeed, my lord, and we will both rest easier now you are here. But tell me, what news do you bring from Court?"

"Before I do, tell me if the gossip I hear is true, that Sebastian has taken a viper to his nest and given succor to the daughter of a Saxon traitor."

"I'd hardly call Alfreya a viper, but it's true she's been living here nigh on two months," Rosalind affirmed. "Why should the news distress you, Rhys? Earl Alfred is dead, his youngest son resides at St. Cuthbert's and is keen to renounce any claim to Tyrswick, and, according to Sebastian, Lady Alfreya herself negotiated very admirably for a peaceful end."

"Do you know outside these walls she is considered a sorceress who can cast spells on wolves?"

"What nonsense!" Rosalind exclaimed with passion. "She's no more a sorceress than I am. It's not like you to pay attention to superstitious nonsense," she said, chiding him.

"It's a long tale," he agreed.

"I can smell it might be," Rosalind told him with a twinkle of amusement in her eye. "I've had a bath ordered; then you can tell me all about it and I won't be jealous of your horse."

* * *

Late into the evening, after most of Tyrswick Keep retired, two lamps glowed softly in Sebastian's chambers, just enough to add a little extra light to the red glow from the banked coals in his fireplace.

Sebastian could see that Rhys, filled with good food and drink, and exhausted from a long journey, yearned to crawl into bed next to his wife.

Except one more obligation awaited him.

They sat by the fire, each with his long legs stretched before him.

After the servant who brought their wine withdrew, Rhys repeated the rumor to Sebastian, watching him carefully for his reaction.

It was to laugh—heartily.

Sebastian raised his cup in salute.

"Well, you have no fear on that count," he exclaimed. "It would be a poor thing indeed to kill one's own familiars. Alfreya's aptitude with a bow is to blame, not some pact with the devil."

Sebastian poked at the coals. The flames flickered and danced.

He took a sip from his cup and let the sweet, pungent flavor of the spiced wine fall down his throat and settle warmly in his stomach.

"That is not the only rumor," Rhys said.

Sebastian shrugged.

"Let them gossip. It matters not to me and, I dare say, not to Alfreya either."

Rhys would not be dissuaded by Sebastian's lukewarm attitude toward the tales. He pressed on.

"They say Lady Alfreya is not a woman at all but a fiend who took on her form after killing her. The story goes she chews off young women's fingers and steals their souls by taking their eyes."

Sebastian's jaw tightened and his eyes narrowed. Disgusting slander! Evil lies…

By and large, superstition of witches and familiars riding across the night sky had disappeared from these lands, but despite being nominally Christian, there were still those who clung to the old pagan ways. Sebastian doubted even the church could rid the world of gossip and jealousy, those two great sins that bit and irritated like fleas, causing annoyance at best and disease at worse.

Rhys offered him a sympathetic look.

"I'm glad you say it is a tale," Sebastian answered coldly. "I cannot begin to fathom the malice behind creating such a rumor over the brutal deaths of two girls."

Rhys shook his head.

"There's been another."

"On my lands?" Sebastian slammed his goblet on the low table beside him. "Impossible! I would have been told."

"It happened on Alnwick lands two weeks ago. The body of a girl ill-used, missing fingers on the hands, eyes gouged out, hair hacked off."

"The Beast is moving south," Sebastian mused aloud.

"And so too is the story that goes with it, which makes the letter I carry with me all the more concerning."

"From Court?"

Rhys nodded and handed the sealed parchment to Sebastian.

The letter was written by the one of the joint chief justiciars, Richard FitzGilbert, who possessed the governorship of England while William sojourned in Normandy. He opened by offering congratulations to Sebastian on his proposal to unite Saxon and Norman by wedding the daughter of the dispossessed earl. It was, wrote FitzGilbert, "a political move most clever."

The contents of the letter pleased Sebastian. He looked up at Rhys with a broad grin to replace the scowl of a few moments before, but the tense expression on Rhys's face suggested, though the document had been sealed, he had been told of its contents.

"Have you considered what it means to give this girl the benefit of your name?" asked Rhys.

Sebastian looked at him levelly.

"It means anyone who slanders her will answer to me."

Rhys took another sip from his goblet and considered him.

They had known each other for years, even fostered with the same household, and Sebastian knew what kind of thoughts raced through his friend's mind. Impetuous was the last thing any man called him. His even temper and considered actions were thought a de la Croix trait, for his sister was of the same disposition. Sebastian knew a hasty decision to wed did not match the man Rhys knew, but he kept his lands well and his people prospered, so who could complain?

When he had arrived, Tyrswick was little more than a sad collection of dilapidated cottages surrounding a Saxon long-house, with villagers living a hardscrabble existence. The baron worked hard to earn their trust and fulfill the potential of the land. And he hadn't even begun to explore the possibility of added wealth in the long-abandoned mines left by the Romans.

No, the people of Tyrswick were unlikely candidates for rebellion.

Anyway, Sebastian had his own reasons for rolling the dice and gambling his future and was disinclined to share them with Rhys. Fortunately, his friend seemed equally disinclined to pursue the matter tonight.

Both men sat in companionable silence by the fire for quite some time before the sound of a pop from the fireplace brought Rhys out of a comfortable half doze with a start. He pushed himself to his feet, clasping Sebastian on the shoulder to bid him good night.

* * *

Frey remained in the shadows of the solar, a cloak and hood thrown over her nightgown against the chill of the night, its dark color permitting her to remain unseen in the shadows.

Sleep would not claim her, not when Drefan lurked like a specter outside, and, with the arrival of Rhys Villiers, this was her only opportunity to speak with Sebastian alone.

She overheard the low indistinct murmurs of conversation through the thick timber wall separating this room from the baron's bedchamber. She knew Sebastian talked late with Rosalind's husband, so she huddled in the dark corner, hugging her knees, and waited.

After a period of time, Baron Villiers left and Frey listened intently for the sound of his own chamber door opening then closing, to echo up the stairs from the floor below, before she edged across to the entrance and glanced through the crack left between the door and the jamb.

Perhaps Sebastian slept, which was why Lord Rhys left. If that were so, Frey would have reconsidered her plans. By the light of the fire she could see the abandoned chair. To see the second chair meant she must peer around the door.

It too was empty.

Frey frowned. Did she doze and Sebastian slipped past her unseen? She took a further step or two into the room and looked.

The bed was…

Before Frey could complete the thought, she was grabbed roughly from behind and held firmly against a man's broad chest. A large hand covered her mouth and suppressed an involuntary scream.

The man recognized her and relaxed but did not remove his hand.

"You picked the wrong night to slit my throat while I slept, princess."

Sebastian's whispered voice filled her ear. He held her still for long moments before speaking.

"Are you recovered? You will not scream?"

Frey nodded and shook her head in answer to each question, and she was released, her heart pumping furiously.

"Do you suggest I pick some other night then?" she said, wiping her mouth to remove the sensation of his hand.

Sebastian ignored her barb and poured a small measure of spiced wine into his goblet. He handed it to her and watched as she drank.

"Why do you assume the worst of me?" she asked.

"Habit," he answered, arms folded across his chest. "Now tell me what you're doing in my chambers while others sleep."

"I have to speak to you."

Sebastian's eyebrows rose in surprise. It might have been skepticism, but Frey couldn't be sure.

"And it couldn't wait until morning?"

All of a sudden Frey's courage left her, and she wondered if her senses had taken leave of her too.

She was an unmarried woman, alone, late at night in the bed chamber of a man whose mere presence made her feel powerful sensations she struggled to understand. What on earth was she doing?

She shook her head softly.

"This was a mistake."

As she turned to leave, Sebastian grabbed her wrist.

"It's a mistake to not finish what you start."

Frey tugged, but Sebastian held firm, looking at her with a mistrust she hadn't seen since the aftermath of the battle with the wolves.

"Sit down," he ordered. "It seems your past returns to haunt us, princess."

Frey gave him her most implacable stare and defied him for long seconds before slowly and deliberately lowering herself onto the chair left by Lord Rhys. Despite her show of external bravado, her chest tightened as she watched Sebastian slowly reclaim his seat.

"Drefan," she stated.

The word dropped like a lead weight between them.

"You've been less than forthcoming about what this man is to you, and I've run out of patience," he told her.

"You want to know what he is to me?" she echoed bitterly.

The banked coals of emotion long suppressed glowed and burst into flame with this breeze of change; they heated Frey's temper and stoked her courage.

"I hate that man more than I hated the Normans," she told him.

"He kept my father angry and drunk while he drained his purse and fed him fantasies of reclaiming our home. He promised great and mighty armies to march victoriously into England. He wormed his way into my brother's affections and pretended he was a friend."

Frey paused and chanced a glance at Sebastian. A single slow blink was the only reaction he showed.

"That doesn't tell me who he is to *you*," he prompted.

"He's nothing to me. He's a dog," she sneered.

The warmth of Sebastian's chambers receded as memories of Drefan's flattery and his cold-hearted deception played out in her mind's eye.

"Drefan claimed to have contracted marriage with me, and my father was rarely sober enough to ask, but that didn't stop Drefan from taking—"

Frey's voice caught and long-suppressed tears of bitterness, shame, and anger breached the embankments of her lids and fell in rivulets down her face.

"He used me, he used all of us, and now he's back."

CHAPTER TWENTY

Sebastian stood and hauled an unresisting Frey into his arms. He held her silently, allowing her rage to play itself out. Anger thrummed through him, but he mastered his emotions and kept his mouth shut.

A desire to erase every heartache, every hurt, tugged at his core, but the past was an enemy he couldn't slay for her. He knew that well enough on his own account, but he dealt with it, pressing forward until the wounds healed and left nothing but the scars. She would have to learn to do the same.

Soon Frey stilled. She laid her cheek on his chest and snaked her arms around his back. It felt right.

The only sound now was the comforting crackle of the fire in the grate and, from outside, the occasional sound of an owl and other night creatures who called the night their domain.

Sebastian could feel her breathing slow and steady against him and he wondered if she dozed on her feet until she spoke.

"Drefan is here," Frey said, her voice a little above a whisper. "That's why I came here tonight. He sent me a message."

Sebastian pulled away and immediately missed her warmth against him. Frey obviously felt it too. She pulled the cloak around her and edged closer to the fireplace, staring at it as though it held the cure to her misery.

An odd pang pierced his chest and he considered the origin of it. To his dismay, Sebastian discovered it was jealousy. Despite the anger building within him, he was proud that he listened calmly nonetheless, while Frey related the arrival and content of Drefan's message.

He would send a patrol out on the morrow to see if he could flush the fox from its lair. He meant it when he told her he would not have rebellion foment on his land.

She turned around and her pretty blue eyes watched him, as usual, trying to second-guess what he might do. He determined to use her full attention to his advantage.

"Now you have a decision to make, don't you, Lady Alfreya?"

* * *

Frey's eyes narrowed at the bitter tone in Sebastian's voice. She saw him clench and unclench his fists and wondered how hands that held her so gently just moments before were now so hard and unyielding.

He picked up a scroll from the bench and held it upright like a torch. His eyes glittered as they watched her.

"Villiers brought this from London," he told her. "It names your husband."

Frey's eyes flicked to the document and back to him, and she licked her lips in nervous anticipation.

"Who is it to be?"

Sebastian shook his head and Frey's heart sank like a stone in her belly. Despite his fine words about her being home, the Crown evidently decreed differently.

She cursed herself for a fool. It had been months since she tried to press Sebastian for an answer to his cryptic promise. It suited her not to question, if truth be told. She *liked* being back at Tyrswick, and since returning, she'd allowed herself to believe a minor baron in a far-flung corner of England would have the influence to make good on his promise.

Sebastian's face was taut; his mouth was now sober and grim.

Frey shook her head to clear it.

"You make no sense at all. What choice? I have no choice. Either I wed the man in that decree or"—she shrugged—"what…?"

"*I'm* giving you a choice, Alfreya."

Her confusion must have spoken plainly on her face because Sebastian sighed and continued.

"Wed me."

The low, calmly spoken words sent a frisson of alarm tracing up her spine and, if she were honest, a measure of desire too.

"How prettily you make the suggestion, my lord," she said scornfully. "Many a maiden must swoon at the quality of your lovemaking."

Anger flashed across his face and settled in his eyes, where the flickering glow of the fireplace and the lamps made it seem lightning inhabited them.

He turned and stalked a few paces to put more distance between them, then spun to face her.

"Then go to this Drefan if that is your wish. Your angry words still speak of a great passion for him. But be warned, your memory will be dead here, buried along with Diera in that crypt, never, ever to return. And if I find you and that man on my lands, I will kill you both."

Frey shook her head, hoping to shake loose some sense.

"What about him?" She pointed to the scroll, abandoned on the table, that contained the name of the man chosen for her by the Crown.

Sebastian's response was to look at her even more dangerously.

"They are your only choices, princess."

"Show me the parchment!"

Sebastian tossed her the document and she perused it to find the congratulations and felicitations of one of the chief justiciars of England.

As she read each line, anger brewed like a North Sea storm and broke when she came to the conclusion.

"You lied! You offer me no choice!"

She flung the letter back at him. It struck his chest and fell to the floor, where it rolled itself up and rocked from side to side until it stilled.

"Either turn me out with the devil himself or marry a…a…"

"Spit it out, Frey! You've never been shy about your Saxon insults before," he sneered. "Can you lower yourself to marry a Norman dog?"

Frey felt as though she had been slapped. Heat and cold alternated in waves and for one horrible moment, she felt she would faint. At length she dragged in a lungful of air. She fell back into a seat, her head sagging.

Baron Sebastian de la Croix was a good and kind man; she knew that. He deserved a good Norman wife with a marriage that offered political and strategic advantages, not a penniless Saxon cast-off with a dubious temper who claimed too much on his good humor and forbearance.

"I'm sorry," she whispered into her lap. And she was, too—for the whole sorry mess.

Frey was hauled to her feet, her hands trapped in both of Sebastian's.

"Are you telling me 'no'?"

She couldn't look at him but shook her head and was answered with a long-suffering sigh.

"Then speak plainly," he said. "The night grows late and I'm tired."

"You'll regret it."

"What?"

"Marrying me."

Frey ventured a look up at him and was surprised to see tenderness lingering in his expression. It frightened her more than his anger. If he felt more than pity for her he might mistake it for love, and she was certain to the core of her being that love was an emotion she was no longer capable of giving to any man.

"Please don't look at me that way," she begged.

"What way?"

"As though there could be more between us than…kindness. It would be a mistake to believe so. Please don't ask me for more."

"Kindness?" Sebastian wore an expression of distaste, as though he had swallowed something bitter. "You think I marry you out of *kindness*, out of *charity*? Please spare your pity and mine, Frey."

Sebastian was now mercurial, his expression changing from disgust, anger, hurt, resignation to something that, to Frey, seemed predatory.

"As my wife there is something else you are obliged to offer me," he said, taking one step toward her and no more.

"Yes, well, I shall be prepared to suffer through it," Frey replied primly, not liking the direction of this conversation.

"Suffer, you call it?" He took another step forward and stopped.

Frey held her ground. She didn't fear him, no matter what mood he was in.

"I'm no sheltered virgin you can intimidate, Baron."

Her bravado elicited a grin as he took another step forward. She was aware he was now so close he could reach out and grab her. Part of her longed for him to do so. If he did, she would be blameless and he wholly responsible for the wellspring of wantonness he unearthed in her.

Arousal throbbed with each beat of her heart. But he stood still and parts of her body stretched toward him of their own volition. Her nipples, puckered and erect, strained toward him, her fingertips yearned to breach the divide, to touch his firmly muscled arms and pull herself nearer.

Sebastian leaned in to whisper in her ear.

"Kiss me."

Moisture flooded her sex and a sigh of longing escaped her lips.

"On my word, I will not touch you," he said, making a show of locking his fingers behind his back. "Kiss me."

Frey pulled back quizzically, uncertain of the game he played. The answer to her question was a grin with a touch of merriment in his eyes.

"Unless, you're *afraid…*"

Frey straightened, knowing she was being shamelessly maneuvered but unable to resist a challenge.

She stepped forward and stretched up to him—the wretch stood to his full height—placing her hands on his shoulders for balance while she stood on her toes. Frey gave him a quick peck on the cheek and stood down on the flats of her feet. He watched her keenly, but gave no indication he was moved.

Frey was dissatisfied; she had been staring at his lips all evening and now wanted to remember how they felt. She returned to her toes and pressed her lips and her body slowly to his, feeling him shift slightly on his feet. He was not as immune to her as he pretended.

Good.

Her lips coaxed his apart and she allowed herself a moan of satisfaction as she felt the nether part of him stir into life and grow firm. As their tongues played and mated, the feeling against her belly increased her own desire.

Breathless, Frey forced her mouth from his and trailed kisses along his darkly stubbled cheek until her lips and tongue discovered an earlobe, which she sampled with abandon.

She knew she was playing a risky game, but, oh, it felt good! Aroused almost beyond breaking point, she wondered at his self-possession. *More, more, more…*her body craved his. She waited for him to abandon his restraint and take her.

Frey felt the movement through his shoulders first and she knew he unclasped his hands. She felt a surge of triumph.

"Yes," she whispered to him as those powerful arms moved around her. She leaned in farther, her weight taken by his arms as she pressed her breasts against him.

"Yes, yes," she whispered.

Then Sebastian pulled away. Frey, to her embarrassment, squeaked in protest.

"In your bed alone tonight, remember how you must suffer me," he told her, his voice hoarse and cracked.

She looked down along his body, his erection magnificently outlined in his hose, then up to his face, unmasked in its need and desire.

She permitted herself a rueful half smile. "Then it seems we suffer together."

CHAPTER TWENTY-ONE

Frey woke with a start, the glow of the morning sun and the shadows of the leaves from the tree above shifting in the mild breeze, playing a game of chase along her arm. Blinking against the light, Frey sat up and looked around a large meadow, treeless but for the yew she slept under.

"Frey! You're awake!"

She turned and found a visitor beside her where there had been no one before.

"What are you doing here? You're dead."

"Oh." Diera frowned, confused, and brushed a hand down her long yellow braid before settling her hands in her lap. Her hands were stark white against the deep blue of her kirtle.

"Not everything is as it seems, Frey," she said.

"What do you mean?"

Diera shrugged.

"You'll know."

A gust of wind blew a cloud across the sun, plunging the glen into deep shadows.

Frey shivered, not just from the chill, but also, in the certainty one knows only in dreams, that she and Diera were not alone.

Frey picked up a fallen branch from the yew and all of a sudden it was a bow. She became conscious of a familiar weight on her back that told her she wore a quiver full of arrows.

She got to her feet and turned away from Diera.

Her heart pounded as she faced a lone figure about six yards away. He—Frey was certain of that because of his bulk—was shrouded in a forest green cloak that fell to the floor, arms tucked into the wide sleeves, and his face, looking to the ground, was obscured by the cowl.

Diera started muttering indistinctly as the wind picked up in strength, but Frey could hear snatches of her words:

"For now we see through a glass, darkly, but then face to face: now I know in part; but then shall I know even as also I am known…"

They were repeated over and over, faster and faster, ever increasing in pitch.

The cowl started to shift as the figure slowly raised his head. Dread terror filled Frey, but she found an arrow in her hand and, with a precision born of practice, she sighted her target and released the projectile.

Her aim was true, but as the arrow pierced the garment, the robe fluttered into a shapeless, uninhabited puddle of green fabric.

* * *

Frey put the dream behind her as she broke her fast in Tyrswick Keep's great hall. She had not seen Sebastian that morning, but that was probably just as well. How could she face him after last night? The remembrance of searing passion lingered still, and Frey wondered whether it wrote itself on her face as well.

The hall was mostly empty. Servants started clearing the benches from the morning meal and catered to those break-fasters who lingered. Frey warmed her hands around an earthenware mug of spiced milk and considered her fate.

They were to be wed, but she was still uncertain of Sebastian's motives.

Perhaps he simply considered her and Brice a problem to be solved for the sake of peace on his lands and for the security of England. There was, without doubt, passion between them, but what foundation for a marriage was that?

Sebastian was bound to make the announcement tonight, but, as yet, no one in the household knew except for Baron Rhys, who glanced suspiciously at her from time to time from across the table shared by the senior members of the household.

In that case, Lady Rosalind knew also. No wonder the woman appeared highly distracted this morning and was being coaxed into eating by both Rhys and her companion Gwenda.

Might there one day be a genuine marital affection between her and Sebastian as she witnessed between Rosalind and Rhys?

She didn't know.

Orlege entered the hall and, on seeing Frey, held her gaze. In answer to a slight frown, Orlege shook his head and disappeared through the door. Frey's frown deepened as she excused herself from the table and followed.

She found him behind the back of the stables where the warmth of the autumn sun was a welcome respite from the shadows that hugged the cold to their breast.

Here, a scent of herbs—sage, thyme, lavender—plucked by the breeze from the nearby garden enveloped them.

"The baron ordered Larcwide to accompany him on patrol this morning," he said.

Frey nodded. "I told him about Drefan last night."

"Aye, that would explain it then."

"Did you find the messenger?"

"I spoke to the lad before he left this morning. He said when he was about three miles away from the keep, a knight he thought he recognized asked him to take a letter to the baron. He didn't think anything of it."

"And what of you? What do you think of it?"

"I think it means trouble."

Silence fell between them, colder than the shadows cast by the Keep.

"Do you hold me to blame still?" Frey asked after a moment.

"Some, maybe." Orlege shrugged. "Hardly matters now. What's done is done."

"But you resent me," Frey pressed.

This time he turned with his face full of resentment and agitation.

"I've discharged my duty to your father, what more do you want from me?"

Frey dropped her head for a moment, wounded. Orlege, along with Larcwide, were her most trusted men, and this estrangement had worn away at her for months.

Orlege exhaled deeply, making clear that he did not want to continue the conversation. He scuffed the ground with his booted feet and in doing so, dislodged a stone, which he then kicked into the garden.

"I'm no good with words. I don't know if I can make you understand," he said. "I'm a soldier. I pledge my life for my lord. He goes into battle and I go with him. I use a sword, a battle-axe, a pike staff, a bow to attack and defend. Understand?"

Frey shook her head.

"I would willingly take a life to preserve yours, my lady, but I don't know how to fight rumors or battle gossip and evil words."

"Whose?"

Orlege's face hardened and he refused to answer at first, though the question plainly vexed him, going by the twitch of a bitter smile that fashioned itself on his mouth.

At last, his face turned away, he spoke. "First it was about your virtue, living unprotected among rough fighting men, then your damned bow and arrow against the wolves," he said.

"It got worse since they found the girl killed like Diera was months back, and this morning I hear from Baron Rhys's men there's another rumor saying you're in league with the devil and have bewitched the baron of Tyrswick into giving you sanctuary."

He faced her again. "What weapons can I use against *that* enemy, my lady?" he spat. "How do I kill slander?"

And, as though he had revealed too much, Orlege stalked off, shoulders slumped.

Frey stared into the distance, where the wooded hills around Tyrswick rose, fancying if she looked hard enough, she could see Drefan's golden hair glint in the sunshine. Instead, the hills seemed to enclose her in arms of green.

She shuddered, remembering her dream.

On the walk back into the Keep, Frey observed the people around her, watching them for any signs that they watched her in return and considered her evil.

Was she so unaware of the level of antipathy toward her? She didn't think so. Frey had been welcomed warmly by those who had served her father, and she believed she had the good opinion of those who were new.

But who could tell? And did Sebastian know of this?

Before Frey could long ponder the questions, she was bumped by a rushing and unseeing Heloise, who was pale and wore her panic plainly.

"Heloise?"

Frey pulled the poor girl out of the path of a hurrying servant who carried a tub of steaming water. It told Frey all she needed to know.

"Heloise! Is it Lady Rosalind? Does the baby come?"

* * *

Sebastian de la Croix was not a difficult man to spot among the group of riders emerging over the rise; he rode in the center, flanked on each side by two men Baldwin would recognize instantly—the supposed stick-up-the-arse Gaines and the old man Larcwide, who was, laughably, man-at-arms to that Saxon bitch.

Another two men behind them Baldwin knew also, but ignored to keep his crossbow sights on the three men leading. His body twitched subtly as he mimed their execution.

Tyrswick Keep's patrol drew nearer to him, then turned away, the riders following the contour of the countryside.

Now, the party presented itself to Baldwin broadside. It would take but few moments to carefully sight the baron's head through the heavy shelter of a scattered tumble of rocks that hid him from view. Baldwin started at the sound of rustling behind him and lost his quarry. He turned quickly to find Drefan propped against a rock, casually slicing an apple with a small knife.

Despite being a man of means, Drefan played the part of a peasant today, dressed simply in gray breeches and shirt. His boots were dusty and travel-marked, but anyone who looked closely at them would know they were of the highest quality.

"Patience, my good friend," Drefan counseled in a soft drawl. A breeze tugged at his longish blond hair and made the dark arch of his brows stand out more starkly against his face.

"It would be so easy, so quick," Baldwin responded, dropping back behind the boulder that had been his hunter's perch and deftly catching a round, shiny apple Drefan lobbed his way.

Baldwin took a bite. The crunch and sweetness of the flesh was satisfying, but it would do little to salve the bitterness that festered in him with respect to his former lord.

"That's exactly my point," said Drefan. "You don't want it easy and quick. If you want to destroy a man, you don't take his life. You let him live. Then you take his peace of mind, his possessions, his loved ones… everything he owns. Then he'll beg you to kill him."

CHAPTER TWENTY-TWO

Frey was grateful to find the solar empty. Solitude was what she craved at the moment. Despite the increasingly chilly autumn evening, Frey stood on the forebuilding roof to watch the colors on the long ripples of cloud bleed from gold to pink then purple as the sun finally sank beneath the hills to the west.

Her legs ached from numerous trips up and down the stairs since adopting the mantle of chatelaine in Lady Rosalind's stead. Rosalind might be occupied having a baby, but there was still a household to run, and Frey felt more use doing that instead of remaining in the bed chambers, listening to the cries of pain increase in frequency and duration.

However, Rosalind had had an easier time of it than most, thank God, and Baron Rhys knew enough to stay well out of the way, Frey reflected, as his wife delivered him the boy child they wanted.

She smiled briefly to herself, thinking of Heloise's resentful stomping at her assumption of the role of Mistress, but even the girl's nanny realized, seeing her in the hall distressed and near to tears, the youngster was in no fit state to do anything much of use.

Poor Heloise, she so wants to be grown up.

As childishly petulant as Heloise could sometimes be, Frey felt some pity for the girl. She was dreadfully spoiled, and Frey considered what she was doing at the same age.

Remembrance of the fighting at Durham and the late-night escape with her father and brother played itself anew in her mind.

Although she had not known it then, she made a life-changing decision that night in taking the young Sebastian at his word and making their escape.

Frey remembered she'd seen something she could use as a litter, a flat-sided wheelbarrow made for carrying bales of hay, and she dashed from her hiding place to get it. When she returned, her father had collapsed from the pain. Brice was staring at him, eyes wide in horror and mewling sounds of hysteria bubbling from his lips.

She had no time to be gentle. A slap on the boy's cheek stopped the sound.

"Go to the door and look about," she hissed. "And be careful!"

With the fear of discovery growing ever stronger, Frey roused her father sufficiently for him to aid her efforts to haul him onto the litter. Now bearing a load, it was difficult to move. Fear caused Frey to surge forward even as her muscles strained, and at last the wheels turned, bringing the cart closer to the door.

"Is it clear?"

Brice rapidly shook his head.

Frey lowered the litter and crept to where Brice stood hidden in the shadows.

Him!

Between the door of the barn and the breach in the palisades wall was the young Norman who had turned his back on them and walked away when he could—and should—have exposed them. He had his back to them again now and was engaged in seemingly easy conversation with another man about his own age. Whatever they discussed ended in laughter and the second soldier moved away out of sight.

Illuminated by the flames from the burning Saxon compound, Frey could see one side of the young man's face, bathed in gold light, then the other as he looked this way and that.

Without glancing back, his arm down by his side, he made one terse wave of his hand. Its meaning was clear.

"Go, go, go," Frey breathed.

Brice pushed on the back of the litter while Frey pulled, steering the little hand cart out of the compound and into the night.

With the recollection, she considered how incredible it was that the young Norman knight who had showed her and her family mercy that night had become the baron of Tyrswick, the man she had fought against for so long without even recognizing him—and now she appeared destined to be his wife.

She shook her head in disbelief. Sebastian's wife? She had been destined to be another's wife before now.

Suddenly, with that thought, she felt watched by him, by Drefan, even now, just as he had done in Edinburgh, always with that mocking half smile of his.

Frey looked out over the meadows and the hills beyond the Keep. It was now fully night, with the shadowed landscape darker than the star-filled sky above. Frey shuddered and it wasn't all to do with the cold. The thought of Drefan being so close after all that went before had cast a pall over her mood ever since his note arrived. No wonder she had sought the solitude of the solar forebuilding roof this evening, but now the sense that he was out there watching made her uneasy.

She retreated inside and tried to warm herself by the fire in the main room, but the chill was inside her. A moment later, Sebastian exited his chambers and joined her by the hearth.

"Why are you not in the hall celebrating the birth of my nephew?" he asked softly.

Frey glanced at him, then focused her attention on the flames. Sebastian was dressed as he was, a man at peace in his own domicile, relaxed in dark blue hose, white shirt loosely tied at the neck, and a soft brown jerkin. She wished she could share that ease.

"I'm tired and I was looking for quiet." Frey shrugged. "Besides, it's a family occasion."

"You're family, at least you will be as my wife."

The promise of finally belonging again was like honey mead—warm and sweet—and her soul drank it greedily. Frey shook her head in mute resistance, giving herself the excuse the fire was too warm, so she could step away from him and sit on a cushion-covered settle.

"Are you not afraid for your reputation, Baron?" she said, looking up at him, her voice leaden with disdain. "Being seen unchaperoned with a woman rumored to be a witch, with wolves as her familiars? It might impede your chances of a more successful match than I."

His look was contemptuous.

"I thought you had too much sense to listen to superstitious nonsense."

"Nonsense it may be, but other people think it."

Frey looked away and fiddled with the cuff on the sleeve of her maroon kirtle as she continued, "All of Tyrswick for miles around seems to hold you in the highest regard. They'll question your wits for marrying me, so it's just as well you have an order from the Crown to compel you. Surely, they won't believe my powers extend that high."

"Thank you for being considerate of my feelings."

Something in Sebastian's sober inflection made Frey raise her head. A twitch of humor leaked from the corner of that sensuous mouth of his and ignited a spark of emotion in Frey.

"I'm practicing to be a good wife, *dearest*," she retorted.

Her barb hit a target, but not the one she aimed at. Instead of hurt and anger, Sebastian laughed.

Frey was perplexed.

"I do not understand you," she emphasized with a shake of her head. "Why do you have to be so kind?"

"You would prefer me not be kind?" he asked, amusement still coloring his voice.

"Yes. Yes, I would have you not so kind."

"And why, pray tell?"

"Because it would be too easy for me to—"

Frey threw both hands over her mouth with horror before the words "love you" could slip out, but it did not escape Sebastian, who pounced on it like a cat.

"Well, princess, as we seem to be in agreement on something, perhaps we should go downstairs and share the good news since it has the Crown's blessing."

Exasperation got the better of her.

"Will you be serious for a moment?"

And Sebastian was. His easy smile flattened to a tight line, the twinkle of humor in his eyes went out, and Frey instantly regretted being the cause of their absence.

"You seem so certain of everything," she said. "How can you be? No one knows what tomorrow will bring."

Frey stood and unconsciously reached for him, his large hand sitting coldly in hers.

"I fear you are too impetuous," she insisted, "and a few years hence you will come to regret your decision and resent having settled for"—Frey swallowed—"something less than you deserve."

"Perhaps you underestimate yourself, Frey." Slowly, his fingers curled around hers, and those mesmerizing green eyes softened.

"You've refused to speak of love between us and that I understand. But love is not the only foundation on which a marriage is built. You are in need of a husband—and I'm conceited enough to believe I would make a tolerable one—and I am in need of a wife. You're experienced in running a household and know and love this land, so you would not pine for a more active life in York or London."

Sebastian stepped closer, and Frey's hand, caught up now in both of his, found its way to his lips, where the warmth of his breath and the butterfly-light touch of his lips poured molten heat through her.

"We could make this arrangement work if you are willing," he intoned. "Are you willing, Frey?"

Frey's eyes flickered closed for a moment.

It would be easy to fall in love with Sebastian. His compassion was a balm that could heal the wounds of the past if she would let it. Could she allow herself to surrender to what this man promised?

Voices of doubt that had cried out so loud and so often over these past months were now subdued. Not gone completely, but they were reduced to an indistinct hubbub below a stronger voice that plucked at the string of her soul.

Trust him.

When she opened her eyes, they were looking directly into Sebastian's own, which were waiting for her answer.

"Yes, I am willing."

The hands holding hers squeezed lightly, but his lips pressed firmly on her knuckles.

"Tonight belongs to your sister and her husband," said Frey. "Our announcement ought to be made tomorrow."

"Agreed," Sebastian answered, picking up Frey's cloak from over a chair and draping it around her shoulders. He wagged his eyebrows comically.

"See what an easygoing husband I'll make?"

Frey fought the temptation to throw her arms around him in an embrace and shook her head, unable to disguise from him a lighthearted smile instead.

Yes, she thought. It would be easy to surrender.

* * *

Since the arrival of Rhys and the sanction from the Crown to contract marriage, Sebastian found himself thinking about Frey more often, and those thoughts frequently ended with an image in his mind of her writhing in ecstasy beneath him. Although separated by dozens of people in the Great Hall, Sebastian looked for Frey every few minutes and just as frequently found her looking back at him with a small, secret smile. It warmed him and in a way aroused him too.

Despite her professed dislike of bedding, he saw she was a woman of great passion who kept that part of herself hidden behind a brittle façade. He was irresistibly drawn to her. Frey was a treasure to be uncovered and be treated with reverence.

He had come to the somewhat uncomfortable conclusion he was in love with Alfreya of Tyrswick some months ago, but he was content to bide his time until permit was granted.

He was only too aware of the Crown's intense interest in which alliances were formed by marriage. It paid to be sure certain barons did not become too powerful and therefore a threat to the monarch. While Sebastian ruled Tyrswick well, his loyalty not in doubt, he still needed to foster the support of the Crown in case Malcolm decided to break the truce and send his Scottish forces south.

A battle such as that he had trained for since his youth and was confident, with the support of King William, he would be victorious. However, the battle between himself and Frey was another matter altogether, though he was equally determined to win.

He would not be content to simply have use of her body; she had conceded that much to him and he agreed. No. Sebastian de la Croix was determined that Frey surrender her heart to him as well.

At the sound of his name, Sebastian turned to find Heloise looking up at him earnestly.

How old was she now? Fourteen summers old? Fifteen?

He wondered if Rhys had considered a husband for her. Rosalind was about her age when they wed.

Heloise was as much as sister to him as Rosalind, so he smiled at the girl.

She blushed in response and bobbed him a curtsey. "I need to speak with you my lord."

"I'm at your disposal, dear lady."

Heloise led him to a quiet, shadowed corner of the Great Hall where the light did not quite reach.

Sebastian positioned himself comfortably on a seat from which he was able to observe Frey in comfortable conversation with Dorcas and Gwenda, and he waited for Heloise to speak.

The girl noticed his distraction. There was an odd look on her face, one that spoke of some hidden emotion.

"You're an aunt now. You must be pleased," he said.

"Oh. Yes. Yes, of course I am. Rosalind will be a wonderful mother." Heloise hesitated before continuing. "I need to speak to you about a serious matter regarding the Lady Alfreya."

Sebastian was peripherally aware of Heloise's displeasure that Frey assumed the duties of mistress of Tyrswick Keep but was not much in the mood to waste time and energy on domestic disharmony while Drefan posed an uncertain external threat.

Still, whatever her grievance was it couldn't be too severe.

"And what serious matter is this?"

"I believe she has a lover outside these walls."

Sebastian's eyebrows disappeared under his fringe.

"And how would you know of such a thing?"

"She receives letters from him all the time." Heloise paused, dramatically. "I've seen them."

Sebastian straightened in the chair and folded his arms across his chest. His men-at-arms would know what the gesture meant from their lord; Heloise did not.

"And why have you made Lady Alfreya's lovers a concern of yours?" Sebastian asked frostily.

Heloise blinked at him with an expression that for all the world told him she thought the question was plainly self-evident.

"I love you and I would not have you hurt," she answered plaintively. "Lady Alfreya does not belong here. She belongs with the man who has vowed to come for her."

Then her words came in a rush.

"You need a wife who loves you and will not play you false. I would never do that, Sebastian, believe me. Were we wed, I would be the best of wives to you…"

Sebastian was struck by the absurdity of the conversation and started to laugh, but he quickly stopped at Heloise's crestfallen face.

"Come now, don't fall to tears," he soothed. "You're a big girl now."

"That's right. I'm not a little girl anymore."

She wiped the tears from her eyes and, as she brushed her fingers down her sky-blue gown, Sebastian saw the signs he had missed—the budding breasts, the definition of a waist. And large eyes that spoke of unmerited adoration.

Oh hell. Rosalind *was* about her age when she and Rhys wed.

He had walked right into a bramble patch and every move he made would only ensnare him further.

Think, man, think!

"Heloise," he started gravely, taking both her hands in his. "I am deeply humbled that you have entertained the thought I might make you a suitable husband. And I believe you would make some man an excellent wife indeed."

At this, Heloise's gaze lifted and something like hope danced in her eyes.

Sebastian wished he were somewhere else, anywhere else. Trial by combat could not be as fraught; in fact, he would even have volunteered to take Rosalind's place in childbirth than face this.

"I'm sorry, Heloise, I'm not the man for you."

Heloise's face fell and Sebastian's heart along with it.

"Why?"

He considered telling her she was like a sister to him, that he was in love with another, that he valued his friendship with Rhys too much to further bind their two families when Heloise might make an advantageous match with another noble house.

Here he was, baron of Tyrswick, a man none would call coward, who faced enemies in battle with courage and fortitude, yet brought to his knees by a slip of a girl and her tears.

If she were a man, they would come to blows and shake hands at the end of it. However, her weapons were not his, and he had no defense against them.

So he took the coward's way out.

"Your brother brings news from the chief justiciars in London. They have authorized my marriage to Lady Alfreya."

Heloise stared at him openmouthed for a moment before closing her lips and giving every impression of renewed composure.

Then she snatched her hands from his with a sharp cry and ran from the hall.

CHAPTER TWENTY-THREE

Despite the cold driving down from the North, the first day of the Hallowmas revels dawned sunny and clear. For three holy days—All Hallow's Eve, All Saints Day, and All Souls Day—all work ceased in Tyrswick Keep and in all the villages beyond to mark the end of the agricultural year.

The graveyard by the village church was trim and tidy, ready for the Office of the Dead to be read in two days' time, when family members would remember loved ones and prayers were said for the souls of the deceased.

Villagers from around the district left their winter preparations of curing meats and making preserves to take part in the revels in a field just outside of Tyrswick village.

Two large tents had been erected on the field and surrounding them were dozens of covered stalls selling goods from all parts of the globe. Merchants hawked the finest silks and spices from the Far East, ribbons and satin from France, intricately woven lace from Flanders, as well as local produce, of which there was plenty.

Sebastian insisted on accompanying Frey for a walk among the stalls, and she accepted his arm. They walked in the company of Baron Rhys and Lady Rosalind, along with Heloise and a couple of men-at-arms, to accept the good wishes of villagers.

While some of the superstitious, clinging to the old ways and old gods, prepared their fetishes and muttered about ill omens under their breath, the majority of Tyrswick was delighted by the unification of Saxon and Norman England.

Frey faced the announcement of the betrothal with a great deal of trepidation. She knew Gaines held her in disdain and sensed Baron

Rhys, who treated her with lukewarm courtesy, was heavily influenced against her by Heloise.

She glanced back to spot Heloise sullenly staring ahead.

How could she have been so blind?

She had no idea Heloise's feelings for Sebastian ran so deep, so it was a blessing that the past week had been busy. The only time they crossed paths was at the main meal, where it was a simple-enough matter to avoid one another.

Rosalind and Rhys fell a few yards behind, stopping to examine wares at a stall, so the rest of the party paused to watch a cluster of minstrels playing the lute, lyre, timbrels, and flute.

At the end of their performance, the small audience who had gathered applauded and dropped coins into an open case.

Sebastian patted Frey on the arm where it was tucked into his.

"Rhys and I should head back to our tent soon to prepare for the games. Will you come to watch?"

The slight uncertainty in his voice touched her. This thing between them was like a newly sprouted seedling drinking thirstily of the rain of little acts of gentleness.

"Of course." She smiled at him, and the smile she received in return warmed her from within. "You've promised, archery, and I will certainly be there to critique your training methods."

Sebastian's smile broadened. "Then I'd better make all haste, I would hate to disappoint my lady."

Sebastian slapped Rhys on the shoulder and the two men departed down the row of stalls from whence they came.

Lady Rosalind passed a package to one of their escorts and took Sebastian's place at her arm.

"You'll discover one of the advantages of being married to a baron is having someone to carry purchases," she confided.

Frey thanked God for Lady Rosalind, the family peacemaker and the only person besides Sebastian who made her feel truly welcome.

Theirs had become an unlikely friendship. Rosalind was gracious and eloquent, a woman who commanded a quiet respect, so different to Frey in many ways. Yet Sebastian's sister went out of her way to treat her as an equal, even doing her best to counsel Heloise from her disappointment, which had appeared to grow more acute.

A brightly colored piece of silk caught Frey's eye, drawing her to a rainbow-hued table displaying small lengths of silk in myriad shades.

She couldn't resist. The silk was a vivid blue-red, an exact match for the lions rampant on the de la Croix cipher, and was beautiful to the touch. Frey ran the gossamer-light textile through her fingers and asked the price.

"For a foot-long square? Surely that price is for a bolt of this fabric," exclaimed Frey on hearing the stall holder's price.

"But it is the finest silk from the East, my lady," the swarthy man protested. "Such a color is made with only the finest handpicked safflowers from the Holy Land. Why, it's the very shade of red as bled by Our Lord!"

Frey raised a skeptical eyebrow and heard Rosalind choke back a snigger at the hyperbole. She turned to Rosalind and held up the fabric.

"What say you, Lady Rosalind? I must confess to being quite taken with the color, but now I'm not so sure it is what I'm looking for."

Rosalind appeared to give the matter serious consideration.

"I do agree it is an interesting color, but when you hold it to the light, I can see the weave is not of the finest quality. How much did you say the man wanted for it?"

Before she could answer, the stallholder rolled his hands in seeming anguish and named a price one third less than he had told Frey.

"Well, it is up to you my dear, but I recommend you set a good example for your marriage. I'm sure the baron would not be happy to learn his betrothed was profligate with coin," continued Rosalind.

Frey pretended to consider her advice before replying gravely.

"Of course, my lady. I should not want to displease him for, although he is kind to me, he is stern and will want a full accounting of my expenses."

"You are very wise," approved the other woman. "Especially since three rows over I saw a much finer piece of silk that was half that price."

"Really?" Frey exclaimed, moving away from the table. "Let's go there now."

The merchant interjected swiftly.

"My lady! If only I had known you were the beautiful young woman betrothed to the baron of Tyrswick, I would not have insulted you with such a price. Pray forgive me and my misspoken words," he said, and named a new price just a quarter of the original.

Suppressing a smile, Frey turned to Rosalind.

"You are far more experienced in these matters than I, my Lady Rosalind; does that sound like a fair cost?"

"Perhaps," she pondered. "But I believe you could obtain a better price if you haggled."

* * *

Heloise drifted toward the back of the group, her chaperones too engaged by the performance of nearby jugglers and acrobats to notice her detachment from the assembly.

She idly browsed through the stalls of beads, ribbons, and trinkets, staying within sight of the party, which, to her mind, did not break the promise she made to her brother to not wander off on her own.

Following the end of a performance of mummers, a crowd of villagers surged past, threatening to push her out of sight of her brother's men-at-arms, but a firm yet gentle hand at her elbow was there to steady her.

"Forgive me, my lady Heloise, permit me this service to you."

Heloise looked up into the bright blue eyes of the young man only a few years older than herself. "I think I know you."

"I would be honored if you did," he said, offering her a courtly bow. "My name is Baldwin; I used to be a knight in Baron Tyrswick's service."

The face and the name instantly rang true.

"I remember now!" she said, taking in his clean, well-made clothes. "You were at the Keep when I arrived, but then you were gone. Tell me, what do you do now?"

"Leaving Tyswick was the best decision I ever made. I'm employed by a wealthy baron as his man-at-arms. He is on his way back from a pilgrimage to Lindisfarne."

Heloise nodded absently, wandering a step or two away and looking across to where Alfreya and Rosalind were exchanging confidences as they watched the jugglers. She scanned the sea of faces, failing to find her brother or Sebastian. When she returned to Baldwin, he held two small paper cones filled with comfits purchased from a nearby stall.

"Is that Lady Alfreya?" he asked, feigning innocent curiosity. "The one betrothed to Sebastian de la Croix?"

"It is. But *I* don't want to talk about her, although everyone else does." Heloise pouted. She started to move away more decisively this time, and Baldwin fell into step with her.

"Why is that?" he asked. "You'll have to forgive me, I've been away for so many months."

He pressed the second cone into her hand.

She halted her stride and considered him. Her judgment was swayed by the fact she stood in a crowded fair no farther than thirty feet from her brother's men-at-arms.

"I shouldn't accept these," she said, attempting to hand the candied nuts back.

"Nonsense! I can easily afford these and, besides, I think you need someone to talk to."

"I hardly know you, it wouldn't be appropriate."

Baldwin shrugged.

"Suit yourself, but I would have thought I was the perfect confidante."

Heloise watched his retreating back for a moment.

"Why?"

He turned.

"I'm only here until after All Souls Day. You can tell me all your secrets knowing you'll never see me again, and I'll never let on."

Heloise hesitated.

"Your loss," Baldwin said carelessly, turning and striding away again.

"Wait!" Heloise cried out.

Baldwin walked back to her. Heloise fought to contain a blush.

"I don't want to be disloyal to my brother or to Sebastian…," she began.

"But you love the both of them very much." Baldwin nodded. "Follow me," he said. "You can tell me everything while we watch the knights at their sports."

Heloise followed.

CHAPTER TWENTY-FOUR

In a dry, grassy corner of the field, a tourney tent in stripes of red and blue stood for the comfort of the noble household of Tyrswick. Inside it, a brazier with glowing coals kept the tent warm for William Villiers, the earl of Goscote's new son, who fussed a little at being placed in a cradle, having just been fed by his wet nurse. Rosalind made herself comfortable on a cushioned chair and rocked the lad to sleep.

Dorcas, Heloise's nanny, the only other person in the tent, dozed on a chair. Most of the party sat outside on a temporary viewing platform, where the bohort would be conducted.

Unlike a tourney in which experienced knights would line up on either side of a field and engage in a melee—first the knights on horseback, then the archers, and lastly those with a prowess with swords—a bohort was an informal event for squires to show off their skills.

Frey climbed the platform, her eyes seeking out Sebastian although he was not difficult to find. Dressed in his surcoat of red and blue, he directed Ebon alongside Lord Rhys, who was mounted on a dappled gray. He too wore a dress surcoat, his of rich emerald green and gold with an embroidered eagle rising from the center of it.

Larcwide mounted the steps and stood beside her.

"Do you fancy to make a little extra coin, my lady?" he asked quietly, grinning at her mix of curiosity and suspicion.

"Wagering, Larcwide? I'm shocked," she said, although a growing smile belied the sternness of the words. "Who should I be watching for?"

"Young Robert's swordplay has been coming on."

"He has an exceptional teacher."

Larcwide accepted the compliment with a grunt.

"Who's keeping the book?"

"Orlege."

"Are you sure that's wise?"

Larcwide's response was to laugh, then quieten when several heads turned in their direction.

"Well, Lord Rhys's men *are* very proud, my lady," he said. "And Orlege is not above boasting. It might have been suggested to our lads they take their time to get the measure of their opponents without giving away their strength."

Frey crossed her arms and raised an eyebrow, to which Larcwide added hastily, "Not that I would ever say who would give them such advice, mind, but suffice it to say that Tyrswick's squires have rather taken to more advanced types of martial skills than those from Goscote."

Larcwide paused expectantly, looking hopeful.

"Does Sebastian know any of this?"

The old man-at-arms shook his head slowly and grinned.

Inwardly, Frey sighed. This had the potential to end badly.

Larcwide's grin broadened when he saw Frey's posture soften and she reached beneath her sleeve for her small leather purse.

She pressed a coin in his hand and whispered, "Put me down for a shilling on Robert."

A fanfare of horns pierced the early afternoon and a crier announced the beginning of the event with all the seriousness of a tourney. At the sound of the clarion, Rosalind emerged from the tent, having changed into a gown of deep green, the same shade as her husband's surcoat.

Frey felt a twinge of dismay she hadn't thought to do the same. She was dressed in her practical, plain gray-blue walking dress.

Sebastian and Rhys urged their mounts to a trot before the viewing platform where the two men bowed to the ladies. Rosalind unwound a length of gold ribbon from her hair and with great ceremony tied it to her husband's wrist.

Rhys raised his arm triumphantly, the shimmering length of satin fluttering in the breeze.

Frey's dismay turned to panic. All of Tyrswick would next be watching her and, although she and Sebastian were not yet wed, what kind of impression would she make if she didn't offer a similar gesture?

She remembered the length of bloodred silk in her pocket and pulled it out, seeing as she did that it was an exact match for the color of the lion stitched across Sebastian's chest.

He edged Ebon around and Frey leaned forward, tying the length of silk around his elbow, where in the breeze it poured out like liquid flame.

Their eyes met and Frey saw something unreadable there, but it filled her with longing. As she was about to withdraw, Sebastian took her wrist and brought it to his lips. The heat of their touch seemed to reach through her gloves, branding her.

The crowd roared its approval and the spell was broken, though not before Sebastian gave her a final salute and rode away to join Rhys and their assembled men.

* * *

On a far edge of the field, Heloise stood beside Baldwin and watched the very public display of regard between Sebastian and Frey.

"The cheating snake," she complained. "She has a lover, you know."

Baldwin feigned shock.

"Surely not!"

"It's true," she insisted. "He writes her letters. But Sebastian is too blinded by the death of his own lover to see that Alfreya is nothing more than a cheap substitute."

"The baron had a lover?"

"Yes, but she was killed. She is buried in the crypt at Tyrswick Keep."

"Oh," said Baldwin. "You know, it is a pity you do not know the name of Lady Alfreya's lover. Perhaps if the baron knew—"

"Oh, but I do know his name," Heloise cut in. "He signs himself Drefan."

Baldwin put on a performance that would have impressed the professional play actors at the fair. He rocked back on his heels, put his hand to his mouth, and opened his eyes wide. As expected, Heloise looked alarmed at his reaction and reached for his arm.

"Baldwin? Are you ill?"

He staggered back, taking her with him to stand behind the small group of people who watched the games.

"No, no…it's just…my lord's name is Drefan."

It was Heloise's turn to look shocked.

"Why, that would explain why he has lingered here instead of heading straight to York," the young man added.

He watched Heloise pause in thought for a moment before addressing him.

"Do you think I could meet with your lord?" she asked hopefully.

Baldwin smiled.

* * *

Although a bohort was supposed to be a friendly competition between allies, the young men of both Tyrswick and Goscote treated the games seriously indeed.

The tug-of-war competition may have gone to Goscote lads thanks to the heavy weight ring-in of a knight at anchor, but the Tyrswick squires quickly showed their superior prowess at swordplay.

When Robert won his match, no one cheered louder than Frey.

The competitors were evenly matched throughout the day, with Sebastian and Rhys both playing master showmen, whipping up the crowd to cheer for one side over the other.

The final display of the afternoon was an archery competition, and here too Frey discovered the competitors equally skilled. Like the others watching, she was nearly hoarse from cheering when Sebastian raised his hand just before the last event of the day.

Rhys, still on horseback, joined him, and the two men conferred in the middle of the field.

As the conference continued for a minute, the crowd became impatient and started stamping their feet just as the two knights appeared to come to an agreement.

All eyes were on Sebastian as he rode over to the crier and spoke to him.

Then the knight lifted his head in the direction of the tourney tent. Even from this distance, Frey felt certain Sebastian looked directly at her, and she could not make her eyes leave his. So consumed, she missed the crier's announcement and the reaction of the crowd until nudged by Rosalind.

"Are you really?"

"Am I really what?" Frey asked distractedly, her eyes still on Sebastian as he approached the stand.

Rosalind laughed. "Weren't you paying attention? The crier has just said you would be representing Tyrswick against Rhys's champion squire."

"I'm going to be doing what?" she responded, turning to Rosalind. "Where did you get the ridiculous notion that I—"

"Unless you believe you are too out of practice, princess."

Frey looked up. Sebastian sat there on his horse, a smile playing around his sensual mouth and merriment dancing in his green eyes. She couldn't speak.

"Perhaps that day with the wolves was a lucky amateur shot."

"Lucky? You think luck saved your life, Baron?" Frey demanded, standing up from her seat.

The crowd, apparently under the belief she had agreed, roared their approval.

Sebastian held out his hand to her.

"Show me how lucky I am, princess."

She took his hand and was swept onto his saddle. Before she could catch a breath, they were galloping down the green toward a bull's-eye target that stood on a three-legged easel.

"Sebastian," she whispered, "are you sure? It's one thing for me to practice with Larcwide after his lessons, but another to represent you and Tyrswick."

"You'll be my wife in two days' time, and then you will *be* Tyrswick."

Their conversation ended there.

Frey dismounted and looked over at her opponent. He was about her height but had the build of a man.

She felt sorry for the lad; his face suggested he was unsure whether to be honored or insulted at being told to compete against the wife-to-be of his lord's best friend.

Frey donned the expression she habitually wore when she commanded in the field. She met the young man face to face, greeted him with a firm handshake, and wished him all the best.

The town crier joined them, taking his role of event steward seriously. He compared the bows they were to use and satisfied himself they were equal in size. He then counted out six arrows, making the crowd count along with him.

Frey knew this game. The closest to the bull's-eye, the higher the points.

The crier looked at her. She was to shoot first.

Taking a pin from her hair, Frey fixed back the right outer sleeve of her kirtle to prevent it fouling her shot, then ignored her fellow competitor, instead watching the direction of the breeze as it rocked the leaves in nearby trees. Frey picked up the bow and pulled back on the string. The draw was heavy and she tested it a few times before selecting her arrow.

Her focus turned to the target, a large white disc with a red circle in the center about a hand span in diameter and surrounded by a larger black ring.

Frey licked her lips and steadied her breathing.

Breathe in, position the arrow, breathe out.

Breathe in, line up the target, breathe out.

Breathe in, pull back the bowstring, breathe out.

Breathe in, release the arrow.

Exhale slowly while it remains in flight, crossing fingers that a sudden cross wind doesn't queer the trajectory.

Frey's arrow hit the outer edge of the thick black ring, a creditable first shot.

Rhys's squire bettered it by an inch, landing his arrow in the middle of the black.

Frey readied her second arrow and released it. It fell just outside the red bull's-eye.

The squire's second sat just inside the red.

With one arrow left, her only chance to win was to make the next shot perfect.

The applause of the crowd drifted into her consciousness. Distracted, she turned toward the sound, unerringly finding Sebastian in the sea of faces behind her. He nodded and mouthed something she couldn't hear, but his steady gaze filled her with her confidence.

Frey mounted her final arrow and pulled back on the drawstring; the muscles of her biceps quivered under the strain and then settled, helping to hold her aim true.

Breathe in, breathe out, breathe in, breathe out, breathe in…

Frey released the arrow. The twang of the string sounded unnaturally loud. She watched the fletching on the rear of the arrow bend with the force of flight as it left the bow.

Breathe out.

And the arrow hit true, quivering in the center of the target. She turned to flash Sebastian a grin, which he returned.

The squire stepped up to the mark and readied his final shot. It fell just outside the red.

Frey thrust her bow aloft in one hand as the crowd erupted in cheers, and she turned, accepting the acclaim. Then she was swept into Sebastian's arms. He lifted her off her feet and spun her around. As he did so, he whispered into her ear.

"Well done, Frey! I'm proud of you."

His words brought raw emotion to the surface. No one ever told her they were proud of her.

It meant more to her than any declaration of love.

CHAPTER TWENTY-FIVE

The tent flap swept open, the cool afternoon breeze at his back alerting Drefan to his guests. He did not face his visitors. Instead he warmed his hands by the brazier and watched the distorted form of the girl reflected in the polished copper kettle that sat nearby.

The girl remained on the threshold, casting her eyes about, hesitating. The little bird was cautious, as she ought to be. He watched her turn to look at the furnishings, a long bench covered with comfortable cushions, the coffer that held various jugs and jars, and then lastly his two companions.

The twins, not much older than this girl herself. He turned his head to watch them dress. One was helping the other adjust the waist ties of their matching ochre and olive gowns.

Their presence reassured the girl—as it was supposed to. She entered. Baldwin followed behind. The little sparrow had hopped right into the snare.

"My lord, forgive my intrusion, but as fate would have it, I have found someone I feel compelled to introduce you to," said Baldwin.

On cue, Drefan turned and Heloise gasped.

He knew himself to be a fine-looking man with a haughty, aristocratic bearing. It suited him. His hair was fair and his eyebrows dark, almost black. A strong, straight nose was positioned over full lips.

Now he was ready to play the role of Lady Alfreya's devoted lover.

"Lady Heloise Villiers, may I introduce Baron Drefan d'Aumont," continued Baldwin. "My lord, Lady Heloise is the sister of the baron of Goscote and sister by marriage to the baron of Tyrswick."

Heloise acknowledged Lord Drefan's bow of greeting with a curtsey.

"My dear! Then you must have news of my darling Alfreya," Drefan exclaimed. "Please sit, be at ease, and tell me how she fares. I fear my attempts to let her know I have returned have been failures."

He turned to the two young women and gave them coins with the instruction to enjoy the markets. They each thanked him with a kiss on the cheek and left.

Now it was the three of them alone, although Heloise didn't seem to notice as she accepted his invitation to sit, take refreshment, and unburden her soul. Now there was an irony.

Drefan said little, indeed needed to say little, as Lady Heloise Villiers told the story from the day of Sebastian's distraught, nay *reckless* behavior following the death of a Saxon noblewoman and then his return with the earl's daughter and the Crown's approbation of their betrothal.

He listened to her tale with intense interest and without interruption.

"Do you mean my letter did arrive to Alfreya's hand?" Drefan blinked as though confused.

"It did, my lord, I watched her read it," she averred earnestly.

Drefan looked over at Baldwin, who was standing by the brazier, and exchanged a meaningful look with his knight. "Tell me," he said, taking a sip from his cup. "Lord Sebastian. You say he was very distressed by the death of the Saxon noblewoman."

"Indeed my lord. He even had her body interred in the crypt at Tyrswick Keep. I believe he was in love with her."

Drefan offered the poor idiot child a sad smile of implied empathy and let her keep prattling on like the hen-witted fool she was.

In his mind, he examined this nugget of information the girl had given him.

To be certain, giving a Saxon noblewoman—a stranger to him—the conspicuous honor of burial in what rightly was the de la Croix family crypt was odd behavior from a man known to be rigidly reliable and conformist.

Drefan recalled Alfred's telling him of his narrow escape from Durham because some fool of a young knight didn't stand and fight or sound an alarm. Surely, it would be too much to expect de la Croix to be the same man.

Most unexpected.

Excellent.

Already, in his mind, he planned his next step. First, confirmation of his suspicions that, if true, would provide the catalyst needed to embolden King William's son, Robert Curthose of Normandy, to do more than threaten to rise up against his father.

He drew his attention back onto the girl, having already half listened to her relate a conversation in which she confessed her long and everlasting devotion to de la Croix.

"What can be done? They are to be wed in two days' time," she concluded.

Her fragile innocence was quite sweet, he supposed, if he was given to such emotion, which he was not. Drefan adjusted his features to affect a look of benign compassion.

"I see you are deeply devoted to Lord Sebastian, my dear, but I wonder whether that is enough?"

The question had the desired effect. Heloise straightened, ready to defend her feelings.

"I love him!" Heloise declared with passion. "I would do anything for him."

With a quick look to Baldwin, Drefan fixed his most winning smile on the girl.

"That's what I'm counting on."

* * *

Robert lit two of the stone cresset lamps in the Tyrswick tent as the three men sat around the radiating warmth of a brazier.

"What have you learned, Dom?" asked Sebastian, stretching his legs toward the heat.

"Well, praise be to God, there have been no other murders apart from the one you learned of, my lord," answered Dominic, nodding to Rhys.

"What I have been doing is trying to learn of anything in common that ties all these acts of evil together."

Rhys snorted, unimpressed. "We *know* what these crimes have in common. The girls who were disfigured and brutalized are of age, pretty, and unwed."

"Rhys!" Sebastian rebuked, but the friar didn't need his defense. With equanimity, the clergyman continued.

"Knowing who he likes to take tells us only what attracts the Beast, not who he is and certainly not how to stop him," he said.

"Then what *have* you learned, Dom?" Sebastian inquired.

"Well, in the weeks prior, a traveling band of tinkers and odd-jobs men would arrive in the village..." Sebastian raised an eyebrow. "Really, Dom? Is that the best you can come up with? A traveling band of gypsies? The convenient scapegoat for any and every crime and misdemeanor across five parishes?"

"The local people don't suspect them. I do," Dominic said. "According to the villagers I've spoken to, the travelers arrive in town, stay for no more than three weeks, and depart. But they have been discounted out of hand because the girls always went missing two to three days *afterward*.

"It's in talking to the village priests that I've learned the party has the same description. Four men, two donkeys, and a cart filled with tools. The priests remember them because they were never seen for mass."

"The quality of the sermons perhaps?" Rhys quipped.

Dominic quirked his lips in wry amusement.

"Very possibly. Nevertheless, it is another thing these events have in common."

"Do we know where these men are now?" asked Sebastian, returning to business.

"We don't, but I have heard reports of a group matching their description heading back north. They may be looking to winter in Northumbria."

Sebastian nodded and stood, drawing the meeting to an end. "I'll have patrols keep an eye out for them."

As the three headed outside, Sebastian felt a tap on his arm.

"I haven't had the chance to congratulate you on your betrothal, Sebastian."

"Is this a genuine felicitation or one of those that lies behind a false smile?" Sebastian grumbled.

"Since when have you ever known me not to speak honestly?"

Sebastian conceded the point with a sigh.

"Never. I know not everyone is happy. Gaines and Rhys have made their reservations plain."

"Are you marrying them or Lady Alfreya?"

Sebastian pinned him with a look, but Dominic shrugged it off.

"You have the Crown's approval and presumably the young woman herself is willing. Since when did you care for the opinions of other people?"

Silence stretched out for several long moments until Dominic was struck by a spark of revelation.

"This is more than just a political and strategic marriage for you, isn't it?"

When Sebastian answered, his voice was low and uncertain, his head bowed.

"I love her, Dom, and I think I always have, but she…"

"Fight for her, Sebastian," said Dominic gravely. "Alfreya's past still haunts her. Win her mind and win her heart and she will surrender willingly to the love you offer."

CHAPTER TWENTY-SIX

Frey sat on a bench facing the open-air stage. Warmth enveloped her as the weight of a wool mantle was pressed on her shoulders from behind. She looked back at Sebastian. He studied her briefly with an expression that, if pushed, she would have described as wistful. She opened her mouth to ask if aught was amiss, but Sebastian, sitting beside her, had already turned his attention to the entertainers.

Frey continued to view his profile in the lamplight.

He was to be her husband the day after tomorrow. A life together, forever joined. The thought beat steadily in her chest. Forever, forever, forever.

It was easy to acknowledge her desire for him. The smell of him lingered on the cloak she wore; it aroused her so she had no doubt coupling with him would be pleasurable.

Over these past weeks, she had watched him, not just the play of his muscles as he trained his men, his sharp reflexes and surprising agility, but also the gentle way he would cradle his nephew, and the authority he wielded.

It would be easy to love him as his men did, out of respect and loyalty, but Frey yearned for something more and knew in her heart of hearts that it would only come if she let go and fully surrendered her past and her fears. It was as though she stood on the edge of a great rock face with a voice in her ear that whispered, if she would only step off, she would fly and soar high like the terns that swooped and dove along the North Sea cliffs.

But she was afraid.

"You there!"

The magician, a man in his late forties, tall with a great theatricality to his manner, pointed right at her.

Frey was taken aback. Could her private thoughts be so publicly manifested on her face?

"He wants to know if you would like to be part of the trick, my lady," said Robert, who stood behind. "He says he can make a woman disappear into thin air, then bring her back."

Frey's first reaction was to shake her head and decline.

"Come now!" cajoled the man. "Surely my lady, the Amazon of Tyrswick, is not afraid?"

Afraid.

The word resonated through her. Perhaps she should stop being ruled by fear. Frey squared her shoulders.

"I am not afraid," she answered softly.

Sebastian's voice rang through the crowd, "Alfreya of Tyrswick is afraid of no one and of nothing."

Buoyed by the accompanying claps and cheers, Frey stepped forward and took the hand of the conjuror.

He called for another volunteer from the crowd. Young Robert surged forward.

"Now, young man," the magician told him, waving demonstratively at the brightly painted box he had unveiled on the stage, "examine this and testify to the people it is indeed a sturdy and complete box."

Robert jumped up to the platform and walked up to the object. Much like an upright coffin, it stood in front of a length of black curtain that hid the back stage from the audience.

"Go ahead, test it! Do you agree this is a solid box?"

Robert leaned in and rapped on the back and sides and nodded his agreement.

With great deference and courtesy, the magician assisted Frey up the risers.

"No need to fear, my lady, all you need to do is just stand in that box."

She did so with a wan smile.

The magician made a further show of asking if she was comfortable before taking hold of a large panel of wood that leaned against the side of the box and turning to the audience.

"I'm going to put this on the front of the box, say a few words of magic, and, when I remove it, the lady will have gone," he announced.

"You'd better bring her back," said Robert, seriously. The audience laughed.

"Indeed, I will, young man. Don't be concerned!"

Frey's smile demurred and the front of the box was secured, but even as the front was closed, she heard movement behind her. The back of the box was as much a removable panel as the front, and, from an aperture in the backstage curtain, a young blonde woman in an olive and ochre kirtle was shushing Frey to remain silent and gesturing to her to slip out of the box.

Going along, she exited behind the curtain.

"Say nothing," said the woman, stepping to one side, but before Frey could nod, a hand clamped firmly over her mouth from behind.

She struggled fruitlessly. Her assailant, much taller and stronger, manhandled her from the backstage into a neighboring tent in which a figure waited in the semidarkness.

"You're looking well, beloved." Drefan stepped forward from the shadows into the lamplight. "Playing whore to that Norman dog suits you."

To Frey's relief, the hand that covered her mouth disappeared, and she drew a deep breath, ready to shout a few choice names, but the hand returned, holding a blade at her ribs.

"You have some gall, Drefan," she hissed. "As soon as I tell Sebastian you're here…"

Drefan surged forward and gripped the hair on the back of her head cruelly. He nodded once and the blade disappeared. With his brutal grip, he forced Frey's head around to the view beyond the parted doorway of the tent. At the edge of the crowd she saw a young man standing close beside Heloise.

"You do remember Baldwin, don't you, my dove?"

As though the man sensed he was being talked about, Baldwin turned, faced away from Heloise, and waved a quick salute.

"You won't say anything to de la Croix until we're well away from here if you value what happens to that pretty little girl over there," he whispered.

Drefan pulled Frey's head back and threw her into the arms of the knife-wielding man.

"Our time here is short," Drefan told her. "I want to make sure you don't forget my face and my name. I'll be coming for you."

Drefan gave his accomplice a curt nod. The man hauled Frey outside and dragged her up behind the backstage curtain. The blonde was nowhere to be seen. The man shoved her into the magician's box just moments before the front panel opened, leaving her blinking owlishly at the crowd, which erupted into cheers and applause.

Her eyes sought Sebastian in the crowd, and she walked toward him blindly. She watched his expression change from amusement to concern as she drew near.

"Frey? What's amiss?" he asked.

To her distress, she couldn't form the words; her teeth chattered and sweat beaded her forehead.

"Are you ill? Come sit down inside the tent."

With a gentle hand at her back, Sebastian steered her toward their marquee. Once seated and with Sebastian's warmth beside her, Frey started to feel more calm.

"Heloise," she forced out. "Where is she?"

Sebastian looked at her for a second before calling behind them to where a clutch of familiar faces from the Keep had gathered in concern at the couple's sudden departure from the performance.

"Gaines! Find Heloise."

Gaines left with a grunt of acknowledgment.

"Drefan is here," said Frey. To her distress she realized her hands shook. "I've seen him."

"When?"

"When I was in the box."

Sebastian frowned.

"You were only gone a minute."

Frey explained to Sebastian everything that had taken place and watched his normally open expression harden.

"Robert!" he yelled, the sound of which made Frey jump. "Find Orlege, tell him Drefan is here and he's to take all the men he needs and search the tents. Start with the magician's and hold him."

"Frey?" Sebastian chafed Frey's cold hands with his. "Frey, listen to me. We will find Heloise…"

"I don't need finding, I'm right here."

Frey started at the voice and saw a matching expression of surprise across Sebastian's face. Standing behind Heloise in the doorway was Gaines.

"Lady Heloise was right outside, my lord."

Frey didn't miss the sarcasm in his tone. By the way Sebastian shifted she knew the disrespect didn't go unnoticed by him either.

"Then see if you can aid Orlege," said Sebastian, dismissing his man-at-arms and turning to Heloise.

"Explain to me where you've been."

"Here," she stated, stepping farther into the tent and folding her arms across her chest defiantly. "I've been right here under your nose all the time."

Rhys barreled in and looked at Heloise, then at Sebastian in confusion.

"What the hell's going on? The men are going tent to tent and I was told Heloise was missing."

"No, I wasn't, brother," said Heloise in exasperation. "I don't know what Lady Alfreya's been saying, but I've been here all along."

"Alfreya saw Drefan here at the fair," said Sebastian levelly. "I'm not going to take any chances with her or your family."

"Agreed. Heloise, we're leaving now," said Rhys tersely, forestalling a squeak of protest from his sister with a raised finger.

Sebastian squeezed Frey's hand and stood.

"Go with Rhys. If Drefan is still here, we'll find him."

* * *

Weariness weighed heavily on Sebastian as he led the last of his men along the road to Tyrswick Keep.

The moon had passed its zenith. It was now the early hours of a new day.

The search for Drefan had proved fruitless, and the magician innocent. His real backstage assistant was found bound and gagged in one of the tents. Drefan had disappeared so completely, he might give the magician some pointers.

Orlege's frustration at his failure to find Drefan seemed to weigh heavy on him. Sebastian appreciated the man had gone to great lengths to assure him of his loyalty, and the fact that young Baldwin was now in league with the Saxon traitor was another matter Orlege appeared to take personally. He had offered to lead patrols daily until both men were found.

"What does this man d'Aumont want, Sebastian?"

The question startled him out of a half doze as his mount walked on.

"He could have taken Frey if he'd wanted, but he let her go," replied Sebastian thoughtfully. "It seems he's intent on tormenting her, for what reason I cannot fathom, but what concerns me is he seems intent on casting his net wider."

Rhys regarded him with a fatigue that equaled his own.

"You mean Heloise."

Sebastian grunted his assent.

"I spoke to her," Rhys continued, "and she denies knowing this d'Aumont or seeing this Baldwin. She says Alfreya has set against her because of you."

Sebastian's answer was a long-suffering sigh.

Rhys fixed him with a serious gaze. "She *is* my sister and I believe her."

"And Frey will be my wife tomorrow," said Sebastian. "You will be leaving at the spring thaw and Heloise will be betrothed by summer, so the issue is neither here nor there."

Steam rose from their mouths as they breathed and from the flanks of the horses; the jangle of bridles and the steady *clop* of the animals, weary as their masters, filled the silence between the men.

"I know I asked you this before, but are you certain about this girl?" asked Rhys at last. "Are you sure she's not in league with d'Aumont?"

"Yes. On both counts."

"Well for your sake, I hope that's true."

Sebastian gave no further response and felt he didn't owe Rhys any. To be sure, he'd asked himself the same questions aplenty over the past three months, but Rhys didn't know Frey as he did.

Exhausted, Sebastian rode into the inner bailey and gave the order to close the gates.

Every step to the final story of the keep taxed his tired muscles, but the comfortable and familiar warmth of his chambers beckoned. The fireplace called to him like a siren and he gravitated toward the heat to melt the chill in his bones.

His steward, Beyard, had anticipated his master's needs. Water heated on the fire for him to wash, but first some warm spiced wine would ease the chill from the inside.

"Allow me," a soft, feminine voice offered.

He watched Frey step forward into the firelight and pour some of the heated water into a bowl. He waited for the frozen words in his head to melt and make their way to his lips.

"Frey…you shouldn't be here."

"Where else should I be?" she shrugged. "You are my husband, or at least nearly so."

Sebastian allowed her to unclasp his cloak and closed his eyes. Despite the removal of its weight, he actually felt warmer without it. He started when he felt the tug of the strings at the neck of his tunic.

Slender fingers brushed against his bare skin, sending sensation straight to his groin. Sebastian opened his eyes and swiftly caught Frey's hands in his.

He took in her face, her bright blue eyes dark with desire, moist lips slightly parted.

"Do you know what you're about Frey?"

Her answer was to step closer.

"Make me forget him, Sebastian."

CHAPTER TWENTY-SEVEN

Sebastian released Frey's hands and imprisoned her lips instead. She responded willingly. Her hands trailed up the battle-hardened muscles of his arms; her fingers explored the broad expanse of his back through the linen of his shirt. His hands spread across her back, working heat through the layers of fabric as their lips mated and tongues dueled, sparking warmth that trickled down her arms, her breasts, and her belly before banking and growing warmer between her legs.

Frey thought she knew what desire was, thought that she had been in love before, but never had it touched her heart and her spirit as this man had done.

Not because of his beauty—Drefan too was a very handsome man—something tugged at her, pulled her toward Sebastian, to mesh and knit itself together into something indivisible. Did she love him? She wouldn't lay claim to, but if any man was capable of rousing such a worthy emotion from her, it would be Sebastian.

Frey drew deep breaths as he released her lips and caressed her cheeks and then her neck. His firming desire nestled below her belly and, driven by instinct, she rubbed herself against it, stoking her own need. Sebastian's arms dropped to her buttocks, where he pressed her firmly against himself and the embers of her desire ignited into flame.

"There's no turning back after tonight," he told her. "We may say our vows before an assembly tomorrow, but now in front of me and God, I want your word."

"Yes," she breathed. "I am willing and I want you. Make me yours."

Sebastian groaned and swept her from her feet and carried her over to his bed. She received his kisses eagerly, clinging to him as he dipped to pull back the furs that covered the bed. A moment later, she could feel the soft feather mattress at her back.

The chill of the night air swirled about her as he stood to release the bed curtains that would shroud them in darkness.

"Don't," she whispered. "I want to see you."

"Then keep your eyes open, princess," he responded, hauling his shirt over his head and dropping it on the floor behind him.

With the firelight behind him, he looked every inch the warrior, the glow of the fire limning his muscles in gold. She reached out to touch him, but he remained out of grasp. He untied the strings of his chausses and rolled them, one-by-one, off his feet before untying the drawstring of his braies.

The fabric released with a tug and Sebastian stood before her in all his glory. Her eyes were drawn to the magnificent length of his erection, and something within her opened and demanded its presence.

Frey was not conscious that her expression had changed, but it must have done so, because Sebastian's own turned to one that promised pleasure beyond her experience.

He climbed into the bed and drew the woolen blankets and furs over his waist.

Frey parted her legs in anticipation of his entrance.

He lowered himself on his arms over her and whispered, "It does a man good to know his wife is eager for him, but there is more to this sport that I'm looking forward to teaching you."

Frey groaned, a release of pleasure and frustration.

"Then I shall be an attentive pupil. I don't like to be bested at anything."

"Ah, my dear heart, in these games there are always two winners."

Sebastian settled himself over her and started with nips and licks at her ears.

Frey's nipples hardened and rubbed against the clothes; the sensation spread and moisture pooled between her legs. She clung to his shoulders and kicked at her skirts to allow her legs to part farther and draw him near.

Sebastian rested on his knees, trapping her restless legs between his thighs.

"I want to see all of you," he demanded softly, and, as he spoke, his hands stroked up the outside of her legs, bunching her skirts as he did so.

He was agonizingly slow while she rapidly unlaced the sides and neck of her kirtle and the chemise beneath.

With bare skin exposed, the sensation of cold danced along her body, adding to the awareness of him that infused her whole being.

His hands released the fabric, skimmed her belly, and spanned her waist, pulling the fabric taut across her breasts.

Frey's hands kneaded his shoulders, demanding silently he cease his merciless tease and bring her relief. Freed from the skirts, her legs twined around him on their own and her hips rocked, enticing him to come to her.

He kissed her lips gently before lightly nipping at them. Such acts brought added heat and color, which he soothed with his tongue.

Sebastian's hands dipped and with purpose pulled both remaining garments over her breasts. She aided him by raising her arms and her wadded clothing landed with his on the floor.

Fingertips teased and touched her full breasts and Frey felt them ache, heavy with the burden of desire.

Sebastian's manhood slipped along the soft downy curls between her legs and they shared a mutual groan before he drew, frustratingly, away. His head dipped to taste where his fingers had trailed. His tongue darted out to flick a rosy nipple.

Frey cried out with the sheer pleasure of it and curled her fingers tightly into the ebony waves at the nape of his neck.

To be sure, she had never felt anything like this ever. It was as though she melted. Before another thought could coalesce, the wet warmth of his mouth covered her breast and his tongue licked and swirled.

Please, please, please, this should be over now, Frey thought desperately. Surely such sensations were unnecessary for consummation, but…*Oooohhhhhh!*

And no more coherent thought was possible as Sebastian claimed her other breast.

Her hips moved restlessly, trying to capture the hard warmth of him she had experienced so fleetingly between her legs.

"Did you say something, princess?" came his husky response at her chest.

"Please," she begged. "I need, ah I…"

"No words," he told her before swiftly claiming her lips. She poured her concentration into matching his kisses, and she did not feel him shift position until she felt the sensation of his fingers softly stroking between her thighs. Her legs parted and he slowly dipped a finger between her netherlips and, with his thumb, coaxed the blooming bud of her sex to life.

One finger, then two filled her, gently stretching.

Stroke upon stroke added sensation upon sensation until the conflagration of desire burst into life and consumed every doubt until all she could do was surrender herself to the sensation and to the man who brought her a pleasure hitherto unknown.

Frey came back to awareness of Sebastian's fingers still stroking and her hips rocking in counterpoint.

"Please, Sebastian, join me," was her breathy plea, and he did, entering her slowly inch by inch, her body stretching to accommodate his girth. He stopped and looked down at her with such tenderness she thought the sensation of her release might overwhelm her a second time.

He rocked his hips and Frey cried out with pleasure, clenching her sex to prolong the pleasure.

"You're mine," Sebastian told her.

He stroked into her again, then again, and again until the wave of bliss rose and Frey was helpless to do anything but let it rise and overwhelm her. She abandoned herself to it when Sebastian's movements became erratic and rapid as he called out in his own release.

CHAPTER TWENTY-EIGHT

Frey didn't know why she felt different, but she did. Surely this day would be just like the day that dawned before it, and just like the one that would follow tomorrow.

She hoisted herself off the stone window coping and took one last look at the blue November sky above, then turned to her wedding gown, the same shade of pale blue, embroidered at the square neck and sleeves in white and silver thread.

It was the most expensive dress she had ever owned. It was lined in the softest white satin, which peeked from beneath the split sleeves of the outer robe.

Two maids waited in attendance, and Frey allowed them to undress her and place the new garment over her head.

As the stays were tightened, she watched her transformation in the reflection upon a rectangle of polished steel. The corners were engraved with the interlocked squares of the old Tyrswick cipher and, on the top and the bottom of the plate, was a lion rampant with the initials "S" and "A" intertwined. It was an expensive wedding gift from the people of Tyrswick, which touched her deeply.

Her pale hair was brushed by the maids until it shone, then the sides plaited and curled around her head and held in place with pins tipped with pearls the size of peas. The rest of Frey's hair was plaited with blue and white ribbons into one thick braid and coiled at her nape to be pinned in place.

She could hardly believe she was the same woman who just this summer spent her days in rough and filthy tunics and hose. Part of her felt unworthy of such splendor. She stretched down to stroke the soft kid boots, the color of clotted cream, which had been made especially for her. They fitted beautifully.

Rosalind entered the chamber carrying a small inlaid casket. Frey envied her, in her gown of deep red, the color of garnet, how she carried herself with a poise and grace Frey struggled to master.

"Frey, you look beautiful!"

Frey blushed, mortified by her uncharacteristic skittishness.

"I want to be worthy of your brother."

Rosalind hugged her tightly, and when they parted, Frey was surprised to find tears dancing at the edge of her lashes.

"That's all I ever wanted for him—a woman who would understand his honor and loyalty, who would take her equal share in his responsibilities. I didn't dare hope he would find a bride who would love him as well."

Love?

Frey cast her eyes downward, afraid Rosalind would see what a fraud she was.

She couldn't love Sebastian.

Love was a fable. The best a woman could ask for in a marriage is for a husband to be kind and fair. On that score Frey had no complaints. She had no dowry, no lands to offer an advantageous match, and he showed unmerited consideration to her brother and even furnished her wedding finery.

Frey swallowed against the lump in her throat and raised her head to give Rosalind a truthful answer.

"I promise that I will give him no cause to regret taking me for wife."

Rosalind's response was a beaming smile. She turned away to unlock the casket she placed on the small table. Light from the window struck the contents within, and the glittering silver and flashes of blue made the interior glow.

"You're soon to be the baroness of Tyrswick, one of the most prosperous counties in Northumbria, so you need to look the part," she said.

The maids stepped aside to allow the baroness of Goscote to place around the neck of their mistress a necklace of silver. Fine links looped a thicker rope of silver and, at the end of each of these festoons, held an oval of polished blue topaz only a shade or two lighter than Frey's eye color. A square sapphire set in gold with round rubies at each corner was placed on Frey's finger.

"There, now you look like the wife of a baron," Rosalind approved.

Frey looked at her reflection once more and wondered who the noble woman was whose reflection stared back at her. The more she stared the less she recognized herself.

Frey started as bells from the chapel in the outer bailey began to peal.

"It's time, Lady Alfreya," said Rosalind, her voice serious with the gravity of the occasion.

Frey swallowed before standing and steadying herself. Across her shoulders, the maids draped a woolen mantle of the softest wool from Scotland, trimmed in light yellow rabbit fur along the cowl and hem.

There was a knock at the chamber door and Rosalind called, "Enter."

The door opened and Larcwide and Orlege stood at the entrance dressed in mail and the red and rich blue that proclaimed them to be in the service of Sebastian de la Croix, the baron of Tyrswick.

They stood to attention as the bride emerged, but then Larcwide breached protocol and took Frey's hand, kissing it.

"You are the most beautiful creature who walked the face of God's earth," he told her.

"Should I get too big for my boots, I shall have you to blame, dear friend," Frey laughed and squeezed his hand.

Frey took Orlege by the hand too and squeezed it. It grounded her.

"Thank you, both of you," said Frey, taking a deep breath. "You are more than men-at-arms, you have been true friends to me and Brice, and you will always have a special place in my heart."

Orlege said nothing and looked away, clearly embarrassed by the informality and the heartfelt words. Larcwide gave her a paternal smile and squeezed her hand back in response.

"Let's get thee wed, my lady."

* * *

Frey emerged from the keep, flanked on each side by her two trusted knights. A crowd followed behind her to the chapel.

It was different from her first visit all those months ago. The air was heated with the bodies of witnesses and well-wishers standing shoulder to shoulder. At the end of the aisle stood Sebastian, surrounded by the glow of candlelight and flanked by his two witnesses, Lord Rhys and Henry Gaines.

Dressed in fresh brown robes, not travel-stained and dusty, stood Friar Dominic, who would be conducting the service.

In the corner, a clutch of brown-robed monks, intermingled with white-robed novices, stood with their heads bowed in prayer.

To Frey, the crowd disappeared as she kept her eyes fixed on Sebastian dressed in full court regalia. Warmth filled her from the smile he offered and the one she found herself offering him in return.

At the altar, Sebastian took his hand in hers and they knelt for the service.

Dominic's rich, deep voice filled the space.

"The Apostle Paul writes to the church in Ephesus, 'Wives, submit to your husbands as to the Lord, because the husband is the head of the wife as also Christ is the head of the church, he himself being the savior of the body. But as the church submits to Christ, so also wives should submit to their husbands in everything. Husbands, love your wives just as Christ loved the church and gave himself for her.'

"Sebastian de la Croix, do you give yourself to Alfreya of Tyrswick to have as your wife from henceforth as you both shall live?"

Sebastian's response was strong, sure, and affirmative.

"Alfreya of Tyrswick, do you give yourself to Sebastian de la Croix to have as your husband from henceforth as you both shall live?"

For a moment Frey panicked, fearing her voice lost, but as she drew breath her answer came equally certain.

"I do."

She received a smile of encouragement from Dominic, who continued, "For as you have confirmed before our Lord God and the people assembled here as witnesses, I declare ye man and wife."

There was a sacred pause before a sweet, pure sound of a young male voice filled the chapel.

By Your grace I've been set free

By Your grace I've been set free

Following the descending scale, the bowed heads of the monks raised and baritone and bass voices reverberated in harmony as they chanted.

No eye has seen, no ear has heard

The wonders of Your glory

The Kindness of Your mercy

No eye has seen, no ear has heard

The mysteries revealed to me on the Cross of Calvary.

Although her head was bowed, there was something about the voice of the boy that seemed familiar, and she found herself listening for it as the hymn continued.

Finally curiosity won and she raised her head, finding her brother standing in the front row of the choir.

Frey was unaware she trembled until she felt Sebastian's fingers intertwine with hers. He leaned in to whisper in her ear.

"Happy wedding day, my love."

* * *

Despite her lovely new kid boots, Frey wished for nothing more than a stool and a tub of warm water to soak her toes.

The wedding feast went long into the night and with it a seemingly unending round of dances, toasts, and greetings from well-wishers.

The servants had outdone themselves for the wedding feast of their master. Expensive beeswax candles filled the room with light as well as the sweet aroma of honey. Grand tapestries in jewellike hues of red, blue, gold, and green were especially brought out for the occasion. The head table glittered with the treasure of Tyrswick; silver and pewter platters filled the table. Turned wooden cups used every day had been replaced with pewter goblets.

Ten courses, including oysters steamed in almond milk, jellied eels, roast capon, goose, and pork stuffed with truffles, filled the tables.

Freshly baked bread made from the flour of Tyrswick's own mill was served with fresh butter, honey, and fruit preserves.

Honey mead was gifted by the monks of St. Cuthbert's and shared liberally among the wedding party while red wine spiced with cinnamon, clove, nutmeg, ginger, and cardamom warmed the hearts and the bellies of other guests.

Having lost sight of Sebastian some little while ago, Frey took the opportunity to search out her brother and speak to him for the first time since she embraced and kissed him following the wedding service.

The monks, twelve in all from St. Cuthbert's, were seated along one side of one of the large trestle tables, talking in groups of two or three, while a knot of brown-robed clerics was holding what appeared to be quite an earnest conversation with Friar Dominic.

Brice was seated at the end of the table. A carved walking stick stood by the edge of the table within reach, a permanent reminder of the cost of their father's folly.

"Did you know? I have permission to stay with you and the baron until Twelfth Night."

"So I've learned. I'm glad," Frey answered, tousling his hair. "I've missed you terribly."

Brice shook his head in protest of the ministration and continued, "But you didn't know I'd be here, did you Frey? At your wedding?"

"No. That was a very great surprise and I haven't yet had the chance to thank Sebastian," Frey replied, looking about the room for her husband.

She felt Brice clutch her hand. When she looked at him, she found his young face was in earnest.

"Frey? Are you happy? With Lord Sebastian as a husband?"

Frey squeezed his hand and considered her answer.

She had never given much thought to the idea of actually being *happy*. An end to constant day-to-day uncertainty for Brice and her father's men had been her only focus before, and, over the past three months, she felt the satisfaction of a job accomplished.

Under other circumstances, she might have been content with just that, and yet…there was something to be said for being wanted by such a man as Sebastian.

Whether it was the wine or the long day, the face of Drefan briefly swam into her mind's eye before she ruthlessly crushed it.

Drefan would never darken the door of her heart and mind again. She made that promise to herself when she went to Sebastian's chambers, and to keep her word meant as much to her as the wedding vows she spoke.

"Are you thinking about—"

Frey silenced him with a finger to his lips.

"His name is never to be spoken. Do you understand?"

Brice vigorously nodded, and Frey pulled her finger away.

"Sebastian is a good man and I will make him a good wife, and that's all that needs to be said of it."

Her younger brother grinned at her impishly.

She raised an eyebrow in response and allowed the flicker of a grin to wipe away the severity of the expression.

"Tell me what has you amused little brother."

"I was thinking about St Alfreda."

Frey remembered the story of the tragic saint.

"I think Tyrswick Keep is much nicer than any swamp."

CHAPTER TWENTY-NINE

Sebastian nodded in all the appropriate places but paid little attention to the conversation going on in front of him. He watched, captivated, as his new wife produced the most radiant smile in response to an apparent jest made by her brother. Something had changed between them and it had nothing to do with having Frey in his bed. Well, perhaps not *nothing*.

The significance of her coming to him was not lost on him. He knew Frey made an important decision last night. He did not believe she loved him; it was too early to make such a declaration, but it was a start.

What they had between them was very new and tender, like the spring shoots that would emerge from the ground in a few months' time. Given warmth and nurturing, their marriage would flourish and strengthen like a mighty oak, but until then this sprouting tenderness needed special care.

Although unaware of being observed, Frey looked up and their eyes met. Her smile broadened as though including him in the joke.

A warmth flared in his chest more satisfying than the mead that filled the silver goblet in his hand. Sure, he must be grinning like a lunatic, but tonight, he didn't care.

Something reckless overwhelmed him. The tight rein he kept on his emotions loosened. The analytical mind that always thought before acting had been sent on a sabbatical. That part of him that always remained subservient to his more rational self decided it would be a good idea to kiss his bride.

Now.

He strode over to the bench where Frey sat with her brother, took his hand in hers, and called out loudly over the noise of conversations in the hall.

"Minstrels! I wish to dance with my wife!"

The red-and-green-clad musicians scrambled for their instruments, and, as they hastily tuned up, Sebastian seized Frey around the waist and kissed her thoroughly. He felt her resistance at first until her natural passion rose and she softened in his arms, her lips parting to his.

For a brief few seconds, they were the only ones in this room, until his ears remembered their function and the sound of appreciative hoots and yells filtered through to his brain.

Sebastian thought he might be drunk. Perhaps a bit.

He had been very drunk once when he was a squire and found himself ambushed by three of his more sober colleagues, who stole his purse of coins and blackened his eye in jealous retribution over their losses at dicing.

This did not feel like that.

He watched Frey losing some of her reserve throughout the evening and actually dance with Rhys.

"I think Rhys is beginning to warm to Frey, don't you, Brother?"

Sebastian wrapped an arm around Rosalind's shoulders and hugged his sister.

"And I know his change of heart is in no short measure due to you. Thank you."

"I wouldn't have done it if I didn't believe you two belong together."

"I'm going to miss you come spring." He added weight to his words with a kiss on her cheek.

"Come now, you will have other things to occupy you than having your sister underfoot. Rhys and I need to get home to Leicestershire and arrange for Heloise's marriage." Rosalind smiled.

"Rhys says there is a newly elevated baron in a county twenty miles away who he believes would be a suitable match."

Rosalind's smile softened. "It would be nice to see her settled. I've been concerned for her over these past few months. None of us had any idea her girlish fancy was serious."

Sebastian shook his head, absolving his sister of any guilt over the matter. He cast his eye across the hall and did not see Heloise among the revelers.

"She's been behaving oddly ever since…secretive," he observed. "And whenever I have given her greetings, her manner has been colder than a witch's tit."

Rosalind swatted his arm for his uncouthness.

"She's a young woman who has had her heart broken. Just give her time. You will always be her favorite brother-in-law, and she will be a doting aunt to your children, you'll see."

The dance ended with the announcement that a course of sweets would soon be served.

"I'm going to check on William," announced Rosalind. "Cook promised sambocade cheesecake as one of the dishes, and I don't want to miss out."

"Go," Sebastian smiled. "I'll save you a slice."

Rosalind walked off with a wave of a hand in acknowledgment.

"Perhaps half a slice!" Rosalind pulled a face at him and continued on her way.

* * *

Heloise edged her way toward the passage that led to the stairs while watching Sebastian lead *that woman* into the newly cleared center of the hall. As she had been instructed, there should be no one who could find fault in her actions, and she carried out her duties assiduously. She smiled and laughed throughout the day and whenever anyone enjoined her in conversation, she offered nothing but good wishes and affected an air of familial pride to anyone who watched.

A rope of gold beads, a gift from her brother for the wedding, hung around her neck. She rolled one around in her fingers and waited until she was sure she would not be missed before slipping down the stairs.

Heloise moved quietly past the guards' quarters and then past the kitchen, where the sound of banging pots and barked commands announced the wedding feast at Tyrswick had another few courses to go.

It was easy, so very easy, to slip into the outer bailey and toward the stables. Heloise tugged her wolf's-pelt cloak around her and stopped at the entrance, eyeing the distance between the keep and the stables.

A few steadying steps against the chill and the wind beginning to rise, then Heloise darted forward, keeping her attention fixed on the dully glowing lamp that marked the stable entrance. All the householders in the keep were upstairs celebrating, even the groomsmen. They would not come to check on the horses until much later.

So fixed was Heloise on her destination that she didn't hear the crunch of a booted footstep to her left until the body it belonged to stretched out and snatched her midstride. Nothing more than a surprised mewl escaped her before a hand ruthlessly clamped over her mouth and propelled her toward the stable opening.

"Shh," hissed the voice. "It's me."

* * *

Later, Heloise watched Rosalind pass up the stairs and round the corner to the guest chambers just as she reached the landing on the Great Hall. Heloise stopped to warm her hands by the fire. She did not notice Sebastian until he spoke to her.

"There you are! You'll miss out on the dances standing here by yourself," he told her.

She blushed. Sebastian swept her hands into his. "Your hands are freezing!"

His notice of her discomforted rather than flattered.

"I know where you've been," he announced.

Heloise jumped. She worked to pry her tongue from the roof of her mouth.

"You do?" she exclaimed, eyes darting for the door.

Sebastian grinned and folded her arm through his and led her toward the knot of dancers.

"You've been down in the kitchen pestering the cook for a taste of the syllabub, haven't you?"

The minstrels began a new tune, and Sebastian led her through the steps effortlessly.

The words lingered for a second or two before they sank in. She sunk with them. If she told the truth, he might save her from this unwise and dangerous course of action.

The dance took them a few steps away from one another, but Heloise kept her eyes on Sebastian as they split—he taking the hand of a second dancer as her hand was taken by another dancer around whom she turned before her hand was reclaimed by Sebastian.

Then the dance progressed in two concentric rings, the inside ring moving to the left while the outside moved to the right.

She watched as Sebastian danced farther and farther away from her.

In life, as in this dance, Sebastian would return to her. Each step and each action would eventually bring Sebastian back to her for good. But eventually was not enough.

CHAPTER THIRTY

The seasons turned from autumn to winter, bringing flurries of snow that melted away by noon. But as December heralded shorter days and longer nights, the focus of the keep turned inward.

The cooks and kitchen servants stayed by the warmth of their fires, deliberating on the final menu for the Christmas feast and how to manage the inevitable leftovers into pies that would form the basis of Tyrswick Keep's main meals between Christmas and Candlemass.

Patrols were short and Sebastian suspended sessions for a month.

Little happened in and around the greater Tyrswick holdings at this time of year, and nothing requiring the intervention of the baron and his men, but Sebastian knew men with little to do were apt to get into the greatest mischief.

He set them to work on replenishing the armory. Arrows, spears, lances, bows, and swords were fashioned and forged with the aid of the blacksmith. Armor was cleaned and new links were added to the mail of young squires who had grown.

When those tasks were done, hands experienced at carving shields and straight shafts for spears and arrows were turned to domestic woodwork, and Tyswick's store of turned platters, goblets, and cups grew.

Frey had much the same thought regarding the management of the household servants, and when she broached Sebastian about her plans, she was delighted to find he gave her full reign to run the household as she saw fit.

He told her with a smile and a kiss, of which she was rapidly becoming accustomed, that as his wife she had his full confidence. And with the authority she now possessed as the baroness of Tyrswick, Frey injected the same structure and discipline inside the Keep as Sebastian demanded of his men outside it.

All the same, housemaids didn't mind the mending of clothes and blankets when their laps were kept warm as they worked. Others not so occupied were seated at looms, completing tapestries to curtain walls, keeping in warmth and holding out the bitter cold that seeped through the stone masonry.

Even the children of the Keep and the younger members of the household, prone to restlessness at spending so much time indoors, were sent out to forage for sprigs of holly, trails of ivy, and other evergreens to dress the Great Hall.

However, while the days were filled with activity so as to wrest the most out of every usable second of daylight, evenings were for leisure.

Larcwide and some of the older men watched as two others sat studiously at a table, contemplating their next move in a game of draughts. Every now and again heads would lift and the displeasure of other occupants of the Hall were made known when the sounds of wooden skittles being felled or the laughter at the antics in a play-acting game became too distracting.

Sebastian taught Frey the game of draughts and, despite a few initial missteps, she could now boast of being a worthy opponent. Her brother was a better one.

"Ah!" Brice announced triumphantly, having landed his counter on the last row of the board.

"I should wonder what they do all day at St. Cuthbert's if you have time to become so expert," she grumbled, then added cheerfully, "but now that you are living here, you will have all the more time to teach me your skill."

Brice looked uncomfortable. His head dropped and chin trembled.

"Frey, I wanted to wait until after Christmas, but I ought to tell you something now," he started, first tentatively and then with increased excitement as he shared his news.

"In summer, I might be going to a town in the south. It's called Oxford and the church has started a school there. Brother Abbot Ranulf says I have a fine mind and if I keep up my studies, he will recommend I study under Gerland, who is the greatest mathematician and computist in all of England."

While Brice spoke avidly of integers, modulos, and divisions, Frey swallowed past a lump in her throat and inwardly mourned while outwardly she managed a smile and told him with all sincerity that his mama would have been so proud of him.

* * *

That night alone with Sebastian in their bed, Frey didn't hide her tears.

"You could speak to the abbot; you could make him stay," she pleaded.

Sebastian wrapped his arms around her and wiped away her tears with the sleeve of his nightshirt.

"I probably could, but I won't," he said, dropping a light kiss on the crown of her head. "Most boys his age would already be fostered to other families. You admit yourself that even his lameness notwithstanding, your brother has not the stomach or the will to be a knight."

Frey shrugged and rested her head on Sebastian's chest, saying nothing.

"And, as Providence would have it, Brice seems to have an academic gift. It would be a shame if it were not exercised to its full potential."

"Brice idolizes you. He'd stay if you asked it," she told him.

"And Brice would stay if *you* asked," Sebastian countered. "But imagine all the things you'll have asked him to give up. The chance to learn with the finest minds of Christendom, the chance to travel. Just think, Frey, all the things he could do if you gave him your blessing to go and be the man he was meant to be."

Frey sat up and crossed her arms.

"I hate it when you're right."

At a glance she could see Sebastian smirk. "Get used to it, princess, I'm more often right than wrong."

"'Tis a wonder there's enough room for two of us in this bed, with you and your enormous self-regard," Frey huffed.

Sebastian laughed, then his voice turned husky.

"Would you like to see my enormous self-regard?" As he spoke Sebastian trailed his fingers softly up and down her arms.

In spite of her disappointment at losing Brice, Frey smiled and shook her head at her husband's jest. The melancholy evaporated, and in its place was a sensual stirring his touch evoked in her.

Following the stroke came a kiss.

One, then another, brought warmth and desire up her arms and across her shoulders, then her neck where Sebastian presented a bounty of kisses.

He propped himself up on one arm and with the other, untied the neck of her bed shift.

In one swift motion, the neck of the garment was past her shoulders, exposing her breasts. Her nipples puckered and hardened in the cool night, but they were soon worshipped by the warmth of his tongue on one, then the other.

Limited by the fallen shift to the use of her lower arms and hands, Frey encouraged Sebastian on with soft words and brushes of fingertips edging up the hem of his own shirt. He moved over her and Frey's legs parted to receive him eagerly, and they were joined flesh to flesh.

Exquisite sensations like those she had never known before Sebastian warmed her and filled her with a compounding yearning, not just for physical release, but also the communion of souls that bound them inexorably in a union that grew and strengthened with every day they shared.

With it came a dawning realization that what she was beginning to feel for Sebastian was not simply gratitude, desire, or even affection— all three words were a grossly inadequate expression.

As Sebastian skillfully brought her to climax, Frey knew without a shadow of a doubt in her heart that she started to fall in love with her husband.

* * *

The days of Advent led to the arrival of Christmas and, following a tradition established by Sebastian from his first year as baron of Tyrswick, the household of the Keep walked or rode down into the village to attend the first of three masses to mark the holy day.

The Angels' Mass was held at midnight on Christ's Mass Eve. The small stained-glass window of the church spilled light and color from the hundreds of candles lit inside, which added much welcome warmth inside the building.

The sweet scent of incense removed the sting of frosty air as well as the odor of unwashed bodies.

Following the mass, the party returned to the Keep and chilled bodies were treated to a feast of warmed pies, both sweet and savory, served with warmed spiced wine.

Some of the household would retire straight after the meal for a few hours' sleep before the Shepherds' Mass dawn service, while others eschewed their beds in favor of sharing the fire with friends.

Return from the third Christmas celebration, Mass of the Day, marked the end of Christmas formalities and the beginning of the feasting.

An enormous roast boar was the centerpiece of the Christmas table, along with several roasted geese. A Christmas pudding called a frumenty, a thick wheat-based dish filled with currants and dried fruit and spiced with cinnamon and nutmeg, finished the final course for the evening.

Despite the lateness of the hour after such a busy day, the younger members of the Keep determined to work off their excessive feasting with dancing. One of the knights obtained a mandolin and started singing a folk carol.

Tomorrow shall be my dancing day:
I would my true love so did chance
To see the legend of my play,
To call my true love to my dance.

"In a manger laid and wrapped I was,
So very poor, this was my chance,
Between an ox and a silly poor ass,
To call my true love to my dance."

While others chatted, dined, or danced, Frey glanced around to see Heloise sitting to one side on her own.

The girl had studiously ignored her at the wedding, sparing only a few mumbled words as she kept her eyes fixed on Sebastian. Since then, she was little more than a ghostly presence, only haunting the meal table in the evening.

Concerned for the girl, Frey broached the subject with Dorcas, who seemed quite surprised Frey thought there was anything strange about her mistress's behavior. Why, the older woman proudly boasted, her charge attended mass in the village church every day over the forty days of Advent.

In the light of the woman's fulsome praise of her mistress's exemplary behavior, Heloise certainly looked devout now, with her head bowed and hands clasped over her lap, sitting in a corner.

In the spirit of good will dictated by the season, Frey decided to put aside her reservations and attempt a conversation. After one of the courses, she left Sebastian's side at the high table. Heloise remained with her head bowed, but when Frey approached, the girl's hands unlocked and fumbled with her fur muff for a moment before emerging with a string of jasper rosary beads.

"Art well, Lady Heloise?" Frey inquired.

"Quite well, Lady Alfreya," Heloise replied politely but formally.

"We missed you sitting with the family at Mass. There's no need for you to sit at the back of the church."

"It suits me quite well," she said, standing and looking down at Frey. "Excuse me, it's been a very long day and I would like to get some rest."

Frey shook her head as she watched her young sister-in-law leave the hall. She debated whether to discuss her concerns with Sebastian, but as she watched him in deep conversation with Gaines and his steward, she decided against it.

What happened within Tyrswick Keep was her responsibility, so if she was unhappy with the way things were done, then she had the authority to deal with it as she wished—as Sebastian reminded her just after they wed.

Frey shrugged and returned to the high table. Heloise Villiers would be leaving in spring and likely married soon after, henceforth ceasing to be Frey's problem.

CHAPTER THIRTY-ONE

Snow started to fall at Tyrswick on Boxing Day and continued each day for a sennight, coating the ground with a soft, powdery white that deadened sound for miles around.

The bleats and lowing of sheep and cattle warm in their pens leaked out from the doors when owners checked on their livestock. The sound of Tyrswick River, which ran despite the freezing cold, seemed so much louder in the absence of other sound.

It was cold this morning, and Frey snuggled down between the blankets, keeping her eyes closed as she listened to Sebastian rummage around their chamber. He was awake just before dawn, as he always was, while Frey pretended to be asleep. One chest was opened, its hinges squeaked, and she heard the sound of a casket being lifted out.

"Hmmm, I wonder where I put it?" he muttered.

"Whatever it is you're looking for could be found here under the blankets, where it's warm," she suggested.

"No…," he replied absently. "I've already been there."

And Frey could hear the casket being returned to his coffer. Curiosity was not a good-enough reason to leave the warmth of their bed nor to open her eyes.

"Never mind," Frey answered. "You'll find it at a more civilized time. Come back to bed until it's light."

"It's light already."

"Then look when it's *more* light. Perhaps in spring," she grumbled.

Frey gave a light purr of satisfaction as Sebastian responded by sinking back into the mattress.

"You're cold."

"Then keep me warm, wife."

He wrapped his arms around her, rubbing her back until she fell into another semidoze.

When she awoke, it was to a strange sensation—a light tickle on her arm. She dealt with it by rolling away onto her back, but then it returned across her shoulder. Whatever it was stopped as she swept her hand across.

Then it returned across her chest and now, alarmingly, in the valley between her breasts.

Frey's eyes opened wide to see Sebastian watching her with a sensuous half-sleepy grin that warmed her from the inside whenever it was thrown in her direction.

She looked down to where the sensation continued and, from beneath the neck of her nightshift, Sebastian's hand emerged trailing a finely made gold chain, from the links of which hung beautifully wrought garnet beads encased in strips of gold. She sat up and Sebastian raised the necklace to let it dangle in front of her eyes. Frey could see the red wink of the stone as slivers of morning sunlight leaked between the wooden window shutters.

She reached out to touch the object. It was a singularly beautiful piece, something a fine lady at court might wear.

"Happy New Year, Frey."

Frey swallowed.

"You spoil me, husband."

"You deserve it and more. Come, lean forward. Let me see you wear it."

Frey did as he asked and she found the weight of the necklace and beads resting against her chest.

Sebastian sat back and admired his gift before focusing on her with equal regard.

"We've been wed two months; do you have any regrets?"

It was on the tip of her tongue to answer they made vows before God and man, so it was too late to express regret, when she caught something in his expression, something so fleeting that had she not been looking, she might have missed it.

Frey caught herself more and more recently noticing things about her husband, subtleties of expression that made themselves known through a slight movement of his jaw, a twitch of an eyebrow, the curl of a lip revealing his mood a split second before he spoke or acted.

She suspected only Gaines knew his moods as well as she.

His expression now told her the question was not made lightly or to tease. She tried some words in her mind and discarded them. In their absence, she stroked his cheek, dark with morning stubble.

"No regrets, Sebastian, never any regrets."

Frey hesitated and Sebastian raised his eyebrows, inviting further explanation.

She owed it to him, that and much more.

She had promised no more secrets and, since arriving at Tyrswick Keep, kept her word. Yet just a short while ago, she forced herself to acknowledge there was one secret she kept from him. One she'd only just become aware of keeping.

Frey drew a deep breath and looked directly into his soft green eyes, which were now filled with curiosity and speculation.

"I didn't think that I could," she started. "I mean, I didn't know whether I was capable of…"

Frey shook her head and started again.

"Would it be inconvenient to declare I have fallen in love with you?"

Sebastian's eyes widened and his nostrils flared with surprise. He took his hands in hers and held them firmly before bringing one, then the other, to his lips to kiss.

"Love never arrives when it is convenient, but when it does, it is always welcome."

* * *

Sebastian persuaded her back into his bed for a while, but when her maid knocked on the door to attend her, Frey insisted that he bathe as well as shave, something he never did in the mornings. She also presented him with her New Year's gift, a soft lamb's wool tunic made from Tyrswick's own wool and knitted by Frey herself.

Frey left him to bathe, and he used the time to consider her words of love to him.

He suspected, well, hoped, that his wife returned his love, and to hear it confirmed with her own lips, of her own volition, was worth more to him than the gifts they exchanged.

He was surprised how much he needed to hear them spoken. Now Sebastian felt the world was on balance, truly righted for the first time, and he was sure that he was on a firm foundation.

On her return to their chambers, Frey was dressed in a mulberry-red kirtle with cream fitted undersleeves and wearing his necklace. It looked magnificent on her.

"You are the most beautiful woman I have ever seen Frey, but aren't you dressed too formally for breaking fast in the hall?"

All she would offer in reply was a secretive smile and a promise that all would be revealed.

As he took in her form and desire filled him, Sebastian made a vow to hold his wife to that.

The lord and lady of the Keep were decidedly late arising this morn and when they did descend to the Great Hall, Sebastian slowed his stride, surprised to see his men-at-arms dressed in livery.

As though they were at a state occasion, the men escorted the baron and baroness of Tyrswick to the high table. As Sebastian looked about, the servants were all formally standing to attention by rank, and he wondered if they had been surprised in the night by the arrival of the king himself.

Sebastian turned to Frey and nodded at the assembly.

"Would you care to explain this?"

Frey offered him an enigmatic smile. He was intrigued. He suspected she had been up to something for days. Little clues were there for the reading—the greater industry of the man and maidservants, Frey ending her day exhausted. Even Rhys commented that his men were grumbling because they had been put to work in the service of Tyrswick.

Sebastian saw her nod to Beyard, Tyrswick's one-armed steward, who sent a boy from the room. The youngster quickly returned ahead of a great silver bowl being borne by one of the large men from the kitchen and watched as he placed it at a table below. The steward waited for the boy to pour a cup and, with his good arm, Beyard handed the cup to his lord.

Frey whispered in Sebastian's ear, "*Waes hael*. Good health. It's a very old Saxon custom to welcome the New Year."

Sebastian nodded his understanding and stood, raising his goblet high.

"*Waes hael!*"

At once, a loud cheer went up with responding calls of *waes hael!* before the sounds of a carol broke out.

> *Here we come a-wassailing*
> *Among the leaves so green,*
> *Here we come a-wassailing,*
> *So fair to be seen:*
> *Love and joy come to you,*
> *And to you your wassail too,*
> *And God bless you and send you,*
> *A happy New Year,*
> *And God send you,*
> *A happy New Year.*

Sebastian laughed, delighted by the entertainment. Beneath the table he squeezed Frey's hand.

"Thank you, my love, for the finest beginning of a new year Tyrswick has ever seen," he said.

Frey shook her head and squeezed his hand back before releasing it to stand.

"I have another gift for you," she told him. "Something the housemaids and I have been working on for two months, but you will not see the effect of it unless you come down here."

Sebastian glanced across the hall into the sea of faces. Each expression told him they knew something he did not.

He wasn't sure about how he felt about being unaware of something going on under his very nose. Surprises sat ill with him, yet another quick look back at Frey and the look of excited expectation on her face satisfied him that it was motivated by good. At her beckoning, Sebastian stood and followed his wife from the platform onto the floor to stand several feet back from the fireplace, the remains of the Yule log still burning brightly.

"Would you like to give me a clue?"

Frey shook her head and the gathering laughed, clearly enjoying this little bit of theater between master and mistress.

Frey directed Robert and another squire to take hold of the lengths of cord twenty feet in length that dropped on either side of the fireplace.

In a loud voice designed to carry across the Hall, Frey spoke, "My lord, I would direct your attention to the breast above this fireplace."

Sebastian duly looked up to see a rod about fifteen feet above the mantel around which was draped what was obviously a tapestry.

At the count of three, the squires tugged the cords and a massive ten-foot-wide, twelve-foot-long wall hanging unfurled, its bottom edge fluttering before settling. Across the chimney breast was a tapestry of the likes he had only seen in great houses of Normandy. A border of sky blue and gold interlocked squares, the old cipher of Tyrswick, framed the new red lion rampant on a background of blue and white stripes.

When it descended, Sebastian was glad the occupants of the hall gasped then erupted in cheers; it masked his own surprise. He turned and hugged Frey to him. Over the din he heard her say, "I love you my husband."

His heart ached, filled to bursting with the love and admiration he felt for his wife. He drank in her beaming features like a thirsty man and wondered how quickly he might empty the hall and make good the tempting thought of laying his wife across the high table and making love to her.

He refrained. This was her moment. This Christmas season was the first real test of the baroness of Tyrswick, and, judging by the sea of happy faces in front of him, she acquitted herself well.

Larcwide had caught his eye when he entered the hall and gave him a nod that said all he needed to know. Frey may have surprised him with the magnificent tapestry, but he still had one more gift to surprise her with.

He raised a hand that asked for silence.

"I'm not a man for making grand speeches, so I'll make this one short."

That in itself was enough to elicit a cheer. Sebastian grinned along with the jest and continued.

"This tapestry is more than impressive ornamentation, although a finer example could not be found even in White Palace itself. It shows that when Tyrswick is unified, it will never be defeated!"

A roar of ascent filled the Great Hall, and the New Year feasting began. Sebastian turned to Frey.

"You think yourself clever, my wife, to organize the women into keeping my gift under wraps, but I wish to show you are not the only person in this Keep who can hold a secret."

Sebastian beckoned Larcwide. The man-at-arms placed on the table before them a magnificently tooled leather quiver filled with arrows fashioned from the finest yew, but it was the bow that captured Frey's attention.

It was a hickory longbow, smaller than the one Sebastian's men used, but perfectly proportioned for its intended owner.

He saw the moment when the realization dawned on her. Her head swiftly turned and the vivid blue eyes that warmed him like a bright summer's day were wide.

Her hand went to the gold and garnet necklace. "My lord, you have already given me your gift."

"Is there a law that says a man may not present his wife with two?"

She shook her head slowly and ran her hand over the bow longingly.

"It has been months since I've held a bow…perhaps I have lost the art?" she breathed.

"I shouldn't think so, but there is only one way to be certain," he answered. "Because it is the pride of Tyrswick that the baron's wife is a skilled archer, and you can show me your prowess when we hunt in the spring."

On that sunlit afternoon while the Keep enjoyed the crisp air and the brisk activity of snowball fights in friendly competition between the houses of Tyrswick and Goscote, Frey put her new gift to use and was thrilled to find she had not lost her eye or her aim.

CHAPTER THIRTY-TWO

Frey wrapped her red cloak around her more securely against the blast of frigid air and buried her nose deeper into the cowl. It was black out, so dark it seemed to make little difference whether she had her eyes open or closed.

The wind picked up strength, making it difficult going, yet something compelled her to continue. A small pinprick of light, little more than a candle in strength, came into view. The light danced and leaped as though entertained by the wind whose task was to snuff out the little flame.

Although it was so small and some yards distant, Frey could feel the flame's warmth, so she pressed on despite the wind. Soon the light gave shape to the landscape around it. The little yellow glow underlit the bough of a spreading yew and, sitting next to the candle, a person with head bowed.

"Hello there!" Frey called.

Diera! Frey recognized her from the moment she raised her head and the candle caught the golden yellow strands.

As Frey approached, the warmth increased and she released the painfully tight hold on her cloak. Even the wind that howled around about her in protest seemed muted here.

"Darkness is coming," said Diera, so softly Frey strained to hear.

Frey frowned and looked about her.

"It's dark now."

"It's not dark now. It will be soon. Darkness is very near."

A flash of lightning illuminated the meadow and Frey swiftly turned. There was something else out there! She lost sight of her quarry the moment the angry crack of thunder split overhead. The candle spluttered and guttered in its earthenware holder, determined to shine against the forces opposing it.

Frey backed slowly toward the yew and peered out over the darkness. The restless murmuring of thunder much farther away filled the night air. She stopped when her feet nudged something firm. Frey turned. Diera lay on her back, one hand resting over the other, the whiteness of her skin stark against the deep blue of the gown she wore.

Frey bent down to see if Diera slept, and, as she reached out to touch her friend, the girl's lids opened, and a pinprick of fear edged its way up Frey's spine. Instead of Diera's familiar brown eyes, the sockets were empty red and tears of blood ran down her cheeks.

"The darkness is here!"

Diera screamed and the blood-curdling sound hit Frey in the chest with the force of a blow. It was then she became aware of someone standing behind her. Frey rose and spun around just as another flash of lightning rent the sky.

A figure stood just three feet away. It seemed to absorb light itself; not even the flash of the lightning or the glow of the candle could give it form.

It took a step forward, then a second, reaching out a hand before Frey heard another scream.

Her own.

Frey awoke with a start to hear the end of a roll of thunder from the series of storms that marked the start of spring. Rain lashed the wooden shutters and wind gusted through the narrow gap between them in a high-pitched whistle. The wind eddied around the room, rustling the drapes surrounding the bed. Then the whistling was choked off by a loud bang that sounded closer than the thunder.

Now she was wide awake and her heart beat loudly. She reached across for the familiar warmth and strength of her husband but found the bed empty.

"Sebastian?"

The lack of response brought to the fore the tendrils of fear that lingered from her dream.

The darkness is here!

Suddenly the comforting cocoon of the bed became stifling and its darkness oppressive.

Frey clawed open the curtains. The low-banked fire was the only light in the room. A silhouetted figure sat by the now-open window, and, for a horrible second, it was the formless figure from her dream.

"Sebastian?"

The figure shifted.

"It's still night, princess. Go back to sleep."

The endearment, once issued with sarcasm that would rankle her, was now part of the language that was theirs alone.

She ignored Sebastian's admonishment and slipped out of bed. A jagged streak of lightning lit the night sky through the window, and Frey paused, waiting for the crash of thunder so close even the solid stone that made up Tyrswick Keep seemed to shake with it.

When the rumble ended, Frey's hand was enveloped in one of Sebastian's. He gave it a quick tug, and she found herself cradled in his lap. Frey rested her head against his chest and took comfort in the steady beat of his heart at her ear.

"Storm wake you?"

She shook her head.

"Bad dream?"

Frey nodded and nuzzled farther into his embrace.

He made no further inquiries; instead trailed a hand up and down her arm. She stayed like this for long minutes, warm and comfortable before she spoke.

"Do you still dream of Diera?"

He shrugged.

"Not for many months. When you came to the chapel those months ago, I was saying good-bye."

Frey thought on that for a long while.

"She still comes to me in dreams," she said.

"What does she say?"

"She says darkness is coming."

Sebastian's embrace became warm and solid.

"I haven't forgotten her. She needs justice. All those poor young women do."

Frey looked up and met Sebastian's eyes. Even in this half-light she could see the weight of responsibility lay on his shoulders. She ran her hands along them. Such broad shoulders—strong, fair, and just. There was no second-guessing his motives. There was no doubt he would bring Diera's murderer to justice if it was at all possible.

She laid a kiss where he was most vulnerable, the place where she could see the pulse in his neck beat strong and steady. Her kisses grew bolder, lavishing his neck with open-mouthed adoration. Without hurry, she reached his mouth and savored its warmth as he welcomed her exploration.

"Come to bed," she said, giving him a tug on the wrist when she stood. He followed and they settled into bed.

Sebastian seemed to sense the different mood in her tonight. Rather than dominating this time, he lay passively on his back, an arm flung over his head, watching her with a guarded scrutiny, but he didn't resist or object when she straddled him.

"I have you where I want you," she said huskily, running her fingers lightly down his bare chest, where nut-brown nipples tautened.

The dreams about Diera haunted her more than she would be willing to admit to herself, let alone to Sebastian. Her friend should be alive.

Frey was consumed by a hunger that didn't quite seem hers. It was as though Diera lingered at the edge of her consciousness, demanding through her to feel alive, to feel the potent physical and emotional force of their coupling.

One of Sebastian's hands trailed lazily through her hair.

She leaned forward, her fingers and lips moving farther down his torso, along skin that prickled and rose up in lines of gooseflesh where her fingernails lightly scraped. As she moved down, her breasts skimmed his chest, adding to her own pleasure.

She was someone else for a moment, someone who would not second-guess her choices, her decisions, and weigh them up against the demands of others. Here, she could demand and take. The thought was heady.

* * *

Whether he slept for the remainder of the night or merely dozed, Sebastian couldn't tell. He was conscious of the warmth of Frey beside him as she slept, sated from their lovemaking a few hours before.

He was honest when he told his wife he no longer dreamed of Diera, but the nightmares had returned. And now the savaged body laid out on the altar was not Diera's, but Frey's.

That was bad enough. Occasionally, however, he confronted the killer—sometimes just before, sometimes just after the deed. But every time, he was too late to prevent her death, and every time it gutted him as though his heart had been ripped from his chest.

But dreams were just dreams. Simply disjointed workings of the mind.

Sebastian shifted and watched Frey sleep peacefully beside him. He lingered over her figure, composed of fine-boned limbs on which delicate feminine muscles sat honed by practice at the archery butt. He followed the swell of her breasts, the flare of her hips to where they disappeared under the blankets that covered them both.

He thought her revelation three months ago that she loved him would alter things, but they hadn't. He suspected the change in her feelings for him happened the night of the Hallowmass revels when she encountered Drefan.

Drefan. The fact the mole had gone to ground over the winter frustrated him.

Sebastian was a man who preferred immediate, clear-cut engagement. On the battlefield or over a game board, his skills were formidable. His word was his word. He had no patience for political machinations in which alliances shifted under his feet like sand. That was why he was happy to stay the hell away from London and York, even Durham.

Drefan was elusive and his motives unclear. The fact he involved Heloise was disturbing.

Well, thank God the Goscote party was now on its way back home to Leicestershire, and the next time he'd see them, Heloise would have a husband of her own.

Sebastian rolled onto his back and closed his eyes, allowing the sound of the driving rain to focus him into a meditative state.

He put the issue of Drefan aside and considered the other great issue he faced: the Beast of the North.

It was spring, which meant, if Dominic was right, the band of travelers would be on the move soon and another young woman's life was at risk. Many itinerant workers trod the same roads year after year, and villagers planned their season by the workers' arrival. If his and the friar's estimation was true, it would mean these men would be on their way to Tyrswick lands.

Sebastian would be ready.

CHAPTER THIRTY-THREE

Torrential spring rain, along with the snowmelt, turned the most unassuming streams into raging torrents, gouging the landscape and threatening to flood some of the small, low-lying communities around Tyrswick.

The inclement weather had gone on for weeks, and this day was the first fine one in some time.

The Keep was a hive of activity. Tempers that had begun unraveling at confinement indoors were now soothed with a flurry of doings. Almost every inch of sunlit space was filled with freshly washed linens, workers inspected and planned repairs to weatherworn roofs, children ran about.

Frey was delighted when Sebastian agreed for her to accompany his patrol of the villages around Tyrswick, a journey that would take four days, but perhaps longer, conditional upon the damage done by the winter ice and the spring thaws.

Depending on the need found, the baron would allocate resources for building and repairs to help ensure the lands returned to being as productive as possible, as quickly as possible.

Frey learned that, in years past, Beyard would have accompanied Sebastian, but as mistress of Tyrswick, the people were as much her responsibility as her husband's. Besides, from the vantage point on her horse in the courtyard, it looked like Beyard would be occupied for quite some time.

She grinned as she watched the one-armed steward intervene in an escalating dispute between one of the senior housekeepers and a lad who had been thoughtless enough to start a bonfire of soiled floor rushes too close to her freshly washed linens. Beyard was thrusting himself between them as the woman attempted to take a broom to the boy, despite his being twice her size.

The harsh scrape of metal on metal as the external gate opened drew Frey's attention back to the patrol, which numbered twelve. Seven, including herself, would be the forward party, and the five following would drive and guard their wagon, heavily stocked with tools and food not only to see to their needs, but also to provide immediate surcease for stricken villagers.

"Ready to ride?"

Sebastian flashed her a grin to set her pulse racing. He looked magnificent on Ebon, and his glossy black hair lifted lightly in the breeze that pushed fluffy white clouds across a vivid blue sky. Dressed in his livery, he was every inch the rightful lord of Tyrswick.

The thought gave her pause. It was a year since her father had been slain in battle, quite possibly killed by the man who was now her husband, a man who she had long been taught was her enemy.

Familiar prejudices withered in the light of the truth. Her father was killed by stubbornness, his inability to accept war with the Normans was over and they were all Englishmen now.

She said a silent prayer for her father, hoping he might have found the peace in the next life that he never found in this one, as she urged her horse into a trot to catch up with Sebastian. He'd stopped on the other side of the drawbridge. As she crossed, she looked down to see the first of the Keep's defenses, a deep ditch filled with water.

"I didn't think we had that much rain," she said.

"We haven't," he answered. "Let me show you something."

They broke away from the main party and rode several hundred yards to where the boundary of the Keep met Tyrswick River.

A structure like a low stone gate stood parallel to the river and straddled the channel that skirted the walls of the Keep. Instead of a door, a series of heavy wooden planks strapped with iron were suspended over the water.

"It's a sluice gate," he said. He pointed downstream to where the river flowed by the village. "We couldn't risk the wheel on the mill being damaged by floodwater, so we had the gate built at the same time," Sebastian explained. "When the river rises above a certain level, we raise the gate to divert water. Not only does it protect the mill and the village, but it also gives the Keep another defense.

"Let's head down into the village to see if the gate did the job."

Thanks to Sebastian's forethought, Tyrswick village had weathered the rains well. The mill was in perfect order and would be ready to start grinding the grain immediately. That meant fresh bread. Large quantities would be required to feed the starving if there had been significant damage done to other areas.

During the course of the day, they visited a number of villages downstream of Tyrswick and, fortunately, they too seemed no worse for wear.

"Nothing a few days of sunshine won't cure" was the oft-repeated assessment.

The muddy roads made the journey slow going, and, at several stops, additional horses and more manpower were required to dislodge the cart from mud nearly a foot deep. Frey was exhausted, but she'd sooner rip out her own tongue than voice a complaint.

Their journey ended farther down the valley when they entered the village where they would spend the night.

On the rise overlooking the hamlet, they could see paths between the cottages turned to black mud, planks providing the only stable crossing over them. One of the cottages had been unroofed in the wild weather and, as the late-afternoon sun disappeared, men scrambled across joists and down ladders, abandoning repairs for the day. The village hall, the largest structure in the settlement, was a thatched wooden building that would be headquarters for the Tyrswick party.

There, they were greeted by a white-haired man in his sixties who introduced himself as the village beadle. "You honor us with your presence, my lord," he greeted.

"How do you fare here?" responded Sebastian as he ducked his head to avoid the low lintel on entering the hall.

The space was already crowded. One corner served as a dormitory for the dispossessed. Children lay dark-eyed and exhausted, listlessly watching the activity of the adults.

"We had flooding through the village five nights ago and two of the crofters' cottages have been swept away," the beadle explained.

"Everyone is accounted for apart from a shepherd and his boy. They went out three nights ago to round up their sheep and they've not been seen since."

Sebastian considered the logistics and manpower he brought with him.

"There's no more we can do tonight. We'll search at first light."

The beadle shifted on his feet uncomfortably before addressing his newfound distress as host.

"My lord, I didn't know you intended to bring your lady with you. You have the use of my cottage, but it's hardly worthy enough for the baroness."

"You'll find I'm accustomed to sleeping in barrack conditions, Beadle," Frey answered.

The beadle looked at her askance and turned to the baron for conformation.

"I'm sure all the arrangements will suit us well, and we thank you and your village for the welcome. We promise not to be a drain on your resources."

The latter part of Sebastian's speech cheered the beadle immensely.

"Oh, one more thing," said Sebastian, "have you word of itinerants about?"

"Not here, my lord. No one from the south would have been able to cross Tyrswick River. It's flooded bad. One of the lads told me it's a hundred yards wide in some places."

The story was confirmed by Friar Dominic later at supper.

"The river has gone down some but it's still going to be several days before anyone is going to be venturing this far north," he said around a mouthful of stew.

Sebastian reached across to refill his tankard from one of the dozen kegs stacked against the back wall.

Out of the corner of his eye, he watched Frey in conversation with some of the village women. She seemed unaware of the gravity of the discussions before him.

Good.

Sebastian sipped from the cup, thoughtful for a moment.

"Then the road to Alnwick is passable, and there is a roundabout way to Durham. They may elude us still."

Gaines pushed his empty trencher away.

"I don't like this. We're chasing ghosts," he announced. "Four mysterious men come to a village—they may not even be the same four men, mind, and sometime after they leave, a girl goes missing and shows up dead. Who accuses them?" He glared at Dominic. "You?"

Dominic refused to be baited.

"I accuse no one," he shrugged. "I propose we ask and we observe."

Dominic rose from his seat, leaving an empty bowl at the table, and addressed the two men as he left.

"'For now we see through a glass, darkly; but then face to face: now I know in part; but then shall I know even as also I am known.'"

"Phantoms," Gaines grumbled. He watched the friar touch the baroness on the back and offer greetings before moving farther into the crowd.

"I say we increase the number of our longer patrols in the areas where the Beast has struck. He may come back and he'll feel the weight of justice around his neck before he can take another life. Besides," Gaines lowered his voice, "a man and a boy are missing. They could just as easily be victims of the Beast. You don't buy into the friar's nonsense do you?"

Sebastian looked at his man-at-arms cautiously. They had been through a lot together, and he always relied on Gaines to keep him grounded, but something about Dominic's logic was compelling.

Torn between two trusted advisors, he considered the merits of the arguments of both men and came to his decision.

"Increasing the number of long patrols weakens security around Tyrswick. And we have worked hard to assure the Saxons we're not brute-heeled murderers drunk on power," he said, "so let's use that. The goodwill of the villagers is the best defense we have. If by issuing a warning we make the people more vigilant, then so much the better.

"As for the man and his boy, if they have succumbed to anything it will be the wet and cold. The Beast chooses victims who are weaker, more vulnerable.

"We're here and Eanfirth is only half a day's ride once the river is passable."

Gaines slumped in defeat. Sebastian smiled to himself. He knew his reasoning was impeccable, and Gaines would just have to leave his doubts at the door.

* * *

"You wished to speak to me, my dear?"

Frey licked her lips nervously. She liked Friar Dominic, yet he always looked at as if he knew her thoughts.

Did God tell him?

All of a sudden the question she wanted to ask him fled, so she asked another.

"Does God talk to people in dreams?"

She found Dominic smiling patiently with a twinkle in his eye as though he knew that was not the question she wanted to ask.

"He spoke to Jacob in a dream and to Joseph, the one with the many-hued coat, and the one who escaped Herod with Mary and the infant Jesus. There's no reason to think he wouldn't still talk to people through dreams."

Frey screwed up her courage but found she could not make herself look at Dominic directly.

"I think he's speaking to me about the Beast of the North."

She waited for a laugh, any sign of derision. At silence, she looked up to see him considering her thoughtfully.

"Let's take a walk outside, my lady, away from where we might be overheard."

The sun had set, leaving only a gray half light. Frey and the friar walked away from the long house and a few cottages to sit on the edge of a stone-ringed well.

"I keep having these dreams. I think I see him but it's not clear," she began. And, once she began, the words tumbled over one another as though eager to escape the confines of her mind.

She told him how Diera would appear to her in the dreams, sometimes whole as she saw her last, other times brutally mutilated, but always frightened of the mysterious figure in green. She would feel safe under the broad and welcoming arms of the yew tree while the weather would rage about her as though angry with the disorder in this world. Then the figure in green would disappear in a puff of smoke despite being shot directly with an arrow.

Dominic's response was not what she expected.

"Do you believe in evil, Alfreya?"

CHAPTER THIRTY-FOUR

The roar of Tyrswick River in full flood drowned out any possible conversation between those standing farther than three feet away from one another.

"We'll follow downstream for one more mile 'til we reach the tributary before we double back," Sebastian yelled before trudging on.

Progress was slow going, but the search party slogged on, determined to find the shepherd and his son before the unfortunates spent a fourth night out in the elements.

Frey had persuaded Sebastian to allow the shepherd's wife to join them, despite his misgivings. The last thing the woman needed to see was the dead and bloated body of her husband or child trapped, half submerged under a log.

But even he had to admit someone who knew where the shepherd may have taken the sheep would help narrow down the search.

He watched Frey walking alongside the village woman, trudging step after laborious step through the sticky silt that spread across the meadowlands where sheep would usually graze.

Cunning woman, Frey. Insisting that the shepherd's wife join the search party ensured *she* would not be left behind, though Sebastian had been sorely tempted to do just that. He didn't adjust his stride for the women, however, and kept up a determined pace for the past five miles. Even some of his men, including Gaines, could only keep the rate going for another hour.

The local woman wore a satchel with dry clothes for her husband and boy and was no doubt familiar with this area. She was wide of girth and took strides to match, grimly plodding on without complaint.

Frey wore her bow and quiver. Her only concession to the conditions was a walking staff, which would, if needed, also serve as a stretcher pole.

He watched her brush a sweat-soaked strand of hair from her eyes and raise them to his as if daring him to make comment.

He smiled. Even dressed in rough tunic and hose, and muddy up to her knees, she was beautiful, and his heart was filled with a proprietorial pride.

Their journey took them up an incline where granite rocks forced the river through a narrow fracture. The ground here was dry, and the elevation provided opportunity to look out over the valley and farther downstream.

Sebastian walked past several men who had stopped to light a small fire and prepare their noon meal. On the lea side of the hill, a flock of sheep stood grazing and, from what Sebastian could see, several of the ewes were lambing.

"Robert! Fetch Mistress Eames."

Moving with surprising speed for someone of her build, the woman was soon at Sebastian's shoulder with Frey not far behind.

"Are these yours?"

The woman peered down the grassed slope before letting out an ear-splitting series of short whistles. Sebastian winced.

Soon one ovine head lifted. The bellwether bleated, separating himself from the herd to start up the rise.

"Aye, they be ours," the woman confirmed.

Soon, the rest of the sheep were on the move, with newborn lambs following their mothers.

"If ye be seein' to 'bout husband and bairn, I'll see to takin' this lot back t'village."

"Will you not stay for the search?" asked Frey with surprise.

Mistress Eames shrugged. "There be no point findin' 'im if he ain't nothin' to come back to."

Her logic was irrefutable.

* * *

Following the repast and the departure of the shepherd's wife, along with a Tyrswick knight as escort, Sebastian settled next to Frey on one of the small boulders littering the top of the hill and scraped the worst of the mud from his boots.

"You should have gone back with her," he said.

It earned him a sour look.

"Don't you treat me like a soft-born flower, Baron," she retorted. "I can keep going as long as you can."

She softened her harsh words with a slow, seductive smile.

"Besides, where else would I rather be than beside my husband?"

Her words were having an effect on him.

Temptress.

If she wanted to play, then he would be honor-bound to join her.

"I seem to recall you have a fondness for outdoor sport, princess," he drawled. "Now the weather is warming, we should see how long you can keep going."

A flare of her nostrils and the widening of her bright blue eyes told him his aim was true.

He leaned in closer, so close he could feel her body heat.

"There's a stream just beyond Tyrswick walls and a waterfall that is shaded and cool in summer. It's secluded. I can't wait to introduce you to how good it feels to swim in bare skin. Think about it, princess."

Frey's breath hitched and she licked her lips.

"Then summer cannot come too swiftly, my lord."

The sun had moved to its mid-afternoon position, and the search party turned to the north to check upstream of a tributary that normally ran slow and clear but which the melting snow and rains had transformed into a roiling, dun-colored maelstrom.

"It's usually easy to cross here," yelled one of the local men. "Most times the water is only knee-deep and only as wide as a man."

Sebastian could see nearly twice as much water churned through.

"Eames won't have gone too far from his flock," said Sebastian. "What might bring the man up here?"

"There's an old hunter's hut somewhere around here. If the storm got too bad, he might have decided to take the boy there," he man answered.

"Do you know where it is?"

"Aye." The man pressed forward to take the lead.

* * *

Frey put one foot in front of the other, her calves and thighs protesting their labor, and followed the rest of the party. Sebastian and Gaines took the lead with the villager. Two other knights walked ahead of her and another soldier followed behind.

She adjusted the weight of her quiver across her back and pushed herself forward, looking down to avoid exposed tree roots, felled branches, and other debris that made the walk treacherous.

Her clothes were damp and cold. Mud coated her hose to the knees. By the chalky sensation on her skin, a smear even streaked her cheek.

She was content to remain in her own thoughts. Her conversation with Friar Dominic weighed heavily on her.

She knew the evil that men did for power, glory, or gold, the sins identifiable and their motivation plan, but the concept of evil as an entity? It seemed to beggar belief.

God she could believe in readily, although in her experience he was as stubborn as she was and with a stranger sense of humor.

But the idea of an intangible evil? Surely such was make-believe, like the stories of fairies and hobgoblins told to make children behave. And yet when Dominic told her the hand of evil was at work, there was a quickening in her spirit as though somewhere deep in her being she knew the words he spoke were true.

"You're telling me the man, this…creature, who killed Diera is close?" she had asked him before their departure.

"Closer than we all realize," Dominic confirmed.

255

"Then why does Sebastian not go out after him?" she demanded with passion. "He could find him and send him to the hell he deserves!"

"Because evil does not always wear the same face."

Dominic paused, waiting for her to compose herself.

"I've prayed much and contemplated on this, Alfreya. I wanted to talk to you because I believe Sebastian is the one who can stare evil in the face and win. Not simply because he is baron of Tyrswick and the law of these lands, but because he has been chosen to do so. The devil and his minions know this and they will try to stop him."

Frey stepped back, his words frightening her.

"You think I'm a mad man, 'but God has chosen the foolish things to confound the wise.'"

She shook her head slowly with each step away.

"Examine your heart and you'll know I'm right. Pray for him, my dear, that's all I ask you to do."

But Frey couldn't just leave it to prayer. Her insistence in joining this search party was not borne of stubborn bravado, but for a very real fear for Sebastian's safety.

At the sound of yells from the front of the group, Frey looked up and then across the churning water to the welcome sight of a man and his boy, wet, bedraggled, and clearly feeling the effects of exposure.

The child, aged about eight, was thrilled to see the search party and took several weary steps toward the water. "Stay there!" Sebastian yelled, waving his arms. "Stay there! Tell him to get back."

At last the shepherd understood the instructions and laid a firm hand on the boy's shoulder to prevent him moving forward.

Excitement and relief overcame fatigue. Frey found the energy to jog to where Sebastian huddled with Gaines, Robert, and his other men.

"…I doubt even the shepherd could make it across unaided, and with the boy not at all," she overheard Gaines speak.

"Agreed," responded Sebastian. "Nothing we've seen for the past three miles is remotely suitable for crossing. How much rope and line do we have with us?"

Frey moved in closer to stand at Sebastian's shoulder. Despite the damp and sweat, he was warm.

Feeling her beside him, Sebastian gave her an odd look before returning his attention to Robert.

"We have four lengths about four yards long, my lord, and two of twine," answered Robert.

"The trees on the other side look as though they may hold. If we can get a rope across, they could use it as a handhold," suggested Gaines.

"If the shepherd tied himself and his son to the rope, we could haul them across," added Robert.

Sebastian glanced at the swollen water course. "Either way, it's a plan."

The huddle broke up and Sebastian yelled across the rushing water. Eventually the message was understood and the shepherd put a little distance between himself and the straight, wide tree trunk, gathering the lad to his side.

Sebastian lined up his mark, making adjustments to compensate for the expected drag of the trailing twine knotted ahead of the fletching, waiting for word the twine was securely tied to one of their lengths of rope.

Frey remained in the background, wishing to be of assistance but determined not to be a distraction. She hugged to her chest the bag of dry clothing Mistress Eames had left with her.

She glanced up to the treetops, where the wind that cleared the skies made it difficult to get a clear shot. Although she had faith in Sebastian's abilities, she knew the attempt was not without risk. The arrow falling short of the tree was the least worst of the possible outcomes.

Sebastian stepped sideways to compensate and, as Frey watched him take a deep breath, she breathed with him and prayed.

The arrow was launched.

Out of the corner of her eye, Frey saw the length of coiled rope jerk and raise its head like an awakened snake.

A cheer followed a split second after.

Frey jerked out of her reverie to see the shepherd already rushing to the arrow. Moments later he was pulling across the twine, then the rope. The man snatched and tied the line around the trunk just below the embedded arrow, then two men behind Frey tensioned their end of the rope around a tree.

The shepherd urged the boy on ahead of him, but the timid lad needed coaxing when the pull of the current threatened to drag him under the line. None-too-steady on his feet either, the man hoisted the lad onto his back and doggedly moved forward, the water reaching his knees, then his waist before he was halfway across.

A crack heard clearly over the roaring water was so loud Frey checked the sky for a storm before she saw the true cause.

"Look out!" she screamed.

CHAPTER THIRTY-FIVE

Upstream, a tree heavy with rain and weakened by rot, wind, and erosion of the riverbank plunged gracelessly into the water, leaves quivering violently as though with fright.

The fear on the shepherd's face as he looked upstream was naked.

He moved as fast as he could along the line. The force of the current and the slippery stones beneath his feet slowed each step as the fallen tree, leadenly tumbling in the hurrying water, came toward him and his child.

Then it struck them. Two heads disappeared beneath the torrent.

No, no, no! Frey chanted to herself. There was nothing to do but watch in horror.

After a heart-stopping second, the shepherd's head emerged. He had managed to hang on to the rescue line as the tree rushed beneath it.

"Papa! Papa!"

The panic-stricken voice of the child faded into the roar of the cascade as, tangled in the branches of the tree, he was swept downstream with ever-increasing speed.

"See to him!" Sebastian commanded, pointing to the father as he sprinted along the riverbank in pursuit of the boy. Without thought, Frey ran after him, but with his superior size and strength, he quickly outpaced her.

When she lost sight of him, she followed the trail he left behind. Sword, bow, quiver, aketon, cloak—anything that would weigh him down.

As Frey rounded the bend, only a couple of hundred yards away from the roiling junction of the tributary and river, she saw that Sebastian had overtaken the fallen tree, but only just.

Before she could catch her breath, Sebastian leaped at the tree.

He made an unsteady landing on the trunk, the action propelling the tree toward the other bank, where overhanging branches impeded its forward progress. The young boy's hysterical screams grew louder as Sebastian edged himself nearer and stretched out his arm.

Fear for her love—this man who was hers, heart, mind, body, and soul—beat a relentless tattoo against Frey's ribs. Over the roar of the rushing water, she could see him speaking words of encouragement to the lad who clung to a limb in a death grip. The child reached out to him and, in a swift movement, Sebastian hauled the boy onto the trunk.

She could see the youngster was badly cut and grazed, and the tree rocked with the movement, threatening to throw them both back into the water.

"Frey!" Sebastian called, his voice even, but his expression tight. "Get a line over here now! It's not going to hold."

Her? But what could she do that he in all his strength could not?

Her hesitation was only fleeting, but it was observed by Gaines, who was the first to catch up with them. Frey could see the expression of disgust that flitted across his face as their eyes met. Gaines hated her, that much was clear, despite the effort she had made to be a good wife to Sebastian and to unite Tyrswick.

She raised her chin. No matter what he thought of her, she was the baroness and, by God, she would use every inch of her authority.

"Rope! Now!"

The man jumped like a startled rabbit and repeated the command to poor Robert, who scrambled on the double.

Frey ignored her shaking hands, shucking off the quiver and bringing her bow into position. Sebastian's position on the log was even more precarious as debris building up behind the tree threatened to push them away from the opposite bank and back into the flow.

Robert handed her an arrow with the rope tied directly to the shaft.

Despite the chill of the late afternoon, beads of sweat ran down her cheeks as she lined up a target, a small clear patch of gray bark not bigger than twelve inches across on an object that bobbed and rocked.

Poorly judge the shot and she'd miss, or worse—hit Sebastian or the boy.

She started at Gaines's sudden breath beside her ear. "Now you have it, Mistress," he intoned softly. "Convenient, would it not be, if the Saxons regained Tyrswick at the hand of the wife of a Norman baron? Let's see how much you really want Tyrswick."

"Get the hell away from me," Frey hissed.

Gaines stepped away and Frey took a deep breath. She spared Sebastian a glance and his expression gave her confidence.

She commanded her hands to steady, took aim again, and released the arrow. Weighted by the rope, it fell short, but close enough for Sebastian to lean down and grab before it was swept away.

He snapped away the arrow and, with swift, practiced movements, he tied the rope to himself, then lashed the child to his chest, thrusting off as the log finally dislodged and tumbled wildly away.

The rope tensioned and the force of the flowing water pushed Sebastian and the lad below the surface.

With muscles straining and teeth gritting, Robert, Gaines, Eames, and two other knights heaved on the line, struggling against the weight of a grown man and a child being dragged farther downstream.

Frey grasped her bow tightly and fixed her eyes on yellow-gray water, watching for her husband and the child to reappear. Long tense seconds passed before an explosive surge broke the surface.

Sebastian gasped for air, as did the boy, who also coughed in body-shaking spasms. Sebastian rolled onto his back, taking the boy on top of him, and kicked powerfully against the current while his men on the bank hauled them ashore.

"Papa!"

The crying boy struggled free of the rope and, weeping tears of fright, rushed into the open arms of his father.

Frey turned from the reunion, ignoring Gaines as he ordered the men to ready for the return journey to the village.

Sebastian stood apart from the bustle, his back to her, resting his forehead on a raised arm, allowing a few wet, choking coughs to escape.

"Art hurt?" she asked softly. She could see his cuts and bruises were minor ones, which he would not count.

He answered with a curt shake of his head, but he did not turn to face her until he had pulled in another lungful of air, which ended in a racking cough.

Frey wondered if he hit his head while underwater. She reached up and ran her fingers through the wet locks, searching for telltale lumps.

He halted her exploration with his free hand around her wrist and hauled her to him, so close she could feel his warm breath on her cheek.

Sebastian didn't embrace her as she longed for him to do.

Here, before the men, he was baron of Tyrswick, a warrior, a leader. Her tender and thorough lover was a part of him that was theirs alone.

Still, the powerful physical communication between them was palpable. She knew he felt it as she did; it flowed between them as it had done when they faced down the wolf pack so many months ago.

The spark of passion was merely an ember then, newly ignited, but these months and their marriage had provided ample fuel so now it burned brightly and threatened to combust into a conflagration.

The look in his eyes told her everything she needed to know of his thoughts. The desire to possess her as soon as possible was etched plain on his face. She knew her willing answer was to be found on hers.

The very thought made heat run through her veins.

She licked her lips and touched his sodden clothing. Sebastian watched her hungrily.

"We need to get you dry," she whispered.

He quirked his lips into a predatory half smile.

"And I was thinking about getting you wet."

* * *

The village celebrated that night, overjoyed by the safe return of the shepherd and his son, not to mention the recovery of the flock.

The story of the baron's heroic rescue, aided by the baroness herself, quickly spread, ensuring he and Frey remained the center of attention well into the evening. He noticed she was uncharacteristically agitated and wondered at the cause.

Sebastian knew Frey's sense of duty matched his, but tonight she had been reluctant to leave his side whereas she would ordinarily mingle with the rest of the gathering. In public, she was always careful to demonstrate the utmost propriety, but as they sat at the high table, her hand found its way into his beneath the tablecloth and held on tight.

Not that he was complaining; he enjoyed having his wife by his side. Her hand parted from his and stroked his thigh.

"You seem particularly eager for attention, princess," Sebastian said quietly, his eyes following the beadle and Gaines making their way toward them from the far end of the room.

"Mmmmm? Did you say something, my lord?" she inquired sweetly.

"Excuse me, Baron?"

Gaines's arrival with the beadle at his shoulder wasn't a welcome one. From the expression on Frey's face, it was to her even less so. Her flirtatious expression fled and a stony mask took its place.

"If I may be excused, my lord," she said, glancing as his man-at-arms. "I find myself in need of fresh air."

Without waiting for leave, she stood, greeting the beadle as she left the table without a second glance.

Sebastian frowned. Something was amiss. He looked at Gaines, who merely gave him a neutral expression.

"We've had news from Eanfirth," the beadle began.

"So the southeast crossing is now passable?" Sebastian asked.

"Aye, but there's more than that…"

Pinpricks of awareness spread across the back of his head. He did not wait for the explanation.

"Another? How long has the girl been missing?"

The beadle blinked, surprised that the need for revelation had been bypassed.

"Since this morn."

Sebastian pushed himself back from the table and stood.

"Gaines, tell Robert and Duncan they are to be ready to leave at dawn with you and me. And inform Larcwide he's to pick a couple of men and escort Lady Alfreya back to Tyrswick. The remaining men can stay here for two days to finalize repairs."

At this, Gaines revealed a small smile of approval.

"Very good, my lord."

"Where's Dominic?"

"I believe the friar is outside," answered the beadle.

"Ask him to join us out at the stables."

The man hurried off on his errand.

Sebastian also made his way to the door. Outside, he addressed Gaines as they made their way to the stables.

"Dominic will ride with us."

"Why?" Gaines asked. "It's not going to take four men and a priest to deal with one mad dog."

"No one has known more about the Beast of the North than Dominic; he's been on his trail for months. The Beast has eluded discovery so far, but this ends now and before another young woman loses her life."

"The Beast?" Gaines stopped in his tracks, his voice rising angrily. "We don't even know it is the Beast!"

Sebastian glared at him. Gaines's voice softened, though only, it seemed, in deference to being overheard. "All we have is Friar Dominic's suspicion that four itinerants at Eanfirth are the same ones from the past year."

"He's a man of God."

Gaines gave Sebastian as close to a look of contempt that he would ever dare give.

"Do you think God gives him their names? Perhaps the good friar should ask God a few questions about why he turned a blind eye to the slaughter of innocent girls."

Before Sebastian could respond, Gaines's voice dropped to a conspiratorial whisper.

"Did you ever stop to think how he knows so much?"

Sebastian was aghast. In the ten years they soldiered together, never before had Gaines spoken such arrant nonsense.

"Where's this coming from, Henry?" Sebastian asked, deliberately addressing his man-at-arms by his Christian name instead of his most oft-used family name.

The man looked sternly back at him.

"I'm just saying that things have not been right ever since last summer when we found the body of that girl you placed in the crypt."

Gaines paused as though contemplating adding more. Sebastian could see his expression change. It seems his man-at-arms did have more to say, and it had obviously been festering for months.

"Sebastian, *you've* changed."

The baron straightened and folded his arms, a gesture he recognized in himself as defensive. He was putting distance between himself and a man he wasn't sure he recognized right now.

Gaines plunged on.

"You and I have known each other for a long time. I *know* you, better than anyone alive. We've covered each other's backs in battle more times than I care to count. You're predictable as sunrise in the morning and sunset in the evening. I could rely on you.

"But ever since you married that woman—"

"My wife," interrupted Sebastian, severely. "Watch how you speak of her."

"And that would be my point. You will hear nothing said against her—"

"Has she been a good mistress of the Keep?" said Sebastian, cutting him off again.

"I've heard no complaints."

"Have you ever witnessed anything to suggest that she is anything less than exemplary in her behavior?"

"No, but that's not the point—"

"That's *exactly* the point! You judge her by prejudice."

"No. I judge her by the company she keeps. Like her former lover who, do I need remind you, promised to raise an army against Tyrswick?"

"Go no further, Henry, for the sake of our friendship as well as your place at Tyrswick."

The threat was like a splash of icy water. Gaines's heated expression immediately cooled to shock, but he kept his mouth closed.

Sebastian lifted his head to draw Gaines's attention to the approach of Friar Dominic.

"I hope you're not going to accuse him to his face of being the Beast of the North," he said. "The friar may be shorter, but I'm certain he could whip both our arses."

CHAPTER THIRTY-SIX

Frey lay wide-eyed and awake long after the rest of the village slumbered. She turned in the unfamiliar bed, sorely wishing for her soft and comfortable one in Tyrswick. She listened to unfamiliar noises in an unfamiliar room and waited for Sebastian to return.

She had seen him step outside with Gaines and wondered what they were meeting about that was taking so long. The hackles that rose at dinner at seeing the man flared again.

How dare he? The personal insult to her integrity was just a minor jab compared with the below-the-belt blow of doing so when Sebastian's life was imperiled.

Did Gaines mean her to miss?

The thought hit with a jolt. The friar reminded her evil could wear many faces; could Gaines be one of them? Who could she trust with her husband's safety if not the man who had sworn allegiance to him?

The sound of squeaking door hinges heralded the return of Sebastian. She could tell his presence by his footsteps. Soon the bed curtains opened and he slipped in behind her and greeted her with languorous kisses along the length of her exposed neck.

Frey offered a sigh of contentment and snuggled back into the warmth of his body. His warm *naked* body.

"You were magnificent today," he told her as his hands slipped up under the hem of her night shift and drew the garment over her head. Rough, callused fingers softly skimmed across her skin, raising delightful gooseflesh.

Her sigh became a hum and she stretched before him, breasts presenting high and ripe to the touch. And he did touch, softly and reverently. "Perhaps I should pledge fealty to you and have you fight by my side," he whispered. But his actions gave lie to the soft words when lips and tongue began a campaign of domination in which he encountered no resistance at all.

* * *

At the sound of an osprey calling overhead, Frey wheeled her mount around and stopped to watch five men venture farther and farther down into the valley. Sebastian was easy to spot on Ebon, the horse's rich black flank glistening in the sunlight.

Beside him, Gaines sat on his horse, and on the other side rode Friar Dominic. She had never seen the friar on a horse before. Behind them, Robert rode alongside Duncan.

"My lady?" Larcwide called. "We need to leave now if we're to make Tyrswick by nightfall."

Reluctantly, she pulled her focus away, sending heavenward a plea and a prayer that Sebastian would remain safe and if Gaines were indeed treacherous, Friar Dominic would know and offer warning.

But every mile that separated her and Sebastian was a chasm filled with regret. Any goodwill forged by their lovemaking in the night withered and died with the morning sun when Sebastian told Frey that she would be going back to Tyrswick without him.

She had watched him dress in the surcoat that bore the Tyrswick coat of arms.

"It's not a suggestion, princess, it's an order."

"I'm armed and I'm with the finest warrior knight in England, what fear have I?"

"Flattery and your own skills notwithstanding, I can't be distracted from my mission by worrying about the well-being of my wife."

She handed him his belt, which he mounted around his hips.

"You need someone to look out for you."

"That's what Gaines is for."

"Gaines? He—"

Frey's argument was silenced with a finger to her lips and a warning look in his eyes.

"It's not negotiable, Frey."

They eyed each other in a battle of wills for several long moments before her eyes slipped from his and she nodded her consent.

"You'll go back to Tyrswick?"

"I'll go back to Tyrswick without complaint on one condition."

"I said no negotiation."

Frey shrugged and gave him her most determined look. He sighed.

"Oh, very well then, what is your condition?"

"You watch your back around Gaines. He's not to be trusted."

Frey could see now the hardening of Sebastian's features.

"I've known Gaines for a very long time, princess. Be very sure before you make accusations of one of my best men." His voice verged on the edge of bitterness. "It's clear you do not like one another, but do not expect me to choose. Neither of you will be satisfied with the outcome."

Frey now swallowed her disappointment and it settled as a nagging ache instead. Suddenly she became aware of Larcwide's scrutiny and turned it back onto him.

He had aged, her faithful man-at-arms and friend. His hair was all gray now, and the creases around his eyes more pronounced.

Knowing he had her attention, Larcwide moved off and she made her horse follow at a slow canter, catching up with him, then settling to a walk.

They rode in silence for some time, Frey lost in her thoughts, when Larcwide finally spoke.

"You need to understand the difference between men and women, Alfreya."

The use of her first name startled her from her reverie, and she considered him cautiously, unsure whether she wanted to hear what he had to say.

"I've been married for nearly six months, my friend, do I need further instruction?"

Larcwide ignored her attempt to deflect him with a jest.

"Men are designed to do one thing at a time and do it well. Women seem to do fifteen different things at once," he began awkwardly. "He needs you to let him go and do the things he needs to. He's not rejecting you; he's not dismissing your skill. Do you understand what I'm talking about, lass?"

The truth of his words resonated with her, so she nodded.

"He loves me."

"Aye, he does."

"Gaines doesn't like me."

"No, he doesn't," Larcwide concurred.

"I don't trust him to keep Sebastian safe."

"Do not doubt the man's loyalty to his lord. I've worked alongside him these past few seasons. I trust him and Sebastian trusts him. He does not have to like you. He just has to be loyal to his liege."

Frey let the matter drop.

The countryside changed as they ascended the valley toward Tyrswick. They passed through copses of trees that had withstood Viking invasions, and past vineyards and orchards planted by the Romans. They skirted small enclosed fields tended by crofters.

There were rumors still in the villages of a fortune in gold and silver that the Romans had left behind, hidden somewhere in the mines burrowed into the hills.

She smiled. If there had been such a treasure, her father never found it and neither had her husband, despite the assurance of one villager that a hermit up there knew of its location and kept it guarded.

Land that had been covered with snow was now blanketed in the soft green of spring grasses. Crocuses added color to the paths along with newly spouted yellow buttercups and the soft purple of the heather.

The hills wore a mantle of a darker hue of green, peppered with silvery-gray granite rocks over which sat a vivid blue sky studded with small white clouds.

Familiarity with this beautiful landscape comforted Frey at an elemental level. This was Tyrswick. This was home.

She paused in her thoughts. This place couldn't be her home now without Sebastian. They could be in the far corners of the Norman Empire, even down to the Mediterranean Sea, where she heard tell of olives and oranges growing all year round.

That would become home if her husband was there.

How much she had changed in a twelvemonth. Only last spring, she stepped across the Scottish border into England for the first time in nearly seven years filled with hate and vengeance in her heart for the bastard usurper of her family's rightful inheritance.

Now she was wed to the very man she swore then was an enemy. All it had taken was the remembrance of an act of kindness for her to see Sebastian for who he really was. What if she lost him now? Her heart would break and never recover. Of that she was certain.

They stopped for a noonday meal and decided to press on to make it back to the Keep before nightfall.

Without a laden wagon to slow their progress, the party of three were making good time through the countryside, even at the leisurely pace they set.

They had passed a few people on the journey—mostly farmers, the occasional swineherd, even a gooseherd who caused them to stop as he shepherded his flock across the track up to the grain trough and pen where they would be safely corralled for the night.

On the crossroads that took travelers either north to Tyrswick village or west toward Cumbria and the Scottish border crossings, a peasant traveler dressed in roughly woven wool stood in the middle of the path waving his arms frantically.

"Sirs! My lady! Thank the good Lord you've come! My wagon has overturned a mile or so that way." The man pointed to his left. "The wife and bairn need help."

"How badly are they hurt?" asked Frey, already turning down the road the man had pointed.

"I fear my good wife has broken a leg, but my little girl won't wake up."

Larcwide hesitated only a moment.

"Talbot, to the village, quick as you can, lad. Get some men here with a litter and send someone to the Keep to tell of our return."

The young knight followed the orders without a second thought and soon disappeared around a bend, leaving Frey and Larcwide with the middle-aged man.

"Quick! Follow me."

The man ran down the lane, then veered off the path into a ditch out of sight of the two riders on horseback.

"Where are you, man?" Larcwide yelled after him.

"Down here!" a disembodied voice called through a thicket of trees.

Frey could hear the whinnying of horses and dismounted, taking with her a rucksack that held some bandages and small jars of ointment.

"I don't know how they came to be down here," she said. "We can't go through on horseback."

Larcwide, too, dismounted and landed heavily. Frey turned to her man-at-arms. His face looked as gray as his whiskers.

"Are you well?"

"Aye, my lady, just my age catching up with me."

At her alarmed look, Larcwide shook his head and nodded toward the trees. "I'll be fine. Let's go see to the people who need help."

Only a few yards through the trees, Frey could see the upturned wagon. It seemed the party had tried to take a short cut through a field. Long, thin brown tracks where the wagon had made its way through the mire were evident.

The anxious father was running the two hundred or so yards to where the overturned wagon lay. Even from Frey's slightly elevated vantage point, she could not see the injured woman or child.

From among the upturned boards of the wagon, she could hear a weak cry. She rushed immediately toward the sound.

"My lady!" She heard Larcwide call but ignored the warning implicit in his voice and outpaced the man.

She ran with the stranger who then halted at the wagon's edge. Frey rounded the corner and saw a figure huddled in a cloak; from the size, it must be the farmer's wife, rather than the child.

Without looking at the man, she placed her hand on the covered shoulder and asked, "Where's your child?"

There was a pause. Frey looked up and glanced at Larcwide, who had caught up with her now but bent in an attempt to catch his breath. She then looked at the peasant.

She asked the question again of him, but there was no reply, just an odd look on his face.

As though sensing something was wrong, Larcwide straightened himself and reached for his sword.

The shape shifted under Frey's hand and moved to sit up, but she ignored it, concerned by the florid hue blooming on Larcwide's face.

"Mistress, move toward me now."

Larcwide's voice was tight.

"What's going on here?" she asked, rising to her feet.

Beside her, the figure in the cloak also rose. Frey turned swiftly as the cowl fell.

Drefan stood before her.

As she took a step back, Drefan gripped her arm tightly.

"Did you ever doubt me, my dear? I've come back for you."

CHAPTER THIRTY-SEVEN

The Tyrswick party reached the village of Eanfirth by mid afternoon. Sebastian could see that it too suffered damage from the spring rains, but nothing requiring resources beyond what the villagers gathered for themselves.

He rapped at the door of the cottage belonging to the village priest. On entering, the party was greeted by a comfortable dwelling and a warm fire burning in a stove on which heated a pot of aromatic stew.

The priest bowed to Sebastian, showing deference with which, he mused with some humor, Dominic never obliged him. Father Cornell was a middle-aged man about the same years as Dominic, but where the friar was built like a prize pugilist, this priest was wiry and half a head taller.

Over a meal, they discussed the band of traveling tinkers.

"When Brother Dominic told us the Beast of the North might have wintered with us, I can tell you I was quite alarmed," announced the priest.

"These men have visited our village in the past and have caused no trouble, but when young Mary went missing yesterday, I thought it wise to send word to Dominic."

"Have you ever thought about speaking to these men, instead of secretly harboring suspicion?" Gaines asked rudely.

Sebastian shot him a look. It was ignored by him, though not by the priest.

"Of course I have! With the exception of the fact that they've never set foot in my church, the only fault I can find is a general lack of personal hygiene. Their quarters smell rank, so no wonder they don't mix with the villagers other than to do the odd jobs."

"When did you last see them, Father?"

The man straightened and turned his attention to Sebastian.

"Three days ago. I was doing my rounds of the village. They've been living in the blacksmith's shed since just before the first snowfall."

"Did they seem anxious to move on?"

"Not especially. But they've been talking about it for weeks, saying it would be as soon as the flooding from the spring rains subsided."

"Then I'm glad we arrived when we did. The River Tyrs has indeed begun falling." Friar Dominic interjected, "Can you tell us more about the missing girl?"

"Little more than you know already," Cornell shrugged. "She's a good girl, never one to give her parents a minute's worry, not one to go running off."

"Well, we have only a few hours of daylight left," said Sebastian, standing. "We'll have to wait for first light tomorrow for a search. But let's talk to these men and not waste any more time."

The priest took the lead to direct them to the blacksmith's shed.

The heat was a visible presence the moment Sebastian walked through the door. The glow of the coals and the shimmer of heat haze rose from behind the anvil. The taciturn smithy, his bulging arm muscles glistening with sweat, nodded a greeting to the party before pointing his mallet to another door behind him.

A smart place to spend the winter, Sebastian thought.

While the heat of the forge burned up the smell of everything but hot metal, the room behind was cooler and reeked of a stench so foul Sebastian was forced to swallow hard against gagging. Gaines and Robert were less successful, and behind him, he could hear the sounds of their dry retching.

The only illumination was sharp shafts of light that forced their way through the slatted timber walls. To a casual observer, the room might have been empty but for sacks slumped against the wall.

Then one of them moved.

"'Ere, 'oo do you think ye are, disturbin' our rest?"

"Get to your feet and show some respect to the baron of Tyrswick!" Gaines growled.

One, then another, then a third sack rose to its feet.

"A baron?" the second sack said. "We be right honored, ain't we, Tinker?"

The third sack spoke. "That we do, Carpenter. Show some respect there, Thatcher, no need to be rude to our visitors."

Sebastian watched the interplay between the three men and noted only Tinker looked him square in the eye. Clearly, he appointed himself spokesman for the group.

"I hope we're not being accused of wrongdoin'. Someone's always trying to accuse us of something or other."

Sebastian allowed a slow grin to spread across his face. It also helped to make his breathing shallow. He wasn't sure how much longer he could stay in this confined space with such malodorous baggage.

"What say you, Gaines, perhaps we should accuse these three of witchcraft?"

Gaines grunted his approval. "A dunking chair for these three would be a blessing to us all."

"Get them out here. Robert and Duncan, you stay and conduct a search."

From the corner of his eye, he saw a look of distaste cross the young men's faces and he sympathized. He gave a lingering glance about the room now the men had been removed, trying to establish the odors into some sort of order.

There was the smell of unwashed bodies to be sure, and the stench of rancid meat mixed with redolent herbs, plus the reek of excreta of creatures large and small inhabiting a small space.

The sound of raised voices outside broke into Sebastian's examination. He quickly clasped Robert's shoulder and nodded to Duncan.

"Do this well and you're on your way to winning your spurs, lads. Good luck."

He left them to the unpleasant task ahead.

The heat of the smithy's forge and the tangy scent of molten iron that lingered at the back of one's throat was a welcome antidote to the pestilent smells of the other room. Sebastian found himself hoping uncharitably for a stray ember to burn down the entire building in the night.

Outside, the late-afternoon air was fresh and cool. Sebastian took in a lungful before straightening his back and, with authority evident in his bearing, approaching Gaines and the three itinerants.

Daylight had improved their appearance somewhat. They were strong and fit for the manual labor that took them from village to village; their clothes were gray and colorless from numerous washings, and a variety of patches, more or less neatly applied, spoke of a hard life on the road.

Carpenter and Thatcher spared nervous glances back to the blacksmith's shack. Tinker showed no such fear. Clearly the man was going to brazen it out with him.

"Why are your friends so nervous?"

"There are many thieves about. A man can't be too careful about holding on to what he owns."

Gaines stepped forward and backhanded him.

"Watch who you're speaking to."

Stumbling, Tinker dabbed a filthy hand to a small cut by his mouth. He shot Gaines a venomous look and focused his attention back onto Sebastian. This was not the first interrogation Sebastian and Gaines had conducted and each knew his role well. It was a surprise just how much men might reveal in a glance or a nervous tic, especially if they were unaware that they were subject of such scrutiny.

Gaines played a valuable role in stealing the attention of the interrogated man to give Sebastian time to observe and assess. In the case of Tinker, the man was trying to buy time.

"A fourth travels with you. Where is he?"

Several changes of expression told Sebastian the man was considering which of several answers to give. The two men behind him shuffled their feet in the silence.

"It's no good, Tinker, just tell him so we can be away from here," whined Carpenter.

Tinker gave a short nod.

"We ain't seen him in four days," he told Sebastian. "Listen, what's this all about?"

"Have you heard of the Beast of the North?" Sebastian asked.

Tinker frowned and turned to the two men behind him; they shook their heads, bemused.

"It seems that for the past year wherever you've been, there's the brutal murder of a young maid."

Thatcher cursed vociferously and shoved Tinker at the shoulder. "I told you he was a wrong 'un."

Tinker shoved back. "You never complained when 'e paid in his share, did ye? Ye stupid drunken bastard."

An argument developed and, while it was words only, Sebastian allowed it to continue, learning among the bickering and swearing that the missing man's name was Tanner, and they considered whatever he did out of their sight no concern of theirs.

"Enough!" Sebastian yelled with such force that even Gaines behind him started. Sebastian suppressed a smile and returned to business.

"Does this Tanner go missing often?"

Carpenter regained his voice.

"He do. He goes off fer maybe a sennight sometimes when we leave a village. Each time you'd think he's gone for good, then he shows up with not even a by-your-leave, but he always pays in his share from what he's earned."

A cry of horror from within the smithy was quickly accompanied by the sound of running feet. Robert emerged first and threw up in the grass. Duncan rushed up ashen-faced and skidded to a halt in front of Sebastian.

"What is it, lad?"

"We…we've found something."

"Speak up," prompted Gaines.

Duncan turned to Gaines, then back to Sebastian.

"Fingers! People's fingers. Dozens of them!"

* * *

Before the full horror of his presence could be realized by Frey, Drefan dragged her away from the upturned cart as six armed men emerged from the trees, some surrounding Larcwide, others righting the cart.

She could hear Larcwide yell her name above the creaks and groans of the shifting conveyance. Surprise and panic coalesced into action. Frey lashed out with a well-aimed knee to Drefan's groin, and, as he doubled over, she wrenched her arm free and ran to put some yards between her and the man she hated.

An ambush! And it was no false flattery to believe she was the target. Her safety and that of Larcwide depended on sounding the alarm at Tyrswick Keep.

"Run, my lady, keep running!" she heard Larcwide shout, and after only a moment's hesitation she did so, sprinting toward the thicket of trees and to her horse waiting on the other side.

The sound of steel on steel filled her with dread. An experienced and wily warrior Larcwide might be, but he was no match for four younger men.

Then the ground tilted toward her and hit with a bone-jarring thud. Air fled her lungs as she landed heavily. The sensation of a vicelike grip on her ankle worked its way into her consciousness.

Despite the bruises, she twisted and lashed out with her free leg and connected with a solid mass that grunted in its effort to hold her. Then her other ankle was imprisoned before she was roughly flipped onto her back.

"Remember me?"

Although he was more roughly dressed and no longer clean-shaven, Frey recognized her new captor.

"Baldwin!"

"That's right, Alfreya of Tyrswick. You don't think I would disappear without wishing you a fond good-bye, do you?"

She was hauled to her feet and, for one absurd second, was grateful for the hold on her upper arms; she was unsure if she could stand unaided. Frey swung a leg, looking for a connection, but Baldwin was faster, avoiding the blow and twisting her left arm so it was wrenched behind her into a shoulder lock.

Frey cried out and Baldwin pressed his advantage, raising her disabled arm higher, sending sharp, excruciating pain down the limb.

"Stop struggling, you stupid bitch, or I'll dislocate your shoulder," he hissed.

Frey shook her head, not to disagree, but to dislodge a lock of hair from her eyes. She stared at Baldwin malevolently yet did as she was told. His grip eased somewhat and the agonizing pain receded to a throbbing ache.

He lowered her arm and grabbed the other, binding both securely behind her back.

She turned her eyes away, searching for Larcwide.

In the field, the battle between Larcwide and Drefan's men was over before it began. Her man-at-arms's sword lay at his feet, and his arms were upraised in the universal gesture of surrender. Just one man watched the prisoner.

The cart was now on its wheels and four men were at work. Two inserted curved iron ribs across its width and the other two followed behind with a canvas to turn the cart into a wagon.

Another man readied the horses for harnessing.

As Drefan made his way toward her, he limped, she noted with silent satisfaction. Frey stood straighter with all the dignity she could muster and glared at him imperiously. If he thought to intimidate her, he had another think coming.

He reached her and stopped a foot away. Several well-chosen epithets bubbled in her throat, but before she could give voice to any of them, Drefan swung hard. The back of his knuckles connected forcefully across her cheek. Frey slumped against Baldwin, her eyes watering with agony.

She straightened herself and took two large gasps of air to fight the heat and pain.

"You dog," she bit out hoarsely. "It takes a big man to hit a woman, doesn't it?"

A flash of anger ignited in Drefan's eyes, but he mastered his temper quickly.

"I'll not let you goad me, my pet, not when the end is so close."

"End? What end?" Frey asked, but he turned his back to her and whistled loudly. His men paused their activities.

"Get a move on! We leave now!"

Frey watched the men redouble their efforts.

"Leave for where?" she demanded.

Drefan half turned back to her.

"Will you ride like a lady or do I have to truss you up and toss you in the back of the cart?"

"Do you really think I'll make it easy on you?"

Drefan shrugged and started walking away.

"Tie her up, Baldwin."

"With pleasure," Baldwin drawled. Frey instantly regretted her choice.

Baldwin shoved and Frey was propelled forward, frog-marched toward the cart. As they approached, Larcwide surged forward, surprising his guard. Frey strained against the bonds, hoping to loosen Baldwin's hand. Her left shoulder throbbed painfully.

Larcwide stumbled but righted himself as though he felt her pain. Then he clutched his left shoulder, agony etched on his face.

The older man raised his eyes, mouthing something wordlessly, and took a few more halting steps toward her before his face contorted in anguish and surprise as a paroxysm shook him bodily.

"Larcwide!" Frey screamed as Baldwin dragged her closer to the wagon.

The old man clawed violently at his chest and sank to his knees.

"Help him, somebody help him!" Frey pleaded, bucking wildly in her captor's arms and heedless of the tears running unchecked down her face.

She watched in horror as Larcwide fell face first onto the grassy meadow and did not rise again.

CHAPTER THIRTY-EIGHT

Sebastian stared at the darkened ceiling of the priest's cottage from his bed, listening to the rhythmic breathing and the occasional snores of the other occupants.

Something did not sit right with him, something just out of reach. He stretched his mind to reach out, but the darkness of night was like a tangible thing barring his thoughts of a way forward.

He closed his eyes and tried to ignore the disquiet. Tomorrow he would need his wits about him and men he could rely upon. Such dark quiet brought to mind Frey's distrust of Gaines. He had to admit he watched his most trusted friend closely today to see whether there was something different about the man's manner. If there was, it was outside of his reckoning.

Instead, they fell into the long-learned ways of working together as they had always done. It was good.

The three itinerants had been aghast at the mummified fingers that belonged to five sets of hands and vociferously denied any knowledge of how Tanner had come by his collection.

Sebastian believed them, but there were enough obviously stolen trinkets and goods among their belongings to justify a thorough flogging for each of them.

A search through Tanner's belongings found carefully wrapped braids of hair of various lengths and colors—again, five in total.

Diera's body, hands mutilated, hair hacked, eyes gouged, was vividly recalled. He closed his eyes tightly against the memory, though once it would have brought him to his knees in torment. He supposed he ought to feel a measure of shame at his selfishness. Diera was dead, killed cruelly and needlessly, but now the memory brought a strange kind of relief, because it wasn't Frey.

Not Frey, not Frey, not Frey…

Sometime later he awoke, the weak light of a new morning accompanied by the sound of several calling roosters heralding the sun's arrival over the trees. After quickly dressing and breaking fast, he checked on preparations for the day.

He found Dominic concluding a conversation with one of the villagers.

"I've learned there's a Roman excavation in the hills," the friar said to Sebastian without preamble. "There's an old hermit who lives in the caves, an eccentric chap who usually comes down to scrounge food. No one has seen him for days."

Sebastian considered the information. Tanner could not have gone far with the girl, and the old mine was as good a place as any to begin their search.

"I'll have some men track the hermit down," Sebastian decided.

"Before you do, I want you and your men to take communion."

Sebastian raised his eyebrows. "It's not Sunday."

"It doesn't matter," Dominic shot back. "You know as well as I do this is a different kind of killing than a drunken brawl or a murder for profit. The very nature of it is evil."

"That's why I plan to be well armed."

Dominic offered a wry smile and quoted, "'The weapons of our warfare are not carnal but they are mighty through the Holy Ghost.' Go check on your horses, Sebastian. I'll see you inside."

* * *

Frey was jostled awake.

"There's no time to sleep, Frey. Wake up!"

She opened her eyes to see Diera's warm brown eyes fill her vision, her face lit by flickering torchlight.

"I'm awake."

Frey sat up, aware they were under the arms of a spreading yew tree. In a cloudless night sky, she could see an endless spray of silver stars. Around her, torchlight danced exotic shadows on the ground and the trunk of the yew. The feeling of expectant trepidation that accompanied other visits to this place was absent.

She looked about. The hooded figure in green was nowhere to be seen.

"Evil wears many faces," said Diera.

At the phrase, Frey snapped her attention back to her friend, who was dressed in her midnight blue robe.

"Who told you that?"

Diera merely blinked.

"Who told you that?" Frey demanded urgently. "Sebastian is going out today to find the Beast of the North, to deal with the man who killed you!"

Frey received no reply, only a pitying look and a slow shake of the head.

"Is he in danger?"

A dread terror rose in her breast, a fear that quelled every other emotion.

"Is Sebastian dead? Answer me!"

Diera stopped her movement.

"Sebastian has been appointed, but this is not his time. Justice will be done this day, but the time of my reckoning is not yet."

"I don't understand."

Diera's reply was a look of benign compassion.

"Pray for your husband, Frey, and I'll pray for you."

She reached out and ran gentle fingers over Frey's head and stroked her cheek tenderly before moving down her arm to hold her hand. A lethargy came with her touch, and Frey felt the overwhelming urge to yawn.

"Rest now. More answers await in the morning."

Frey closed her eyes and felt a tug on her hand, encouraging her to lie down.

Her final conscious thoughts were a prayer for her husband and a prayer for Diera.

Frey slept and was certain of it because, when she awoke, her body ached mightily from the previous day's abuse, especially her shoulder, where Baldwin wrenched it. This was no dream.

Overhead she recognized the shapes of oak leaves silhouetted against the early dawn light. Her hands were free, but her ankles were hobbled to prevent escape.

The camp was quiet. It seemed morning hadn't sufficiently broken for the other men to stir and yet she was filled with a certainty that she was being watched. She turned her head. Just a few feet away with its back to her was a figure cloaked in green.

Green!

Frey sat bolt upright and silently and fruitlessly reached behind her for her quiver and bow before recalling their confiscation.

This was no dream. The figure in green was real. It turned away from the sun now peeking over the darkened hill to the east and faced her.

"I see you're awake," said Drefan, sardonically.

"You! You killed Diera, not the Beast of the North!"

His reaction was not what she expected. Drefan nodded once and followed with a slow clapping of his hands.

"You were always too clever for your own good. Yes, well done. I killed Diera, but only you and I will ever know it."

* * *

The morning was late by the time Sebastian reached the entrance to the abandoned mine.

He was aware of several of these cuttings around Tyrswick and the one nearest the Keep was a rich source of coal that he had been quick to exploit.

There were rumors of the Romans mining lead and even hiding a trove of silver on Tyrswick lands, but he had been too occupied with the defense of Tyrswick and ensuring its agricultural success to go chasing after rumors of treasure. What he had already uncovered was more than enough for one lifetime.

Perhaps that was something for this son to explore, should he and Frey be so blessed.

A yell from a couple of his men several yards to his right broke his reverie, and he jogged to where they stood.

The bent body of a shaggy white-haired man lay on the ground, his fingers clutching a scrap of cloth. Sebastian noted his men ventured no closer than a yard away, and as he approached, he understood why. A particularly awful stench wafted from the corpse.

Sebastian bent to give the cloth a tug and the rag came away with some difficulty. Rigor mortis gripped the body still and, coupled with the lividity of the skin, this suggested the man had been alive just a day earlier.

Sebastian sniffed at the fabric. The odor was there but slight. Sebastian bent down again. The smell of it, like cat's piss, was stronger on the hermit's beard.

He waved a hand at Dominic.

"Dom, you know something about herbs. What does this smell like to you?"

The friar didn't venture any closer, instead resting his weight on his staff.

"You can tell from the color of his lips and the rictus, not to mention the disgusting odor, he's been given yew-leaf tincture."

Gaines took a step back and ordered two accompanying villagers to take the old man's body back to the vicarage for cleaning and burial.

"That might explain how the Beast keeps his victims subdued; just a little in wine to disguise the taste would be enough," he added.

Sebastian straightened and looked at Duncan and Robert.

"Pull yourself together lads and prepare the torches. It's not the first body you've seen and it won't be your last, but there's a girl in there who might yet be still alive and, by God, we're going to make sure she stays so."

The two young men rallied and set about their task. Sebastian gave his equipment a final check and Gaines did the same. His sword sat within its scabbard; a dirk was strapped to his right thigh.

Sebastian allowed himself a small surge of pride. His two squires were similarly prepared and looked as though they could actually be competent with both. Larcwide and his incessant drills had done wonders.

Twenty feet through the mine adit, the men were confronted with branching tunnels.

"Which way, Sebastian?" asked Gaines, contemplating both.

Sebastian turned to his party and counted the number of unlit torches they carried. Duncan and Robert carried a dozen each, bound and slung across their backs and held two in each hand. He had seen the iron rings installed three yards apart along the tunnel. Evidently the ever-efficient Romans deemed that sufficient light to see.

Their supplies were possibly enough if they relied on them to light their way down one tunnel, as long as it was no farther than a thousand yards in length.

"Go left—let's explore that for a few yards. One torch for every other ring. That will give us about an hour."

Thirty yards in, the tunnel opened out into a natural cave. Sebastian and Gaines entered together, Sebastian circling left and Gaines to the right, while Dominic and the two squires were instructed to wait at the entrance.

The torch in his hand appeared dim. He looked up for its cause. A fissure in the roof of the cave opened at an angle to the surface, bringing a shaft of light and, from the erosion on the floor, a small measure of water when it rained.

"Baron!"

Sebastian turned immediately at Gaines's tone of voice—urgent and strained.

He hurried toward the light from his torch, which now lay on the ground. Its flickering light revealed a prone form where Gaines kneeled. His audible sigh indicated palpable relief.

"She's breathing! She's alive!"

Sebastian ran the torch over the girl's length. There was enough light to reveal her hair had been hacked off, but the Beast had not got so far as to gouge out her eyes or to remove her fingers.

"No injuries, thank God."

"None that we can see, anyway." Sebastian shrugged. "Robert! Duncan! Get over here and get this lass back to the village."

The young men swiftly assembled their stretcher and eased the still-unconscious girl onto the canvas. She didn't stir, which did not bode well.

"Tell the healer that she'll need to be purged of yew," Sebastian ordered, making his way back down the tunnel to where it forked. The squires followed swiftly after, and he watched them disappear into the blinding sunlight of the mine entrance.

"Dom, you go with them. Gaines and I will handle the Beast from here."

"I will not, Baron."

Sebastian turned to face the equally determined friar and looked him up and down. Dominic could hold his own in a straight physical confrontation, of that he was sure, but this was another matter altogether. It required armed, expertly trained soldiers to deal with the monster who lay ahead.

Gaines refused to hide his scorn.

"You're unarmed, man, unless you plan to beat him to death with the crucifix around your neck."

A flash of anger crossed the cleric's face but was quickly extinguished.

"Have you two not been listening to me about the true nature of the Beast of the North? Just because you wield steel you think you are adequately prepared for what you are about to face."

Dominic turned to the darkened tunnel. He pulled a torch from an iron ring and walked away, calling back as he did so, "'We wrestle not against flesh and blood but against principalities and powers, against spiritual wickedness in high places.'"

"He's a madman," Gaines pronounced softly.

Sebastian cursed under his breath, lit a fresh torch, and followed.

The tunnel narrowed and the trio were forced to walk single file.

After several hundred yards, Sebastian accepted another lit torch from Gaines. Every now and again, a haunting moan could be heard, accompanied by a breeze that caused their lights to cast unnatural shadows along the walls.

There must be another entrance nearby, Sebastian decided. A gust of wind blowing through the network of passageways caused the moans, along with a creaking latticework of timber supports from the original excavations. In spite of himself, Sebastian felt tendrils of fear work their way along his spine. His instincts had served him well in previous battles, and they told him now that they were foolish to continue much farther alone.

The girl is safe. Mission accomplished. Go home, something told him. Make love to your wife. Return to this godforsaken hole another day with an army of men."

With every step he took, the thought became more insistent.

Sebastian stopped at another branching excavation. He was about to give voice to his concerns, when a cry filled the air and he was knocked bodily to the ground, his head hitting a rock.

Sebastian shook his head to clear it, hearing the sound of scuffles and curses. For one panicked moment, he feared he had lost his sight until he saw the shadow of a man haring down the right-hand passage, the figure lit briefly by the guttering remains of a dropped torch as it expired.

He could hear a groan of pain as he righted himself and reached in his pocket for a flint. Groping about, he sought the extinguished torch and found it at last. In a swift motion, he sparked the flint, and the pitch-soaked head, still hot, caught alight once more.

Gaines writhed on the ground, clutching his calf. Blood flowed through his fingers. Dominic was gone.

"That crazy bastard monk cut me!" Gaines swore through clenched teeth.

"Easy man, let me see it."

Sebastian prized Gaines's fingers apart. A six-inch gash ran down the man's calf. Thank God for his boot, but for which the cut might have severed an artery.

As it was, the wound was serious, but not mortal.

"Are you sure it was Dominic who stabbed you?" asked Sebastian as he tore a length of fabric from his tunic and began binding Gaines's lower leg tightly. The man grimaced.

"Yes. No. Oh shit, I don't know...."

Sweat poured down the face of the man-at-arms as Sebastian eased him to his feet, bringing with him Dominic's abandoned staff.

"Do you think you can make it to the village?"

Gaines gave a curt nod while attempting to put weight on the injured leg and failing.

Sebastian stooped to pick up the bundle of remaining flares.

"I mean alone."

He received a sharp look from Gaines that he knew well.

"No. If you're determined to go on, I go with you."

"Don't be stupid, man. You can't walk."

"Yes, I can," Gaines replied stubbornly, and placed almost his full weight on the gashed leg. He cried out again and, but for Sebastian catching him around the chest, would have fallen.

"Henry, please," said Sebastian, "use the staff, crawl if you have to, but get back to the village and send Robert and Duncan back here with some of the villagers."

Sebastian unsheathed his sword, glancing in the direction in which Dominic had disappeared, then turned back to Gaines, who now looked stronger, probably fueled as much by anger as pain, he thought.

With a shake of his head, Gaines made a few hobbling steps back in the direction of the entrance, his injured leg crooked up, supporting his weight with the staff.

"You're both mad!" he said.

"Probably. Now get going."

Sebastian turned away and began walking.

"Sebastian?"

He stopped and looked back at Gaines.

"What?"

"Godspeed."

Sebastian gave his friend a grim smile and strode on.

CHAPTER THIRTY-NINE

Frey recognized she was in shock—numb, both inside and out. The rope binding her hands and ankles made her captive, not only to the men who took her, but also to the swaying of the cart, which rolled southward toward Durham. The covers of the wagon were drawn, allowing only the faint glow of daylight through the weave of the canvas.

Pins and needles spread up her arms and across her shoulders, a blessed distraction from the nausea in her belly. Her mouth was soaked dry by the cloth gag made necessary as a result of the deep teeth marks one of Drefan's men now wore on his hand. His mistake for getting too close.

She wanted to weep but did not. She would sooner burn in hell than show weakness in front of Drefan. He had said no more to her after this morning's revelation, and unanswered questions burned within her. She prayed Diera's soul might have the rest promised her on the inscription in Tyrswick Keep's chapel.

She only learned of their destination by overhearing two of Drefan's men stop to talk to a merchant making his way north.

Why Durham?

A small flicker of hope rose. If Rhys and Rosalind were still there paying their respects to the bishop, then maybe she could get word to Sebastian. But in order to do that, she couldn't be trussed like a prize turkey.

Come on, Frey, think! The plea turned into a prayer.

The cart, laden also with a couple of chests and several sizable sacks, dipped and juddered its way through a rut in the road, and the rope at her wrists rubbed against irritated skin, accentuating her helplessness.

She closed her eyes against the pain and the beloved face of Larcwide swam into view.

This time tears did leak from the corners of her eyes. Another person dear to her was dead because of Drefan.

She remembered soon after their arrival in Scotland, Larcwide took her and Diera aside one evening while her father drunkenly snored in their chambers. Frey had only just turned fifteen.

He had been uncomfortable with schooling two naive young highborn women in the ways men might use their wiles or their strength to get what they want, but as Frey now recalled the memory, Larcwide had always taken his duty to protect seriously and had seen the way the men in Malcolm's court were looking at them.

"You have to be smarter than them."

The words, spoken long ago, struck a chord anew. Her life and her husband's life depended on it.

Several hours later, the cold bite of the early evening air flooded the stopped wagon, and, having been hauled roughly to the tail of the cart, Frey looked up as the first stars of the night twinkled cheerfully in the indigo sky.

Frey's feet dangled over the edge of the tailgate and the desire to kick out at the manhandling brute nearly overwhelmed her resolve to wage war with her wits rather than her temper.

She ushered in deep breaths through her nose to calm herself. To her surprise, the man, one she had not seen before, offered her a look of something like compassion, although she couldn't be certain in the dimming light.

"I seen what a nasty bite you gave Poldarth. You won't give me that trouble, will you Lady Alfreya?" he asked kindly.

Frey shook her head vigorously. She sighed in gratitude as he loosened the knot behind her head, then those at her wrists and ankles.

"Thank you," she croaked as he pulled the rag away from her mouth.

The man gave a slight frown of disapproval.

"You shouldn't have been tied up for so long. Wait there while I fetch my good lady wife."

At that the man walked away into the small crowd setting up camp for the night. It seems they had become quite a caravan.

She stretched her arms experimentally, almost relishing the pain of her muscles protesting their lack of use, and watched the activity before her.

Two other carts similar to the one she rode in stood to one side, their horses out of harness and grazing quietly nearby. Laughter, both male and female, erupted from one end of the camp where a cooking fire had been lit.

The atmosphere could almost be described as festive. Frey briefly considered making a run for it, but even if her legs were up to the task and she could outrun her pursuers, where would she go? No. Durham, if that indeed was where they were heading, would offer her more opportunities.

Soon a middle-aged woman carrying a basket bustled up to her.

"There, there, my dear, you've been through quite an ordeal, but it's all over now. You're quite safe here," she began. "My name is Mistress Duignan."

Frey opened her mouth to speak but instead let out a choking cough.

"*Tsk, tsk,* that won't do at all," she said, and rummaged around in her widemouthed wicker basket to hand Frey a leather flask. "You drink this up while I put some salve on your ankles and wrists."

She drank greedily, the taste only registering with the last mouthful. It was pungent, earthy. In a panic, she shoved the container back into the woman's hand.

"What's this? What did you give sume?"

"Only valerian, my dear. Your husband wants you well enough to give your testimony to the bishop in Durham."

The tranquilizing effect of the drug on an empty stomach worked rapidly. It took Frey a moment to register her words.

"My husband…He's here?"

"Of course he is, my dear! Greatly relieved he is, too. I can't tell you how sick with worry he's been," Mistress Duignan smiled benevolently. "My Lord Drefan has asked me to take special care of you and that's what I intend to do."

* * *

In the blackness of the mine, there was no reckoning the passing of the day, no reckoning of direction, either.

Sebastian ruefully considered the twine sitting at the bottom of the bag of flares that slapped across his back as he ran, an admonishment of his impetuous action; one that would have earned a tongue lashing, if not a flogging, for his men if any had done anything as similarly reckless.

He should have used the twine to tie along the iron torch rings and guide his way back. Now, after several turnings, Sebastian had to concede he was lost. Moreover, there had been no sign of Dominic either.

He stopped, mastered his harsh breathing, and listened.

The baleful howl of the wind was softer here, and the sound of steady dripping indicated water nearby, a supposition backed up by the smell of damp air and slime-covered walls, glistening as they reflected the torchlight.

Then sudden screams, anguished but faint. He hadn't imagined them.

The blanket of fear, which had only been hinted at back along the passage, settled oppressively around him, warning him to turn back.

He could die down here and no one would know.

Frey would never know.

Who would protect her? Did she know how much he loved her?

The thought of her spending endless lonely years without him was infinitely more terrifying than the thought of his own death.

"Oh, Frey, my love. I don't want to leave you!" he intoned.

Terror sunk its talons into his heart, and, with each beat, the pain became a physical agony. The tormented cries of the poor soul in this mine might have been his own.

Then a memory of her smile, the recollection of Frey's courage, the feel of her naked flesh under his hands as he brought her to the peak of desire, the sure and steady realization of her reciprocated love played across his mind.

Perfect love casts out fear.

The talons withdrew and Sebastian basked in a feeling of peace as though a warm sun emerged from behind a dark cloud. A breeze from somewhere pushed at his back. Sebastian took a step or two forward just as his torch died.

As his eyes grew used to the dark, a glow emerged from around a corner some twenty yards distant. He might have missed it had the torch not gone out.

Then the cries began again, but there was something beneath them. A low deep chant of which Sebastian could hear snatches.

"Pater noster, qui es in caelis, sanctifice turno mentuum."

Reflexively he joined in the prayer under his breath.

"…Thy kingdom come, thy will be done, on Earth as it is in Heaven…"

Sebastian continued forward until he encountered the spur off the main tunnel, half blocked by a cave-in. Light glowed eerily beyond the rock fall. The voices were louder here, and Sebastian eased his way over a broken prop. A keening wail echoed around the walls. Sebastian pulled out his sword and crouched.

He eased the blade out into the void, using the polished surface as a mirror. A dozen lit torches flooded the cave with light.

Dominic stood in the center, his crucifix glinting in the illumination. The friar's entire focus was on the figure before him, a man whose face was contorted with hate and fear. He clutched a bloodstained knife in his left hand.

As Dominic prayed, the man juddered violently, then halted his involuntary movements with a sharp call to attention as though he were a doll in the hands of an unseen puppet master. Unerringly, the man's head snapped in Sebastian's direction as though he could see him from behind the rubble.

"Come out, come out, baron of Tyrswick! We want to play."

We? Were there more men here?

Sebastian, sword brandished, cautiously entered the space, scanning the flickering shadows for an ambush. Dominic didn't seem the least bit concerned; he remained single-mindedly focused on the man before him. As a soldier, Sebastian fell back on his training—circle the perimeter, eliminate any surprises.

There were none. Only the three of them.

"Tanner?" Sebastian asked.

"Yes?" said the man.

"By what name are you called?" the friar demanded.

Sebastian frowned. What on earth? Dominic already knew the man's name.

Tanner kept staring at him with large, curious eyes. Sebastian stared back. The fear he experienced earlier welled up once more.

"I'm talking to you!" said the friar with authority.

Tanner's head swiveled sharply back to the cleric.

"Our name? Multis," he spat contemptuously, pronouncing a strange sibilance on the name. "But we are known by many names."

Dominic took one step forward, and Tanner's hand, which clutched the knife, sprang up defensively.

"Dom…" Sebastian warned, but his words went unheeded as Dominic took another step forward.

"*Ego praecipio tibi in nomine Jesu Christi exire,*" he said, before repeating in Norman. "I command thee, in the name of Jesus Christ, to come out."

At that, Tanner let out an ear-piercing scream and shuddered violently. The knife clattered harmlessly into the dirt before he too dropped, convulsing.

Before Sebastian could move, Dominic rushed forward and knelt, placing a hand on the man's chest and continuing to pray under his breath. Tanner's chest convulsed once, twice, and a third time before he lay completely still. Sebastian stepped forward. The man looked as though he were dead.

Sebastian sheathed his sword and knelt down beside Dominic. The final words of the Lord's Prayer lingered on his lips.

"For thine is the kingdom, the power, and the glory, forever and ever amen."

Tanner's eyes opened wide and he drew a deep breath as though he had been a drowning man. His eyes focused on Dominic's before he burst into tears and pulled himself into a fetal position.

Sebastian was startled at the change in the man from belligerent to quiescent. Was this really the Beast of the North, responsible for the deaths of at least six women? Sebastian stood and looked down at the man.

"Are you the man they call Tanner?" he asked.

Tanner started as though he had only just noticed Sebastian's presence.

"Aye."

"Stand up."

With Dominic's assistance, Tanner rose unsteadily to his feet.

"You hereby stand accused of heinously killing six women and brutalizing their bodies. How plead you?"

Tanner blinked uncertainly for a moment before revelation washed over his face.

"Oh God. Was that me?"

The horror of his deeds hit home, seemingly dawning on him for the first time.

"Yes. It *was* me, it…made me…I…"

"May God have mercy on your soul," said Dominic, shaking his head sorrowfully.

Sebastian continued.

"By the confession of your mouth before two witnesses to the charge of six counts of murder, I, baron of Tyrswick, condemn thee to death—"

"Five!"

"—You will be hanged by your neck until you are dead and your body left to rot as a warning to others who would blaspheme against the laws of God and of William, king of England and Normandy."

"No! It were five! I killed *five* women, as God is my witness!" Tanner yelled.

"We have your trophies," Sebastian shot back. "Their fingers—"

"Aye! But fingers from the hands of five, not six."

Sebastian shrugged.

"Five or six, does it matter?"

Even in the face of condemnation, Tanner was affronted.

"I may hang, but I'll hang for the right number of crimes."

CHAPTER FORTY

Sebastian closed his eyes, ignoring the disapproving eye of the village priest's housekeeper as he propped his feet on the table and rocked his chair back on two legs, its back and his shoulders resting against the windowsill.

He was tired and his mind wandered toward the prospect of a soft, warm bed. Frey's soft, warm body in a bed. Naked. The thought of making love to his wife warmed him as much as the fire that burned in the nearby hearth.

It was late. On his return to the village and ensuring that Tanner was in secure custody—more for his own safety than any threat he now posed—he checked on Gaines.

The healer had done a neat job on the vertical line of stitches that ran down his calf. And despite his insistence, the old woman good-naturedly but adamantly refused to let him see the girl, assuring him that her body at least had suffered no lasting harm. Now, he waited while the priest and Dominic heard Tanner's final confession. He would hang in the morning, and notices would be sent out to the villages where the Beast of the North had struck.

Despite taking a moment to enjoy his private fantasy of Frey laid out before him, another thought intruded, one so insistent he reluctantly left his wife's side. Five murders, not six. Tanner was resolute. If he told the truth, and it seemed likely he did—for why otherwise confess to the other five—then which was the odd one out?

It had to be Diera. Tanner said he'd taken the fingers of both hands, but Diera was missing only those of her right. There were forty rotted and mummified fingers in Tanner's bag. It was, Sebastian considered with grim logic, a complete set of fingers for five victims.

Diera. Why? And by whom?

Sebastian examined the possibilities.

Unlike the other girls, no one would mark Diera as missing. Everyone presumed she had gone back to Scotland. Her body was identified by the small gold ring with the old Tyrswick insignia. Demon possessed or not, Tanner hardly seemed a man who would ignore a valuable piece of gold. And, given his predilection for the fingers of both hands, there seemed no reason for him to vary his pattern.

That could only mean Diera was killed in the manner of the Beast by someone who *wanted* Sebastian to believe the girl was the daughter of Alfred. But why? What purpose did it serve and who would do such a thing? He didn›t know why, but he could think of one man who would do it if it served his ends.

Drefan.

As though punctuating the thought, the cottage door flung open and Talbot and Orlege barreled through, both sweat-soaked from a long, hard ride. Ignoring the henlike fussing of the housekeeper, protesting about the heat being let out and mud brought into her house, Orlege marched up to the table.

"My lord!" he began.

The man looked him squarely in the eye, with a look that hinted at turmoil. A glance over Orlege's shoulder revealed Talbot's stricken face.

Frey!

Sebastian stood, his heart beating faster in his chest in anticipation of the bad news.

"Tell me everything," he ordered. "Leave nothing out."

* * *

For some time, Frey floated in a half dream, one in which she was warm, comfortable, and safe. All she would have to do is open her eyes to see the familiar furnishing of her chambers in Tyrswick Keep. Sleepily, she reached a hand across the bed. It was empty. Sebastian must have risen early to train with his men. She should join him.

Frey, with her eyes still closed, made a halfhearted effort to rise, but her limbs were much too heavy, so she settled down under the covers and listened to the sound of the household at work.

Strange, she thought. The sounds were much louder than they normally were. Did someone leave the chamber and staircase doors open?

A conversation started nearby and grew louder.

"…Oh, much better, my lord. She slept like a top."

The slight Irish burr of Mistress Duignan's accent gave her away.

"I'll put some more salve on the poor girl's limbs, and, by the time we get to Durham, she'll be as right as rain."

"Good," a male voice answered, his response too abrupt for Frey to identify its owner at once.

He continued, "She will need to stay quiet for the remainder of the journey."

Frey's eyes opened immediately. Drefan.

She was back in a cart, but it had been made up with a proper bed and there were two handsomely carved coffers, along with a box she expected might fit a wash bowl and pitcher.

It was a traveling boudoir fit for a lady.

"Lady Alfreya is prone to hysteria and self-harm. I want her to be given belladonna before we leave today. She will travel better if she sleeps."

She clutched the bedclothes and seethed as the conversation continued right outside the wagon. Belladonna? Did the man wish her dead? To be sure, it was an effective sedative when used correctly. When misjudged, it offered the patient only the sleep of death.

Mistress Duignan obviously harbored misgivings.

"I'm sure that won't be necessary, sir. Belladonna is too potent for such a wee thing. A couple of healthy cups of valerian will quiet her nerves."

Apparently, the woman's assurance wasn't enough, so she added with haste, "My lady has been as quiet as a lamb. In fact, she still sleeps. See for yourself."

Frey snapped her eyes shut and concentrated on breathing slow and relaxing her body. The flap opened and she could hear the sound of Mistress Duignan clambering aboard and Drefan soon after.

Afraid she could not keep the charade of sleep, Frey made a great show of stretching and yawning.

"Diera? Is that you?" The shaky uncertainty in her voice added to her appearance of befuddlement.

Mistress Duignan patted her hand.

"No dear, it's Mistress Duignan," she soothed maternally. "Remember? I put that lovely salve on your hurt wrists and ankles."

"You're very kind, Mistress Duignan." Frey gave her a tentative smile.

"I have someone here who wants to see you very much."

The woman stepped aside and Drefan leaned forward.

"Good morning, Alfreya. I trust you slept well."

His mockery was ill-disguised and, prior to her decision last night, she would have seized the bait and told him openly what a rat-faced bastard he was or scorched him with withering sarcasm. However…

"I did, my lord."

She watched his eyebrows rise in mild surprise.

"Mistress Duignan, you may leave us."

The woman departed. Drefan leaned forward as though he might kiss her. Frey sank reflexively back into the pillows.

"That was a fine performance you put on, but do not think I am fooled. I'll be keeping my eye on you."

"You had me drugged so I can no longer stand on my own feet," Frey hissed. "What threat do I pose you?"

"That's better." Drefan sat back, satisfaction spread across his features. "Meek and weak does not suit you."

"Sebastian will come after me."

"Yes, I'm counting on it."

As much as she willed her temper, her body betrayed her. Frey's eyes widened and her nostrils flared in alarm.

"What game do you play?"

Drefan shook his head, refusing to answer her questions. He opened the wagon's flap and nimbly jumped down.

"I don't play games and de la Croix will soon learn it."

He flashed her a devilishly handsome grin, the same one that deceived her those years ago in Edinburgh, but she knew it for what it was now. Her own expression hardened in response.

"Be a good girl and I might even let you live. You can beg me as Diera did."

* * *

Sebastian eased off as Ebon struggled with his ruthless pace. The twenty-four miles from Eanfirth to Tyrswick was a comfortable day's ride on horseback, but he pushed his mount and his men to go quicker. They had departed at first light, and a league from Tyrswick village, in the hour after noon, he slowed and turned to Talbot and Orlege.

"Show me where you found Larcwide's body."

Talbot led them to the place in the meadow where he found the man-at-arms.

"He bore no wounds and his equipment had not been stolen," the squire said.

"Heart failure," concluded Orlege with a profoundly sorrowful shake of his head. "His heart simply gave out on him."

Sebastian read the field as he would read the landscape on a hunt.

Trampled areas of grass suggested a band of men. A rectangular yellow patch of grass, out of place in the green, proved the men lay in wait on a canvas groundsheet for at least a day before they sprung the trap. A narrow parallel track told him they took Frey and some additional weight on the cart with them.

"There's nothing more to see here."

He followed the track back up to the road and called Orlege to fall into step with him.

"Send Robert and Duncan on to Durham with the letter for Baron Goscote and widen the patrols. We find Drefan and we'll find Frey."

Sebastian paused to clasp Orlege on the shoulder.

"And we'll give Larcwide a warrior's send-off. He was a good man."

* * *

The following day, the mood in Tyrswick Keep was even more subdued.

Tyrswick's squires formed a guard of honor while a detachment of household knights, including Orlege, carried Larcwide's coffin from the chapel.

Even the sky was overcast and a light drizzle made the graveside vigil a more miserable affair.

"It shouldn't have happened," Gaines grumbled afterward. Several pitchers of spiced wine had been consumed over the course of the wake. "Left on the field to die like that. It's not right."

Sebastian spent the next two days alone in his chambers in private mourning. He knew his servants thought his actions to be eccentric.

If they only knew.

It was not Larcwide he mourned, although his wise counsel and steady presence would be sorely missed.

He had discovered in Frey's coffer, hidden among undergarments, four letters from Drefan, urging Frey to maintain her courage and have faith in his promise to rescue her from her unwanted marriage to the bastard Norman.

The manner of the writing suggested that correspondence had begun around the time of their wedding and continued until February when the worst of the winter weather cut Tyrswick off from the rest of the world.

Was her love for him a sham?

He could not accept that, but a voice in his head, sounding very much like Gaines, Sebastian hated to admit, allowed the doubts to burrow parasitically into his soul.

And weeks passed.

Patrol after patrol returned without sighting or clues to the whereabouts of Drefan and Alfreya. He thought again of Diera and his suspicion that Drefan and not the Beast of the North was responsible for her death. His certainty of just a few weeks ago withered and died as self-doubt took root.

And, though he racked his brains, he could not ken any reason why Drefan would have killed Diera with the intent her body be mistaken for Frey. Was there an advantage for Drefan in having him believe so? Or had Sebastian become so fixated in his hatred for the man that he would ascribe any wickedness to him?

More likely, Sebastian supposed in his clearer-thinking moments, poor Diera had simply fallen foul of some murderous copyist of the Beast in the lawless world outside the villages.

Yet if that was the case, how to explain that Diera was found only recently killed so close to Tyrswick many weeks after she had been supposed returning to Scotland?

Thinking about it was starting to hurt Sebastian's head, so he descended to the yard where, between patrols and management of the affairs of the county these past weeks, he spent every spare moment in punishing rounds of training. The pig leather hide that was his punching bag received a brutal pummeling, and swordplay practice with his men took on an intensity hitherforth unknown since the Invasion.

For Sebastian, each thrust of his sword, each punch landed on the bag was, in his mind, directed at Drefan.

Sebastian laughed to himself bitterly. He had Frey's description of the man, and Orlege's too, but he had no real idea what his enemy looked like. He was fighting a specter.

He'd allowed himself to go soft since Frey came into his life. He had bought into the lie of peace without price, and now he was at risk of losing the one thing that meant everything to him.

He began to consider it possible Frey was dead and, at his lowest ebb, wondered if that conclusion was not preferable to succumbing to the alternative worst case, the poison that brewed in his mind since the discovery of the letters.

* * *

Six weeks ground glacially by without a single word of hope, then early summer brought unexpected visitors. A guard stationed on the ramparts sent word down to the training yard that an armed delegation in the livery of the bishop of Durham was approaching.

Sebastian mopped the sweat from his brow and handed his sword to Robert, his newest knight. He called for Gaines and Dominic to join him in his chambers.

Sebastian poured a pitcher of hot water into a bowl. He sluiced his face and quickly washed the worst of the dried sweat from his body.

"They're about to arrive in the outer bailey," announced Beyard. "Cook has arranged a repast for them to give you time to repair yourself."

"Good," said Dominic as he folded his arms and looked contemptuously out of the window. "If the bishop's men are anything like the bishop himself, they won't object to gorging themselves on someone else's purse."

Gaines raised his eyebrows. "It's a good job diplomacy is not listed as a virtue, Friar. I always wondered why a man of your talents never went any higher than traveling cleric."

"I have no time for men who claim to be servants of God serving their own interests over his," Dominic responded crisply. "And the bishop is such a man."

"Gentlemen!"

Sebastian's punctuation brought both men to order.

"We don't have time to argue among ourselves," he told them as he dressed in his own court livery, a fine linen shirt and hose and a resplendent surcoat in white with the scarlet lion rampant finely stitched on his chest.

"We all know the bishop does nothing unless it has an immediate and personal reward, and he wouldn't send such a numerous delegation without reason. I suspect I've been enough of a thorn in his side these months that he's finally been forced to act on Frey's abduction.

"Let's hear what they have to say."

Sebastian entered the Great Hall and looked up at the magnificent tapestry Frey had designed for him. If her dedication to him was a pretence, she could not have done that. He felt her love and presence in the room at that moment and a surge of optimism. His bride would return home.

However, to his surprise, no men gathered at the trenchers apart from his own household.

Beyard approached, his mouth in a grim line.

"Sir, they've refused to disarm and refused to enter the Keep."

Dismayed, Sebastian, followed by Gaines and Dominic, Orlege and Robert, descended to the outer bailey.

Standing in the forecourt was a senior knight, a man into his middle age. He might have been handsome once, but easy living under the bishop's lot had thickened his waist and his chin.

He stood to attention, accompanied by two younger men, both serious-faced, whose hands were poised on the hilts of their swords.

"The bishop honors us with such an auspicious delegation," Sebastian began. "So what's this I hear that you refuse to accept my hospitality?"

The man straightened and unfurled the scroll in his hand.

"Sebastian de la Croix, baron of Tyrswick?"

Sebastian frowned.

"I am he."

"You are hereby accused of sedition against William, the rightful king of England and Normandy. You will answer to these charges in Durham."

A fleeting look to Gaines and Dominic reflected twin expressions of surprise. Sebastian turned back.

"Who accuses me?"

"The charge comes from Lord Drefan d'Aumont of Angou, who further charges that you abducted and raped his betrothed, Alfreya."

CHAPTER FORTY-ONE

They had traveled for an entire month before arriving at Durham, and Frey knew that was nearly four weeks ago. Her courses began the day she arrived at Durham Castle, and four days ago she experienced the telltale ache that accompanied their imminent return.

She stood on a small balcony, safe within the massive stone walls of the castle, and rubbed her abdomen, unmindful of the spectacular scenery across which farms and pasture lands had created a patchwork of orderly plots from midway up the hill and the start of Shaw Wood, down to where the sun had blessed the River Wear, wide and muddy brown, with a sprinkling of gold.

Where the river turned a sharp bend to pass the castle on a second side, a clearing had taken place for the bishop of Durham, William Walcher's, new obsession—a cathedral and monastery.

Her vision swam abruptly and she clung to the parapet for support.

She was still being drugged and, despite her best efforts to avoid heavily flavored wines, there was little she could do to avoid food, although she did her best to eat sparingly.

The healthy weight she gained since living at Tyrswick had been shed, leaving her as thin and weak as she had been in her final weeks as an outlaw.

"Come away from the window, you'll get ill in all that fresh air," Mistress Duignan clucked, placing a woolen shawl across her shoulders. Frey immediately shrugged it off, anxious to feel the sun on her back for a few moments more.

Seeing her duty done, the titian-haired woman sat by the fireplace and resumed her knitting. Frey returned to the room, light-filled and pleasantly furnished, most suitable for a married lord and his retinue.

But a prison was a prison, no matter how pleasant the view.

After several minutes of restless pacing, Frey slumped into a chair and reluctantly picked up some needlework. She stabbed at the fabric more in anger than dexterity and watched resentfully as her jailer slumped farther and farther into her chair, then started to snore lightly.

Frey bided her time silently. The passage of minutes was marked by the shadows being cast across the floor.

She had learned that around the time they reached the far edge of the wide floor rug, the evening meal would be delivered by Drefan's twin whores, who, laughably, passed themselves off as her maids. Some evenings Drefan would arrive too; on others, she would not see him all night.

The only sounds in the room were the occasional pop from the fireplace and the rhythmic snores of the woman who dozed beside it. Frey watched the sun creep over the carpet until its shadow mark lay halfway across. It would now be approximately ten minutes before the rug lay in full shadow.

Still Mistress Duignan slept and, finally, Frey rose stealthily and crossed to the far end of the room, where a stout oak door opened out to the hall.

She reached out and touched the handle, feeling its substance in her hand. With growing confidence, she pushed down on the latch and the resulting click sounded unnaturally loud. A swift glance around saw Mistress Duignan unmoved.

Now was her chance!

The door opened with minimal fuss, nary a squeal on the hinges, and Frey tugged the weighty timber cautiously. Just a little bit more and she would slip around it into the hall.

But to Frey's surprise, the door suddenly swung inward of its own accord, the heavy oak pivoting rapidly on its hinges and slamming back against the stone wall.

Frey fell back in shock as a wakened Mistress Duignan screamed behind her. Drefan filled the doorway, his two blonde mistresses drifting behind him with the evening meals on trays.

"What's this, my lady? I arrive early for our meal and find you trying to slip away?"

He came toward her and she retreated in equal measure until she felt a windowsill at her back.

Drefan reached out and his hand gripped her chin cruelly and pushed.

Frey scrambled to brace herself as he bent her backward through the open window, leaning over her. She steadied a line of sight on him against the glare of the sun now in her eyes.

"You'll be hanged by nightfall if you kill me now," she hissed.

His answer was grin.

"You overestimate your importance."

To emphasize the point, Drefan pushed harder.

Frey lost her footing and rested against a mere twelve inches of stone coping, her knees bent and heels digging against the inside wall for purchase.

With his hold on her face tightening, her scream was little more than a squeak.

"That's right, my little mouse. You're mine to toy with for as long as I please. Should I decide on defenestration for you, all anyone will think is the poor lady Alfreya, not right in the head, chose to take her own life rather than face the Norman dog who even now rides to Durham."

Drefan hauled her back into the chamber and shoved her toward a cushion-covered settle.

Sebastian! Unreasonable hope filled her breast, and the expression must have shown itself, as Drefan's own face changed as she sat.

"You love him."

Frey sat straighter on the bench and met his gaze. Drefan burst out laughing and clapped his hands once.

"Perfect!"

"He will kill you," Frey answered steadily, although she wondered at Drefan's apparent delight.

"De la Croix is a sentimental fool! Before the sun sets in three days' time, you will have ripped out his heart piece by piece until he is a husk of a man who would be defeated by a stiff breeze."

Scorn flushed her face, red hot and venomous.

"I'd sooner rip out my own heart."

"It's too late, my pet. It's already done. Don't you remember your impassioned words?"

Drefan stepped away from her and threw out his arms, acting the scene and using the floor as if he were a professional mummer. "'Every time I come close to that Norman dog, I wish I held my dagger to plunge into his chest again and again and again.'"

His blonde mistresses stood on either side of Mistress Duignan, each laying one restraining hand on the old woman's shoulders as they giggled their appreciation of his performance. The old woman gaped as Drefan continued.

"'I would take his life without pity as he took my father's life without remorse. Would you do the deed for me, Drefan? You would if you were serious about your love pledge for me and, oh my love, how I would show my gratitude and give you my body as yours—'"

"Enough!" cried Frey, feeling her fingernails pierce through the silk on the cushions beneath her as she clenched her fists in anger. Yes, those were her words, and she was horrified to hear them again, but they were written many moons ago, a full twelvemonth past, when she was still at war with the Normans and the hatred with which Drefan had poisoned her mind still blazed in her.

She swallowed and continued in a more measured tone.

"My husband will never believe those letters to be recent."

"My dear, it's likely he already does, especially when he reads my replies."

"You never answered my letters!"

Drefan folded his arms and grinned.

"Oh yes, I did. A reply to each one sits bound in a satin ribbon among your clothes in Tyrswick."

Frey's eyes widened. How? When?

Drefan saw the questions on her face and answered them obliquely.

"Lovelorn girls are always apt to make rash decisions."

"Heloise," she responded leadenly.

"She was a very useful idiot," Drefan admitted. "Not only did she place the letters but she also informed us of events inside the Keep, all of which will date the letters within a half year of today. And should he discover they are false, he will surely learn who secreted them among your possessions. What damage do you think it will do to his relationship with his brother-in-law and ally?"

Frey had no response. She knew Sebastian loved Rhys as a brother and considered Heloise as his own sister. Would it be better for him to think that she had betrayed him than his own family?

She drew breath.

"Sebastian," Frey began slowly, "is not a man to be underestimated."

"Neither is the bishop and his court. The letters not only confirm my version of events but also help support a compelling case that will convict de la Croix of being a traitor to King William."

A stalwart Norman knight like Sebastian, a traitor? Why the very notion was absurd. Two months of aching fear now found their release in derisive laughter.

"You truly are an addle-brained lunatic. No one is ever going to believe such an accusation."

Drefan gave her a parody of a downcast expression.

"Oh…Now you've underestimated *me*, my pet. A very, very bad thing to do.

"You think me ill-prepared, but I have been dedicated to nothing else for many years. There is nothing that has escaped my attention. For instance, de la Croix's traitorous allowing of your escape from a Durham barn with your father and the brat."

Frey regarded him with shock. How did he know?

She composed herself. "Sebastian is loyal to King William."

"Sebastian is weak."

Anger burned in her at Drefan's sneering judgment.

"Mercy is not weak; mercy is strong. And Sebastian risked his own life that night he let us go—"

She stopped abruptly, realizing she had only further confirmed his accusation. "No one will believe you," she said.

Drefan smiled. "But they will believe you."

"I will not support your case against my husband!"

"Never mind." He gestured back toward the women. "We have witnesses to your admission and they will happily testify."

Frey slumped. He had won.

"All this for Tyrswick," she muttered bleakly.

"On the contrary, my lady, I have been pledged a prettier prize than your drunkard father's mere district. King Malcolm has promised me the whole county of Northumbria when he invades England and is victorious."

Frey heard Mistress Duignan gasp behind her, and Drefan glanced over to give the woman a vicious, mugging smile before returning his attention to Frey.

"Who knows? It may be more. The Norman Empire is stretched and cannot support its own weight. Who can say how far south Malcolm might push?"

Frey dropped her head.

Drefan turned to the older woman, who sat in shocked silence behind Frey.

"You have displeased me, Mistress Duignan."

He nodded to the women flanking and restraining her.

"Take her to my chambers and wait for me there while I deal further with Lady Alfreya."

* * *

The conversations that echoed about the cavernous Great Hall of Durham Castle, one of the most impregnable fortresses in the north, stuttered and fell silent as Sebastian and his party entered.

With a swift wave of his hand, Gaines gave the signal for a dozen knights to disperse into the crowd with but one instruction—determine the size of Lord Drefan's company. Gaines, Orlege, and Robert, as Sebastian's most trusted men, had an additional mission: to identify the location of Lady Alfreya and to report to him, discreetly.

The Tyrswick men melted into the crowd largely ignored as most eyes—some friendly, others filled with contempt or simple curiosity—remained focused on Sebastian.

Only one man approached, Ligulf of Lumley, the most senior Saxon earl still in power in the North. The man exuded authority and wielded a strong hand that kept the hot-headed younger Saxons in check, but the earl was also a pragmatist. He knew William the Conqueror would never relinquish England, the jewel in the crown of the Norman Empire.

Lumley's position as senior advisor to William Walcher, the bishop of Durham and King William's personal appointment, was mutually advantageous, so long as peace was maintained.

From the look in the man's eye, it would appear Lumley believed peace should start in the Great Hall.

"Greetings, Tyrswick."

Despite the man's age, his double-handed grip on Sebastian's forearms was strong and firm.

"Greetings, Lumley." Sebastian nodded out across the sea of tables whose occupants were now making a great show of disinterest. "I see my arrival has caused a stir."

"What did you expect? One of King William's favored knights accused of plotting against him? Court hasn't been this well attended since Walcher's investiture."

The earl led Sebastian toward a quieter corner of the hall. He leaned forward slightly and lowered his voice.

"What's this nonsense about, Tyrswick? These are no trifling crimes this Lord Drefan D'Aumont of Angou charges you with."

"Falsehoods to be sure," Sebastian responded crisply. "But my first concern is for my wife."

"*Your* wife? Well, that appears to be the subject of some contention too."

"Have you seen her?"

Lumley shook his head.

"Only a glimpse when she first arrived, then she was spirited away to their quarters. This man claimed she had been so ill-used at your hands that her mind and body were damaged."

Sebastian became aware of the pain of his fingernails digging into the flesh of his palms. He unclenched his fists and enunciated his words coldly and precisely.

"I would never hurt Alfreya."

"Calm yourself, my lad," said Lumley, his expression kind. "I know you would not—"

"But he would!"

Sebastian's raised voice quieted the hall again. He spared the faces a glance and returned his attention to Lumley.

"I want her away from him now! I'll be demanding an audience with His Grace."

"You're in no position to demand anything, Tyrswick, not while these charges hang over your head. Walcher has set aside Friday afternoons to hear court matters. You can petition him then."

"Three days from now? What the hell does the man do all day?"

The earl's mouth lifted in a sardonic smile.

"You've not heard the latest? He's made grand plans for a cathedral and monastery right at the end of the peninsula. He spends half his time cloistered with draughtsmen and the other half banging the cup for contributions."

"So, no time to deal with matters relating to the peace and security of the North," said Sebastian with rueful bitterness.

Lumley shrugged. "Walcher isn't a bad man, he's—"

"—just so heavenly minded that he's no earthly good? That's how a friend of mine describes him." Sebastian hung his head briefly and closed his eyes. "To hell with it," he said, looking back up. "Three days, Lumley! I'm going to push for an audience now."

"Good luck with that, young man. You'll have to get past his chaplain, Leobwin, and his cousin Gilbert. They are the ones who wield the political power here."

"I have gold enough to grease the wheels," Sebastian retorted.

Lumley gave him a stern look.

"Take some advice from me, Tyrswick. Use the time to prepare your defense, make sure your men stay out of trouble, and renew some acquaintances here. The goodwill of your peers will be vital at the trial."

Sebastian weighed his options for a moment before offering a quick murmur of agreement. Lumley all but sighed in relief.

"In the meantime, I'll ask my wife to lead a delegation of noblewomen to check on Lady Alfreya's welfare," he offered.

"Then you have my most pronounced thanks," said Sebastian.

The earl clasped his forearm. It was meant as an expression of solidarity, but Sebastian recognized the warning in it. Feuds flared quickly here and much blood had been spilled in them.

"If we are going to stop the invasion from the north, we have to stop fighting among ourselves," said Lumley.

Sebastian frowned at the rapid change of subject. "These shores have not seen a Viking raid in nearly ten years."

A shutter came down on Lumley's expression and prickling awareness crawled its way up Sebastian's spine.

"You mean Scotland, don't you?"

Lumley said nothing to confirm, but a slight shift in his posture revealed more than words.

"It's inevitable. But I would rather it later than sooner."

A stir near the entrance to the Great Hall stole the older man's attention briefly before he turned back to Sebastian.

"We've had our minor differences, Tyrswick, but even I know you're loyal to the king. Don't do anything rash, eh?"

With a clap on the shoulder, the earl departed, deliberately avoiding the party now spilling through the double doors.

Emerging from the center of the crowd was a tall man, dressed finely in olive, trimmed with ochre. Sebastian sized him up. He was easily as tall and as broad as Sebastian himself.

The man carried himself with aristocratic ease born of self-assurance. His blond hair drew the observer to his dark arched eyebrows, which framed gray eyes. Even without a description, Sebastian felt he would have would known him.

He was face to face with Drefan.

CHAPTER FORTY-TWO

Frey huddled beneath the bed linens. She was too conscious of her vulnerability to drift into sleep, though she was exhausted. Her mind and body compromised, leaving her in a half-waking state.

She was not a woman prone to tears or tantrums when her monthly courses came, but now a hysterical bubble of laughter threatened to spill from her mouth at the thought of them. She swallowed the bitter laugh with a half sob.

Drefan's temper this afternoon was as ferocious as she had ever known, but he had not the appetite for anything else. The thought of a woman's blood curdled desire quickly even in men used to war and wounds, and for that she was grateful.

He roared but did not come near her, not even to deliver the beating he sorely wished to give. Drefan needed her alive, for the time being, anyway. Frey uttered a silent prayer for her elderly jailor. Mistress Duignan would be the one to bear the brunt of Drefan's brutality. Frey hoped she had strength to withstand it.

Instead, Drefan raged at Frey, then tormented her with Diera's awful misfortune and that of her fellow travelers.

"You hoped I was still in Scotland raising an army for you, but I wasn't," he had sneered.

"My party was in and out of England all the time. Sometimes we were close enough to hear your men snore at night. And when your father was dead and the group left for Scotland, we followed them and killed them. Except Diera, of course. Not straight away."

Though horrified, Frey had not been able to resist asking the question. "What did you do?"

"Oh," said Drefan lightly, "she was safe enough while she remained compliant and of use to me. And after she was disciplined for her first escape attempt, I thought she was cowed. She traveled with us for four weeks."

He looked at Frey emotionlessly.

"But you can never trust a woman, so when she tried to slip away again, I killed her."

He heard Frey's involuntary gasp at his brutally dismissive tone and smiled. He looked at his hands, front and back, then held them up for her to see.

"With these hands, as a matter of fact. With these bare hands."

"Why?" demanded Frey, huddling into the corner of her bed farthest from him. "Why did you kill her?"

He seemed to consider his words for a moment, his eyes becoming distant.

"Because I could," he said at last. "And because she reminded me of you."

Then he gazed at her more directly once again.

"I did regret it, honestly, Alfreya. I mean, what was I to do now? I'd have to dig a grave. Then I recalled the stupid villagers all abuzz about the Beast of the North and what he did to his victims, and it seemed much simpler to gouge Diera's eyes and cut off her fingers and hair, then just dump the body. You can see my logic. Just add another to the Beast's tally and I didn't need to get my men to dig a hole."

Frey had stared at the wall in shock for some time after he left the room.

She started awake. Perhaps she had dozed after all. She stopped to listen.

The wing of the castle that held the guest chambers was silent. It must be well after midnight.

"Get up!"

Frey heard the voice clearly; it was the voice of Larcwide.

"Get up now!"

She stirred, unsure of the direction the voice had come from. It seems as though it was all around her, in fact *through* her.

A sense of urgency filled her with energy, where the moment before had been lethargy. Frey sat up slowly and eased out of bed so as not to disturb the one of Drefan's twins who had been instructed to sleep beside her.

The woman did not stir.

Frey's hand connected with the solid reality of the door handle and it moved. She inched the door open and stood back against the wall, fearing a repetition of this afternoon's encounter with Drefan. Frey breathed out to the count of five and then breathed in.

Merciful silence.

A glimpse down the moonlit gallery revealed no one about.

"*The chapel*," the voice prompted.

Frey hazarded a guess and turned right, not looking back.

The dance of candlelight through the stained-glass sidelights of Durham Castle's chapel cast shadows of red, yellow, and green along the floor. Frey stepped through the entrance. Two shapes, bodies hunched over in prayer, sat in the front pews on either side of the red-carpeted aisle.

From habit, she dipped her hand in the holy water stoup and crossed herself. Frey was conscious of the open space and felt vulnerable so close to the door, so she moved farther in, edging along the back wall, past the two confessionals and the narrow oak staircase that rose to the choir loft. She found a deeply shadowed seat within the six rows and waited for the two figures to leave.

Stubbornly, they did not, their murmured prayers continuing.

Impatience, even panic, threatened to overwhelm her. What if Drefan should find her here? What protection would there be in a small room with two devout insomniacs?

"*Sanctuary.*"

The idea brought a measure of peace but no further clarity. Should she pray?

"Sanctuary," the voice insisted.

"Sanctuary!" Frey cried, startling herself as much as the two worshippers with the spoken word.

A richly dressed woman and a man clothed in the dull brown of a monk's robe turned swiftly to face where she now stood among the pews.

"My name is Alfreya of Tyrswick, wife of the baron of Tyrswick," she told them. "I throw myself on the mercy of Almighty God and demand the right of sanctuary from the Church."

The monk stood and pulled back his hood. For one horrible moment Frey feared it was Baldwin there to take her back. The face revealed was a welcome one.

"Dominic!"

* * *

On too little sleep, Frey's temper strained to the breaking point.

"Take it back!" she snapped.

After the interrogation she received at the hands of Lady Aldgyth of Lumley and Lady Maeve, the wife of the bishop's counselor Lord Gilbert, the poor lady's maid was a convenient scapegoat for her frustration. The girl was at first frightened at the explosive outburst, and then bemused.

Frey was forced to admit that, on the face of it, her objection sounded absurd.

Refuse to receive a coffer full of beautiful clothes and matching shoes?

She barely spared it a glance before waving away the two squires who carted the box. She could easily refuse when they were bought by Drefan. Frey wanted to leave no uncertainty in anyone's mind whom she favored.

She took a deep breath and continued in a more conciliatory manner.

"Please inform Lord Drefan there is nothing of mine in his chambers. If he will not accept the return of the clothes, you have my permission to distribute them among the poor."

The young woman's eyes lit up. It seemed she considered herself most eligible for her ladyship's charity, and Frey was in no doubt the spoils would be distributed among Lumley's servants within the hour.

Good.

From the moment she came under the protection of the Earl Ligulf of Lumley and his wife, Lady Aldgyth, her every word, every gesture, was observed and discussed behind covered hands and closed doors by every denizen of Durham Castle.

Did you see those bruises?

Well, she doesn't look feeble-minded.

She's awfully thin.

Have you seen both men? Who wouldn't love to have *her* choice?

She was on trial as much as Sebastian.

Frey's actions now could win or lose support for Sebastian among the other knights called on in two days' time to side with the accused or the accuser.

To commend or condemn.

The ladies brooked no dissembling on Frey's part. Their questions were thorough, relentless, and intensely personal. Not even Abbot Ranulf in St. Cuthbert's Abbey would dream of asking such intimate questions.

Frey answered with equal frankness and, after an hour, the two older women gave one another meaningful looks and mercifully left her alone.

Frey returned to the mahogany coffer that remained closed in the anteroom hastily prepared as a small bedchamber for her. The chest had arrived before dawn this morning, but she'd had no time to open it.

She ran her hand over the familiar woodwork. It was the first piece of furniture given to her. No elaborately carved and inlaid piece could ever mean as much to her as this sturdy and reliable piece of craftsmanship made by Tyrswick Keep's carpenter.

She lay her cheek against the surface as though being close to it she could be close to Sebastian and fingered the latch, watching it pivot on its hinges.

Tears begged for attention behind her closed lids. Stupid feminine weakness, Frey cursed, and stubbornly refused to give in to them.

It was ridiculous surely, but it seemed that if Frey concentrated, she could smell the freshly cut grass and the fragrance of the meadow flowers of home. With a new sense of purpose, Frey opened the lid.

A single sheet of paper lay folded on top of the freshly laundered, familiar clothes from Tyrswick. It was a note in Sebastian's own hand.

It contained one word.

Courage.

A sharp rap on the door brought Frey back to herself. Wiping stray tears, she bade the visitor entrance. When she saw the grim expressions worn by Lady Aldgyth and Friar Dominic, she stood.

"What's amiss? Is it Sebastian?"

Lady Aldgyth bustled past her into the chamber beyond and called for two maids.

"My lady," began Dominic, "I had hoped this wouldn't be necessary, but it seems you will be required to give evidence."

Her heart quickened. To give evidence would be to see Sebastian and set to rights the lies spun by Drefan.

She lifted her chin with confidence rather than feigned bravado.

"I welcome the opportunity, Dominic."

* * *

It was obvious to Sebastian that Bishop Walcher would dearly love to be somewhere else; probably holed up with his advisors, dreaming of ever more elaborate embellishments to his cathedral.

The man turned to Drefan and waved his hand impatiently to direct evidence to support the charge of treason be given.

Drefan remained silent and still until all eyes were on him.

Sebastian was reminded of the magician at the All Hallows Eve revels—impressive theater as long as one didn't look too closely. He made that mistake himself once.

It would not happen twice.

Sebastian had his own trick up his sleeve. He vowed to Frey long ago that he would see that Diera got the justice she deserved, and one way or another he would deliver.

Did his hatred of Drefan derange his judgment? No matter. This morning at the breakfast, he announced his intention to denounce Drefan on a charge of murder.

Sebastian's declaration and subsequent refusal to immediately name the victim created such uproar in the Hall that Walcher could no longer ignore it. He angrily demanded both men convene in the Bishop's Hall to settle immediately the matter of both the accusation of murder and the case of Lady Alfreya.

Now here they stood, face to face, in front of an audience of their peers who would also be their judges.

Sebastian, every fiber of his being tensed for action, looked directly at Drefan, whose cold gray eyes stared back implacably.

What concocted "evidence" would Drefan bring?

Sebastian was an exemplary soldier. London could have no quarrel with him; tax revenues had increased year on year as he improved farm yields and, in two years, turned the abandoned Roman coal mine into a safe and profitable enterprise.

This year, he intended to turn his attention to an abandoned lead mine, which, local legend had it, also hosted a rich vein of silver.

The Crown did well from Tyrswick, Sebastian considered, and his own conscience was clear. His only disobedience was back in the days of the Harrying, when he spared the lives of the wounded Alfred and his children, and none but him and Frey knew of it.

"My friends," Drefan began. "It might seem to you here that this is merely a falling out between two men over a woman."

Sebastian fancied he heard behind him a quiet snort of derision from Gaines, who sat on the front pew on his side of the aisle, along with Dominic, Orlege, and Robert.

"But nothing could be further from the truth," Drefan continued. "This is about the future security of England.

"I myself have only recently become aware of a conspiracy between the baron of Tyrswick and the late Earl Alfred to conspire with King Malcolm of Scotland to invade England."

The Bishop's Hall was in uproar once more.

Sebastian watched the reaction of the crowd closely. Those lords who refused to pledge their support for him ahead of time showed little emotion. His own supporters openly jeered Drefan, with the exception of Lumley. Was the man wavering in his support? Sebastian had no time to speculate on what that might mean. The earl was highly influential among the Saxon nobility who remained in Northumbria. The support of Saxons hinged on his opinion.

Drefan's prosecution continued. Damn it if the man didn't look like he was enjoying himself, Sebastian thought.

"Have you never wondered why a knight as renowned as de la Croix retires to a quiet backwater when he might have had his pick of the Welsh marshlands or even a holding in France itself?" he asked.

"Then let me give you the facts of the case. This shameful affair has its origins during the Harrying of the North. In the Year of Our Lord 1070, in a battle outside this very city, a pact was established. A young, ambitious squire, de la Croix, disobeyed his lord's orders to secure a hay barn where Earl Alfred sought refuge."

Sebastian's heart turned cold.

By God, the man would try to damn him with the truth.

CHAPTER FORTY-THREE

Frey examined her reflection in the length of polished steel. As Lady Aldgyth's maids tied the stays of the deep blue kirtle, the gown formed itself across her breasts and waist. The two young women gasped at the color and, begging her ladyship's pardon, could not help but remark that the fabric matched the color of her eyes.

Frey brushed down the sleeves, fitted tight to the elbow then slashed wide to reveal the bloodred lining that also edged the square neckline as well as the edges of the sleeve.

The same fabric formed the underskirt and, as she turned and sat on a low stool, slashes of red peeked from the beneath the rich blue of the kirtle. Gold brocade ribbon decorated the neck, elbows, and sleeves.

The weight of the gold-and-garnet-trimmed chain, Sebastian's gift on New Year's Day, settled across her décolleté. The other maid fastened soft leather shoes to her feet.

Finally, a gossamer-fine veil in white covered her braided blonde hair, held in place with a gold circlet.

One last lingering inspection in the mirror and she was satisfied with her preparation. Frey, wearing the colors of Tyrswick, was dressed for battle.

Escorted by two of Walcher's own household guards, with Friar Dominic by her side, Frey stood at the entrance to the bishop's Hall. Part of the new wing of Durham Castle, the large room was sumptuously appointed with wall hangings and tapestries and long rows of highly polished brass candelabras that shone with the morning summer sunlight streaming through the transom windows set high in the wall.

Her eyes sought out Sebastian. He stood as a soldier at ease, as did Drefan opposite. Each was dressed in their finest court attire, but neither could out-do the bishop in splendor.

The white robe worn by William Walcher, bishop of Durham, was simple in cut but not in fabric. His garb was snow-white linen, almost blinding in its intensity, over which he wore elaborate mulberry-red vestments embroidered in gold. A small miter made of cloth of gold covered his graying head.

He sat on a high-back oak chair on a dais a foot higher than the stone floor.

His throne, though made of quality oak, seemed plain on first glance. The back resembled the arched stained window behind, its relative austerity relieved by red and gold embroidered cushions. A smaller chair was placed at his right hand for his chaplain Leobwin.

Frey became conscious that her presence at the far end of the hall was causing a stir.

"When the bishop signals, walk toward him and do not look at Sebastian or Lord Drefan," Dominic instructed softly at her ear. "Remember, 'God has not given us a spirit of fear, but of love, of power and of a sound mind.'"

Frey gave a single nod of acknowledgment and promptly ignored Dominic's instruction. She kept her eyes on Sebastian as she had done a summer ago. This time, instead of suspicion, his mesmerizing green eyes greeted her with love, encouragement, and pride.

This time, instead of in defeat, Frey walked toward him victoriously with an equal measure of love and pride.

Only when she traversed the hall did she stop before the bishop, where she curtsied and kissed the sacred gold signet ring engraved with a miter and the appointments of his office.

"You may arise, my dear," the bishop told her kindly, and then, with a sidelong glance at Drefan, added, "I had been told you were too ill to be presented to court. I'm glad to see for myself the report is untrue."

"I believe you'll find there are many things you have been told which are untrue, Your Grace," Frey responded.

The bishop straightened and looked out among the audience for the hearing and addressed his next remarks so all assembled could hear.

"My lady, do you swear by Almighty God to tell the truth to this assemblage?"

Frey's voice rang out confidently.

"I do."

"Then be so good as to identify yourself to the court."

"I am Lady Alfreya of Tyrswick, wife of Sebastian de la Croix, baron of Tyrswick," Frey answered loudly and with assurance.

"Are you here willingly?"

"I stand before you willingly today, Your Grace, but I was not brought to Durham Castle willingly."

Frey heard the murmurs of the assembled crowd but didn't turn. She wondered whether the interest being shown here was as much related to the cause of justice as the amount of coin wagered on the result.

"According to Lord Drefan, your testimony is you were taken against your will and subjected to outrages. Are you saying this is not so?"

"It is so."

At the seeming contradiction of her words, the room erupted in a din that forced Walcher's righthand man to yell for order. Frey remained silent at the interruption and kept her attention fixed on Walcher's face. He was difficult to read; indeed, he seemed almost bored with the proceedings, as though he had something better to do and somewhere better he had to be.

If she could convince him of Drefan's perfidy in this, it would undermine the charge of treason against Sebastian. By providing Walcher a nice, neat resolution, perhaps he would be inclined to dismiss all counts.

As the crowd hushed, she continued, "Lord Drefan is the man who took me against my will in a scheme to defame Sebastian de la Croix and claim Tyrswick for himself through me. I have been legally wed to only one man, and that is the baron of Tyrswick."

The volume of the hall increased again, but a couple of loud raps from the bishop's shepherd crook on the tiled floor silenced the crowd.

"What Lord Drefan does not know is that even if the baron were stripped of his title, the lands will return to Earl Alfred's heir, Brice, who still lives."

Another thought occurred to Frey and, relishing the high drama, she turned to Drefan.

"You set the trap for Brice that would have killed him from infection but for the healing of Brother Halig at St. Cuthbert's Abbey."

His astonished expression lasted for a blink of an eye and no more, although she could see the man begin to recalculate his plans. Warming to her theme, a cascade of thoughts tumbled into her mind and flowed like a stream across her consciousness, leading her to a further conclusion.

"The wolves!"

Frey pivoted to look to Sebastian, who nodded in reply. It seemed he had come to the same conclusion the split second she did. She turned back to Drefan and pointed an accusing finger at him.

"You created the land slip and drew wolves upon myself and the baron deliberately to kill one or the both of us!"

The court was in uproar yet again, and no amount of rapping of a cane nor shouts for order could calm the crowd for minutes. Eventually order was restored, but not before Sebastian had enfolded his wife in an embrace, heedless of the crowd.

"Welcome home, princess," he whispered in her ear.

She clung to him like a vine and he breathed in the smell of her. Wildflowers.

"I love you with all my heart," she replied.

He responded by strengthening his embrace.

"I'm looking forward to you showing me how much, but we're not out of the woods yet. Be strong for a little while longer."

"I shall," she assured him, "but Sebastian, Drefan has confessed to me he killed Diera. He disguised her murder—"

"As one committed by the Beast of the North," Sebastian concluded.

She looked at him in amazement. "How did you know?"

"I'll explain later," he said as the crowd began to still. "We must retake our seats now."

"But I have something else to tell you—"

She was silenced by the rapping of the crook, which was now winning over the babble of the crowd.

Frey swallowed dryly and accepted Gaines's hand to take her to his own seat.

* * *

"We have dismissed the charge of abduction and ill-use of Lady Alfreya of Tyrswick as one without basis," continued Walcher. "Now we come to the more serious matter of an accusation of treason against Sebastian de la Croix, baron of Tyrswick, by Lord Drefan D'Aumont of Angou, cousin by blood to Edgar the Atheling, cousin by marriage to Robert Cuthose, son of William our king."

Sebastian was surprised.

An indirect connection to the Crown? Well, that explained the man's arrogance. It also settled another matter.

Regardless of the truth, regardless of the good opinion of Sebastian's peers, Drefan unchecked could bring this charge again and again, even before King William himself.

There could be only one way for this nightmare to end—a wager of battle.

Sebastian drew himself up taller. If that was his only recourse, then it was what he would do.

He would be ready.

"We have all been deceived," said Drefan. He paused dramatically then went on. "I thought I was doing my duty to bring justice to a woman once pledged to be my bride, but I now see I am the one who is being ill-used by two conspiratorial families.

"Let the court ask if the Lady Alfreya will recall that fateful day for herself, when her father Earl Tyrswick and her younger brother sheltered in a hay barn in a village not far from here," said Drefan.

"Is it not true that Sebastian de la Croix, then a young knight, willfully ignored his oath to the Crown and failed to report to his lord that the rebel Earl Tyrswick and his offspring were hiding in the barn? And further, that he allowed them, even guided them, in their escape from the rightful custody of the Crown?"

Walcher's eyebrows had risen during the telling; in fact, they had risen so high they had disappeared beneath his miter.

"Lady Alfreya, is this true?"

The noise of chairs scraping back on the stones sounded harshly.

Sebastian met Frey's eyes and read the fear in them. He knew with a certainty that just the merest indication from him and she would lie for him.

No. He would not let her.

"You will know the truth and the truth will set you free." He would not be responsible for damning her soul and his.

"The truth, Frey."

Anguish crossed her face. She knew as well as he did what her answer would do.

"Courage, my love."

He watched as Frey licked her lips just once, squared her shoulders, and answered with passion.

"My father, brother, and I were spared that night by a knight who is the exemplar of chivalry and valor."

There! That's the beauty and bravery he fell in love with that night all those years ago. His own spirits lifted. A flicker of delighted malice flittered across Drefan's face before his features settled into a practiced neutrality.

"Evidence of my veracity, my lords, from the damsel's own lips!"

Drefan went on.

"What was promised between the participants on that night can only be a matter of conjecture, so I leave it to you to speculate why the baron entreated London for approval of a hasty marriage with no effort to find whether the man who had prior claim on Lady Alfreya still lived. After all, it's not like the woman breeds."

Sebastian opened and closed his right hand slowly, the small action a tool to master his anger when his immediate desire was to bury his fist deep into the face of the man before him.

"Day after day, as drunk and as maudlin as Lord Alfred was, his story did not vary. His lands held a king's ransom and were at disposal to any who would liberate England from the, ah, foreign invader." Drefan paused to ensure he had everyone's full attention.

"King Malcolm of Scotland was very interested indeed."

Bishop Walcher was unimpressed with the theatrics.

"Hearsay," he dismissed with an offhand wave, "from a man no longer alive—"

"Answer me this," Earl Lumley interjected, rising to his feet. "Why would any knight with land relinquish his title and everything that goes with it to support an invasion against his liege? It's suicidally preposterous."

"Not if he thought the rebellion was going to be successful," Drefan answered without missing a beat. "King William is, I regret to say, occupied trying to quell rebellion from his own son. England is vulnerable."

Belatedly, Walcher reasserted his authority.

"If you have genuine proof of any wrongdoing by the baron of Tyrswick, I suggest you bring it now, because I'm beginning to think that you're wasting our time, my lord, and I have better things to do."

"Pardon, my Grace," murmured Drefan with an obsequious bow. "An honest knight once in the employ of the baron approached me, concerned that his lord was withholding from the Crown a trove of silver, which might well be payment from Malcolm of Scotland."

Sebastian frowned. Who the hell?

At the end of the hall, a familiar face appeared. Baldwin, dressed in the olive and ochre colors of Drefan of Anjou's household retinue, carried a small yet weighty casket, judging by the strain on his arms.

At the Bishop's nod, he approached and placed the casket at his feet and, with great ceremony, turned a lock and opened the bowed lid. To be sure, silver streamed across the floor and glittered in the sunlight.

Leobwin picked up one of the coins and passed it to Walcher, who examined it.

"Baron?"

Walcher tossed the coin to Sebastian who caught it deftly.

Sebastian ran his thumb over the impression on one side and then the other. Definitely silver, definitely a Roman denarius with the head of Septimius Severus on one side and VICTORIAE BRIT on the other.

He tossed it back to bounce with a chink and settle among what looked to be at least two hundred more coins.

"Do you recognize these, Baron?"

Sebastian answered firmly, "I do not."

"One of your men says differently," Drefan responded mildly.

"A man I stripped of rank and sent packing—"

"A man grievously wronged for defending the interests of the Crown and daring to question the relationship of his lord and a woman who a few days earlier was supposed to be his sworn enemy!"

Sebastian glanced rapidly between Walcher and Drefan, ensuring he had both men's full attention. "This man has the temerity to accuse me of deception and dishonor, when he abducted my wife and embarked on a campaign of terror against Tyrswick, including the brutal murder of the young woman who was Lady Alfreya's companion!"

Sebastian let a quiet satisfaction settle into his spirit at the look of sudden alarm in Drefan's face.

He pressed his advantage.

"This man sought to hide his vicious crime by disguising it as the work of the Beast of the North."

"Lies!"

"The truth!"

Silence descended at the unexpected intervention of a feminine voice.

Frey had risen from her seat and walked to beside Sebastian. The scent of wildflowers filled his nostrils, the warmth of her presence a palpable thing.

"Drefan of Angou admitted his crime to me, that he sorely used my maid and friend Diera, then killed her with his own hands."

"Do you accept the word of a woman?" demanded Drefan.

Sebastian watched Walcher's expression wavering to uncertainty as Drefan continued to vehemently protest his innocence.

Enough.

"If Drefan of Angou does not yield," called Sebastian, "then I demand trial by battle."

CHAPTER FORTY-FOUR

His chamber was in darkness by the time he returned to it, with only the glow of the banked fire to relieve the overwhelming blackness. By it, he could see the shape of Frey unstirring beneath the linens.

They had been separated immediately after the court hearing, with no chance to speak.

Gaines informed her that he had to go with Earl Lumley and escorted her to his chambers.

That was hours ago.

Frey was understandably upset by his demand for a trial by battle. Another sin to be heaped on his shoulders.

He recalled the afternoon.

"Sebastian, no!"

He had ignored Frey's protest and kept his eyes fixed on Walcher. The bishop turned to Leobwin and conferred in low voices for several moments.

Walcher sat back in his chair and addressed Drefan.

"Do you withdraw your charges against the baron of Tyrswick?"

"I do not."

"Do you deny the accusation of the murder of"—Leobwin supplied the name—"the maid Diera?"

"I do."

Walcher turned to Sebastian, his face grave.

"Do you deny the charge of treason against the king of England?"

338

"I do."

"Will you withdraw the charge of murder against Lord Drefan of Anjou?"

"I will not."

The Bishop issued a put-upon sigh and rose. "Very well. A trial by battle two days hence, and may God be with you both."

Now Sebastian undressed quietly and slipped between the sheets. Indeed, his wife was deeply asleep. Dried trails of tears marked her cheeks and he rubbed the offense away.

Frey's eyes opened sharply—the past two months having left her wary—then threw her arms around him. If she wept, she covered it.

A lump grew in his throat. He never wanted to be the cause of his wife's tears, only of her passion and her joy.

"Did Ligulf interrogate you further?" she whispered. "He's fixed on the notion that Malcolm will soon invade England."

Sebastian nodded. He took his wife's sleep-clenched fists and kissed the knuckles of one hand and then the other before enfolding both in one hand and drawing them to his chest.

"I know."

"He's not the only one. Drefan believes so too. That's what else I needed to tell you. The rebellion of which he accuses you is one he foments himself."

Sebastian sighed. "Nothing surprises me about that man."

Frey shifted and Sebastian welcomed the weight of her head on his chest.

"I'm surprised Malcolm continues against King William even as his son is hostage to the Crown."

Sebastian stroked Frey's arm and felt the tension ebb way with the motion.

"Malcolm has sons aplenty; he won't miss one."

Frey emitted an unladylike snort.

"Ligulf's biggest battle," Sebastian continued, "will be convincing the bishop to bring Northumbria to readiness. The Scots bearing the incorruptible body of St. Cuthbert himself into Durham would be the only way to get Walcher's attention."

Silence stretched between them and Sebastian wondered if Frey had drifted back to sleep.

"Are you ready?" she said finally.

For a moment Sebastian wondered whether he should deflect the question with a jest, then decided against it. Frey understood the gravity of his decision; he would not insult her by making light of the battle to come.

"I am."

Frey wound her arms around him.

"Drefan will not fight fair."

"Then trust Gaines and Orlege as my witnesses. They will ensure he doesn't get away with anything underhanded. Besides, I have an advantage Drefan does not."

Frey raised her head and looked at him questioningly.

"I have a very strong incentive to stay alive," he told her. And, at that, her tears glittered in the firelight and rolled down her cheeks in rivulets of molten gold.

"I love you, Frey. I think I fell in love with you on that very first night we met. Your courage, your fire, stir in me a passion I never thought possible to experience."

"Damn you, Tyrswick," said Frey, her voice low and harsh with need. "How do you expect me to be brave when you bring me undone? I love you so much, and I am afraid for you. I want to hold you this night and every night until we die old and gray."

She spoke on a sob.

"Please don't leave me."

Sebastian could take no more. He engulfed Frey in his arms and rained kisses across her hair, down her face, until his lips claimed hers, hungry and demanding.

Frey responded with equal fervor. Her hands caressed him across his back and along his neck before her fingers threaded through his hair and gripped, keeping him with her.

His tongue mated with hers, dueling for control. He won, shaking off her hands and pinning them above her head with one hand, while the other gripped the light linen night dress. With one swift movement the garment was rent from neck to hem.

Using his superior strength, Sebastian shifted, holding Frey beneath him. Her night dress opened like a curtain, rosy red nipples crowning the breasts set high and firm on her chest. He took one in his mouth and played with it with his teeth and tongue until she squirmed beneath him, breathily demanding more.

As he turned his attention to her other breast, his free hand slid between her legs. The slick heat of her drew his fingers unerringly to her core. Two fingers plunged into her again and again, while his thumb stroked her red and swollen bud.

Frey arched her back in ecstasy, a keening wail accompanying the clench of her inner walls as her climax overtook her.

He felt alive. He *was* alive—more than he had been in the two months of Frey's disappearance.

Sebastian savored the intensity of his erection, fueled by his wife's passion. He breathed in the tangy, earthy scent of her arousal and revelled in the feel of her around his fingers.

And now he experienced the equally desperate need to taste her. And he did.

The silky curls at the junction of her thighs pleased him with their softness, luring him deeper. Frey cried out again, the rhythmic rocking of her hip stuttered and bucked as yet another orgasm shook her.

Sebastian was unashamedly erect and it took all the willpower he possessed to stop him from plunging into her sweetness. As if sensing his restraint, Frey's thighs spread wider in invitation, her legs sliding down his back, urging him upward.

The need to be fully joined overwhelmed him, and he entered her in one swift motion. She called out his name and with her inner muscles held him to her. He had no idea where he ended and she began.

They were one. One in body and one in spirit.

He held himself still and stroked Frey's face, softly urging her to open her eyes. Soft dark lashes opened to reveal the deep blue beneath.

"Look at me, Frey, look at me as I make love to you," he whispered, echoing the words he spoke to her when she first came to him that night, afraid of Drefan, afraid of him.

Her lips parted and the kiss she offered was sweet and warm. Frey teased him, nuzzling him before offering chaste kisses along his stubble-coated chin. The red heat of his passion softened to a warm glow that filled his entire being with peace and belonging. Then she squeezed her inner muscles slowly and provocatively. Sensation shot directly to his groin and he eyed her. Frey wore such a sweet expression as she kissed his temple, he wondered whether the contact had been accidental.

Then she did it again, holding him firm for a beat or two before relaxing, then squeezing.

"Wench."

He barely recognized the husky voice as his own. He rocked his hips once and Frey moaned wantonly.

"Mmmm, but I'm your wench," she answered, squeezing him again.

Then, it was too much. Sebastian thrust into her again and again, the sounds of her encouragement driving him hard. His own release, long denied, hovered on the brink until Frey cried out her passion once more and he tumbled over the precipice.

* * *

Frey stretched full length beneath the sheets. The fine linen rubbed against her naked flesh, reawakening parts that had been thoroughly and pleasurably used not once but twice during the night. The scent of Sebastian lingered although he did not tarry abed.

He had kissed her awake in the half-light period before dawn and made love to her again before leaving to consult with Gaines and Orlege on protocol and tactics for the battle tomorrow.

"Dear God, please don't take him away from me," she pleaded softly.

Sebastian had left word not to disturb his wife, and Frey didn't bother to call for her maid; she was quite capable of dressing herself and needed this time in solitude. Every fiber of her being urged her to stop him and recant the demand for a trial by battle, but she did not.

She would not.

Frey knew as well as he did the only way to be rid of Drefan and his threat for good would be to fight. Drefan had nothing to lose. And he must face retribution, in this life and the next.

First, the "misfortunes" that dogged Alfred's campaign, which saw Brice nearly lose his life and did cost Diera hers, then enlisting Heloise in the plot to undermine Frey's marriage to Sebastian. Her own abduction…

Even a warrior of superior skill can be defeated on the battlefield if his mind is bested first.

The letters.

Frey worried her lip. Had Sebastian discovered them? Did he know they were false?

The need to find him and assure him of her love was overwhelming.

She dressed swiftly.

Robert waited at the door in his knight's livery and informed her gravely that he, along with Talbot, would be her escort and guard at Durham Castle.

The past few months had altered both young men; they seemed to have grown taller and their physiques had broadened. No longer carefree youths, both were now serious young men for whom, she later learned, Larcwide's death bore hard. Frey wasn't sure if the change was to be celebrated or mourned along with her old friend.

They escorted her from the suite of chambers and into the Great Hall to break fast.

As she sat, another six men she recognized from Tyrswick left their places and surrounded her table.

Now, this was too much.

"Robert…"

The young man who just three months ago would have quailed at the censure in her voice, crossed his arms and planted his feet.

"My orders are explicit, Lady Alfreya. Your life above all others."

Frey ate without further comment while she inwardly warred.

She was a capable woman, a warrior herself who chaffed under the protective detail her husband demanded. Yet to protest now would be a potentially fatal distraction for Sebastian. A slow count to ten helped somewhat.

Oh yes, she would complain all right, but the day *after* tomorrow, when she would demand Sebastian take her home to Tyrswick, where she would have the run of the Keep and the freedom to ride and hunt across the moors without requiring a small army of guards.

She could wait.

A Castle Durham page tapped Talbot on the shoulder and drew him away from the table to whisper something in his ear. With a lift of his chin, Talbot alerted Robert, who rose also. The two young knights spoke in hushed tones before Talbot turned back to the page. He pressed a coin in his hand and the lad scampered off.

"What's amiss?" Frey asked on Robert's return. His face was grim.

"Not here, my lady. Let's walk along the terrace."

Out of the Great Hall, they walked out into the inner bailey, a space easily as large as the entire footprint of Tyrswick Keep. In the center of the bailey, in preparation for tomorrow's spectacle, carpenters were erecting tiered stands to overlook a post and rail enclosure, measuring twenty feet by thirty feet in area.

Frey gave it a reluctant sidelong glance as she was hustled across the open courtyard through another wing of the castle complex until they reached the terrace lawns sitting high above the River Wear.

Not a word had been spoken since they left the hall, and Frey's patience was at an end.

"Not another step farther until you tell me what's going on, and I mean now, Robert."

The young knight drew his fingers through his hair in a nervous gesture that belied his air of confidence.

"Two bodies were found floating downstream this morning. Do you know who they might be, my lady?"

Frey frowned.

"A man and a woman tied together," Robert continued. "Their bodies might have been weighted by rocks but had broken free. The woman was—"

"Stout, past her middle years, with red hair; her husband gray haired," she interrupted.

"You did know them?"

"Mistress Duignan and her husband. They kept me guarded but were as much misled by Drefan as others. They were kind to me," Frey answered softly. "Another crime to lay at Drefan's feet. So what are we to do?"

"Nothing."

Frey started. She hadn't heard Sebastian come up behind her until he spoke.

He was stripped to the waist and sweat-soaked, his dark hair curled slightly at the nape. He was her magnificent warrior.

He accepted a cloth from Duncan, who followed in his wake, and wiped the worst of it from his arms and neck.

"They will have to wait their justice on the morrow, when Drefan goes to meet his maker."

"We thought it best to let you know as soon as we heard the news," Talbot offered.

"You did right, lad," he said as he accepted his tunic from Duncan and finished dressing.

"You three help Orlege and Gaines with the equipment. I'll escort Lady Alfreya."

When they were alone, Sebastian reached for Frey's hand. Her fingers curled around his larger ones. She swallowed. This would be one of their few moments alone before tomorrow. Now was her chance to ask about the letters. Frey screwed up her courage.

"When Drefan took me, he told me about replies to letters I was supposed to have written." She paused and waited, hoping Sebastian would interrupt to tell her he spotted the ruse from the first.

He did not.

"I never received those letters…I wrote letters…damn it, this is coming out all wrong."

His moss-green eyes regarded her cautiously and she started again.

"I love you, Sebastian, and I would never play you false—have *never* played you false. I wrote the letters before I knew you. Every assumption I ever had about you was wrong."

He answered with a slow grin.

"I know."

Frey stamped her feet. "Then why did you let me run on like a gowk!"

Sebastian's grin broadened.

"Because a man never gets tired of hearing his wife admit she was in the wrong and that she loves him."

That earned him a scowl. Sebastian laughed.

"And you should be nicer to Gaines from now on because he was the one who stopped me acting like a—what was the word you used, a gawk?"

"Gowk. It means fool."

"I found the letters and, yes, for a time I did believe you'd played me false, until Gaines pointed out that no woman, regardless of the contempt in which she held her husband, would ever leave without taking her clothes and jewelry."

Frey was still put out.

"So I should be grateful for Gaines's poor opinion of women generally?"

Sebastian laughed and folded Frey into his arms.

"Yes, my love, I'm sorry to say that you should."

CHAPTER FORTY-FIVE

The blare of trumpets called the crowd to order. Outside the arena, a crier addressed the crowd, outlining the rules of engagement. In the center, Sebastian stood fully armored. Facing him stood Drefan, equally protected. Although only his eyes were visible, the malice in them was unmistakable.

Lumley stood between them.

"The law is quite clear that I am to inform you of the rules before the contest," he informed both men.

"As each of you are noblemen and each has brought suit against the other, you are both deemed to be plaintiffs.

"This matter will be ended in one of three ways. The first is to cry 'craven, I am vanquished.' The man who cries craven will forfeit land and title and will be banished from Northumbria. The second is with your lives. If each man remains undefeated at sunset, then the matters under consideration here will be considered satisfied.

"Are these rules understood?"

Beneath their armor, both men gave curt nods.

Lumley paused.

"By coin toss you will decide on choice of weapon—staves, swords, cudgels, or battle axes."

"Heads goes to the baron of Tyrswick, tails to Lord Drefan d'Aumont of Angou."

As the morning sun broke over the tops of the trees and a cock crowed in the distance, the gold coin in Lumley's hand glittered.

Sebastian watched the coin as it spun in the air and dropped with a soft thud into the dust.

"Your choice, Lord Drefan."

"Swords."

The call went forward, and, from the far edges, two men came running to the center, each with broadswords. The earl assiduously examined both before allowing the two men to claim their weapons.

Sebastian welcomed the feel of the steel in his hand. His blade was well weighted and perfectly proportioned.

"May God defend the innocent," Lumley told them.

Sebastian and Drefan followed him to the rail. The earl took his place next to the bishop of Durham, who sat on a cushioned campaign chair three levels up on a tiered grandstand.

On the same row, Frey stood, and Sebastian's heart beat a little faster. She was dressed in Tyrswick colors again. Woven through her hair, a length of silk in vivid red. She met his eye without reservation and without tears as he knew she would. His pride burgeoned with her show of courage.

William Walcher stood, and the crowd stood also as he delivered a short prayer for the souls of both men. He ended the benediction as Lumley had.

"May God defend the innocent."

Another blare of trumpets and the battle began.

Drefan attacked first.

Sebastian raised his arm and let his shield take the blow, moving as he did so away from the rail.

The blow from the blocked cut reverberated up his arm and across his back, and every nerve was alive to the sensation. He swiftly counterattacked, right-left aiming at Drefan's shoulder. The first blow met with the clash of steel that rang loudly, the second with a dull thud as sword struck shield.

A further downward swinging cut was intercepted by Drefan's sword. Shields clashed as the two men pushed each other apart.

Sebastian lunged, aiming for the center. Drefan jumped back and countered with a swipe of his shield.

The first half hour reminded Sebastian of the drills he had mastered as a squire—attack, parry, thrust, attack, parry, thrust—as he worked to identify Drefan's weakness.

So far he displayed none. He was a competent, disciplined fighter.

The sun rose higher in the morning sky and along with it the heat. Sweat trickled down Sebastian's back. The fabric cuffs in his tunic absorbed the sweat at his wrists.

There was no question they were evenly matched.

This would be a war of stamina.

* * *

Frey had watched tourneys aplenty, was familiar with the cut and thrust of swordplay, and so had been put out when Friar Dominic pressed a rosary of simple wooden beads into her hands at the beginning of the morning.

She had little time for ladies who cowered and shrieked at the sight of male physicality on powerful display, nor patience with the women who *tsk*ed-*tsk*ed and spoke knowingly among themselves about masculine brutality.

Why, in the past, she'd even had a discreet wager or two on a favorite champion, but today was different. Her investment was not in coin, but in the life of the man in the center of the judicial list, fighting for his very existence.

She knew what strength and skill it took to wield a sword well. Larcwide had schooled her in the basics, and with each action Sebastian made on the field, she felt her own muscles stretch and strain in sympathetic response. It wasn't in her nature to be idle, and so to watch her husband from the sidelines, helpless to do more than pray, was a torment hitherto unknown.

At the beginning she thought to distract herself and considered her position, seated three along from the bishop of Durham on the raised dais shared by the nobility. From this position, one, just one, well-aimed arrow from her bow, and their enemy would lie dead, and the spirits of Diera and Larcwide—even Master and Mistress Duignan—could be at peace.

So as much as she had resented the beads that slipped through her nerveless fingers, she was grateful for the occupation now.

Duncan sat beside her and Talbot, one row down. She'd learned the lad was put out his lord had chosen Robert to be his attendant, and Frey could see the young knight spent as much time watching the campaign tent, where Gaines and Robert were stationed, as the fight.

Again and again, Frey worked the prayer beads through her hands.

The shadows in the inner bailey melted away as the day advanced and Sebastian stepped up his attack, putting Drefan on the defensive. Controlled swings left and right were deftly blocked, but Drefan had ceded ground, edging closer to the rail on the far side of the list.

The crowd rose as he stumbled, his shield tumbling from his arm with a noisy clatter.

The man quickly regained his footing and, now shieldless but with both hands to control his blade, he sprang back menacingly and swung wildly, missing Sebastian's neck only barely.

Frey suppressed a scream as she watched her husband duck and the blade scraped noisily along the edge of his helmet.

Sebastian dropped his own shield, pivoted, and answered with an upward-angled drive that missed his opponent's thigh by a finger's width.

Talbot sat bolt upright and turned back to Duncan.

"Did you see that? The baron's helmet shifted; the blow must have sliced the leather chin strap."

Duncan glared at Talbot and pointedly nodded at Frey. The young knight murmured his apologies, which Frey acknowledged with a distracted nod.

The absence of shields spurred both men on. Attacks and answering blows increased in pace.

Drefan concentrated his attack with left and right broad swipes now centered at Sebastian's head. On a return swing, Sebastian swept his blade upward, opening a gash along the length of Drefan's right forearm. Red rivulets seeped through the tunic where flesh was exposed.

First blood.

Drefan dropped his sword and clutched at his arm. Sebastian held his sword at the ready, waiting for his opponent's next decision. Drefan bent at the waist, gasping from the long exertion and the pain of his wound.

"End this now!" Sebastian told him, loud enough for the crowd to hear. "Call craven and it will be over."

Drefan buckled at the knees and Sebastian lowered his sword and stepped forward.

Then with a mighty roar, a scream the likes of which Frey had heard only from the guttural throats of Scottish highland warriors, Drefan rose, holding the blade end of his sword and swinging again for Sebastian's head.

The pommel of the sword caught the side of the helmet, leaving a dent an inch round in the steel.

Sebastian staggered, dropping to one knee with the force of the blow.

Frey may have screamed; who would have known in the din of the crowd? They sensed that the battle was now turning deadly.

Drefan lined up for another blow when Sebastian aimed a sideways kick to his knee and Drefan too dropped to the ground.

The combat turned hand-to-hand as the men grappled for dominance. Sebastian's helmet rolled several feet away in the dirt. Through the roiling dust Frey could see short, sharp blows exchanged and a glint of blade as the combatants struggled to retrieve their weapons.

When both regained their feet, only Drefan was armed.

The tunics and surcoats clean and resplendent that morning were now dust, blood-, and sweat stained.

Drefan continued to hold his sword in the middle of the blade, offering short, sharp jabs designed to pierce through the links of mail. Sebastian leaped back once, then twice, away from the wicked point, eyeing his own sword, which lay three feet to the left and behind his adversary. Every lunge forward by Drefan drove Sebastian farther away from his weapon.

Frey realized her husband's only choice would be to make a dive for the sword, but the consequence of doing so would break the cardinal rule of combat—never present one's back to the enemy.

But there was no other choice. Sebastian made the leap.

Drefan turned, holding his sword like a dagger in both hands, raising the steel above his head.

Sebastian reached for his sword and grasped it, rolling onto his back.

Drefan plunged his blade down as Sebastian raised his, and the honed edge of Sebastian's weapon sliced through flesh from thigh to chest. Drefan sank to his knees with a groan.

By the time his head hit the ground beside Sebastian, Drefan was already dead.

Frey rose with the crowd, although the bishop and his party remained seated.

"Take me down there, now!" she ordered Duncan and Talbot.

The young knights forced their way through the crowd that surged to the edge of the ringed tourney field. Decorum be damned.

Frey ducked beneath the rail and ran to where Sebastian now stood, his back to her in quiet, earnest discussion with Gaines and Robert.

She didn't look at Drefan's broken body, now being attended to by Baldwin and another man she did not recognize.

"Sebastian!"

He turned to her, his face ashen.

Gaines stepped forward between them. "Listen to me, my lady," he told her in urgent hushed tones. "This is not over yet. The bishop still has to pronounce the verdict."

Frey studied Sebastian's face thoroughly; beads of sweat that had nothing to do with the sun overhead poured down his face and dripped unchecked from his chin. She traced his beloved face with her fingers, and she could see pain found its expression around the corners of his eyes and in the taut line of his mouth.

"How seriously are you hurt?" she asked.

"Ribs," he gasped before shaking his head.

"He needs a stretcher."

"No, my lady," Gaines told her firmly. "As the baron and Drefan were both plaintiffs, the bishop may hold off making judgment until he sees whether Lord Sebastian lives. You can be sure that is what Baldwin as Drefan's second will demand. We press for settlement now."

Gaines gave her a look of such compassion that she wanted to scratch it right off his face. If he was being kind to her, it meant Sebastian's condition was grave.

Frey opened her mouth to speak, but no words came out. She tried again and this time found her voice.

"Then what needs to be done?"

Four knights ringed Sebastian and Frey, shielding them from view. Gaines stepped forward and pressed a wad of linen into her hand.

"Keep this pressed against his wound, my lady," he told her. "Sebastian, put your arm around your wife." No one questioned Gaines's familiarity.

Frey carefully embraced her husband around the middle. As she pressed the cloth to his chest, he let out a low moan. Her fingers were immediately sticky with blood. Robert and Talbot arranged Sebastian's cloak to conceal his injury.

"Ready?" asked Gaines.

Sebastian nodded once. His shallow, rapid breathing worried Frey, and, as though aware of her concern, Sebastian looked down and squeezed her shoulder.

"Courage, princess," he murmured.

* * *

Gaines took the lead as the remaining soldiers adopted guard positions around them.

"We'll pay our respects to the bishop and beg his indulgence to clean up. He'll be expecting us to attend the bishop's Hall tonight."

Someone had thought to remove the rail in front of the bishop's seat, and they made their way toward it.

Frey bit her tongue to stop the sobs she knew were just below the surface. She could feel Sebastian struggle for breath. He sucked in lungfuls of air, only to have his breath hitch.

The group stopped in front of the bishop.

Sebastian bowed his head. Frey curtsied in the same movement. When Sebastian arose, he stood taller and addressed the cleric with a voice harsh but strong.

"Your Grace, I am vindicated."

Walcher looked him over before glancing behind them, where Frey imagined Drefan's body was now being removed from the courtyard.

The bishop addressed the crowd.

"I attest, and ye are my witnesses, that God has given the right to Lord Sebastian de la Croix, baron of Tyrswick. If any man says differently, let him step forward now."

The crowd, substantially smaller—many having already left, their desire to see blood sated—fell quiet.

No one stepped forward.

"Then Sebastian de la Croix, baron of Tyrswick, heaven and I declare your vindication."

Sebastian bowed once more as Walcher rose and, with his retinue, returned to the castle.

Sebastian remained with his head bent for long moment, his breath coming in rattling spurts.

Then breaths stopped.

Frey felt the pressure of Sebastian's weight come to bear on her shoulders, and she staggered beneath it. During the few moments that elapsed before Duncan and Talbot ran back with the stretcher,

Sebastian did not move. His head was bowed, legs buckled, and arms stretched out, his body upright only with the support of Gaines and Robert.

Laid on the litter, he looked worse. To Frey's horror, his surcoat, once white, was red with blood. It was his face that was drained of color.

The men rushed with all speed toward the entrance and were some distance away before it occurred to Frey to follow after them. She took a few faltering steps before she realized that people were staring at her.

Frey stared back, bewildered.

"Come child, let's get you inside," a compassionate voice at her shoulder told her.

She looked down as Friar Dominic gently took her hand.

Her gown was nearly black, a part of her mind registered.

Blood. So much of Sebastian's blood.

Too much.

By the time she had entered the chambers, she found Sebastian lay stripped to the waist. Streaks of gore, darkening to rust as it dried, were smeared across his torso like the marks of claws. At the center, an area hastily cleaned for the application of a large linen bandage was sealed on three sides with salve, while the loose edge fluttered slightly. Sticking from the center was a hollow reed.

Frey tried to look Gaines in the eye, but she couldn't see past his arms, bloodied as they were to the elbows. He looked away, rinsing his hands in a bowl while Duncan poured steaming water from a ewer.

"Is he…?"

Frey didn't trust herself to give voice to the rest of the question.

"Nay, my lady. It was a close thing, but Sebastian still lives."

"Then how bad?"

The question was met with silence from Gaines. Frey looked around the room.

There were no answering looks from anyone else in the room. Robert and Talbot kept their eyes resolutely to the ground. They had all seen chest wounds in battle, and almost all were fatal.

"Tell me!"

Friar Dominic clasped a firm hand on her shoulder.

"His life is in God's hands now."

Bitter gall rose in her mouth and she swallowed hard.

Gaines cleared his throat to draw the attention of the men in the room. He jerked his head in the direction of the door and they followed him out silently.

Frey reached out toward Sebastian, her hand shaking.

Sebastian, a man full of life, with a ready smile, was too still, his body waxy and pale against sheets now tinged pink with water-diluted blood from the cleaning of his wound.

Frey was aware of a hushed conversation between the two older men who remained, but she couldn't tear her eyes away from Sebastian.

Spots of deep red, minor puncture wounds, were scattered across his chest and arms. Frey picked up a piece of linen and plunged it into the still-steaming water in the ewer. Lovingly, she wiped and caressed each arm, washing them clean.

Then his chest. Frey's fingers lingered over his heart, feeling for his pulse.

It was there. Thank God it was there.

A gum of myrrh held the dressing in place. The cloth packed around the reed was stained red, but it did not spread. Her hands hovered over the bandage.

"Gaines tells me the sword thrust pierced his lung."

Frey started and looked up. Friar Dominic stood on the other side of the bed, the deep lines on each side of his mouth pronouncing his concern for Sebastian more than words ever could.

The next days passed in a mind-numbing haze of routine. Frey insisted she be the one to clean and dress Sebastian's wounds. No one would gainsay her on the matter.

Fever came at the start of the second night, with pain and tremors so violent it required the combined strength of Gaines, Dominic, and Robert to hold Sebastian still long enough for Frey to administer an opiate.

Then he slumbered so deeply that Frey counted away the hours watching his chest rise and fall, holding each of her own breaths until she saw Sebastian take his next.

* * *

Frey woke with a start.

When did she sleep?

Bright sunlight filtered through the branches of the spreading yew.

She knew this place. It was the place where ghosts lived.

"Pray for your husband, Frey."

Frey turned swiftly. Diera stood before her wearing an expression of peace on her face and dressed in a fine gown of creamy white, her plaited yellow-gold hair a thick rope over her shoulder.

Diera looked like an angel. Then her words penetrated through the surprise of seeing her.

No, no, no, no, no!

Bitter tears, long suppressed, fell unchecked down her cheeks. He was gone. Sebastian had left her. Soon she would see his ghostly visage in this ephemeral place as well, then suffer it every night for the remainder of her life.

Frey turned and ran through a meadow of knee-deep grass, shining ribbons of green and yellow that bent in the gentle breeze as though worshipping the sun in the distance.

She stopped at the rise, panting and out of breath. Tyrswick Keep rose like a sentinel out of the landscape.

Frey ran again, finding herself at the chapel.

She halted at the entrance and looked into the gloom. Light from a window illuminated a point on the floor. It drew her to the spot before the altar where she knelt and traced the inscription with her finger.

est anima meaquiescit

My soul is at rest.

"He's not here."

Frey jumped.

Diera stood behind her with the same beatific expression she wore beneath the yew tree.

"You're looking for Sebastian. He's not here."

"Then why am I here?"

"Because you need to tell him for me."

"Tell him what?"

Diera's smile widened, and it seemed that the chapel filled with light.

"Tell him 'thank you.'"

EPILOGUE

It would be three more long days before Frey could be certain that Sebastian would live. He opened his eyes and squeezed her hand weakly. She nurtured Diera's message in her breast for a further six months before she was sure he would be ready to hear it.

Long before then, news arrived that Baldwin had been found hung one night, by his own hand or by that of others was unknown, though the latter more likely. And the remnants of Drefan's men were now back in France.

The discovery of another trove of silver, coins like those produced by the unmourned Baldwin at the Durham court, came during an exploration of ancient Roman lead workings near Tyrswick, which also yielded a rich vein of precious ore.

Running of the Keep fell to Frey and Gaines jointly while Orlege honored his old friend and mentor's memory by using Larcwide's training systems and drills with the new squires.

But seasons change and so did life at Tyrswick.

As the leaves in the forests around the district turned to red and gold, Sebastian healed loudly, stubbornly, and sometimes not with good grace.

Before the last of the brittle autumn leaves fell to the ground, he regained his mount, but a ride to the village and back taxed the reserves of his energy, so county sessions were held only in the Great Hall of the Keep.

The beginning of winter brought news that Rosalind and Rhys were expecting a second child, and Heloise and her husband their first, along with a message from the young woman filled with remorse and begging forgiveness.

Sebastian started light sparring with Orlege as the first flakes of snow fell in the training yard.

Christ's Mass this year was further declared to be a time of thanksgiving for the good health of the baron and for the abundant harvest and new wealth found in the mines, which brought prosperity across Tyrswick.

And Brice joined them for one last Christmas and New Year to proudly announce he had been invited to Bolognia to study with the greatest minds of Christendom at the new Studium Generale. Sebastian settled a generous sum on the surviving son of the last Saxon earl of Tyrswick so he would never want for money to continue his education.

Soon, thickening branches and budding twigs heralded the arrival of spring as well as a summons to assembly at Durham by all barons. There, Ligulf of Lumley made his case that Northumbria should prepare for an impending Scottish invasion.

His concerns were—predictably—dismissed by Walcher, and, it had to be said, by others too. Sebastian kept his counsel but quietly ordered Orlege to increase patrols.

Yet no matter what occurred outside the borders of Tyrswick, Frey felt only peace.

Now summer arrived. More than a year had passed since that fateful day on the judicial list at Durham Castle.

Sebastian kept his promise and showed her the secluded glen with the waterfall, and indeed it felt good to swim without clothes. They dried off in the sunlight and made love in the shade of a spreading oak tree.

She traced the scar on his chest with her fingers, marveling how something red hot and angry could fade to pink and would soon be white, lingering like a ghost of events past—always there but with no more power to harm.

Frey kissed the scar and across his chest, taking in the warmth of his skin and the firmness of the muscles that lay beneath. She touched every inch of his flesh, giving thanks for its wholeness before she joined him in mutual communion.

Their bodies might be only temporarily united, but their souls were one forever, indivisible.

And now, with their bodies momentarily sated, Frey whispered her news that, God willing, there would be an heir to Tyrswick to arrive on their second wedding anniversary.

Never had surrender been so sweet.

THE END

About the Author

Elizabeth Ellen Carter's first novel, *Moonstone Obsession*, was shortlisted for the Romance Writers' of Australia Emerald Award for Best Unpublished Manuscript prior to its publication in 2013.

Her next novel, *Warrior's Surrender* (2014), won the Readers and Writers Down Under 2015 Readers' Choice Award for Favourite Historical Fiction.

Carter has subsequently won praise and a wide readership for her highly researched historical romance adventures including a number of series and standalone novels.

Her titles *Dark Heart*, *Revenge of the Corsairs*, and *Live And Let Spy* were nominees for InD'tale Magazine's RONE Awards. The novella *Nocturne* was named one of the most anticipated titles of 2016 by Australian Romance Today.

Carter can be found online at www.eecarter.com

Moonstone Obsession
by Elizabeth Ellen Carter

Secrets, lies, and scandals…

Selina Rosewall had given up on love, but while helping her brother further his merchant fleet business, she meets Sir James Mitchell, Lord of Penventen. Their attraction is mutual, but what James wants from the relationship goes further—much further—than Selina could have expected. And she learns that in the world of the Ton, scandal and deceit are commonplace.

For James, it's hard to say which is more dangerous: being a spy or being considered husband material by the Ladies of the Ton. With political machinations threatening to draw England into the violent wake of the French Revolution, the last thing James expected was to fall in love with the daughter of an untitled seafaring family. But when his investigation stirs up a hornet's nest, can he protect Selina from danger that threatens her very life?

"Full of historic details and colorful characters, Elizabeth Ellen Carter's debut historical novel is a wonderfully engaging success. Her charming leading couple is irresistible, and the international plot in which they become embroiled will keep readers' interest from first to last." - *The Romance Reviews*

"Revolutionary France provides a fascinating backdrop to this tale of intrigue, danger and suspense and the carefully researched historical details lend the story realism. I love Ms Carter's writing style; it flows smoothly and her vivid imagery made it easy to picture the scenes." - *Rakes & Rascals*

"In a voice distinctly her own, but with a hint of classic suspense novelist Daphne du Maurier, Elizabeth Ellen Carter has shaped a rich world bathed in reality and fiction." - *Larry Wilson*

In this series:

Moonstone Obsession (Moonstone Romances Book 1)
Moonstone Conspiracy (Moonstone Romances Book 2)
Available in ebook and print at your favourite online book retailer.
Moonstone Promise (Moonstone Romances Bonus Story)
is a free read from eecarter.com

DARK HEART
BY ELIZABETH ELLEN CARTER

Can love survive a dark heart?

Rome, 235 A.D. A series of ritual murders of young boys recalls memories of Rome's most wicked emperor. Magistrate Marcus Cornelius Drusus has discovered the cult extends to the very heart of Roman society.

Despite his personal wealth and authority, Marcus is a slave to his past – conflicted by his status as an adopted son, bitterly betrayed by his wife and forced to give up his child.

Kyna knows all about betrayal. Sold into slavery by her husband to pay a gambling debt, she found herself in Rome, far from her home in Britannia. Bought by a doctor, she is taught his trade and is about to gain her freedom when her mentor is murdered by the cult.

When the same group makes an attempt on her life, Kyna is forced to give up her freedom and accept Marcus' protection. With no one to trust but each other, mutual attraction ignites into passion. But how far will Marcus go for vengeance when he learns the cult's next victim is his son?

Can the woman who is free in her heart heal the man who is a slave in his?

LIVE AND LET SPY
BY ELIZABETH ELLEN CARTER

The King's Rogues Book One

England, 1804: Refused his rightful promotion, Adam Hardacre quits the Royal Navy in disgust and is quickly approached with an intriguing proposition to serve his country undercover.

His first assignment takes him home to Cornwall to expose traitors plotting a French invasion of England. There, he meets newly unemployed governess Olivia Collins, who has stumbled upon a hidden secret from Adam's past – his youthful summer love affair with the local squire's daughter. It is a tragic history that brings Adam and Olivia closer than is wise.

However, with the attraction deepening to something more, neither realize that Olivia unwittingly holds the key to his mission.

As Adam infiltrates the plot, Olivia finds out the shocking truth behind his lost love's death many years ago, and both their lives are in danger. But their growing relationship is clouded by suspicion. Who can and cannot be trusted – anyone or no one?

Or... even each other?

"Exciting and romantic. I couldn't put it down!" – *Kristin Nielsen*

"A lively account of mystery, hidden secrets, wonderful characters, romance, and, of course, spies. This is one you do not want to miss." – *Barbara Michael*

"Adventure and mystery and a love that overcomes tragedy." – *Beth Meador*

Also in this series:
Spyfall (The King's Rogues Book Two)
Spy Another Day (The King's Rogues Book Three)
Father's Day

Available exclusively on Amazon from Dragonblade Publishing

MOONSTONE CONSPIRACY
BY ELIZABETH ELLEN CARTER

Revolution in France, rebels in England, and
one woman caught in the crossfire...

The powerful sequel to Moonstone Obsession

For her unwitting participation in a plot to embezzle the Exchequer, Lady Abigail
Houghall has spent the last two years exiled to the city of Bath. A card sharp, sometime
mistress, and target of scandalous gossip by the London Beau Monde, Lady Abigail
plots to escape her gilded cage as well as the prudish society that condemns her. But
the times are not easy. France is in chaos, the King has been executed, and whispers
of a similar revolution are stirring in England. And because of Abigail's participation
in the robbery plot, the Spymaster of England is blackmailing her into passing him
information about the members of London's upper crust.

When dashing English spy Daniel Ridgeway takes a seat at her card table and
threatens to expose her for cheating, Abigail has no choice but to do as he demands:
seduce the leader of the revolutionaries and learn what she can about their plot. As
she's drawn deeper into Daniel's dangerous world—from the seedy backstreets of
London to the claustrophobic catacombs of a war-torn Paris—she realizes an even
more dangerous fact: she's falling in love with her seductive partner. And the stakes
of this game might just be too high—even for her.

"...this romance is compelling with such vivid characters and adventure that it is
quite easy to get wrapped up..." - *In D'Tale Magazine*

"When I heard the author was turning the female villain of the first book in the
series into the heroine of this one, I found it hard to believe. Abigail deserved
a nasty fate, not a happy ending - or so I thought. I'm delighted to admit I was
mistaken - Ms Carter brilliantly persuaded me to take Abigail's side." - *Demelza
Carlton* (author of the *Romance A Medieval Fairytale* and *Mel Goes to Hell* series)

In this series:

Moonstone Obsession (Moonstone Romances Book 1)
Moonstone Conspiracy (Moonstone Romances Book 2)
Available in ebook and print at your favourite online book retailer.
Moonstone Promise (Moonstone Romances Bonus Story)
is a free read from eecarter.com

www.ingramcontent.com/pod-product-compliance
Lightning Source LLC
Chambersburg PA
CBHW071150100726

47908CB00002B/317